Harp

NIDHI DALMIA

Reviews for *Harp*

Harp by Nidhi Dalmia is a refreshing love story. Author Nidhi Dalmia's debut novel, *Harp*, explores what happens when two people from completely different universes meet. A unique, touching love story set in the times of communist Poland of the late sixties – the Iron Curtain forms the backdrop of the story. Ashok's anxiety and excitement as he travels around the world, and his emotions and persona stay with the readers even after the book finishes. Dalmia's book offers a mix of characters and takes the reader through their remarkable journey, making this a must read. It is well written, racy and colourful.

– Hindustan Times

A deftly crafted and consistently compelling read from beginning to end, *Harp* is an extraordinarily entertaining novel that clearly documents author Nidhi Dalmia as an original, skilled and innately talented storyteller.

– Midwest Book Review, **Oregon**

The book deals with journeys we make across countries, even as we embark on a private quest within to know ourselves better, and to seek what it is we really want from life.

– Business Standard

Nidhi Dalmia...Sculpts *Harp*, a fiction about love, longing and coming of age...encompassing these journeys is also a quest on their part to know themselves better and seek what they really want. These aspects' reflecting real life situations and the universality of emotions resonates well with the reader.

– The Hindu

Harp is a moving book that talks about love, sacrifice and passion. *Harp* is a romantic fiction that transports one to the late sixties and all the changes taking place then. *Harp* also gives a description of socio-economic situation in India and abroad prevalent at the time. It has elements of the Dairy Industry and Business Management.

– India Today Education

Love, longing and coming of age intertwined with cultural, sexual, student revolutions and the music of the 60s.

– Deccan Chronicle

Nidhi Dalmia's debut novel, *Harp*, resonates the words of Charles Dickens as he paints the picture of a dreamy romantic world and transports his readers to 1960s. It's a tale of three friends, Ashok, Lauren and Aparna, told through twists and turns, many emotional voyages traversing through the Europe less travelled.

– The New Indian Express

With degrees from Oxford and Harvard under his belt, he took a decades-long detour to the world of business before finally telling a story close to his heart.

– The Tribune

Harp talks about romance, music and travel. Set in late 60s, it mesmerizes you with really intense description of characters and it takes the readers to the lesser travelled places of Europe, US and India.

– The Patriot, Mechanicsburg

It is a racy and colourful read as he visits cities in France, Norway, Finland, Sweden and Poland. The descriptions are vivid almost photographic like that of a postcard.

The story is gripping and one does not want to put the book down before knowing what happens to Ashok and Lauren. *Harp* is a period book. The style is refreshingly natural... The twists and turn in this unique love story simply make it difficult for a reader to part with it.

– Millennium Post

In his debut novel *Harp*, Gun Nidhi Dalmia offers a glimpse into the bygone era of sixties, revisiting the idealism, music and culture of a generation, who like him believed that the good times would never end.

– Marwar India

Very few books have ventured into the world of Communist Europe in the 1960s and 1970s. And, *Harp* does just that. The descriptions and insights into that world are still relevant. This truly sets apart the book from other stories.

– Women's Era

Harp is spellbinding and one does not want to put the book down before knowing what happens to Ashok and Lauren.

– Travel and Hospitality

In his first novel, *Harp*, Nidhi Dalmia talks about love, passion and sacrifice. Set in the late 60s, this novel takes you through the world of music, literature and travel. A mesmerising story with intricate descriptions of the quaint and remote part of Europe, this is a journey which also delves into Indian culture and morality.

– You & I

How beautifully the author has described Europe. I literally can imagine the places Ashok goes to, specially his train journey. I really enjoyed the depth, the author has added to describe the music, architecture, youth and world of the late 60s. This time was a time of revolution in terms of sex, thoughts and technology.

– High on Gloss

Harp – a deeply entertaining novel authored by Mr. Nidhi Dalmia is a refreshing love story tugs at the heartstrings of every 20 year old.

– Alwarpet Times

Harp may not be a regular love story, but it will hook onto you. It is heartbreaking for a few while comforting for others, it makes you believe in it while the simple essence of the story being truth and hope. The strong and effective characterization followed by impeccable narration adds more beauty to the story, probably teleports you to the scenes and the actual locations. It might be a 400 page long book with 100 small chapters, but it is unputdownable. The writing is simple yet excellent. The minute detailing of the locals from the food to people to behaviour is appreciable.

– Errors and Kaushal

The tale of love of Ashok, Lauren and Aparna moves around in the city of love, that is Paris. And many of us would love to read it for the way the author goes around describing scenes of the couple and the place.

– Come Alive

Author has meticulously penned the story including most of the intricate information pertaining to love clubbing with the lifestyle of Europe.

– Sarath Babu

The story is mesmerizing with really intense descriptions of the places from the smallest parts of Europe; it will take you to the Indian culture and morality. Harp is spellbinding and one does not want to put the book down before knowing what happens to Ashok and Lauren.

– Trinity Mirror

The descriptions and insights truly set it apart from other fictions. The author, who grew up in the late '60s, subtly captures the nuances of the era.

– The Asian Age

Despite being set in a previous context the novel beautifully captures the reader's attention with its theme and exploration of ideas every adult goes through at some point in their life. The character of Lauren inspires people to realize their dreams and goals by not backing down due to society's pressure. The book wonderfully captures and describes the thrill and joy of solo traveling one should experience at first glance in life. The book delves deep into the realities of real life which young adults today can relate to. The book inspires and gives hope to readers that it is never too late in your life to follow your dreams, goals, and passion.

– Caffeine Chronicle

A Cosmopolitan tale straddling different eras and cultures... author Nidhi Dalmia comes up with such a book "Harp", which is a romantic love story which depicts the lives and loves of three protagonists in the zeitgeist and idealism of the 1960s, straddling ...American, European and Indian cultures.

– The News Now J&K

Reviews for *Afternoon*
(Also by the same author)

'War, love, travel. The Sixties India. In his seductive tale of love and longing, Nidhi Dalmia takes us into a world of free spirits constrained by familiar doubts. A delightful read.'
– Sanjaya Baru, *Economist, Writer and Media Personality*

'Nidhi Dalmia's imaginative writing set in Delhi, Kashmir and Berkeley, USA evokes nostalgia for another era, offering a poetic glimpse into the intensity of love and longing in the swinging sixties.'
– Siddharth Kak, *Popular Television Personality and Author*

'Set in the Bay Area, New York, Kashmir, and Delhi in the late 1960s, intertwined with the significant cultural, student, sexual, and intellectual revolutions taking place then, *Afternoon* is a moving tale that superlatively reflects how our lives are shaped by the choices we make as well as factors beyond our control.'
– Sandeep Bamzai, *Veteran Journalist and Author*

'Refreshing, vivid account of the protagonist growing up in New Delhi in the swinging 60s and travelling to the US, exploring human relations unselfconsciously. Great nostalgia for the 60s generations of young Indians and Americans.'
– Salman Khurshid, *Author and former Minister of External Affairs*

'A riveting narration of one man's journey across borders, spanning a conflicted landscape of love, loss, and courage to discover meaning in the parables of history.'
– Ravi Shankar Etteth, *Author of The Tiger by the River, The Brahmin, and Killing Time in Delhi*

'In today's age of social media and instant gratification, *Afternoon* is a pleasant reminder of how humanity thrives on culture, cross-border relationships, and empathy.'
– Raghavendra Rathore, *Design Mentor*

'Afternoon' is a fascinating story bringing alive the mood, atmosphere and the hidden undercurrents of societies of the 60s. The term afternoon representing the waning of day and slowing of rhythms, is aptly reflected in the book through challenges faced in inter-relationships set amid international geo-politics, choices made and acceptance of factors beyond anyone's control, all of which have been subtly interwoven by the author, Nidhi Dalmia.
– Shovana Narayan, *Kathak Guru, IAAS retd., and Author*

To my parents

"...I have come to doubt
All that I once held as true..."

Simon and Garfunkel

"...The sky is on fire
And I must go..."

Joan Baez
(Farewell Angelina)

Two mynas fought noisily in the veranda. Were they fighting or making love? Sometimes one was on top, sometimes it seemed the other. They kicked up dust as they fell on to the patio beyond the veranda, still fighting. Another myna came and peeked from the top of column. Then a whole lot of them arrived on the scene. A council of elders. It wasn't always easy to tell. It was easier with pigeons. They were always making love whilst flapping their wings.

In the room just above, they unclenched with force to be locked again in a different position, very quickly. They couldn't bear to be separated a moment longer than required. It started with him holding her open palm to explain to her what different parts of it represented. This is Mount Vesuvius, he said caressing the left bulge of her palm. The softer and more voluptuous it is, the more passionate you are.

"And what is mine like", she asked, looking directly into his eyes.

He did not let go of her hand.

"Very sensuous", he said, his eyes melting into hers.

Her mini skirt had become pulled quite high when she sat

down. His hand inadvertently touched the cusp where her light golden thighs pulled together formed the border with the skirt line, and contrasted with the multicoloured miniskirt. He got an electric shock. She must have felt it too. He daringly let his hand go to the same spot again. This could not be taken for an accident. With their eyes still open their mouths met and they kissed passionately. His hand lightly cusped the inside of her thigh, which felt soft and smooth. The other hand cupped her rounded shoulder and then felt the softness of her back. She did not stop him. The ecstasy ceased to be a point and became a line. His tongue began to explore her mouth. Was she allowing this? Even participating in this? He devoured her pale, slender neck. His mouth went to her collarbone and he wasn't even aware of unbuttoning the top hook of her blouse. His tongue flicked right and left at the start of the curves. Her chest swelled and became taut. It could no longer be ignored. She put her arms back while still kissing him and undid the other hooks of her blouse. Freed, her bosom swelled even more. His mouth slid downwards.

He might have lost his virginity as might she have, or she might have stopped him, somewhere along the way. It remained suspended in space as one of life's many imponderables, as there was the sound of the first floor apartment door opening. What? How had her parents come back so early? In panic she steered him towards the window and pushed him in the direction of an undignified exit. She shut the window after him and that was that. There was no possibility of discussion or some other way out with the parents, bolstered by acceptable explanation.

He found himself on a narrow ledge. To get anywhere he had to traverse a row of wires coming into the house just next to him. He crawled under them, some shirt buttons coming off in the process and as the ledge turned the corner, saw that he would have to get rid of his shoes, hold the ledge and then jump. The shoes landed with a thud and he waited hoping no one would emerge from the downstairs flat to investigate. They must have flown past the large brightly lit drawing room window. No one did. He let go, his knees bent as he landed. He was winded but safe. He opened the clasp of the gate and fled past the roundabout to the waiting car.

She was packed off to finish her schooling in a well known boarding school in the Himalayas soon after as her parents were getting transferred. She left early one winter morning as term began in January. She phoned Ashok at 5.00 a.m. - saying "Wake up, sleepyhead" and he drove in the still night like dark in the freezing car to say bye but he couldn't see her anywhere on the main street. She must have just left.

Ashok expected a letter from Nalini but nothing came. Maybe she was too far away.

She receded into a distant albeit unforgettable memory.

2

Had I made a difference to anyone in this world, Ashok wondered as he became immersed in ordinary day to day life. All of us want to leave footprints in the sands of time. To somehow make a difference, be different. Who will remember us after we're gone and our contemporaries are gone?

When we're growing up we think we're special, that it'll be different for us. The whole future lies ahead. We look at our photographs in school and college. They speak of our thoughts of being this or that, of doing great things.

It is imperative to have dreams, whether they turn out or not.

Sexual revolution, permissiveness came suddenly and completely to the urban Indian middle class too. There was no gap. Girls spending the night - not going home after parties was taken as commonplace. Ashok went to visit his friend Arun the afternoon after a party. Arun's then girl friend lay pointedly on his bed, as if to make a statement.

Mini skirts began to be seen everywhere. Boys wore flowing kurtas over denim jeans. Bell bottoms followed. Many boutiques sprang up in Delhi selling very colourful clothes that matched perfectly the mood of psychedelia. People read the selected poems of T S Eliot and looked appropriately melancholy or profound.

The avenues were broad and tree lined, Parking was easily available. There were many cars but the traffic was not impossible.

Ashok imagined the West too, to be a magical place. There was so much music, films, books, thinking, movements coming from there in the late 60's - things happening there.

No one knows what life has in store but you know what you like and what you find pleasant from the past, a close friend had said to him in the College cafe one day on one of their last days in College.

3

Ashok jumped into the family business soon after College with earnestness. He picked up things quickly. He was happy with the first visiting card he designed. There was no education like hands on. He worked very hard - till late into the night. Often he didn't stop even in the beautiful, blue evenings to inhale the fragrance of freshly cut grass, mixed with sweat after a game of tennis. He set unrealistically high standards which were not sustainable long term. But what does youth know about moderation or limits? These lessons are learned hard and often only through mistakes.

On top of that both Ashok's parents strongly believed in the value of work and strove to inculcate the value of work is worship in him. His father Brij had an acute sense of timing and which product would do well where. It made him an excellent entrepreneur. But he badly felt the need for a family member to help him and believed the best education was on the shop floor here and in tackling real life problems as they arose.

He started working from very early morning till he retired. He was full of ideas all the time and his active mind as well as his drive allowed him to take very little time off. Since factories ran three shifts there would always be a Supervisor, if not a Manager he could make enquiries of and give his orders to.

Brij was extremely fond of his son but could not relate to him spending hours on theatre, music, literature and cinema. He never had time for these himself. One exquisite Delhi evening with the sun setting red behind the Eucalyptus trees and the evening full of azure tones, Ashok flushed from playing Tennis sat on his bed strumming the guitar with a bunch of friends. His father walked into the room just then to have some connection with his son. There was an immediate disconnect and everyone felt awkward.

But Brij had managed to inculcate in his son his love of Indian Philosophy especially Vedanta and they spent time together, discussing abstruse concepts, the divergences in different chains of thought and what they themselves felt about it. Spirituality was a binding force, even as a School of it taught detachment.

Radhika, Ashok's mother, shared with her son a love of learning and an interest in all subjects. They were curious to know about everything from advancements in Space to developments in Physics, the latest writing in fiction and how the Domino effect was playing out in International Relations.

His father had a Dairy products factory at the edge of town. The brand had become well known through the quality of its products, especially its bottled milk shakes. These were sold in traditional round wide milk bottles in different flavours - strawberry, vanilla, banana (green), pineapple (yellow). This flavoured pasteurised milk was much in demand but other products were also popular.

The butter fresh and yellow (3% salted *a la angleterre*) stored in a freezing room at 4°C was made in shining silver butter churners from Silkeborg. Ashok loved standing there observing the process and putting pats of delicious butter in his mouth, like Krishna the *makhan chor* - the very young butter thief. He stood in the Freezer covered in his fur-like jacket in December and thought he was in Scandinavia.

The ice-cream was sold in bricks, on sticks, in cups and cones. At retail outlets and to distributors all over town cabinets were provided with high capacity compressors, which stocked the multitudinous varieties. Chocbar, choconut, casatta-tutti fruiti in layers along with a layer of cake, pistachio etc. as well as the ice-candy like orangebar. But the most effective were the ubiquitous ice-cream carts spread all over the city at strategic points, outside the Mughal monuments, the temples and colonial monuments like India Gate as well as the schools and colleges. The brand name was written in red on the cream coloured carts. Then in keeping with the times, his friend Vijay's groovy cousin, visiting from Bombay painted the carts many psychedelic colours. They really caught the eye.

She was vivacious and her air of being free and not inhibited was appealing. A refreshing change from many Delhi girls. She was young enough to like James Bond books. Ashok taken with her presented her a set of three. Vijay raised a knowing eyebrow. Ashok put on a green and black Zodiac striped shirt, he had recently bought. He poured himself some whiskey, in a crystal glass, as the ice tinkled in it, feeling very debonair. It was early evening and there was the smell of freshly cut grass from the adjacent lawn. There was an open air Elvis movie on at the nearby Army mess. Drive ins in America must be similar they imagined. Their shoes had special clips on the soles and the heels so they could tap along with the songs. It gave them a sense of abandon and of being part of something. She gave him a dazzling smile that only the very young can manage. She sat between him and Vijay. He would try to take her dancing after the movie and dance her off her feet. She was going back to Bombay the next day.

Back at work the next morning, Ashok learnt that buffalo milk had 6.5%+ fat and cow milk in India had 5.5%. In the West it had only 3-4%. Ashok learned the significance of micro-bacteriology for Dairy products, the important role the laboratory played. He was fascinated by the multiple colours of bacterial colonies, under the microscope. Here was a kaleidoscope of natural psychedelia, more varied than any LSD could produce. These bacteria played such a vital part.

Ashok learned the production of long-life UHT milk, condensed milk and milk powder, especially for the Indian army out in the remotest terrains in the North-East, Kashmir and elsewhere. He jumped at new packaging by Tetra Pak. He made close contacts with the National Dairy Research Institute in Karnal.

The edge lay in Technology and Packaging followed up by dynamic, imaginative Marketing. Ashok decided to get some training personally in Europe.

He could only be at the forefront if he had a good idea himself of what it was all about. He would still hire the best Dairy technologists but he would be able to guide them better, interact with them more closely and provide entrepreneurial input in a more meaningful manner.

Valio, the Co-op Dairy Association in Finland, agreed to give him a fellowship for technical training in their factories spread out all over the country for a couple of months as did the Dairy Marketing Federation in Norway. The latter gave him a choice of training at Tromso or Bergen. Bergen and Trondheim were the largest cities next to Oslo. Tromso was near the Arctic circle and seemed very remote. Ashok chose Bergen. This turned out to be a very pretty town on the West Coast surrounded by high mountains with a fairy tale lake in the middle. A cable car and a funicular took you to the top of the nearest mountain. The neat three or four storeyed houses with red roofs for the rain and snow were in pastel colours - light green, blue, yellow, mauve, violet, pink. They really seemed to be out of a Hansel and Gretel tale. They had to be seen to be given credence. Ashok couldn't believe where he was. He had chosen well.

The French Ministry of Agriculture also gave him a technical co-operation fellowship, for three months, under the overall tutelage of a Professeur J. Casalis. He was to spend one week in each factory of each type of Dairy product spread out all over France. He got a detailed programme - *une semaine dans l'usine du* this and another *dans la fabrique* of that. Ashok was very pleased to get this letter, in French of course, and took a special delight in reading it on his own with the French he had acquired at the Alliance.

Ashok felt the infiniteness of time, anything was possible. If he met a girl he really liked he didn't have to take it further right then. Her address was the important thing. He would look her up when he next went to San Francisco or Alicante. There were so many lovely places he would visit, sooner or later.

His life stretched out into the distance, into eternity - at the end of stucco white plains bright with sunlight.

The only way Ashok could travel was to get scholarships. Foreign exchange could not be taken out of the country. He had no resources of his own. Nor did he want to be a burden on his parents or the family business.

Ashok got in touch with the commercial sections of countries advanced in Dairy Technology and manufacture. He selected names from different fields within that. His strategy and perseverance paid off. Companies agreed to give him short-term intensive training as well as to pay for him.

In the field of packaging, Alfa Laval the maker of Tetra Pak, expressed willingness to host him for a week in Sweden. Express Dairy in London also agreed to train him.

Armed with all these fellowships the young Ashok at the age of 19 strode out on his Odyssey, from his sheltered existence in India. He had learnt to drive a car well in the mean streets of Delhi, he had a way with words should he come across superciliousness and handling these training arrangements entirely on his own had done much for his self confidence.

What if he should come across thugs or vandals? He was physically fit, with regular swimming and tennis. He had taken boxing lessons in school and dabbled at karate and judo. Courage, he would find out, was not a permanent thing but a decision taken at that very moment. There was nothing more dangerous and misleading than typing yourself as per some pre-conceived notion of what you were like, whether through past experiences or the casual, often loosely thought out, or casually expressed opinions of others.

The other lessons he would have to learn himself. Life happens and Experience teaches you, if you let it.

4

Ashok is favoured because he is a boy, thought his younger sister Gita resentfully. He doesn't even know it. He thinks that's the way it is. He would be so mean, she remembered. He would get whatever lovely books, things he wanted and then he wouldn't share them. Would lock them up in a library and then demand borrowing money from his own family. He would justify it by saying that he needed to finance new acquisition of comics, other books. He would also say that we were not careful enough with his precious books. Compared to us he has so much freedom. Neeru his older sister also felt the same. Maybe such resentments are the germs of many a sibling fight, devastating yet common, over possessions, later on.

The three were close too. Close in age, they practised dance steps together from the Fox Trot to Cha Cha. They went to parties together and covered up for each other when required. It gave the parents a sense of security also that the girls were not going alone. But Ashok didn't like leaving the party at 10.30, just when things were getting really interesting because of a deadline on the girls. How archaic is this, they all thought.

Why couldn't our parents have been in the Army, Navy or Air Force - so much more broad minded.

There was a shared interest in the rock and folk music that flooded in from both the UK and the US, the Hollywood films that came to Plaza, Rivoli, Regal, Odeon, with their large pictures of Pat Boone and Elvis Presley adorning the main halls with their marble floors. They taught Ashok to consider girls wearing tight salwars with their kameezes as fashionably hep and the ones with loose salwars as pap *behenji* types, of no interest - traditional and sister like. The parameters of snobbishness and acceptability were being defined.

5

Ashok's parents were extremely upset about his leaving. It was a voyage into the unknown for their young son. They weren't ready to let him go as yet. He would learn about technology but there would be time enough for that. Ashok kept postponing his trip. He wanted them to let him go happily. Finally on the last day of his P Form - it was valid for 45 days, he left. It wasn't ideal, it wasn't the way he had wanted to leave but getting another P Form would be impossible. He had been trying his best to explain himself to them. He hoped they would understand somewhere, somewhat, even if they wouldn't show it. He touched his parents' feet, he hugged them, the whole family came to see him off at the airport. With his heart in his mouth, he left.

The first stop of his trip was Amsterdam. It was February of 1969. He had tried hard to get a Fellowship to the Netherlands. It was renowned for its Dairying from Friesland to all its regions. His dairy technologist teacher in Delhi who worked at their factory had glowing tales of his work and training there. The young Ashok was fascinated and his dreams began. But nothing worked out in that country. KLM however provided a good routing and a competitive fare. The air hostesses were warm, attentive, attractive. Ashok was reading *Durga Saptashati* in Sanskrit, a thin, soothing hard back with blue lettering on the cover-it would calm him down, these prayers to Amba, assuage his anxiety - a time tested method his father relied on and what worked for his father would work for him. He used to sleep with it under his pillow. A very pretty blonde hostess was curious and bent over him, asked many questions. She was clearly impressed. The airline proved to be an excellent choice. Ashok though attracted to this young woman who was giving him so much attention was in a serious mood. He had just left home. He could not be thinking about such frivolities. Better to pray. He had butterflies in his stomach.

The first night in picturesque Amsterdam with its doll's houses next to the canal, its attics, sloping roofs and unique façades was courtesy KLM. Ashok was very tired but wide eyed. The Dutch were very friendly. He asked for a glass of cold milk. It was delicious. Like nothing he had tasted before. He didn't know milk could taste so good. At dinner time too he wanted nothing else. Someone brought up a glass of cold milk to his room. It didn't lead to loose stool like this much milk in India might have.

The air was crisp and cold on his cheeks. There was snow everywhere. He felt the freshness of the cold. He loved it. Winter was not yet giving way to Spring as in Delhi.

He saw the city lights being put on early. There seemed to be a translucent fog hanging here and there. Small European cars with their chrome yellow lights sped by. He saw couples in most of them. The cars weren't filled to the brim like in India. He saw blonde women sitting in passenger seats and imagined them to be well read and interesting to talk to. They would be driving with their heads full of ideas, images, thoughts. They would go home and read something. At least a mystery novel if they were tired and wanted something light.

Was all of Europe so full of charm and character? He would have a lovely time. It lay ahead, full of promise.

There were dreams to be dreamt and fulfilled, promises to be made and kept.

The next morning was very cold and snowy. Ashok put on his overcoat, gloves and snow boots acquired in Kashmir and felt that he had come so far.

He didn't know a soul. He went to a stop outside the Hotel where the bus for the airport would come. He was the only one there. Was this the right place?

A bus drove up and stopped a few yards ahead. It stayed put. What was Ashok to do. He didn't want to miss it. He hesitated, then walked up to it and tugged at the door. It wouldn't budge. He tugged again, harder. Nothing happened. The driver looked impassive.

Ashok went back to the original place. Some Japanese came and stood next to him. At least there were others now. Suddenly the driver started the bus and pulled up. The hydraulic door opened automatically, with a hiss. There were many more people now. The bus wound its way through the picturesque town full of canals and rowhouses next to them. Ashok glanced at his reflection as the bus crossed other buses. What did people think when they saw him? What did his reflection represent?

6

The transit stop in Amsterdam over, his first exposure to Europe, it was time for the dairies in France. A short flight and he was in Paris. He was actually in this fabled place that evoked such images, this ultimate city of Love. It was hard to believe. There could be no better introduction to Europe. KLM, Amsterdam and now Paris. He watched as the autobus went past the Seine, the bridges of Paris. It seemed to be such an elegant city. The wide boulevards and avenues, the Champs Elysees, the Arc de Triomphe, the beautiful façades of the buildings on either side, with the wrought iron balconies and the large windows.

The bus took him to the Air Terminal at Invalides. The system of Air Terminals in the city centres all over Europe made a lot of sense to Ashok. It had all the facilities, you could check in or leave luggage, buy tickets, meet people, leave messages, use the toilets, eat or drink something and you were in the heart of town.

What was Invalides? Was it something to do with a Hospital, was it a World war memorial? Ashok wished he had some perspective.

He walked aimlessly a bit. No one was there to meet him. Large buildings loomed in the distance. Everyone seemed in a hurry. Everyone had someone with them. These were impersonal places. One could easily feel alienated, alone here. He remembered some of the avant garde movies of the times depicting how easily even the locals could feel isolated.

The French Ministry of Agriculture had given him directions where to go, where to stay initially in Paris. It was a small family run hotel, off the Champs Elysees, on one of the streets branching off a small street. It was clean and friendly. They had a cheerful looking *brasserie* coming out on the street.

It was well located and the young Ashok quickly felt at home. Even when he was sitting on an outside table and there was a call from his family in India, they knew where to find him. Impossible in a big hotel without leaving directions.

The young woman wearing specs in the Ministry was brisk and businesslike the next day. Told him where to go in France, how to get there, whom to meet in each factory and where to stay. A report was expected by the end of the sojourn at each factory. He knew where his evenings would go. She didn't speak any English but Ashok seemed to have a flair for languages and a particular affinity for French. He was surprised and pleased at how much he understood with the *niveau* of French he had.

He was to catch a train next morning for Lyon, *une grande ville provinciale*. This was down the Loire valley and beyond. The train was faster than any he had been on. The magnificent French countryside swept past wide windows designed to show the landscape - the tall trees next to wide open country roads, the occasional red or shiny, dark blue car zipping down them, the yellow mustard fields, the bridges and the romantic cottage below, next to the river.

A pretty girl smiled at the lean and muscular Ashok from the seat across. Ashok pursed his lips at the corners and grinned back confidently. The world was at his feet. Life's blows had not yet hit him.

He made his way to the dining salon. Petit dejeuner was a steaming mug of coffee, a long loaf of bread and some butter. People were biting off chunks of the bread and swallowing it down with the coffee. Was this all breakfast consisted of or was it like this on the train?

A factory van was thankfully at the station to meet him, with an amiable white coated fellow at the wheels. Ashok had not yet learnt to travel light. He didn't want to spend his hard earned stipend on clothes in Europe which would be expensive anyway. He lugged the heavy suitcase into the van and groaned. He had got doubles and triples of everything as if he was going off into the wilderness. To last him his whole trip. Even his Chip 'n Dale flannel nightsuit and elegant maroon Indian *bandgala* Jodhpur suit that he would wear at special occasions. He imagined sensuous nights with interesting strangers, who would be charmed by a young adult wearing Chipmunks with bright purple dots. Who knows what Life holds for you but you have your dreams.

Everyone wore long white coats inside the dairy. There were gleaming aluminium steel silver churns and other equipment everywhere, from different parts of Europe. There was an air of efficiency as people rushed around doing or not doing whatever they were supposed to do.

Ashok was to spend a day in each of the specialised production sections, observing everything from the maintenance of the machinery to its process control, minimising its energy and input consumption as per well laid out standards and maximising its output. The focus was *surtout* on Packaging and Quality Control of the product.

There was bright sunshine and blue skies outside, though it

was very cold. This was not the midi for nothing. No danger of Seasonal Affective Disorder here.

Ashok spent two days in the Laboratory, one each in the Bacteriological section and the regular Lab which counter-checked each aspect of quality and kept tabs on weights and measures and other specifics.

Ashok was so absorbed, he lost complete track of time. He wished he could have more time in each place but then he would miss out on the variety of different regions and what each specialised place had to teach him. He resolved to spend much more time in the lab in other places.

The factory was equidistant from Lyon and Dijon. After a couple of evenings Ashok felt settled enough to catch one of the efficient local trains to Dijon. He didn't know a soul there. He paused outside a brightly lit restaurant. It seemed to have many attractive young girls chatting away animatedly. There was a sea of blonde hair. How come there were so many blondes? This was half-way to the South of France and Ashok had already seen a number of people who didn't look that different from him.

There didn't seem to be a single empty table and the maitre d' seemed forbidding and unapproachable. Certainly, it seemed he wouldn't take kindly to imperfect French or any English words. He suddenly felt alone and isolated. He stood uncertainly outside the bright window. He wanted to get to meet some of these pleasant looking women. But how? He had been so confident at parties when being one of the first to walk up to strange new girls. The ravishing ones. Courage can be a matter of a moment.

One of the factories was in the part of France very close to the Italian border. The weekend came. He had discovered how sacred that was in Europe. Nothing would move. He had no plans but his garrulousness came to his rescue. He had just come to this factory three days ago as his training accelerated and had coffee during one of the breaks with a whole bunch of them in the factory café. The following day again he joined them. Did nothing in particular but was at ease. The next thing he knew was they were inviting him to drive down with them into the scenic Piedmont region of Italy with its hills and wine terraces for a weekend of hiking. He was fit, he liked the idea. Then something came to him. "But I don't have an Italian visa". They looked at him and dismissed the problem with a wave of the hand. "When we drive in, nobody will ask you". They seemed so confident, that Ashok thought that it did not seem reckless.

Piedmont was special. He had seen pictures of Tuscany. But it was its own thing. It was an unforgettable weekend, full of laughter, sweat, trekking, thirst, jokes. The wine tasted like nothing else he had tasted before and the wine fields on the slopes and valleys were splendiferous. They went on and on.

The following week Ashok's training took him to wondrous Provence, westwards towards Toulouse and Bordeaux, then back up towards Limoges, Nantes and Rennes, brief stays at specialised facilities near Rouen and Amiens and finally back to Paris where he had started. Some of the smaller factories and production units were clubbed with others in the weekly planning.

Ashok put his mind to the training. He learnt a lot. He had had no idea that the world of dairying could be so vast and fascinating. It had certainly been time well spent. His mind was brimming with new ideas and concepts, things that he would implement.

This was the advanced West. Everything was gleaming, well maintained, more ordered. Ashok quickly felt himself valuing money more than he had ever before. Maybe his sense of values was changing. There was a certain attractiveness about the multicoloured Franc and Lira banknotes. He felt like accumulating it for its own sake.

7

In Amiens arrangements had been made for him to stay at a monstrous soulless, concrete structure. He was only here for three nights. Should he stick it out or make a fuss? No, three days were three days. They should be well spent. He shuddered at the prospect of staying in that cold and impersonal building. Just across this hostel was an *auberge de jeunesse*. Far cheaper than the lodging that had been arranged. He wandered in there. It felt much more congenial.

Opposite the Reception there was a Café for snacks with self service trays. Ashok would have to sleep in a dorm with a bunch of young strangers. Sometimes these were divided into rooms with 6 to 8 beds, bunker style. Others were huge dorms with many beds in them. The bathroom was a row of sinks and toilets and showers in a row. There was the obligatory making your beds and stepping out of the hostel between 9.00 a.m. and 5.00 p.m. but Ashok would be at training anyway. He quickly made up his mind to shift there.

His local co-ordinator a very pleasant person, readily agreed to the new arrangements. Prof Casalis would have to be informed but that was all right.

After the first day's training, the sun still bright in the spring evening, he came and sat in a group of chairs next to the Reception. A girl in white flares came and looked him up and down when he was still standing. Strange, he thought. Was she trying to say something? Was he supposed to feel something? A pretty girl with high cheek bones, she came and stood near the chairs, a little while later. "What are you doing here?" she said in English.

Her name was Martine. She was from another town not far from Amiens, and was visiting it with a group of friends. What had caught her attention?

Ashok told her where he was from. They kept talking. She was really quite attractive, somehow very French. He sat next to her at dinner and they continued their conversation after dinner in the Lounge. He felt like asking her to come out for a walk but the hostel gates shut at 10.30 and it was lights out after that. The girls' dorm was not only separate but the entrance to it was through a door on the other side. Her face lit up as she smiled and said "Good Night".

They didn't fix to meet again. Would he see her again the next day?

At the factory he couldn't concentrate. He kept thinking of her and their discussions the previous evening.

It was another gorgeous evening. Everything was lit up. France could be so beautiful. There she was. It was only 5.00 p.m. Ashok had returned early. She was with a number of people but she came and sat with him in the Lounge. The discussion just took off and he didn't know where the time went.

Ashok could propose a walk outside this time. They walked in no particular direction. There was a canal with tall straw-coloured weeds growing next to it. They walked down a slope towards it.

They gazed at the flowing water and the discussion

continued. Now it was on Trotsky and how had his theories been implemented things might have been so different, how he was murdered in Mexico by fellow communists. The scene was like from an impressionist painting - the wild flowers, the blue water, the yellow banks. They sat down with the weeds almost reaching over their heads, but far apart enough to make comfortable sitting possible and the river scene no less visible.

Ashok chewed on a blade of grass. The breeze was cool and fragrant. There was a sense of timelessness.

The scene was too tranquil to continue talking about the Revolution. He talked about some of his dreams, some of life's conundrums that he hoped to resolve. Life spread out ahead for miles and miles... up to the horizon. Martine smiled knowingly at this. Or was it indulgently?

"You think I'm naïve...", he said breaking a weed and brushing her cheeks with it.

She continued to smile. This is what comes from opening up yourself, your thoughts?

He poked her ear with the weed. Was he teasing her? He had just met her.

They sat amongst the weeds, not far from each other. Well, he was really living life. He was doing what he wanted to do. The breeze became cooler, the evening bluer.

They started walking back towards the Auberge, but he wanted to spend more time with Martine. They came across a corner Café, it seemed family run. They were setting tables outside. The smell of delicious Minestrone wafted past. Was this an Italian family? They looked at the menu-the prices were affordable and the items were mostly Italian.

"Let's eat here" he said. A carafe of red house wine came with the meal. They talked easily.

There was a sign on the way back for a sale of clothes.

"I want to buy a pullover," he said suddenly. Let's go have a look"

They followed directions which involved taking a bus.

He liked a bottle green one and a red one. They were both thick and would keep him warm. Martine held them them up against his olive skin. They looked good on him. She approved. Such help was invaluable.

It was dark now and the street lights were bright.

They passed a group of children playing noisily. *"Vous êtes terribles. Les enfants terribles"*, she said to them, smiling. Why did she say that? She looked charming. Was she showing off?

They made it back to the hostel just before closing time. He wanted to talk to her some more but they couldn't sit in the Lounge. The lights would be put off. He looked wistfully at the door leading up to the Girls' section at the far end of the Hall. No one was looking. It would be so easy to go up the staircase behind it.

Martine caught his glance. He wanted to at least kiss her goodnight. What! He had just met her yesterday. He looked outside.

"Shall we go for a walk" he asked. She was willing. She was such a nice girl but it was clearly impractical.

He went back to the dorm. The lights were already off. Someone in the bunker bed diagonally below him kept making a restless tapping sound. He recognised him as a tall German boy he had talked to briefly. Ashok rustled his sheet impatiently, sibilantly. There was an embarrassed giggle and the noise stopped.

The third day was very interesting, absorbing. Ashok learnt many new things in Dairy Technology. He saw machines filling milk bottles set in a large moving circle at an amazing speed and capping them in red foil. He witnessed SIG butter packing machines and Westphalia centrifugal cream separators.

He had seen smaller versions but these were later models. The butter churners from Silkeborg were exquisite. So efficient. The very latest as were the atomisers for spray dried milk powder. He thought of Martine at lunchtime. He didn't even have her address. This was his last day at this factory. The next morning he would be on a train. He got an hour at the end to finish his report. He did it sitting in the Lab.

There was no Martine at the hostel. Had she left already? Did it matter? Life was full of chance encounters. You can't accumulate or collect people, he told himself.

He wondered what to do? Should he wander off somewhere? He might miss her.

Twenty minutes later she turned up, flushed pink, happy, with the same group of people. Maybe she had planned something with them.

She saw him, waved.

She was leaving the next day. Her address was 160 Boulevard de Chateaudun. She was still living with her parents. She would be free later in the evening. Yes, they could spend some time together.

A cock crowed in the distance. At this time?

He had brought some Livre de Poche today. He would try to read Francoise Sagan, Anais Nin, Georges Simenon *en francais*. Savour Colette and Maigret in their own *langue*, see what it tasted like. Shouldn't be too difficult. 'Don't get stuck on words', he told himself. 'Go for the global sense.' Some tea would be great with this. The Café was open. He bought some in a glass, the tea-bag colouring the hot water amber, the lemon slice making it delicious.

He stood on his toes and stretched.

"What are you doing? Some Yoga?" said Martine smiling, appearing out of nowhere.

"I know some *Asanas*", he thought "but I must learn many

more as soon as I get back. Its such a rich heritage, I must take full advantage of it."

She had been told by friends of a pleasant place, not far from there and not expensive. Natalie, a friend of hers, would also come for an aperitif.

They all ordered Martini Cinzano Vermouth. A day for amber coloured liquids with citron on the side.

Natalie was a thin girl with dark hair. It soon became clear that she found him appealing. This was always gratifying. She talked more than Martine and was nice but Ashok was intrigued by Martine and Martine was charming. He was also aware of some sense of urgency. This was his last evening with Martine. He found himself wishing that Natalie would leave. They would have to be back by the youth hostel's closing time, in any case.

"Paintings many times try to be three dimensional," Martine asked after Natalie left with a *bise* on each of Ashok's cheeks, "but when do they succeed?"

Should Ashok give a serious answer or a clever one. If the latter, it should be quick as well. Practice always helped in such matters. Of late his head was filled with Dairy. His thoughts went to cows giving better milk with music and affectionate treatment. They were loving animals who responded to how they were treated.

"Whenever the perception of the viewer makes it so. Perceptions differ of course. So each person's reality is subjective, especially vis a vis Paintings."

They stopped for a glass of wine at a Bistro. Ashok thought it was lucky that this was France and wine was not only a necessity but cheap as well, especially if it was the house wine.

They made each other laugh and walked home laughing. He stopped a few steps away from the Auberge. It was now or never. He was afraid of spoiling it.

She looked up at him as he stopped. Ashok kissed her. It was thrilling. It wasn't a long kiss but she responded. That was the best part. He smiled at her.

"Your eyes are honey brown" she said, almost in a whisper.

"Please keep writing", he said. "Maybe we'll meet again".

This time it was she who kissed him. It had a different quality and feel to it. Again, it was rapturous.

Their watches were showing 10.30.

They hastily slipped in through the door.

"*Au revoir,*" he whispered as she went to the forbidden staircase leading to the Girls' Dorm.

Early morning he caught the fast train to Paris and there he was with the city still waking up. End of his sojourn in France - last stop.

The factory here was in the outskirts - a large modern set up. He absorbed himself in the training - Martine kept flashing in his mind, he re-focussed on whatever he could pick up here. That is why he was here. Not for romance.

There were continual developments in Packaging and Technology. There was a lot to learn. The last days flew past.

The metro had its own unique smell, its own unique way of opening the doors. Gitane cigarettes everywhere instead of gum. He came to the city and sat in streetside Cafés. Even the streets were brightly lit. Under the various bridges he saw many a young couple. He watched the theatre of life. Sometimes he wished for someone to share it with.

8

Part of Ashok's training was in the Research and Development Lab, which included some pilot plants. One of the girls particularly struck him. His glance kept inadvertently falling on her. The machine she was testing looked very state of the art. She had a thin sensitive face, she was petite. He felt some of those indescribable sensory waves, those vibrations that emanate from other people or are a product of some non-verbal dynamic between the two.

Should he talk to her? Would these chance meetings mean anything? Wasn't everything transient, he told himself.

He couldn't look at life and relationships in such a utilitarian fashion. One didn't have to get something out of everything. That wouldn't be him. Did that include intangibles. His thoughts went to Martine. Would he ever see her again? Surely. He wanted to, but would chance and circumstances enable it to happen? Even if they didn't he was indescribably richer by the experiences of those three days. The young can be very wise.

He saw her leaving possibly for a drink of water. They had a drinking fountain here, very American. He waited behind her. He smiled at her when she finished. She smiled in return.

"*Tres interessant*" he said referring to her high tech machine. Not Oscar Wilde but he had to say something fast.

"*Vous aimez votre travail?*"

"*Ba-oui*" she shrugged.

He had some more questions related to the working of the machine. Could he ask her after work?

She was no great expert but yes, 5 o'clock.

Let's go down, talk over some coffee, he suggested.

He didn't want to sit in the factory café. They could sit at a café near her house. He caught the suburban train and metro with her and several stops later they alighted in a pleasant Paris *banlieue* he had not seen before. A short walk later they were sitting in a congenial bistro. Her place was round the corner, she said.

He wanted something typical, so she suggested kir, champagne or white wine with cherry syrup. Very common, not at all expensive. He loved the sweet taste. Ah! this was the life. He didn't start off with the machine at once.

There was no need. Too serious.

She had been working there since a year. Would continue for the moment. Didn't know how long. It was pleasant working in a Dairy. She too liked the smell of dairy produce.

She had another sister, a younger one, about to finish school. She still lived with her family but would move out soon.

She had been on this machine from the time she finished her in-house training. Sometimes she worked half-days on Saturdays in the main factory to earn overtime, when she felt the need for some extra cash. Her name was Nicole.

She enjoyed going to museums and looking at paintings when she had the time, especially those that had human expressions. Did she like nudes, as well? Some of them were quite interesting and sensitively done.

When he felt they were about mid-way in their conversation, he asked Nicole details of the machine. His bona fides should not be doubted. And he really wanted to know about the machine. She was intelligent and observant. He felt she was observing him as well. Was there a hint of mischief in her eyes? Was there a slight knowing smile? He absorbed himself in her explanation.

The Paris *soir* was still young. The young Ashok was charmed by the city of Romance. Its avenues were brightly lit and its monuments, the facades of four-five storeyed buildings lining the streets and its fountains were as elegant as the well dressed women.

He had no definite plan. He had such little time, he couldn't cover it methodically. There was no point. Better to just enjoy whatever arises as Zen thinkers say.

He just took the bus and got off wherever seemed interesting. He didn't even know the names of the *quartiers*. It didn't matter. The key was to make the most of it. He would never be this age again. The same he would not be here again.

He wandered into an area he later found out was Pigalle. It seemed full of hustle and bustle. A number of women, particularly on certain streets, smiled at him or looked at him invitingly. My God! Why was this?

He suddenly felt like going home exhausted by all that he was absorbing and slept like a log.

The next evening he waited for her again. He hadn't fixed up anything, nor had there really been any opportunity. If she was not free or didn't want to spend time with him that evening - *tant pis*.

But she was. May we sit somewhere nice and have a glass of red wine?

They went to the *Quartier Latin*. The ambience was unique. It was *tres vivant*. It was full of young people, more girls than boys, laughing, walking in the narrow streets, who seemed oblivious to what time it was, middle aged people with a youthful, vibrant air about them. Ashok felt that it seemed to affect plebeianism. It seemed both genuine (in *espirit*) and acquired in terms of actual needs perhaps. What was not affected was its intellectual air.

When he told Nicole this, she said "Ah! the keen observant eye of *l'etranger*."

"Shall I continue?" he said "some of these are professors, some are musicians, some aspiring film makers *toujours* searching for inspiration, some are painters - of course, talented, unrecognised" he added with a smile.

"And some are merely lost souls..." she finished.

Boulevard St Germain with its special atmosphere, Boulevard St Michel, Ashok kept up with Nicole who seemed full of boundless energy as she traversed different *rues*.

When they reached 'Les Deux Magots' she said, "let's sit here. This is where Sartre and other *bien-connus* had thoughtful coffees."

"No doubt came up with inspiring ideas, while sipping the stuff," added Ashok.

The menu prices reflected the eminence of its clientele. All visitors would want to sit and savour the feeling that came with it.

Well, they could afford a Café. Ashok had to balance between saving foreign exchange for the future and getting enough out of the present, which would never come back.

He was feeling peckish now but the food in these Cafés was singularly limited. What happened to the famous French cuisine? All you could get was expensive *Croque-Monsieur* and a few other items.

For proper food they would have to go to a restaurant. He asked her if she could stay for dinner and was pleased when she agreed. They would go back to the student areas and eat there.

How about a Café theatre, she suggested. It was a sudden thought. Ashok had never heard of such a thing. He liked the sound of it. It was a brilliant idea. One of them had a performance slated for that evening and it wasn't far from where they were.

It was in a well lit basement with large windows. It seemed interesting. There was another well attended restaurant on the ground floor. They descended the spiral staircase leading down. All the tables were set facing a portion of the floor which was the stage. It was an intimate setting, quite different from a regular Theatre.

The performance was also something in between a cabaret and a play. Initially, Ashok was horrified at the mention of cabaret. But Nicole and the actual performance itself quickly dispelled the erroneous stereotype he was carrying from India. Moreover, this was not a strip-tease.

He gave light attention as one does in meditation. More would have been a strain and with less he wouldn't have understood.

The presence of Nicole, the entertainment, *du bon vin*, the excellent food made for a stimulating evening. Is this how Parisians lived?

He enjoyed the plot and the spectacle.

Was it chance, an accident, that in both places in a short time, which is all he had, he had managed to meet two quite different but interesting people? Should he take credit for forming some sort of relationship with each or was it the dynamics of the interaction and the chemistry in each case?

He walked Nicole home and enjoyed the walk through the streets. This was live theatre in front of the pavement cafés.

There was attraction. It created an electro-magnetic field, a subtle one but the tension was more palpable.

Nicole read voraciously - mostly fiction, of all types - very good stuff and things he had never heard of. She runs through trashy stuff as well as biographies, romance, mystery, suspense, thoughtful stuff as long as it's still fiction, she explained. She did not seem to have intellectual pretensions but was coming across as intelligent and someone who enjoyed life without needing to label it. Politics she thought was 'dirty cooking' and best kept away from.

They reached outside her parents' home. He thanked her. Only an insider can make you see things in a particular way. She smiled warmly. She had had a good time and it had been a break from the factory routine on working days. As he kissed her cheek, the corners of their lips touched, almost imperceptibly.

His last day of training in Paris passed quickly. It was a busy schedule and included a meeting with the Management. It included going at 4 in the morning for the milking (to the music of Chopin) of some of the best breeds of cows which up till now had only been names in Dairy Journals and Textbooks. They had to go some distance into the countryside for that but the roads were very good and empty at that time of the day. There were very tall trees lining the roads, heightening the illusion of grandness and space. The dawn light was gradually suffusing the landscape from somewhere below the horizon. But a full moon still hung low in the sky between the trees. No wonder so many English authors had been captivated by the South of France and this wasn't even that countryside as yet.

The summing up meeting at the Ministry had taken place

over the mid-morning coffee break. Prof J Casalis seemed pleased with the training and their decision regarding the Technical Co-operation Fellowship. Ashok had managed to set a good precedent for those to follow in the years to come.

He saw Nicole at her machine and smiled at her. He waited for her by the factory door in the evening. Please would she come with him to Montmartre this evening.

It was a good choice. The atmosphere was unique as was the feeling of going up the hill. There were artistes everywhere still and the night life was full of promise. This was the area of Moulin Rouge and the Can-Can after all. Girls kicking up their shapely legs may no longer be shocking but it was evocative of Toulouse-Lautrec, a bygone era and so many nameless things.

They got an early dinner table at a place that seemed typical albeit the name didn't mean anything to Ashok. These places filled up early and if they dawdled at a Café on the way up and then came here, there would be no place. Better to choose early and to choose well.

Ashok couldn't decipher some of Nicole's expressions. Sometimes he thought there was a hint of irony. From what part of her past did it come, thought Ashok. Sometimes it was something else. She was a complex creature. In a way that added to her attractiveness. Taller than Martine but still petite. Very pretty - the sort of looks that grow on you. Nicole had a pleasing light golden complexion, her features were typically French. When she smiled her upper lip curled in a way that made it feel flirtatious. It might or might not have been cultivated, now it was a part of her.

This place was ideal for dancing. Ashok felt an excitement in his legs. He asked Nicole to dance. There was an area between the tables and the stage. He was pleased at how well they moved together. The wine had already arrived and the first glass drunk.

More people came on to the dance floor. Music for fast dancing came on, preparatory to putting people in the mood for the can-can or equivalent. Ashok was pleased to find that Nicole was good at that as well and kept up with him. Who knows what creature lurks behind what façade? If he had been dismissive of her as one of the many girls on the shop floor he would have missed out on this richness. And she wouldn't have dreamt of making the first move. There it was the story of many a life - what might have taken place and what did.

Ashok loved dancing. It would never tire him. He felt the damp inside his shirt and the perspiration on his brow but he was lost in it. The food, the drink, everything became immaterial. There was him, his partner, the music and the movement. It had been like that at College parties which often lasted the whole night. Once a whole lot of them went to India Gate, and bought ice cream at 5 in the morning from a cart standing near Rashtrapati Bhavan. Ashok didn't really expect anyone to be there at that time. But there he was.

The scene had completely changed, the characters were different, he had evolved, moved on but the damp shirt and the losing himself in the dancing were reminiscent of things that seemed a long time back but were actually only a couple of years away.

Nicole was tireless and in no hurry to get back to the table but the spectacle was about to happen, so it was time to *mange* alongside. The courses were superb. The music and the bevy of *jeunes femmes* rushing on stage made Ashok pause *mid-morceau*. They just kept coming on to the stage. How many were there? The beat changed and they stood in an arc and kicked up their legs. They were shapely. The atmosphere was evocative of *a la recherche du temps perdu* but not only that.

They were both surprised to find themselves enraptured by the spectacle. Neither of them expected it to be as good or as absorbing. There are hidden treasures if only you'll open yourself to them.

By the time they had dessert - a sort of sorbet of *fraise* and the cognac it was about 2 a.m.. Late for Nicole who had to be on the job the next morning and for Ashok who was leaving France but the atmosphere in Montmartre was such that the night seemed young. It lent itself to an almost reckless attitude - tomorrow who had seen it?

Nicole and Ashok found themselves laughing and walking down the cobblestoned street that sloped down.

Ashok had an intuitive feeling that Nicole could be quite difficult. But even if so, she was right now in a gay mood.

"Is it safe?" asked Ashok the foreigner thinking of the lateness of the hour and the strangeness of the setting. Cities were cities and anything could happen. In response Nicole gave a confident laugh. Ashok kissed her cheek. After some time, he kissed it again but could not move away. He found his tongue darting against her cheek. As he stayed there he felt her tongue darting from side to side, almost playing with his, on the other side of her cheek. It's as if kissing on the mouth was not yet permitted so they had to make the most of what could be done without that. The young Ashok felt a thrill course through him. He forgot everything else as they stood close together in the coolness of the night. Nobody paid them any attention. This was not India.

As they continued walking downwards, Ashok impulsively put an arm around Nicole. They passed a small Café with *crêpes* written on it. What was it doing open at this hour? Shades of

India Gate? But this was Montmartre. He bought a salted one for himself and with blueberries for Nicole. He had a sudden desire to exchange his half finished one with hers. She ran away from him giggling. She could run quite fast. Ashok had to make quite an effort to catch up. He made as if to snatch her crêpe. She laughed like a child caught. Instead he spun her around and kissed her, the crêpe still in his hand. It became a long kiss and they found themselves breathless when they finally unclenched.

They were out of Montmartre now. A taxi was whizzing past. They hailed it and headed towards Nicole's home. In the back of the taxi he kissed her again. There was passion in it now. My God! He thought. This is like in the movies. Is this really happening? I'm really living life.

He felt the softness of her chest next to his. His mind stopped and he was lost in the embrace.

He took Nicole's contact address - to get hold of her whenever he managed to see her next, which might be months or longer. Her parents would always know her whereabouts. The encounter with her was full of promise. He would love to see her again. His time in France was at an end but his life was just beginning. He had met two such people, Martine and Nicole, in an intensely packed bit of time. He would surely be back sooner or later.

Was a long term relationship in the future conceivable, he wondered. Would she appreciate the wit of Oscar Wilde or Tom Stoppard the way he did? She hadn't grown up with Enid Blyton or Billy Bunter or Agatha Christie or P G Wodehouse. Nor with Little Lulu, Tubby, Nancy and Sluggo, Huckleberry Hound or Woody Woodpecker. Lone Ranger, Cheyenne had transported him to the Wild West and the romance of Wagon Train and the pioneers. These influences were cellular. Were they necessary as a common denominator?

It couldn't be that his eventual partner had to be Indian, British or American. That wasn't him.

9

He left France for the shores of Polska via Frankfurt, not quite with an aching heart but the young experience an intensity that only they know about. It was the month of May.

Maybe he would come across his true love like this whether he was ready or not. Who knows about these things. And these encounters were as much about finding himself he pondered. To understand his sexual self. To know what really mattered to him.

There was no Dairy Scholarship in *Pologne*. It probably wasn't that advanced in Dairy Technology anyway but there was an invitation to visit factories in Warsaw, Wroclaw (Breslau when it was German), the Nowa Huta area and Cracow. Might gain something. Would be interesting to visit Poland in any case.

Warsaw was dull and grey in its architecture, soul-destroying monstrous Soviet style construction, block after block with tiny windows and a non-human scale. Most of Warsaw had been destroyed. There were hardly any resources. The Communists had to re-build quickly, cheaply and on a mass scale. Aesthetic appeal wasn't a relevant parameter. These were more basic, survival issues.

The girls were good looking, many of them. Well defined, well proportioned features, refined faces.

No wonder they were considered the best looking in Europe. He had been hearing this. It seemed well deserved.

In Warsaw, the factory was on the other side of the river - in Praga, the poorer part. The milk bottling equipment was *Angielski* - Udeck. The same pasteurisers, cream separators. Machines from Vulcan Laval, Koltek Oy in Finland. The milk powder was spray dried - an atomiser at the top of the huge cone. The machines were all Western but not state of the art. He had assumed it would be technically more advanced than in India, if not like the West. In fact some of the Management control systems were not as efficient. Indian business could teach them a thing or two. Of course, the Communist era was still very much there. The dairy staff were all white coated but they did not have the same air of briskness about them. There was an underlying lack of care. The lab did not give off the same sense of cutting edge research or of purpose.

Should he cut short his visit and go back to the West. There may be nothing to pick up here. But lessons are not only technical. Besides, his programme was tightly set.

He had been given the choice of staying with a family in Mokotow or one of the Orbis Hotels. The hotel was characterless and depressing. There was a stale air about it, the view was monotonous - of plain grey cement façades and tall buildings. Ashok would feel neurotic here.

The family in Mokotow was warm and friendly, characteristic of Poland, even in Warsaw. Of course, nobody minded their own business.

The husband worked for the Foreign Ministry and spoke some English. The rest of the family, like most of Poland then, had no acquaintance with English. Ashok peered at the letters. They were Roman. How could the language be so completely different. At least in French there were obvious similarities with many *mots en anglais*, even if the *prononciation* was different.

Piotr the husband settled down in the evening with some golden piwo with froth at the top, in an invitingly shaped convex glass. He offered him some. The piwo was surprisingly good and 10 bottles came for 25 zlotys. The official exchange rate was 1 US $ = 24 zl. The unofficial rate was 135 to the dollar.

Ashok was learning to adjust fast. He felt settled enough the next evening to take a tram. A ticket which had to be punched into a machine inside the tram was just 1 zl, bought from kiosks called Ruchs. They sold newspapers, cigarettes, condoms and other items of hour to hour need. These were open for long hours and you could just step out on to a street and find one, not too far away. They were even more ubiquitous than the piping hot sausage stands downtown.

Sometimes there was a Wild West feeling. Groups of men stood around some of the main city streets. As he neared one such group of rough looking young men he felt some tension. Was it his imagination or was something happening. As he drew quite near the tension increased. One of them said in a gruff voice "*masz agnia*". In a flash Ashok thought of *agni* in Sanskrit. The young man was testing him for the group. Young children did it more innocently when they saw a foreigner by asking "*ktura jest godzina?*" - 'what is the time', to see if he understood Polish. Ashok lit a match and offered it to them. He had passed. He was one of them. They let him be. He might have just escaped being roughed up.

He took his place in the queue at the tram stand. A tram arrived with the clanging of bells. It said 31. It was headed for Zoliborz and various destinations beyond. None of the destinations or stops meant anything. What the heck, he would just take it. He would probably never be in Poland again.

The tramlines lay thick across the city. Often two trams

would pass right next to each other going in opposite directions. The trams were brightly lit from the inside highlighting the characters standing or sitting. There seemed to be no passenger limit in these peoples' transports. At rush hour these and the autobuses could be impossibly crowded.

There were two trams linked and Ashok sat in the first row of the one behind. He could look into the tram hooked up in front. At turns and bends the tram ahead would be at an angle to the one behind such that you felt like you were peering into a drawing room window.

A few rows from the back of the first tram sat a vivacious dark-haired girl laughing and talking to a blonde girl standing next to her. Ashok's eyes kept straying back to the dark one. When she laughed which was often, there was such an attractive quality about her. She was good looking. Manners would have kept him from staring at her but in Warsaw people stared a lot he noticed, including at him. Inexplicable but true.

She saw him looking at her. She indicated him to her companion. How come nobody else was looking at her? He couldn't keep his eyes off her.

The tram had travelled quite far now, stopped many times. But it didn't matter to Ashok. He just had to take the same tram number back in the opposite direction. At each stop it would stop for a minute. He saw them getting off. Until now he'd thought nothing of it. Almost without thinking Ashok got off at the same stop. A second later the tram moved off. Very few people had gotten off there. It helped Ashok in not feeling self-conscious approaching them, a hangover from his Indian upbringing. The tram stop was dimly lit and open from all sides with tramlines running off in all directions and at different angles into the darkness. A strong night wind blew at them lifting their hair and carrying leaves with it.

They smiled at each other. The dark girl had such pretty

dimples. He thought of how she'd been laughing a moment ago. It was very appealing. He was glad he'd gotten off.

Ashok couldn't live without music. Even in France he had acquired a small portable record player. Lennon singing about holing up in the Amsterdam Hilton went through his head. On an impulse he said, "Beatles....*musik*....*herbata*...". Would they come? He was a stranger - foreign looking. But they must have liked him enough - felt sufficiently at ease.

He had independent access to his room in Mokotow. With the wind blowing about them he talked to them in his broken Polish a little while longer. It was just as well that he seemed to have a natural flair for languages and picked them up very fast. The training in Sanskrit his parents had given him in his formative childhood years helped. Polish was part of the Indo-European group of languages and although it seemed totally different from English, random reflection revealed words and word roots in common with Sanskrit.

They found themselves in the same tram 31 heading back. It was a little surreal. The blonde one's name was Danuta and the dark, pretty one was Barbara. Ashok knew that much of flirting is actually non-verbal. Facial expressions, the way you smile, the expression in your eyes, the depth of your gaze, the play of eyes.....You might have much knowledge or intelligence and you might be too serious or a bore or an upper class twit.

Ashok put some tea on in the kettle.

"*Mleko!*" they said "yeech" when he asked if he should add that. These were Europeans - the idea of strange English customs like milk with their tea was unthinkable. *Herbata* was with a slice of lemon and sugar if you wanted, drunk in a glass.

He put on a 45 'Don't let me down'. The music was very catchy. They sang along in their cute Polish accents. The 't' was much softer like in French or Hindi.

"Don't let me down
Don't le-e-et me down
I'm in love for the first time
Don't you know its gonna last
Don't let me down
Don't le-e-et me down"

Western music was not available. It added to the novelty. He wished he had something else from the West to show them.

Ashok held out his arms for Barbara to dance. In the music he forgot everything. He moved to the music automatically, without thinking. She came closer and their bodies moved together smoothly. Synchronicity.

Ashok danced with Danuta. But his mind was on Barbara and soon he was dancing with her again. The light was too bright. Everything seemed comfortable. He flipped it off. He felt an irresistible pull towards Barbara. She called him "*Czarnuszku*". The 8 o'clock shadow added to the impression.

He kissed her while dancing. She kissed him back. Their mouths opened more and the kiss intensified. She was as attractive as she was nice looking. Kissing her was ecstasy, Ashok found. How did it happen so fast? Ashok couldn't say but he revelled in it. And somehow the taste of her kiss corresponded to her looks. This is what it would be like.

Danuta flipped on the light. She had been left out too long.

Danuta held out her arms in front of her in a dance pose and said something in Polish which sounded like 'oh yeah? So the two of you can go mmmmm again.' English wasn't needed. It didn't sound crude, it was said nicely. It was amusing but Ashok felt a strong attraction to Barbara and just wanted to be back in the kiss with her.

Tact was called for as well as strategy. He sat between them, put on a 1967 album of the Beatles, the one which had 'I need you' and the cover of which showed them standing above and looking down a stairwell. He poured some more *herbata*. He had bought some dark Wedel chocolate. Given that it was not a consumer society, it was unexpectedly good. He passed that around. His eyes said it all to Barbara. Her look was expressive. Their eyes found each other's. Barbara had laughing dancing eyes. The subtlest of dimples formed on her cheeks at times.

He had brought a few presentation items from Cottage Industries in Delhi. He was going to give them when he stayed with people or when someone was exceptionally nice and helpful.

He took out a small ivory elephant carving for Barbara and a walnut wood paperweight for Danuta. Ivory was still not *interdit* those days. Both were exquisitely carved. They both examined their presents with pleasure. It was obvious that they had never set eyes on anything like this. Such things only came out of India. While Danuta was still examining her *cadeau*, he whisked Barbara off her feet. He liked her proximity and the feel of her hand in his. He didn't want to risk that spark of jealousy in Danuta's eyes again but he knew he wanted very much to kiss Barbara.

The cool night air blew the drapes further apart. Only women could handle women. She was dying for a cigarette and she waved the empty packet of *papierosy*. They had both been smoking in the tram. Would Danuta be a *kochana* and get some for both of them from the nearest Ruch. She held out the *Pieniadze*. It was an obvious ruse but maybe Danuta partly gave up on Ashok. It was hard not to sense his pull towards Barbara. He found her intensely attractive. Danuta was pretty, had a pleasing personality, seemed intelligent. She wouldn't be gone long but Ashok wasted no time. He kissed Barbara and she returned the kiss. The chemistry between them was superb. Their kiss intensified and deepened. They still moved around but both of them lost awareness of the world outside the kiss.

Things had escalated so fast. In the context of the interaction between them it felt OK however. 'Don't let me down' would be memorable in a fresh context as well.

In a few moments Danuta was back. She let them continue dancing and kissing. It still wasn't fully dark outside. At this latitude it had started getting darker later and later. The air that blew in from the window was cool and pleasant. Danuta puffed at her cigarette in the dark. The threesome had to be sustained. Ashok stopped presently to change the music and put on some more *herbata*. Ashok's Polish improved by leaps and bounds, enough for him to tease them.

He walked with them outside and they found a taxi beyond a bridge. He took down their phone numbers and addresses and walked with them upstairs to their first floor flats, opposite each other's. He fixed up to meet Barbara again the following evening. They had said *'dobranoc'* to Danuta first. Ashok didn't have the luxury of time in Poland. He hoped there wouldn't be complications the following day and he would have some time just with Barbara.

Polish lead crystal was famous even in the non-market oriented Communist days and the bowls and other items were superbly crafted. They were available along with handicrafts from the Tatra mountains and other regions, in Orbis and Cepelia shops, where payment could only be made in freely convertible currency. The potato-based Polish vodka was very good and the best export quality was available in these outlets.

Ashok had noticed that the main food items were some form of pig meat with loads of mashed potato on the side, with some beetroot. The meat and potatoes were obligatory. Just as well that the national drink was based on potatoes which were farmed in abundance.

Ashok pottered around some of the Orbis outlets near Aleje Jerozolimskie and Ulica Marszalkowska. He had some French francs left but better to keep them in reserve, he thought. You never know what situation arises. Besides he still had to go to many places for training and didn't fancy lugging crystal all over.

At 12 noon the Polish radio would play a certain Chopin tune in announcement of the hour. That was now playing. His visits to other factories in the area were to start then. He was to be picked up from the front of the Metropole Hotel below the prominent red electric Air India sign with the trademark centaur which could be seen from far away in the city at night. Air India didn't land there but such was the state of fraternal relations between the two 'socialist' nations.

In these other factories in various outskirts of the city Ashok once again found that the technology, the processes, the machines were of the same level as at his factory in India. Even the makes were the same Western ones. There was a bit more mechanisation of handling and there wasn't as much labour to be seen. Other than that they could have been in India.

But he was glad he had come to Poland. It didn't take long to feel how different it was from the West. It was the Second World, in its approach to materialism, its values, its culture. It exposed him to another dimension, one that would start to be assimilated in the West in just over a couple of decades but no possibility could have seemed more remote at the time.

As a foreigner he had to go and register with the District administration in Warsaw, even if he was there for only a few days. His host went with him to the local office inside a small bungalow surrounded by other low set bungalows in a compound. Endless forms in Polish had to be filled. By the end of it he understood that *nazwisko* meant surname, *podpis* meant signature. His host jabbered on in Polish with a lot of *pravdas* thrown in for confirmation at the end of the sentence, explaining what, Ashok wondered. A one time visit also had to be made to the Police headquarters at Palac Mostowski.

There must be a dossier on everyone especially every visitor thought Ashok.

He was interviewed by a pleasant attractive slightly plump blonde lady who at the time seemed middle aged to Ashok but must have been in her mid-30's. She spoke enough English and Ashok felt that somehow she knew everything about his visit to Poland the *rencontre* with Barbara included. Yet there was nothing sinister about it and he got none of the 'I have done nothing, comrade' feeling portrayed in Western cold war fiction. There was a basement in the stone and granite building with grills outside. Ashok remembered walking outside the previous day and thinking that they must be interrogating people in these basements.

She seemed indulgent, understanding with a 'boys will be boys attitude'. Ashok wanted to fit her into a pre-conceived notion but couldn't help liking this person who seemed *sympatyczne*, like a supportive friend in a strange place. As the discussion continued he felt her attractiveness even more strongly. "Why am I being attracted to her of all people", he asked himself. But these things have no answers.

Maybe she was meant to be like that, in that position. Maybe it was just their dynamics.

Evening came and it was time for the tryst with Barbara. Ashok felt that he was living intensely all right. Paris and Amiens seemed so far away and yet it was only a few days ago.

Barbara looked very good again, her dark attractive complexion emphasised the particularity of her features. Danuta was also there.

They decided to go to the *stare miasto* - the old town was one of the few parts that had been restored piece by piece in the rubble that became Warsaw. It still retained its charm and had not yet been subjected to the gross commercialism that started taking over the place in the 90's.

En route in the tram Danuta produced some sweet Polish snacks, somewhat similar to *shakar-paras*. Ashok wasn't in the mood for something sweet, shook his head.

Danuta looked up at him, mischief in her eyes.

"*Dla czego? Nie jest dobsze?*' - 'It's not good?' Her face had an expression of mock hurt.

They went to a well-known sports bar at the other end of the Old Town Square. The girls talked animatedly, their sentences ending with musical Polish intonations. Ashok found their vivaciousness and this way of talking, charming, unique.

Ashok was careful that Danuta didn't feel excluded. They went to a corner restaurant in the *stare miasto* known for its duck meat and borscht. The two friends were very comfortable with each other and Danuta's presence helped enhance the playful atmosphere. It extenuated for Ashok's lack of fluency in Polish. The duck was accompanied by shredded very red looking beetroot and preceded by some excellent turnip soup straight out of the Enormous Turnip. The duck was light not heavy as it often can be.

There were a lot of young people about in the Old Town square, some were yelling to each other across the Square. The atmosphere was one of revelry and gaiety. Contagious.

Barbara seemed to have reached an implicit understanding with her good friend and neighbour that they would not be a threesome after a point.

Danuta made no attempt to accompany them afterwards. Ashok finally had Barbara all to himself.

'Don't let me down' had become their song. He put it on. He'd managed to get some hand made candles. He lit those at either end and the room was suffused with a golden glow and shadows produced by the candle-light. They danced slowly, unhurriedly, without the pressure of Danuta's presence. The night was still young.

10

He was on a schedule, early morning he caught his flight to Cracow - the ancient capital. It was a short journey of less than an hour on LOT - Polskie Linie Lotnicze. The plane was an Antonov 24 - a turbo prop. The fare in zlotys if converted was $7. Cracow was lovely. It hadn't been destroyed in the war and unlike Warsaw had a lot of character and charm. The façades of the buildings evoked France in many ways. The corrugated iron balconies and protections in front of the large windows were very European. The soul destroying feeling that Ashok was aware of, in spite of himself in Warszawa, was missing. Behind the tall trees and the benches in the narrowest of parks were visible captivating buildings, some of them with ornate elevations.

Ashok imagined Cracow as it must have been 400 years ago. The corner villas with reddish roofs set in gardens and the angled walls were quintessentially European. He imagined tutors teaching Chopin in more recent times, to pretty young maidens. Prior to the lesson there would be a *szynka* sandwich and a steaming mug of *herbata*. He passed the *Uniwersitet Krakowski* on the way to the Dairy plant. He asked his hosts if they could take a *chukker*. The students looked bright and animated. The names of the departments were written in Latin at the tops of the buildings, near the base of the triangles which were part of the design on the façade at the top. He felt like studying there but he knew well that you can't be a student everywhere.

The plant itself was more modern than the one in Warsaw. The latest machinery was there and it had an air of efficiency and purpose. Technology does have an impact on people's motivation and how they feel, mused Ashok.

The dispersion in the atomiser at the top of the milk powder plant was much faster. Ashok hadn't known that was possible but frontiers were constantly changing.

The sun was setting amongst the old city steeples and spires. It was spectacular - a scene out of a painting.

Ashok's thoughts went to Dubcek and the Prague Spring. He had still been in Delhi University then. He remembered his indignation and despair at the thought of a world that had almost changed but didn't. It hadn't felt far away at all. This was the age of idealism.

But Polish troops had participated in the suppression of another small satellite state, despite their own long standing history of persecution by larger and more powerful neighbours - sometimes to the extent of disappearing off the map for long periods. How could they?

And operatic paeans were still being sung in false arias on Polish radio to Wladyslaw Gomulki. There's a limit to a political culture of sycophancy.

The next morning Ashok lugged his baggage, wishing that he had left some in Warsaw. It was very heavy - it had stuff to last him throughout his training in Europe. In carrying it he was tilted way over to the other side. He had picked a soft leather black suitcase, which was light and sturdy. But there were no wheels at the time and the lessons of life like travelling light are learnt through experience.

The train chugged its way out of the station blowing steam and coal in Ashok's eyes as he looked out the open window. The Polish countryside with miles and miles of golden fields interspersed with green hedges and groves of tall trees swept past as they made their way towards Nowa Huta. This was the steel area Ashok learnt, but there was this Dairy there worth a visit according to the Polish Ministry of Agriculture which looked after Dairying.

This was really the countryside with small towns having a High Street a single hotel and church on it, people standing around in groups and spilling over on the streets. No one paid him much attention. Strange characters came out of Warsaw. It was more of interest to swill *piwo* in the bar.

Ashok didn't want to spend the night although the hotel room was decent sized and cost only 90 zloty. The night train saw him on his way further West to Wroclaw. From there he would circle back East and end his Polish journey in Warsaw.

Ashok overslept past Wroclaw and woke up in a small town which was not far away. Fortunately the train stopped there as well and after wild eyed and anxious enquiries hopped off there. Even at the enquiry office no one spoke English but he managed to get directions for a bus back to Wroclaw from a middle aged man who in a common human understanding said *"hollera! Dobszy szpi,"* - slept well-in the still early morning. Ashok got a front seat in the red bus as it drove towards the rising sun.

Wroclaw was picturesque with some of the low-rise slanting roofed bungalows set in neat little gardens still intact. Poland was very Polish and *en meme temps* typically European. The lovely evocative sounds of Chopin on the piano floated out of a few windows. He also thought he recognised Liszt.

Some of the Wild West feeling that some of the groups of young men standing around in bunches gave off in places like Warsaw was less evident in more Western parts of Poland.

The factory had white unsalted butter like most of Europe. The English yellow butter with salt had not yet crept in. Some of the packaging machines Ashok hadn't encountered before and he studied them with interest.

11

Wroclaw felt much better than Lodz. It would be an experience to spend the night there. The Odra river - the former Oder river when it was the Polish-German boundary, not long ago, mused Ashok, with the beautiful bridges spanning it was picturesque as was the University with its typical cream coloured close set buildings with the onion shaped roofs and slanting attics atop six storeys. Many parts of Wroclaw, especially the University area seemed un-destroyed, unlike Warsaw. There was a symphony performance on and there were special dollar tickets. Ashok was hardly loaded but even 1$ was a lot here and he could spare a few from his savings.

A pleasant looking young man somewhat older than him, with slicked down hair was sitting next to Ashok. He smiled at Ashok and in the interlude was standing next to him when Ashok ordered a tall thin glass of iced white wine and a canapé with ham on it. The usual language problem was there - no one but no one spoke English - but Ashok had learnt by now how not to let a little thing like that stand in the way of companionship. The young man ordered the same items. The orchestra members seemed talented. Some of them were very young. His girl friend Teresa was a flautist. The State gave patronage and they played music full time. They loved their work which is the only way to work, realised Ashok. Adam himself was a student in the University in the process of writing his thesis for his *pracy magisterski*.

He went backstage with Adam. The performance had been transcendental. A whole group of cheerful people from the orchestra went laughing and talking into the inner lanes the way only natives can. They made no effort to talk in English for the benefit of the *zagraniczne* – the foreigner. Ashok enjoyed being the observer. They were speaking so fast it was difficult to understand even snatches. He repeatedly heard '*Co?*' pronounced 'Tso' which by now he knew meant 'what' and '*wiesz?*' which meant 'you know?'. They emerged onto a brightly lit hall where the noise of everyone talking drowned out everything else.

They sat around a table in a large group.

The Polish girls had a special unique way of flirting. It was very distinct, recognisable.

One of them a very pretty blonde girl smiled at Ashok, asked if he would like some of her *herbata*. Ashok suddenly felt that he didn't understand any Polish, he was tired of trying to understand something which was so different from English.

"*Nie rozumiem, polski*" – don't understand Polish – he said.

The pretty girl said '*herbata*' this time to say that she wasn't saying anything in Polish, she was just offering to share some of her tea. Teresa was flirting outrageously with Adam. Ashok recovered his senses. She played the harp mostly. She was in the final year of music at the conservatoire. Her name was Lauren. She and Adam had studied English Literature earlier.

"*Dziekuje bardzo*" he said thanking her and taking some of the amber coloured liquid in the glass and smiling at her in turn.

She had always liked music. It became pretty clear at an early age that this was to be her vocation, not just an avocation. The selection standards were very high but once in, you didn't have to worry about money at all.

Her grandfather had been killed in the War, among the elite Polish officers calculatedly massacred by the Russian secret police under orders from Stalin in the Katyn forest massacre. The Russian version that it had been done by the Nazis was bought by no one, despite the Politburo making this the official line in harmony with fraternal relations. But even then they were guilty of standing by and just letting it happen when they could have intervened. Mostly the topic itself was taboo. The Polish communists who had been identified and bought to power by the Soviets were not going to let anyone poison the relationship between the two Socialist sister states arrayed against the avaricious, unprincipled West. It did not suit the West to morbidly snoop around the graves in Russia (in the words of Churchill) after the secret meeting between him, Stalin and Roosevelt.

Lauren from the time she was a little girl would ask her mother what would become of her, what would she do in life, who would she marry, would he be good looking and charming, have an attractive personality, where would she live? "Que sera sera" her mother would sing back typically, "Whatever will be will be, The future's not ours to see...."

She was a dreamy girl, with her head in the clouds. She loved music right from the start but also could get absorbed in books and get lost for hours under a tree or on a bench, when the weather permitted it. She was not a loner and had a nice bunch of little girls as friends with whom she laughed and played games. She didn't take to boys much at that age - found them too rough and interested in other things.

Class studies did not interest her greatly but since it was

something that had to be done, she liked to do well in it and get the work expected of her out of the way. This was her *cote pratique*.

And as she grew up like other girls she began to find boys interesting, in a way that was different from the much needed companionship the girls provided, partly to discuss the very same boys.

It had been tough for her parents to bring her up. Her mother had to get a job in a tool making factory. Money was scarce but the cost of living was low and many things were free under Socialism - education, health. The basics like milk, ham, bread, *Ser*, tomatoes, potatoes, red radishes, some other vegetables and fruits like cherry were cheap and by and large not in short supply, unlike some other Socialist countries. Her father's was one of the jobs that had prestige in a classless society but not much money. He had a car though. The highest pay was not more than x multiples of the lowest pay. The rents were very low even in good locations, once one was lucky enough to get an allotment in the mass housing of small apartments consisting of 1 bedroom, 1 bathroom, 1 small kitchen and 1 relatively large drawing room. Of course it was hard for young people to get their turn and older students were compelled to stay with their parents much longer than their counterparts in the West.

Her parents had been highly supportive of their daughter's blossoming but uncertain talent. It would have been easier for Lauren to have pursued a safer and more conventional career. But that would have destroyed her soul and not been in keeping with her passionate, venturesome character.

Lauren had a flawless rose and gold complexion, well proportioned features and expressive thought lines. She was slender, about 5' 6". Ashok found himself wondering whether it was his life script that he moved from place to place coming across these girls that he felt strongly attracted to and moving on; was it serendipity, synchronicity, the nature of his present sojourn; would he see any of them again, should he just enjoy their company, be completely centred in the present or have some other expectation from life, from them.

Lauren had a very pleasant sounding infectious laugh. Ashok felt like joining in even when he only partly understood.

Even if one has talent as Lauren clearly seemed to have, Ashok got an inkling of how tough it must be to develop a mastery of music - practice plus talent plus an innate feeling for the instrument plus something else indefinable.

Ashok found that he was lost again in her perfect complexion. She had just asked him a question. He strove to respond quickly, not wanting her to guess the subject of his reverie. She would only have been flattered.

Adam was holding forth on Ionesco and Rhinoceros. Ashok had loved the book when it came out in the early 60's. Adam seemed to be developing his analysis intelligently. Ashok understood more than he would otherwise have because he knew the context. At least he had found stimulating company. Adam moved on to other works in the Theatre of the Absurd. Waiting for Godot he was enjoying currently.

Some of the others got involved in a side conversation. Lauren grinned at Ashok. "Building Socialism," she said indicating them.

This ability to laugh at the state of things was essential he knew.

Ashok knew he was attracted to Lauren. He wanted to go home with her. Life was short, his stay here was short. But could it happen so fast?

12

The evening ended. He kissed her hands. "*Dowidzenia*" - Polish for *au revoir* she said. "*Dobranoc*" - he responded kissing her good night quickly on the cheeks. She smiled brightly at him and was gone in quick steps into the darkness, probably to a tram stop at some distance.

"I would like to meet her again." He told Adam.

"That could be arranged", said Adam sounding resourceful and worldly wise.

"Now what", wondered Ashok. There he was in far off Wroclaw. Was this not remote? Should he change his programme. For how long and for what? What if something happened to him? What if he was lost? Would he be missed? How would anyone know where to find him?

And yet he was amongst people, amongst friends. He felt safe enough, comfortable enough. He enjoyed Lauren's company, and yet....

Should he let his head dictate as usual, he pondered. Do the sensible thing - the 'right' thing and move on. Or should he stay on so that he could see Lauren again. What of Martine or Nicole? He hadn't stayed back for either. Was he more attracted to Lauren or just learning to act on his heart. Should he return to France, when and how, if so; what about his training, his work, his plans. All of these encounters had potential. But he had been time and space bound to move on. And what about Barbara - she would be there in Warsaw.

He made his way to the train station at Wroclaw, as if in a dream. He would soon be chugging towards Warsaw. At the train station he thought he saw Lauren but it was someone else. He made his way to the right platform dragging his suitcase across the long bridge. The train steamed in, coal dust got into his eyes. He stepped on to the high entrance step using his strength to pull up the heavy suitcase. He found his seat in the right compartment. It was exactly like in Indian trains. It wasn't a chair car. There was a sleeper on which three could sit during the day and another one above it pulled up during the day, with the same arrangement across. Luggage was to be tucked in below the seat.

The value of 'Work is worship' was deeply embedded. A sense of duty, of responsibility, lay heavily upon his shoulders. So what was life, he mused - missed opportunities, connections made and yet not made. Connections almost made and lost because he moved on in the pursuit of his original plans, doing the 'right' thing. Listening to his mind and not his heart? It was hardly so clear cut. There was no certain direction from his heart. It was incipient. It had potential. If pursued, it could fulfil the longing within, the passion within....perhaps. But then he would have had to give up his direction, his real world pursuits for what might well turn out to be inconsequential or elusive ones. There were no certainties. Choices made, paths taken whether deliberately or by default, would have consequences.

The guard blew the whistle. Ashok looked uncertainly about him and jumped out. The next train would probably only be on the next day. His schedule not just in Poland but the countries to follow would be affected. He left his luggage at the left-luggage at the station. 10 zlotys for 24 hours.

Was it Lauren or a desire for an end to uncertainty, for something to hold on to.

He had been strongly attracted to Barbara, Martine, Nicole as well. He hadn't stopped. Maybe he was learning to stop.

Lauren was stunned.

"What are you doing here, stranger?"

"Who knows," Ashok smiled.

They went and sat down on a bench surrounded by bushes, in the park. Ashok bought two hot sausages overflowing with mustard, from a vendor near the park. They tasted really good. There were so many different varieties, many of them with spices.

"I have to practice at the Conservatoire. Why don't you come and listen?" she asked.

"Love to," said Ashok, enjoying the moment to moment, carefree feeling. Was there a tinge of guilt lurking somewhere? There was no place for it.

She practiced with passion, with feeling. Ashok felt it. Was it special for him or was she always like this, he thought. He allowed himself to be lost in the music, to float in it, to be transported by it. He closed his eyes. Did this passion reflect itself in all aspects of her life.

She paused suddenly looking drained, spent. The sounds of the Harp still resonated in the salon. Both of them sat there wordlessly, as if to digest what had passed between them.

13

The late afternoon sun was dazzling at this latitude. They stepped out uncertainly into it. Ashok felt he was shaking. Practical things like where to stay seemed trivial. His arm brushed against hers.

He felt the Unbearable Lightness of Being. He felt he was floating on a fluffy white cloud. His whole being felt *tres tres leger*.

Suddenly they turned towards each other and kissed. Their lips brushed lightly. Then they met again lightly, gently. The potential was explosive.

After that first impulsive kiss, Ashok and Lauren kind of held themselves apart, as their relationship burgeoned. Maybe they were both afraid of letting go. Maybe, they also realized that physical intimacy, becomes not just an expression of emotional and over-all intimacy but also has a way of becoming almost its sole expression and of taking over.

One day Ashok kissed her goodnight. She quivered all over and slumped to the floor, near the door of his room. Ashok was himself in a daze from the kiss. There were circles around his head with yellow canaries flying in them. But he also lowered himself to help her up. This position was even more dangerous and they found themselves kissing spontaneously.

Some days later they kissed again. He found himself nipping her lip softly. She opened her mouth and kissed him. Had her passion been unleashed? His mouth opened in response and their mouths got cupped in an equilibrium of tension. When they stopped, he immediately re-started. It was too pleasant to stop.

This was more desirable than anything else.

One day led to another and Ashok stayed on. The connection between Lauren and Ashok grew steadily as days turned into weeks. Everyone commented on Lauren's gaiety and Ashok felt supremely happy.

She found him a room in an attic with a slanting roof, with a landlady she knew, not far from her *mieszkania*. The old lady was glad to have the extra income of 50 zlotys a day. This much Ashok could manage out of his hard currency savings thus far, especially if he sold it on the open market. Hotels would only accept payment in convertible currency anyway - not in zlotys.

In Eastern Europe, people didn't have to be affluent to be interested in the Arts to enjoy them. There was a large middle class and a large working class. There wasn't that much economic disparity between the two, though interests varied. There was no one rich, except the Communist Party officials.

Ashok was introduced to her *matka*. She was in her 40's. She seemed to live in a dream world - both for herself and her daughter. It was easy to see where Lauren had got her romanticism from. In the middle of the afternoon she would have the record player on with a very light lime green cover depicting a tranquil lake surrounded by trees. The scene was evocative like the eclectic collection from Billy Vaughan which had renderings of 'A Summer Place', 'Tammy', 'Red River

Valley', 'Red Sails in the Sunset', 'Japanese Sand man'. Ashok had the feeling of being transported to another place as he climbed the staircase leading to her flat. Her father too liked to go out every evening for a spin, or a dance. He too was a romantic.

14

Back home in Delhi Ashok's sister Neeru meanwhile fell in love with a handsome charming chap in her MA English class Vikram Kaul. This was where girls and boys got to mix in class, in Delhi University - at the undergraduate level most of the Colleges were still segregated, though a few were Co-ed. They went out for secret coffees and thought it very daring. They were seen and the grapevine reached her parents.

She and Gita went *phus-phus* about it till late into the night.

"He recites Shakespeare sonnets to me Gita, in the far garden seat in the late evening with the garden fragrant and the moon peeping behind the trees"

Neeru sighed.

The parents wanted their daughter happy. They made some enquiries. Vikram's father had a shop selling Kashmiri handicrafts in Jan Path. It was rumoured that he was becoming an alcoholic. When Neeru came over for dinner, he talked enthusiastically about how to make Port and how he used to make it in Srinagar. He offered her a sample. Vikram's mother taught English at one of the Delhi University Colleges. She was entitled to staff housing and that's where they stayed. But what would happen once she retired?

Neeru liked the liberal atmosphere she saw in Vikram's house. But her parents worried about how Vikram might be able to look after Neeru. Moreover Neeru had been brought up in a traditional Hindu way. All festivals were celebrated with full ritual, there was daily puja in the house. She had been carefully bought up with a sense of values. Vikram's family did not even seem aware of lesser festivals like Akshaya Tritiya, Teej or Radha Ashtami. There were no copies of the Ramayana or Mahabharata lying around, no small temple in the house. These festivals marked the passage of the year, the seasons; the rituals associated with them like buying gold on Akshaya Tritiya had meaning and significance.

Neeru's parents wanted only the best for their children. They knew what would make them happy in the long term. They had the wisdom and the experience.

15

As the weeks passed, there were a number of calls from his sponsors in Warsaw. What had happened to his plans? Ashok had been totally irresponsible for a change. All he could think of was Lauren. What was happening to him? He woke up and wanted to be with Lauren. His letters to his friends were full of Lauren. He dared not write to his parents about Lauren. But he would have liked to. There were a number of forwarded messages from the countries that he was due to visit. Ashok did not reply, because he did not know what to reply. There would have been a deluge of anxious communications from his family but he told them he was exhausted from the intensive training and the non-stop travelling and wanted to pause a while in Wroclaw.

For Ashok's family, Poland was remote enough and a provincial town in it even more so. Ashok might well have been in Mars. This was an unheard of Communist country, deep behind the Iron Curtain. No one went there, no one knew about it, no one had any connections with it. Airmail letters took 10 days to reach. There was no direct dialling.

Trunk calls had to be routed through London who then dialled Poland and asked the caller to speak louder and louder to build up the radio circuit. But they had little actual say vis a vis Ashok's movements, decisions regarding his life, other than the traditional time-honoured Indian tool of emotional blackmail, which they had had no scruples in using to the fullest before Ashok left and at every opportunity, since. Ashok was no longer a minor, had a strong mind of his own and had planned his trip such that he was not dependent on his family for finances. He had himself arranged scholarships in several Western countries, saved even small amounts whilst in them to the maximum extent, sometimes at great deprivation to himself and fortunately for him even small hard currency amounts went a long way in the East, where the currents of life had presently led him.

His family had liked the idea of his getting Management training related to his business, but he was very young, had led an extremely protected existence. The family worried about his ability to look after himself, where he would be an anonymous dot in the universe. Ashok was innocent and idealistic. He was emotionally open and women found him attractive. He would fall for them whether they were suitable for him in the long term or not.

Lauren spent more and more time with him. When he wasn't with her, Ashok sat in the scenic parks and read or wandered around the historical sights of the city or in the museums. There was a British Council on the 5th floor of a massive old building that rose darkly against the evening sky, in an array of such buildings joined together in a row. It was a welcome island of English or even an oasis tucked away in an unexpected corner of the Slavonic desert. Or he bought delicious red radishes from old ladies selling them on the pavements and consumed them with relish.

She started staying later and later into the nights with him but still went home to sleep.

They would put on the piano music of Jan Pederewski and Chopin as they kissed. They would listen to Schumann and Beethoven's 5th and 6th, to Mozart and Haydn. They would lie on the long green sofa in the room with raised ends on either side. The sofa was long enough to serve as a bed in case of need. It suited this purpose admirably. Once they started kissing, they couldn't stop. These sessions went on for a long time. The kissing would transport them to someplace else, as would the music. There was no world outside. Time stopped. They got united through their mouths. It was a very intimate contact, in a sense the most intimate contact with someone one felt deeply about. A kiss was all the more thrilling because they were still virgins. Up till now even in Hollywood everything was put into kissing as that was all that was allowed in real life. The sexual revolution was changing that only now.

Ashok's hand went to Lauren's thighs at the cusp of the dress and cupped the slight hollow. Spontaneously. She did not protest. Ashok was on cloud nine. It flattened to maximise the contact and then automatically turned sideways to move slowly, gently to caress the inside of her thighs. They were still held together but not with tension. Ashok could feel the other thigh on the back of his hand. They pulled with passion as their kiss got bigger and more out of control. Somehow even when the situation escalated, they had managed to stop up till now.

It slid in as smooth as butter. There was a little cry from Lauren. There was thunder and lightning somewhere in the distance. Her hymen had been penetrated. They were united at yet another level.

It seemed fitting somehow that they lose their virginity to each other. On the radio there was 'Revolution' and 'Hey Jude'.

It happened during the climax of 'Hey Jude'. That too seemed most appropriate and Ashok never forgot it.

Sometimes in one of the many parks that dot most European cities, Lauren would say she was tired and Ashok would bend and 'push' her from behind. It would elicit smiles from passers by. Poland prided itself on its Europeanness in a way that was infectious. It was affiliation, cultural identification. There were many theatres but much as Ashok enjoyed plays this required an in depth knowledge of Polish. Conversational Polish wouldn't do. The Opera was another matter. Tickets were cheap, not yet affected by Capitalist considerations and easy to get. The quality excellent. And Music especially Chopin was ubiquitous. Magical, transcendent, gentle, romantic, bringing out the most refined and tender feelings. Not just symphony orchestra but individual virtuoso performances.

Almost three months went by. The small bits of money that Ashok had saved in the West, carried him a long way here. July 1969 was in its second half. Man walked on the Moon. There were the wondrous events of Woodstock. It seemed so far away here in Poland. America seemed to be of another World.

The days, weeks, seasons segued into the next and nothing else began to matter but experiencing and being with the other. Another three months passed and then another six. The Companies where he was to undergo training, stopped making enquiries about his programme dates.

Their chemistry had been incredible - their love making was explosive, at times extremely passionate, inflammable, and at times, gentle, caressing, soft, tender, always loving. Once they started kissing they couldn't stop. Each kiss was a long kiss goodnight. They walked to the kitchen with Ashok stuck to her. He found himself holding her breasts from behind. As she turned around they slumped to the floor, sitting with their legs wedged together in front of them. As they became one, somehow spontaneously without any design a rocker was formed, such that as they moved first one would be up in his place and then the other. Their very movement would push the other up. Their bodies formed an arc and there was this up and down rocking movement. It created an experience that always stayed with them.

16

Lauren and Ashok were both very romantic. They matched and complemented each other in this as well as in their passionate love making. It would be hard to say who was more romantically inclined of the two. The moonlight, the cool night breeze in the bushes, the stars sparkling, the redness of *aube*, the freshness of it, the azure blue sky, a beautiful wafted piece of music carried over the wind made them feel the same way. "Every place I go I'll think of you, every song I sing I'll sing for you..." Even when Ashok was not with her Lauren began to see Ashok elsewhere, in the city where she went. Certain songs they heard over and over again and they became their songs: Petula Clark's 'Downtown', 'Please don't sleep in the subway', 'Colour my world', 'Now I've got love going for me', Dusty Springfield's 'I Only want to be with you', 'Goin' Back', Sonny and Cher's 'Walking the Quetzal', 'Baby Don't Go', 'The New Faces–Lace Covered Window', 'Groovin' by The Rascals...

Something had happened to them. Ashok would start a smile at the corner of his mouth and Lauren would pick it up.

Lauren and Ashok would talk late into the night. Or have

laughing fits when they couldn't stop. The late summer night would palely frame the outline of neighbouring houses.

Many of the old elite in Poland are very Francophone - like in much of Eastern Europe and Russia, she remembered telling him. It was synonymous with sophistication. The cultivated in Russian classics always spoke French. They liked the sound of it. Ashok loved the sound of Lauren's voice. The way she talked. Her accent when speaking English. So unique. So her. She was striking to look at and had such a vivacious charming persona.

Poland was home to her music. She needed that stimulation and support. Lauren made him appreciate its culture, its peculiarities. The way you could go into a shop, stand at a counter and have small pastry and *herbata*. The way shopkeepers said *dzien dobry* and *dowidzenia, dziekuje* even though they didn't know you. The chocolate you could get, the variety of hot sausages with mustard you could eat in the street, on a cold snowy day. Its winds, its lovely days of sunshine, blue skies and intense cold. The freshness of the grass in spring and its intense freshly cut smell in the summer. Framing this were typical Polish row houses, the tall trees and the Slavic Cupolas and gables.

Lauren might have been an activist to the extent it was possible in the Poland of the time and she sometimes got into passionate debates with friends at the University. Her fellow musicians were a more taciturn lot.

Lauren enjoyed mystery and adventure novels. She would tell Ashok the story, the characters, the circumstances, lead him to guess who had done what and why and then sometimes succeed in flooring him with the solution. Historical novels, epics, classics, fiction where ordinary people played out their feelings and thoughts, the actions that lead them to. They analysed and discussed the Western movies that were allowed to come to the local Film Club, often taking up where the local raconteur had left the discussion before the start of the movie. They talked late into the night. In the summer it would be light till late into the night and the cock would start crowing pretty early in the morning. They teased each other, laughed like children. They played games which sometimes ended up in kissing. Once he chased her down a University street threatening to put an ice cream down her back, whilst she fled laughing. Sometimes their talk became baby talk. They had taken one day at a time but the nagging thought had remained - what of his Parents, his duty towards them, their expectations of him. They must miss him like only parents can. His parents got newsy letters from him but if they asked about his programme they got no answers. They must miss him very much as only parents can. He could stay here with Lauren, surrounded by her music, living this very Continental life for a long time. But for ever?

He had to think about his career, his life. Neither of them wanted to live in Communist Poland. It was too closed. No world existed outside of Poland. And it was clearly *zatsofane* - backward. The open thinking, the free access to books, media, Western cinema. He missed the intellectual stimulation. And to enjoy the theatre, to get deep into its psyche, his functional knowledge of Polish would have to get much deeper. It was a tough language, very different from English, though his knowledge of Sanskrit helped, much to his surprise. He knew they were both part of the Indo-European group but he didn't think he'd come across words that obviously.

Lauren herself didn't want to live there, though she clearly wanted to remain in Europe. It would have to be Western Europe. Where? France? He had acquired a certain level of French out of interest but they both would have to greatly *approfondir* their *langue*. And what of friends and a life, and their work. The competition for her would be much stiffer. Both Poland and India had very strict Capital controls. Neither of them could take any money there to start off with, not even their savings.

Maybe it was the strict training of her parents, her cultural upbringing. She loved Europe. It was on a pedestal. She was European. She was willing to live anywhere in Europe but Europe it had to be. She could not dream of living anywhere else on a permanent basis. It was as if it was in her cells, much more than could be explained by words like socialisation or *sanskar.*

She couldn't think of living in America for example. So much violence there and so crass, so uncultured, no subtlety about them. Only into dollars. And so racist (unlike Europe!) Negroes being mercilessly beaten by cops. The Communist media had accentuated these stereo-types in their projections.

Nor even England - it wasn't really Europe. Only geo-graphically so. Too strange, peculiar. The rest of Europe always joked about them. And the food and the miserable weather.

She would meet friends for tea in a tea house and she would talk about Ashok whilst the friends listened interestedly and proffered comments from time to time. Sometimes these observations led to her own chain of thoughts much afterwards. The way she could talk to these *kolezankas* she could not talk to others. Ashok came close but still he could not really fulfil the same role, especially when the talk was about him.

"He's always kissing me", she told Wanda" - finding reasons, excuses to kiss my hands, my cheeks, the nape of my neck and most of all my lips."

And Wanda asked with a knowing twinkle "is it too much?"

Lauren smiled - "No, I always respond. I feel free enough to tell him when I'm not in the mood. He senses it anyway. It's not often. And when we get passionate, it is hard to tell who is the more passionate of the two."

Wanda laughed - "I wish I could say the same thing. Once I pulled at my boyfriend's moustache - tried to pull it off in the kiss, it got so passionate..."

17

Neeru started seeing Vikram more and more - until it became everyday. Something had to be done. Things could not be allowed to drift like this. It would have consequences.

Brij and Radhika tried talking to Neeru. Matters of the heart could hardly be decided in a mechanistic fashion, she said. Anyway she was just seeing him regularly. Nothing else was on at this stage.

They spread the word amongst relatives and friends for a suitable match for Neeru. The time had come. She was clearly interested in boys and rather than her bringing into the family someone who would be inappropriate like Vikram, far better that they take the initiative. She would herself get attracted to someone out of the eligible young men they would select for introduction. Neeru found the idea absurd and did not buy 'the parents know best' argument. After a lot of quiet, painstaking research, asking around, making discreet enquiries, they set up the first meeting over tea at the house. Neeru at first refused but subsequently agreed just to please her parents.

4 p.m. on a bright Wednesday evening was set, fine china was laid and dainty cucumber sandwiches laid on a plate. Harish was a nice enough boy and it wasn't his fault that this charade was being set up. He was running a factory in Calcutta and life in the magnificent bungalows with verandahs, lawns and driveways, with tall stately banyan, neem, tamarind trees would be exceedingly pleasant.

Harish was charmed by Neeru and wanted to take her out for a coffee. They were permitted to go the next day with a chaperone. Neeru agreed finding no harm in it. Harish took her on a long drive which found them sitting in a place she hadn't been to before called Holiday Inn in Faridabad. It was close to lunchtime now and though they hadn't been permitted to go out for lunch, some chop suey was ordered. A greasy looking serving turned up with vinegar with chopped green chillies floating in it and soya by the side. They dug into it hungrily and although it was an Indian version of Chinese food, it tasted really good. The chefs were Nepali and often employed for Chinese food in India because it was thought that they would know about it, Chinese looking that they were.

Somehow those days Neeru felt like speaking English with a French accent and Harish was found speaking like that after the outing, so taken by her was he. The parents and Harish were in Delhi for another 4 days. Harish requested and was allowed to meet Neeru twice more. At the end of it Harish declared himself to his parents that he wanted to marry this girl. His parents had already considered things carefully before agreeing to the first meeting.

They conveyed their willingness and interest to Neeru's parents, who in turn told Neeru.

Neeru was flattered. She thought about it. She liked Harish more than she expected. But he didn't sweep her off her feet like Vikram did. She might even have contemplated it had she not known Vikram.

She told her parents. Harish and his family went back at the end of the visit.

The feelings of Lauren and Ashok for each other continued to develop and evolve into really deep ones, something which neither of them could have imagined when they first met. They felt the magic of the moment and the congruity of mind, body, spirit that one feels at times in sports upon finding the sweet spot (when strokes are effortless, brilliant and fluid) or when intense and deeply felt sex unites the two into timeless moments.

Inevitably, sometimes there was friction - for instance when they talked to each other about the other. Often it went off uneventfully. But if it was about difficulties with the other and if Ashok started off 'The trouble with you is...', Lauren would get defensive and react sharply.

Or another time -

"Stop worrying about your parents so much Ashok. It's such a kill joy, becomes oppressive."

Silence. He had explained this to Lauren so many times "At least Lauren I am not afraid of mine, like you are. You are so scared of them and what they will think. It defines your behaviour."

Ashok tried to cram in as much as possible into every bit of time and therefore had a tendency to do things last minute. Lauren liked to leave enough margin and not have to rush around should something go wrong.

Ashok is late every now and then, she thought and that drives me crazy. He knows how irritating this is and yet its almost as if he can't help himself. Once when he was supposed to reach, he was just leaving. I was so mad at him. He says he looks forward to our meeting but then look at this casual attitude towards being on time. He seems contrite and says he'll not let it happen again and then after some time it happens again.

Maybe because he grew up as a vegetarian where Indian food is best eaten with the hands, he doesn't always eat Continental food neatly. The leftovers in his plate can be a mess. He cuts out the fatty bits - says its animal lard. But that's what is so tasty. He takes very long eating sometimes. Tedious.

Lauren was steadfast and yet every now and then during the months their relationship developed and grew, she tried inexplicably to break off, saying it wasn't ok, as if she was pronouncing something from the Scriptures. Then despite everything she would make up with Ashok and the status quo would be restored.

Oscar and Magda were European Europeans - very conscious of their Europeanness and of everything European, the vast schism dividing East and West Europe notwithstanding. They were intrigued by and open to ancient cultures outside Europe like those of Japan and India. But their daughter having so much to do with someone who was non-European, that could be dangerous. It had to be pre-empted.

She had an older brother Wlodek who was going to study Cinema in the famous film school at Lodz. The Course took 5 years. Lauren hero-worshipped her brother. It was his picture she had in her wallet. One day he would be a well known film director in the tradition of a string of internationally known directors from Poland like Andrzej Wajda and Krzysztof Zanussi. Wlodek was even more conservative about his sister getting 'involved' with Ashok.

Lauren was scared stiff of her parents, especially her mother. Always had been. In that sense she remained a little girl. She remembered how she used to cry petrified when her mother scolded her, punished her, look for someplace to hide but there was nowhere to hide except to cover her face against the softness of the duvet on her bed. As she witnessed Lauren's feelings for Ashok reaching intensity, her mom at first tried to reconcile with it. His family was well off, her daughter would be happy. But ultimately just could not accept a non-European son-in-law as could not her young but surprisingly reactionary brother, in contrast to his artistic pretensions and aspirations.

Moreover, Magda had seen Ashok now at close quarters. He was disappointing. Too depressed, too without spirit, too much in his head, God knows what he was brooding about! She had tried to accept him but he himself had made it difficult. She would do everything in her power to thwart this. She would explain things to Oscar and enlist his help further and Wlodek already understood. Lauren herself had good sense, she would see in the end that Ashok was not good enough, see through his frailties. Lauren's grandmother a disapproving witness to her daughter's misplaced exclusivity was powerless to change it.

The bottom line was that the position of Lauren's parents had hardened. They had tried to reconcile to it. Ashok was quite well off, she would have a good life in India. He was cultured and gentle, she seemed happy with him. This was their daughter and only the best life was good enough for her.

Ashok could easily pass for a southern Italian or Spaniard

and was often mistaken for one in Poland. Magda could see that for herself but in the end he wasn't European - whatever that may mean or be.

Autumn turned to extreme cold as the Polish winter set in. The cold weather made Lauren even more beautiful, her skin even more smooth.

Even in the cities, all the open spaces became fields of deep snow. The snow covered trees and traditional houses with sloping roofs were silhouetted against the sky. The Vistula froze and a drive outside the city showed an occasional bridge amidst a landscape blanketed with snow for miles and miles. Not a single green leaf or blade of grass to be seen anywhere. Snow on the pavements, next to the tram tracks, as the trams hurtled through the city in the bitter daytime cold of–20°C or lower. One's breath froze as it came out. Only very thick clothing, heavy overcoats, moisture-resistant boots, gloves, a fur cap suitable for Eastern Europe would suffice. Clothes suitable for the milder winters of Western Europe wouldn't do at all. That, a hot soup, *szynka*, sausage or meat with mashed potatoes plus vodka swigged down quickly were needed even to combat the lunchtime cold. *Cholernie zimno* as the Poles called it.

His Polish visa which was originally for three months kept expiring and renewal which was very difficult the first time, got more and more so. He had to go to Warsaw each time for the visa. And for renewing it the Poles wanted convertible currency. So many dollars per day. Even if he got hold of zlotys, they would be useless. No amount of arguing that he was from a developing country which did not have hard currency and not from the West, got him anywhere. Fraternal Socialist relations were not working well! But the main police woman in the inner chamber, in the forbidding centrally located building in Warsaw, gave him a knowing smile - he wasn't a problem in any way - he was just a young man in love and everyone knew about Polish girls being the most beautiful in Europe! She seemed to know all about him. The police woman herself attractive seemed older to Ashok at the time though she must have been no more than 10 years older than him. Probably has a dossier on me mused Ashok. He found an international student office representative in SGPIS, the prestigious Warsaw School of Economics which had produced the likes of Oskar Lange and Michal Kalecki, quite by chance, in the café of the school. Having time on his hand he had gone there at lunchtime when the visa office shut - just to get to a better atmosphere - one he could relate to more. He gave him a contact at the office of the International Students Union - the Iron Curtain counterpart of the Western one. A friendly looking young man with specs and a wisp of a beard on his chin was there with two other student looking young men. They said his contact wasn't there then but they turned out to be very helpful. They gave him a student card and put on it visiting student at SGPIS at the invitation of the Polish Students Union. When one of them hesitated, another said "*daj, daj*". They even gave him an invitation asking him to extend his stay for another three months to further promote friendly exchanges between Poland and India. This was manna from heaven!

But even this time expired and he came to the end of the road - the visa could not be renewed any further. He could not stay indefinitely in the Poland of the time. Nor could he forever abdicate hearth, home and responsibility towards parents, family business in India.

Lauren was clearly talented, loved her music and would go far. She could not give up that passion - nor could he in all reasonableness expect it or even want it. The practical difficulties of fulfilling their respective dreams seemed insurmountable, overwhelming, *malgre* everything they felt.

Maybe there was a stubborn streak in her which wouldn't let her budge from such cherished ideas as her paradigm of Europe. And perhaps in her heart of hearts unacknowledged she didn't want to be on another Continent from where she had grown up, where she had gone to school, had had friends, pranks, escapades, memories or from where her family lived.

19

One day he caught the train to Warsaw. Time had flown by and it was already close to the end of April. The time to leave had come inevitably, inexorably.

These had been magic moments, unforgettable, lovely times but was he truly in love with her, was he committed to her, was she *the* one? They were both so young.

They had been anticipating that the day would come when there could be no more visa extensions, no postponements ad infinitum of the training to come.

"I can't hang around forever doing nothing but being with you. That is worth a great deal. But I have no other friends, no other life here in Wroclaw - I am here just for you. I have no work. I need a purpose. I don't want resentment to build up. It might, despite us."

Their relationship had developed way beyond what either had expected or imagined. They talked late into the night about their situation but also everything under the sun. About their feelings, their vision, their values. Maybe they would again get together in the future, though their trajectories were different. They would see how their respective paths, lives worked out.

They would try once again to be open to meeting others. They would get in touch again, if and when they felt like it. By phone, by letter, after some time. They would try and minimise the pain of parting.

Lauren came to see him off at the station wearing a green coat that really suited her and waved as the train pulled away. It had a Lara's theme quality to it. A petite figure, standing alone on the platform and then walking away as the train pulled off. Her shoulders were slightly slouched, betraying how hard the time ahead would be, how much her heart would pain, how much she would pine for him. After such a long time with her, when all plans of training and returning home had been thrown to the wind, his departure had an intensity which only the two of them knew about.

Ashok felt the ache in his heart, the lump in his throat. Loyal Lauren, true-blue. A gem.

Ashok didn't want to stay on in Warsaw. He wanted to flee Poland but there were formalities to be completed. Even the notorious Indian bureaucracy paled in comparison. Polish paperwork was complex, contradictory and endless.

He got in touch with Barbara. Some of his heaviness evaporated in her presence.

Barbara flitted around as light as air. His heart yearned for Lauren but whatever their feelings, it had not ended in commitment nor any plans for the future. Otherwise life would have taken a different path.

During the day he worked on submitting his report as well as other formalities to do with the officially sponsored visit to Poland. Barbara's dark-tinged complexion, the radiance shining through that hue, her thin face, her infectious smile, her attractive features, her somewhat pointed nose had their old effect. He loved her company.

He would sow his wild oats before he settled down. Figuratively. That was part of settling down.

What made Barbara so light hearted - almost floating in the wind.

'....Forget all your worries, forget all your cares....' as in the Petula Clark song, was the effect she had.

He spent three pleasant days in Warsaw trying to forget. Barbara was full of humour, which he could understand much better now. They laughed together at anecdotes and the stories were infectious. One joke led to another. He hadn't laughed this hard in a long time. Was he laughing especially hard to relieve stress.

It was so easy to be with Barbara. Or was he just trying to distance himself from Lauren. Barbara might not be as accomplished as Lauren nor so evolved. But did that matter in the final analysis.

Barbara said she would write to him.

He left the shores of Polska with these thoughts. The Finnish, Norwegian and British training Fellowships were still intact. It had taken some phone calls from Poland to extend them, a tough exercise in itself. The Polish operator much like her Indian counterpart would take the number and call back whenever she felt like it and the customer just had to hang around.

20

The Naxalite movement was at its peak when Gita reached her second year of College in Delhi University and she also like many of her contemporaries got swept into it. She spent long hours in the University Campus, away from home but this was what Ashok and Neeru had also done and this was what was normal at the time. Brij and Radhika told their friends and family that Gita was very active in several College and University societies like the Social Service League, the Photography Society, the Hiking Society etc.

The Naxalite Movement was for violent change and did not have faith in the electoral process like the Communist Party of India did or even the Communist Party Marxist, which had split from the CPI and gone much more to the left. But this was the CPI-ML and would not participate in this farce, in these processes that were loaded.

She told Brij and Radhika that she was going to do volunteer work in Bihar and she would be gone for a month. There was a drought there. She would send them letters or post cards regularly and trunk call them once in a while. From bigger cities like Patna it was easier. She soon slipped into Bengal, where the epicentre was. The passion, the desire to act, the commitment was a gale force here if it was a dust storm in Delhi.

She wound her way to the tea estates and saw that the labour was paid by weight, saw also how much they had to collect to achieve that weight. This system had been in vogue since the days of the British Raj. The humid conditions under which they had to bend and pluck were energy sapping. They did their best but what they were able to collect and get paid for was often not enough to sustain the clothing and feeding of the children and to look after the old parents who had moved in with them. They were forced to borrow from the local money lender. The money lent was not for long term betterment of their conditions but for unavoidable yet unsustainable consumption.

The group that Gita was assigned to decided to ask the money lender of the village to waive the loans of the poorest families and if he did not agree to stab him as a lesson to all.

21

From Warsaw to Helsinki, across the Baltic Sea, Ashok landed in stunning Suomi with its unexpected and eye catching architecture. It was modern, imaginative, creative and unlike that of any other in Scandinavia.

He was ushered into the headquarters office of Eero Horetinen, the Managing Director of the Finnish Co-operative Dairies Association, that controlled most of the major dairy production in Finland. Dr Horetinen who was short but sat tall in his high-backed chair was an amiable, bearded fellow with a triangular face. It had probably been his decision to grant the Fellowship. He asked what Ashok would like. A proposed programme was shown to him and discussed. It involved travel to many Co-operative factories specialising in different dairy products and spread out all over the vast country, by road, train and by plane. It was a comprehensive six-week schedule and Ashok loved it.

Initially, he was given a room in the flat of a single staff member in Konala, on the outskirts of Helsinki near the main factory. He was shown the bus stop from where he could catch Bus 39 to the centre of town. But he felt suffocated there and asked to be moved if possible to a student dorm. That's what he was essentially and he would feel at home there.

He became friends with a blonde fellow, with a pretty, girlish face who was slightly taller than him. He reminded him of some of the pretty girls he had come across in Poland. He was called Ahri and was studying Mathematics in the University. He was reasonably fluent in English. At the self-service they chatted about their day and he translated some of the Finnish dishes and what went into them. He became friends a little later with another fellow who for some reason was addressed by his last name Saarinen. Maybe he didn't like his first name or it was too complicated. Saarinen was short and looked older than his years. His avocation was opera and he told Ashok about an opera by a Finnish composer set in Benares, where a Brahmin girl falls in love with the protagonist - the son of a prince who goes to sleep under the tree whilst playing the flute - and the story that is woven around the tragedy that befalls them.

Saarinen introduced him to a downtown cellar where the young, the hip and those with intellectual pretensions hung out. It was called Vanhankellari. It was right in the centre of town and stairs led down to it next to an innocuous looking window.

Ashok became a regular at the Kellari and became friends with a number of regulars who formed pluralistic groups there. It was a huge place with different rooms without doors in the entrance spaces and sections leading from one to the other. The lights were hung low from the ceiling, dim without being depressing. There were some long tables with benches on either side interspersed with passages and followed by similar but shorter tables in cosy corners. Some of the sections were at a slightly lower level connected by a few steps and partially partitioned off with small wooden banisters. There were also round tables which encouraged a different mode of conviviality. This being the young intelligentsia, most people spoke English.

On the scholarship money he got from the Finnish Co., he could have lived well. But Ashok wanted to save up precious foreign exchange. God knows when he might need it and it was impossible to get in India or Poland. He started liking Wiener Schnitzel. A variety of drinks, including some unusual Finnish ones, were available and food though good was cheap in the Kellari. Even that little amount he didn't want to spend when he could help it, so one day he went there for the company but decided not to order anything. A few of his friends pooled together and ordered him a Wiener Schnitzel. Ashok was pleased but didn't take it as a big deal. This is what one did in India all the time. He would have ordered for a visiting foreigner without a thought. But one of them said "We pay for you". Ashok nodded happily and said "Thank you". Then another one said the same thing and a third one to add to the gravitas!

Another evening in the cellar a bunch of them sat across a long table. Some of them were from other Scandinavian countries, with some from Continental Europe and America - hence all foreigners. Most of them were blond haired and blond bearded. The beer tankards were full. The bonhomie was apparent. '*Skol*,' said someone, '*Prost*,' said another. The cheers in different languages went around the table and an appreciative sip was taken everytime. It came round to Ashok before he had time to think. "Cheers" was too lame, it wasn't his mother tongue anyway. '*Madhu*,' he said hastily thinking of Amba Ji '*Garj, garj kshanai moorah, Madhu yavat pibamyaham.*' before she did away with Mahishasur, the demon king who had taken the form of a buffalo. The table resounded to deep and full throated cries of '*madhu*' as the Vikings raised their glasses! Only the horns were missing, but then Mahishasur had already been taken care of.

Ashok accompanied a bunch of his friends to a performance of *Fiddler on the Roof* and went backstage with them. The architecture of the Theatre was modern, stylised as in much of Finland, with an arched roof meeting the ground and a glass front. The play fitted in well with the surroundings. Russia was just next door. He enjoyed the play even though it was in Finnish. He waited outside in the period before they could go backstage. It felt like late at night. There was no one else there. Where were the others? The grass was moist next to the fence - there were bright lights here and there but they only accentuated the late night lonely feeling although it was only 9.30 pm. How would he get home?

Ashok suddenly felt far away - the sense that descends upon every foreigner when he is in a distant land with an unfamiliar culture, no matter how quick to adjust and adapt he might be. Then it goes away unless you hold on to it.

He was reminded of the time in Delhi that he was listening to Joan Baez in the Fiat with the windows rolled down. It was near India Gate. Suddenly he felt someone looking at him, an American girl in a three wheeler scooter. Pretty. Her look conveyed everything - of hearing something familiar, when she felt so far away, when she least expected it. A look of recognition coupled with a 'take me with you' look.

After wandering around a bit and somewhat inefficiently retracing his steps, he followed an alley that seemed to lead nowhere in this theatre complex and entering a doorway found many of the lot from Vanhankellari with whom he had come here, in the first instance.

They were all talking animatedly in Finnish but Ashok wasn't going to let something like a strange language bother him. He was used to languages by now, that employed the Roman alphabet but showed nothing discernible in common with English. He joined a group with two girls and a fellow he recognized from the Kellari. As soon as he got a chance he interjected with something in English and was pleased to get a response from one of the girls - dark haired and sexy looking–'but not totally my type' thought Ashok fleetingly.

They were all going to a dance in a big hall in another part of town. Ashok decided to join them.

It may not be as pleasant an experience as going to The Cellar or Sensations in Delhi but he enjoyed moving to the beat and showing-off, and was at his exuberant best on such occasions.

They drove off in a group of Volkswagens to a different part of Helsinki, that Ashok had not yet been to - still central, but quite different from the part where Vanhankellari was. Ashok had walked down the broad street Mannerheimintie and the downtown area where the big stores were with some huge but empty restaurants on the first floor.

The music was loud, it was still of the late '60's and beautiful. Ashok felt his hips swaying to the beat. Her name was Vera. She danced well but Ashok found himself wishing that it was someone who meant more to him. Then someone cut in on him, someone who looked like the brother of her boy-friend. She looked relieved and Ashok was left all alone. The Kellari and theatre groups could not be traced in this crowd. Ashok decided to wallflower it for a while. He had the assuredness at the time. Maybe, it was a function of youth. Then he abandoned himself to the music and danced on his own.

Like Mick Jagger with a mike and flowing mike wire in hand. He had not bothered to shave since some days - his beard had begun to look like a cultivated one, startlingly black in contrast to his olive complexion and the blonde hair in his chin and moustache, as also to the sea of light hair all around him.

It helped but most of all what caught the eye was the way he danced. Not just the abandon or the flowing with the music or the dancing like everyone is watching or no one is watching but *surtout* the movements of his arms and legs, his feet and head and the air of great self-assuredness about him. His upper lip became a thin line of pleasure which curved upwards at both ends in a barely discernible smile. It was magnetic, attractive, appealing.

He felt he was creating something. He was joined by two girls tall, svelte, blonde who smiled at him and said with their eyes 'you are attractive'. The music went on and on. Ashok was tireless. He wished it would never end. It was magic.

The girls scribbled their numbers on a small notebook page and gave it to him. It was quite late now and they were leaving.

'I am happy just to dance with you' by The Beatles - 'Just to dance with you-oho-happy just to dance with you,' went through Ashok's head.

A blonde, young man with specs whom Ashok recognised by now as one of the organisers let him out into the deserted streets and quickly latched the door behind him. His meaning was clear, make yourself scarce. A couple of guys had followed him to the door. They looked threatening, like they had every intention of bashing him up. The need to blend in vs the discomfort of standing out. They were clearly jealous. But Ashok could not find the prudence in himself to run or even to walk fast. Could it really be? The organiser must have opened the door a few seconds later. Should he expect running footsteps? How should he get home? Somewhat guiltily he thought, should he allow himself a taxi, given the hour or should he as always try to take a bus? He was very tired and might have to wait long for a bus at this time of night even if he deciphered the correct bus to take.

The next day he couldn't find the scrap of paper. He must have dropped it at night. And as so often happens when paths cross in this universe and there is potential of friendship, that was the last he saw of them.

22

The shop floor at the plant in Valio was huge. There was row upon row of pasteurisers, sterilisers for ultra-heat treatment, milk-powder sprayers, milk packaging machines which packaged milk in various novel forms which were both attractive and designed to preserve the milk for longer and longer periods. It was a massive hall, of glistening, shining steel and aluminium of enormous proportions. There were the ubiquitous white dairy coat clad workers, each playing his part of the puzzle. Ashok was fascinated. He could spend days just watching everything. And in that was the learning. Watching with a relaxed mind, which allowed things to be picked up which may not otherwise have been noticed.

He began to recognise some of the faces and they started not just smiling at him but communicating with him about aspects of production or maintenance of the machines. If you work alongside someone no knowledge of language is required. The meaning was clear, the communication, lucid. Some pieces of butter fell into the packing machine's innards, in handling. The operator retrieved it from there, all mixed with grease and dumped it all back into the butter being packed. Ashok watched horrified. These were supposed to be advanced countries, with high standards of hygiene. How could such things be allowed to happen. The other worker next to them shook his head when he saw Ashok's look.

Some Saturday mornings Ashok decided to actually work at some of the jobs. Not only was it a useful learning experience - nothing like hands on, he thought but he also picked up some precious overtime money. Clearly, his help was needed and Labour's contribution to the production or packaging process, recognised and well-rewarded.

Ashok was proud that he had earned his own money. The laboratory and R&D were in another building nearby. It was double-storeyed and even then of a lower height than the factory which had to have a high ceiling because of the huge plants, many of them perpendicular and cylindrical.

There were test-tubes in rows and chemical flasks. Different sections with pilot test plants and testing apparatus. Micro-bacteriology played a very significant role. There were Dairy journals in English, Finnish, Swedish as well as a Library. Ashok spent time in the R&D and in the lab. The laboratory in-charge and his deputies to whom he was assigned got to know him well but did not know how to train him. There was no structure and though they were happy to answer his questions from the articles he read. They pretty much left him to his devices. There was a certain comfort in just sitting there and getting into esoteric aspects but there was also a dissatisfaction of having time just pass. Ashok told himself that he would be getting a valuable certificate of training from a well-respected institution at the end of this time period, but he was beginning to learn an important lesson of life and of growing-up, that the Journey matters at least as much as the Destination, if not more.

And since transfer of capital wasn't allowed out of India, if he ever wanted to move to the West, these certificates would come in handy. But what good would the certificate be if he couldn't actually do the job, deliver. This may seem self-evident, once stated, thought Ashok, but this is what acquiring wisdom involved. And right now this was not the objective with which he had come. So he left the bucolic comfort of the labs and went back to the machines.

Some of the factory colleagues who he had become familiar with would invite him Thursday and Friday evenings to join them in proposed dates. They had their inimitable way of inviting him. They would indicate this with a finger inserted in a circle. Ashok shocked, never went with them but they persisted in their endeavour to entice him, each weekend.

The Finns were quite different from the rest of Scandinavia. They were and were not a part of it. The climate had made them light-skinned and light haired but they weren't quite as fair as the Nordic peoples. Many of them were dark-haired, their customs were unique not like neighbouring Russia nor like Sweden or Norway. Its own distinct self. Their mannerisms, their way of reacting were their own. Yes was 'eii' with a shake of the head. Some of the ways in which they moved their bodies and limbs during musicals like *Fiddler on the Roof* or while dancing were uniquely Finnish. Ashok had not seen those anywhere else. He began recognising them.

Above all the language was a part of the Ugro-Finn branch, completely different from Swedish, Norwegian, Danish which all had close affinity with each other. The only other language that was somewhat similar was that of Estonia across the Baltic Sea and at that time an unwilling member of the Soviet Union. (On a clear day, the lights of Talinn, could be seen from Helsinki harbour.) Were they even a part of the Indo-European group of languages?

Swedish was a second language spoken, especially in Western parts of Finland and in urban centres like Helsinki/ Helsingfors. Many cities had a completely different name in Swedish but it remained the language of the dominant neighbour and therefore resented.

Ashok's training took him to Tampere and to Turku/Abo - the next largest cities of Finland. Each was a train ride away of several hours. There were plants specialising in different dairy products there and he spent a week, in each place. These towns had their history their character and their share of the unique and creative Finnish architecture, which used so much wood, stone and local materials - was environment-friendly and blended well with it even in those days, when it hadn't become the politically correct thing to do so. But Ashok didn't know a soul, English was even less spoken and there was no equivalent of Vanhankellari for him to go to.

He wanted to share his thoughts, his experiences with Lauren. He kept brushing the possibility of this away. He wanted to hear her voice. What was the harm in talking to her? They had not stopped being friends. They had parted because they had so decided and at that point of time had to. Would she take his call? She would have the same hesitation. Why start it again? The parting had been so difficult, so painful.

Despite his better sense he phoned her. He heard the initial surprise in her voice and then the same hesitation at the other end. Her emotions were involved. But they managed to settle down to talking normally and of what they had been doing. They stayed away from feelings and any talk about missing each other.

He found himself phoning her a couple of times more even though he tried to restrain himself.

It was a treat every time. But the pang he felt was unmistakable.

He had cloudberry liqueur which was as delicious as the name, strawberries from close to Lapland, even some reindeer meat which was neither as rich nor as heavy as venison. But the music in the restaurants was the heady, dreamy music of the late 60's. It was ubiquitous. It had universal appeal. Ashok was young and full of confidence. The music would send him into outer space, he would walk up to strangers in the restaurants - groups of women and ask them to dance. He would lose himself in the music and the dance - and nothing else would matter then.

23

As Neeru and Vikram continued to see each other regularly, Brij and Radhika had to either accept him as their daughter's beau or to take a stand with all the repercussions that it might have.

Radhika talked to Neeru alone. She didn't want to give her implicit permission for sleeping with him by talking about it but her daughter had to be warned. She didn't want her getting pregnant. These things happened. It would have been inconceivable in her time but the Times they were a changin'.

The difference with Vikram was too much. It was not possible to reconcile to it. Harish was still interested. Neeru did not understand these things now but it would affect her in the long term.

Ashok is conveniently not there to divide the parents' attention thought Neeru and they are watching me like hawks. One evening she was dropped back bright and starry eyed from a dance party where Vikram had whirled her around and made her feel as if she was dancing in the air. It was 1 a.m. Radhika was waiting for her at the gate with thunder in her eyes. She attributed the reasons for her daughter's gaiety to the worst, forgetting her own youth, as parents are strangely wont to do.

Neeru was gated. The *chowkidar* was given instructions to stop her going out unless he checked with one of the parents.

Three mornings later at 4 a.m., with the night *chowkidar* in deep sleep, Neeru slipped out. She took whatever cash she had, a few change of clothes. There was the early morning freshness in the air. She walked for a bit under the tall trees lining the road, saw a scooter, hailed it and went to Vikram's house. A sleepy old retainer let her in expressionlessly. These old faithful domestics who were like family members always remained inscrutable.

24

Senaajoki was a clean, wind-swept, sparkling white village with a stream running next to it and a small curved picture-book wooden bridge across it. Ashok imagined the three goats on the other side, grazing on the green hillock and the evil creature under the bridge waiting to devour them. The streets were broad, there was a corner café not far from the single-roomed apartment he was lodged in. He turned right and walked to the end of the street next to his building. On the other side of the road was a ditch covered with grass and abutting a thickly wooded cluster, with the afternoon sunlight filtering in and lighting up the trees. There were crossroads at the end of that road. There were no pedestrians to be seen anywhere nor the odd car. Ashok instinctively turned right. It seemed to lead nowhere but at the corner of the road, round another turn was an inviting white stucco café. There were a few cycles leaning outside the walls of the café.

The Senaajoki ice-cream plant was in a village of the same name. The training was for three days but it included a weekend in between. The plant was huge and fascinating. The ice-cream packing machine filled cones with different flavours as they moved in circles and protective foil or other packaging material was wrapped around them. Ashok stared at it for hours. He couldn't take his eyes off it. He was also aware of several eyes upon him. Where had he come across that before?

On the ice cream machines there were mostly girls in white coats.

They looked at him curiously as he stood and observed the machines closely. Some of them were nice looking. As he continued to stand one or two smiled at him. He felt a little self-conscious at all this attention. He took out a sketch pad and started to draw these machines with some of their innovative features. No doubt manuals would be available but drawing it made the concepts sharper and clearer, imprinted them in his mind. It also gave him something to do instead of just observing the machines while being observed.

Ashok's presence had created much interest among the ice-cream machine girls. By the end of the day, he began taking the attention for granted.

But this was now the weekend, he hadn't seen a soul since the morning. Were they all at home or had they gone away, picnicking or to the nearest town Laahtiranti, which was still a town but considerably bigger than the ice-cream village.

The café held the possibility of encountering at least a few of those girls.

Ashok felt on top of the world. All the attention had spoilt him more than a little.

There were stools and a counter outside the café, at the other end. One had to go around the corner of the café, to see it. There were three of them there. They didn't look at him directly but the interest was evident.

His morning feeling of being alone evaporated.

'These girls are nice looking but are they my type?

Should he put his nose up in the air, continue to ride the

crest of this wave of attention…or should he go up to them, talk to them - give in?

Ashok's immaturity lost - pragmatism won, though it was a titanic struggle. One of the three in fact drifted away. The late afternoon sun was quickly setting, in this far northern place. He wouldn't meet a soul and evening was approaching. There might have been lots of people at the factory but he wouldn't see them again till Monday. Sunday, the café would probably be shut. Feeling special, being snobbish was a luxury. Ashok needn't make mistakes and only then learn. Besides, he had not seized opportunities before. Sometimes, they lasted only a few seconds. He was beginning to understand the consequences.

They were some of the girls at the ice-cream cone packing machines.

"May I join you?"—best to be direct, sometimes. They nodded.

"What and why were you drawing next to us?" the dark-haired one asked in slow English as he sat down.

"I just wanted to draw the machine you were working on because I was fascinated by it. It was such a good machine and did everything so smoothly."

"But, you are looking at it for so long, already"—her accent, her English were cute. She had a long, thin, attractive face, long, thin arms by her side. Her name was Irina. The other one was equally thin and young with straw coloured hair. She seemed more shy, perhaps because she was less confident of actually using her English. Her name was Hanna.

"I wanted to draw it to imprint it in my mind. I would remember its working even better that way."

"Oh so you weren't drawing us?" asked Hanna, flirtatiously, belying the impression that had been created moments ago.

"Oh, but I drew you all sitting around it."

"But the fo kus wasn't on us."

"A romantic notion of an artist in your midst, in search of a subject!"

This much English was too much for them.

Senaajoki had numerous village-greens, vast fields, handsome tall brown trees, thick forests all around, log roofs over houses in the distance, clean, wide, well-paved wind-swept streets, surrealistically empty. A pink coloured sky added to the feeling.

"You were also taking many notes."

"For the same purpose."

The conversation was of necessity limited. But interest extenuated for language. They opened up. They enjoyed working in the ice-cream factory. They had never been to Helsinki but they would one day. They had heard that the shopping was fantastic.

Where was he from? Italy? What was he doing here? How long would he stay?

He really had his own factory? It wasn't a co-operative? Most factories in Suomi were like that.

The border between interest and sexual interest is thin in such situations. Simon and Garfunkel "….the borders of our lives".

It grew dark, the café shut. A bright arc of moon was clearly visible over the trees…luminous, enchanted.

He couldn't invite them over. His room was comfortable, clean but there was nothing there. And there was no kitchen, no food, no music, no entertainment to offer. In Eastern Europe, anything he could show from the West would be of interest, a curiosity. In Poland he had left with Lauren, the portable record player he had acquired in France for the equivalent of $50. It produced wondrous music, rich in analog sound. Danuta and Barbara had been fascinated by the music he played on it. The Beatles, the Stones, Elvis, the Kinks, the Hollies, instrumentals from Billy Vaughn and Lawrence Welk.

These were not available as discs behind the Iron Curtain - though people had heard these songs over the radio.

The dilemma was over quickly. What were his plans for the evening? Would he like to come over to Hanna's for a drink and a bite later? It was easy to find.

They wrote down the address and gave him directions. If he got lost, he might find no one on the streets to ask.

The girls produced some Campari. Ashok was attracted by the bright red colour. He had never had it before. This was the thing about Europe, even these young girls just starting out were able to afford it. Ashok decided he would stick to cloudberry in the future, how could a taste be developed for something so bitter, even when diluted with a lot of soda.

A Chess set was pulled out. They ganged up on him. Ashok loved Chess and part of the secret of his success was that he never took it too seriously. In school, he often played with an Alistair Maclean by his side. What better than reading *Night Without End* and drinking a Coke with crushed ice tinkling, when the learned opponent took his time. Ashok felt worn out with pre-calculating permutations and combinations in response to possible moves by his opponent. Nor did he like plotting an over-all strategy.

He told them Chess had been invented in India and Indian rules though different only in a couple of ways were considerably more difficult. He was always glad to be playing international rules.

Ashok also enjoyed targeting the more powerful and significant pieces of the competitor. Aggressive strategy dictated that the king should be the target from the word 'go' and should be trapped through clever and insidious means or better still through choices where the surreptitious knight or the bishop from the other end of the board could kill the king if the queen or some such majestic piece was not sacrificed.

But, Ashok played all sports to enjoy them. In the process, if he became good, all the better, otherwise he still enjoyed it. Part of his enjoyment came from presenting similar Hobson's choices with the hidden knight or the innocuous pawn between say a rook and a bishop.

The local dish was delicious. The girls gave him the Finnish name, so he could know it for the future but Ashok kept forgetting promptly. They teased him and the atmosphere grew more and more relaxed.

Was Finland as liberated as neighbouring Sweden, that too in the country.

Sweden—advanced, rich, very Welfare!

Or was it a more individual thing, he mused, beyond all that and to do with personal chemistry and attraction.

Hanna shook her head in a particular way. It reminded him of Lauren. He felt a sudden longing but he had to live in the present. He had decided to leave the shores of Polska, he was getting training and he had to make the most of his time.

Coffee had that effect on him. He just couldn't sleep. But the next day was a Sunday and he always enjoyed the aroma and the taste. They put on the obligatory Sibelius. And then it was Grieg. The music was splendid. It put everyone in a dreamy mood. The sky outside, visible through the double glazed windows, was bejewelled with stars, like in a Planetarium. The pollution-free atmosphere, the lack of city lights, the thick forests, all contributed to the contrast. The double-glazed provided protection from the intense cold at this latitude. It was bright, warm, cosy inside the apartment.

Did they have any preference for the type of guy they wanted as a partner?

"Dark, handsome...." said Irina

"You forgot tall."

"Does not have to be. I think, I prefer not..."

"Ooh... Just like me, of course."

"Of course." she smiled.

They were equally attractive in their different ways. He didn't want to go home, he wanted to stay there with the two of them, as long as possible. It was getting later and later. There was a comfortable silence except for the music in the background.

Irina said something in Finnish.

"That's rude," protested Ashok.

"I am just saying that I don't feel like walking home now and am going to sleep here."

"So am I," said Ashok seizing his opportunity.

"You can,", said Hanna, matter-of-factly. "The sofa is quite comfortable and I can give you a pillow and a cover when you feel like sleeping."

"And now tell us a story from Home."

Ashok told them a story from the *Panchatantra* - the Monkey and the Crocodile.

"It is a simple story but the moral of courage and using your wits in adversity can be applied at various levels. The King wanted his children to be taught the ways of the world. It would equip them to deal with the intrigues in the Kingdom and to be better rulers. The *Raj Guru* told them a number of stories on successive days."

The tension was tangible now. It had been building up all evening. Something was going to give. He had just met them that day but Time does not always pass in equivalence with its chronological measurements.

The flat was small and cosy with a bedroom and a drawing room. Irina was given a mattress in the bedroom. Hanna didn't bother to shut the bedroom door and left it ajar.

Ashok slept fitfully. He could hear the girls tossing and turning too. There was the ticking of the clock. Finally after what seemed like a long time, Ashok whispered "Hanna" tentatively into the darkness. There was no answer but Ashok felt he had been heard. A little later, a little louder "Irina". He could see the stars outside, from the bedroom window framed in the wall opposite the partially open door.

"Yes" answered Irina

"I can't sleep."

"I can't either."

"Come and talk for a while."

"Alright", said Irina and came and sat by him.

They talked in whispers. Ashok wasn't sure that Hanna was asleep.

Irina's shoulders glistened. Her legs shone palely below the short comfortable nightie in the dim light of the apartment. Her palms rested on her thighs held together. The atmosphere had imperceptibly become electric. She got up to use the bathroom and came back and sat slightly closer. While gesticulating to make a point his hand accidentally brushed against her thigh.. He got an electric shock. He could see she had too.

"What are you up to, you two?" asked Hanna suddenly not intending the double-entendre.

"Couldn't sleep, just talking," said Ashok as they moved apart while Hanna walked into the room, but she had sensed something. A guilty look flashed for an instant on Irina's face as if she had stolen something.

The next day was unusually bright and sunny, the equivalent of an Indian summer across the Atlantic. They had sweets and an aromatic Finnish drink that Hanna came up with. The Finnish sweets were delicious. Ashok had never tasted anything like them. If he gave them some of the best *barfis* in India, they would probably feel this way. He would relate to his remaining days at the factory, differently.

They walked in the green Finnish countryside and deep into

the thickly wooded forest. The sunlight filtering through the tall trees seemed surreal. The path through the trees was so narrow, it was almost not there. They had to walk single file and close together. Irina turned back towards Ashok, probably to say something, but they kissed unexpectedly instead.

The remaining two days at the factory passed quickly. He sensed a heightened interest amongst the girls. Hanna and Irina seemed to have given away nothing. They smiled and nodded at him on the shop floor, continued working. Was there something that many of them could feel?

"When shall we three meet again?" he said to them on the last night. Shakespeare could be used even if he remained unrecognised.

His training took him from place to place. He was a rolling stone.

"I could gather no moss", he said aloud.

"What?" asked Irina.

Was there a future for him with either of them, he thought. Maybe the girls would end up in Helsinki. Could he imagine settling down here, or in Helsinki? Or, either of them going away with him, and being happy, far from home? It had only been a few days but the imagination brooks no boundaries. And could this not have been thought about Martine and Nicole.

Wasn't he acquiring a number of friendships, no less satisfying as the ones from school and college? Wasn't he living life to the fullest, in each situation?

He was still very young. Why should he even think about long-term relationships.

The training in Senaajoki came to an end and it was time for the next factory.

25

Vaasa was the northernmost point of his whole trip. A flight had to be taken to it from Helsinki. Pentti Kosinen from the management of Valio accompanied him. The Co-operative Dairy Association was certainly looking after him well. They took the training and their responsibility seriously.

Vaasa was more than 500 km north-east of Helsinki. Ashok couldn't imagine being so far north. It was hard enough believing that he was in Helsinki and in Finland. Was this the northernmost he would ever go in his life? It was still far enough from Lapland and way below the Arctic circle. He peered outside the car window. Did the terrain, the vegetation look different or was he imagining it? It was a largish town - smaller than Turku or Tampere. The architecture was ultra-modern and typically Finnish. Materials were used imaginatively, creatively, in ways and designs that he hadn't encountered before. Houses used steel and glass too, much before they became fashionable in office buildings but in ways that seemed totally residential.

The Vaasa plant was a brand new, gleaming, stainless steel and aluminium factory. The process control was immaculate, even in those pre-computer days. It smacked of efficiency. It encouraged working. Ashok wanted to stay there. He felt happy, he was enjoying the journey of the training now. It was important to enjoy the process, not just look for the certificate or for the training to be over.

Kosinen introduced Ashok to his first ever sauna. There was one inside the administrative block. It was cold and dark outside now, everyone had gone to their respective warm hearth and home. There was wood panelling everywhere. There was an indoor swimming pool in a central room, lit up, with warm lighting all around. There was a table next to the main stair into the pool, containing fruits, some cold meat slices and wine.

Kosinen took them to an exceedingly warm cabin with a temperature gauge, two levels of wooden benches along the walls, brightly glowing coal or similar fuel, with a container of water in another portion of the room. They stripped completely in a changing room, put on towel robes and Kosinen indicated that they sit or lie on the benches. Ashok climbed on to one at the upper level, using his bath robe as a cushion when the wood of the bench began to feel too hot. He sweated and felt a different sense of being coming over him, suffusing him. Kosinen mixed some herbal essences with the water and sprinkled it on to the coal which sizzled. A delicious aroma filled the room. Ashok was filled with the exoticism of the experience.

After what seemed like much longer but was closer to 15 minutes, they came out of the sauna and Kosinen jumped into the pool.

The water in the pool was pleasantly cool, even though it was freezing outdoors by now. Ashok felt refreshed and invigorated as he splashed about in the blue water. Kosinen glanced at Ashok's body.

"You are very fair," he said.

Ashok thought this was a strange remark.

He shrugged "There are many people in India like me."

They put on white towel robes. Ashok felt a sudden pang of hunger. The cold cuts under the black grapes were delicious. He sliced the fruit and took a thirsty sip of the cold white wine. Life was full of novel experiences, some of them hedonistic. The secret was to enjoy every precious moment while it lasted in this impermanent, ephemeral world.

"This sauna thingy should spread all over the world from Finland", said Ashok out loud.

The next evening was his last in Vaasa. Would he ever again be this far north? Would he see the land of the midnight sun, the Northern Lights sometime?

Kosinen took them to a very pleasant restaurant. There was a live group playing with a girl singer holding a mike in the lead.

She was singing–'If you are going to San Francisco.' These were universal songs. Ashok felt a sharp pang of something.

Ashok went over to a table, three–four tables away and asked a dark haired lady to dance. Did it require courage? Perhaps when he was older. He didn't give it a thought. She seemed much older to him, she must have been in her mid 30's. She clung to him. She didn't speak any English. Ashok had stopped expecting to find anyone who did, in Europe. The music was pleasing. There was a clutch of people dancing. Kosinen seemed content to sit at the table, indulgently. She remained in very close contact. He felt her quiver. He danced with her the rest of that evening, going back to the table to talk to Kosinen and take sips of some other liquor, that he had ordered, similar to cloudberry, found only in those parts.

He liked dancing here with this person to this music in this second floor restaurant with the cold brightly lit street visible below through the large windows but how much nicer if it had been his true love.

A one hour flight on Finn Air and he was back in Helsinki the next day. His time in Suomi was over. It was time to wind up. He rang up some Vanhankellari friends. He hadn't seen them for some weeks. A short straw-haired fellow called Vespi by all who had told Ashok a number of opera stories said, "O-Oh! You're leaving? No!"

'You're sounding like you have regrets now', he thought, 'but you could have taken the initiative more often', but he said nothing.

A number of young people he had met at youth hostels and elsewhere had told him about the ship from Helsinki to Stockholm and travelling deck class on it. Precious foreign exchange had to be saved. He had not much as it is, and what if he wanted to stay longer in Europe?

26

He lugged his heavy black leather suitcase to the harbour, his small, light, attaché given by one of the airlines, in the other hand. This contained all his fellowship documents and travel papers and served as his briefcase. He tilted over sharply to one side to balance the weight of the suitcase. There was a long narrow platform to be traversed. The suitcase was crammed full of his clothes.

One side of the handle came off, Ashok tilted over even more. It was really difficult now. Ashok heard a guy in a tractor pulling a luggage-carrier behind him. He turned around to look. This guy could easily carry it on the mechanised platform. From behind his head Ashok repeatedly got the vibes that he wanted to help him but he wouldn't look at him, ignored him. He should have taken his help. But was not the West a place where no one helped anyone else? You were all on your own. It was a sort of individualism.

There was a covered plank at an incline as entrance, with white painted railings at the side. The Captain and his No 2 stood in their shiny uniforms at the top of the entrance, greeting the first class passengers. Ashok panted up, dragging his leaden suitcase up it. A plump fellow with a Cockney accent said "Ere, let's give you a hand up," and Ashok felt a welcoming hand miraculously lessening the weight.

Ashok found that he met the nicest people on deck. They seemed interesting, adventurous, mostly young. Maybe he wasn't missing out after all by not being in one of the more comfortable cabins and not even having a bed for the night. He leaned back in his chair, and ordered a hot meat and potatoes dish. It tasted delicious and was inexpensive enough for even Ashok to not try and starve through dinner. Beer was the same price as any other drink including water. He sat back and enjoyed it.

There were round tables with four-five chairs around each. This portion of the deck had some sort of wooden cover painted white. He went and sat at the far end. An attractive lonely looking lady in her mid-30s came up from one of the cabins. A blonde-bearded fellow with a thin face joined him. He was from Brighton and seemed to have a lively sense of humour. He was as pleased as Ashok was to find another English speaking person, with common interests. Ashok hadn't bothered to shave since some time and an intense black beard contrasted with his complexion and the blonde on his chin and moustache. Swedes are not known for their singing skills many Finns and other non-Swedes had told him. A portly balding Swedish man started singing for the passengers having dinner, as the tables filled up. Ashok enjoyed the music. The singer paused. Ashok clapped loudly from the far end of the deck, alone. The Swedish singer looked at him and nodded. Ashok stretched out in his chair on the deck. His companion from Brighton, John was already asleep. Ashok had visions of following the older lady to her cabin and knocking on her door with a story.

The overnight journey on deck ended with the outline of houses along the shores of Stockholm visible in the early morning - mist covered. So this was Sweden!

He found a bus going from the harbour to the railway station. The two English chaps were going there too. The train for Norway left in the evening. They had the day to see Stockholm. The buildings were grand.

In the central parts and squares they were ornate with gold work, rich façades, elaborate opera-house like balconies overlooking the squares, designs at the top as if some of the buildings were wearing well-designed crowns. As they moved away a bit from this part of the city, they came across taller, well-maintained six-storied buildings that seemed to be from the nineteenth century. Some of them were of striking colours, others gilded, yet others looked like triangular cross-sections rising up against the sky.

There was a medium sized maroon building, the colour going well with the light, the triangular point of it ending at the corner across the bridge. There were houses along the river front, the street lights lighting them up gently and many bridges spanning the river as it meandered across the city.

"You sure are getting the eye," John said noticing the peripheral and not so peripheral vision that Ashok was managing to attract as they tramped across the city.

The city was exquisite, magnificent - there was a lot to absorb in just one day - too much. He started singing Simon and Garfunkel's,

"Oh, homeward bound,

I wish I was,

Home, where the...

Home, where the..."

John joined in.

He would come through Stockholm again on the way back from Norway.

Evening saw them converging at the railway station, with an unexpected group of English-speaking people, an Australian woman materialised, the Cockney fellow was there and a number of other people came from all directions.

27

The money lender refused. He had to earn a living, provide for his family. This was the job of the Government to uplift the poor. He could not do it. He had already stopped charging interest from some of the worst hit families. He had to at least get his capital back.

In the mid afternoon at 3.30 p.m., the young urban naxalites in Jeans, with their faces masked to avoid recognition went to the money lender's grain shop and stabbed him repeatedly in the stomach. Gita almost fainted at his agonised cries and could not get herself to join in. She was committed to the cause. It wasn't a matter of individuals. They dispersed just as quickly leaving the money lender lying in a pool of blood in the dust with the flies buzzing around.

28

Ashok's train would take him all across Sweden, into Norway. It was the end of May. He wouldn't have to change in Oslo. The same train would cross Norway at night - a fantastic feat of engineering - across the high mountain plateau, the passes and the fjords way below, until it reached Bergen and the West Coast by the morning.

Oslo came and went. The capital of Norway, 'The Doll's House' and Ibsen, the Nobel prize.... The train stopped at the railway station. Some wagons were attached to another engine, he could hear the sound of coupling and uncoupling. He would see Oslo another time. The train trundled on into the night. It would be cold outside.

Late at night, after dinner, he felt the train climbing. The landscape was brilliantly lit. The mountains rose high and the city was left far behind.

Ashok could see the fjords - way below, yet clearly visible in the moonlight. The fjords were narrow, deep in parts, the water pure from the mountains, rushing over and cleansed by the rocks, gurgling, bubbling, frothing-white with the force and the pressure. The terrain in-between was densely forested but in parts it was sparse with craggy rocks and bushes. What was clear was that the fjords were a spectacular distance below the mountain passes which the train was on.

Sometimes there would be a solitary house on a mountain top. The snow in the higher altitudes reflected the moonlight. Sometimes it seemed to be a plateau as the train went on and on. It was a marvellous feat of engineering. Sometimes a cloud or high peaks blocked the moonlight and it was pitch black outside. Most of the passengers were sleeping. They must have become used to the drama of this journey, from the East coast to the West.

Morning came. It was 7 a.m. There were a whole lot of strangers talking in Swedish and Norwegian, the former with more variation in the lilt and tone to distinguish it, for Ashok. Sometimes, he heard a sharp intake of breath when a 'yes' was whispered.

It was early morning at the station. The passengers quickly disappeared along with their baggage. There was a small cabin not far from the platform. The station master was sitting there in a dark blue uniform, smoking a pipe. Ashok knocked. The station master looked at him. Ashok asked him how to get to Bergensmeiriet.

"Where are you from? Have a cup of coffee", he offered.

"Could I leave my luggage here? I've to go to the toilet."

He returned to find a steaming cup of black coffee in the cabin. He'd had no breakfast, was tired and travel-worn. It was very welcome. He took a sip gratefully. It was very strong. He was a tea-drinker after all.

The Company had given him a small attic room with a sloping wooden ceiling meeting the floor next to the bed. It was a sparse room. There were no cooking arrangements. From the small window could be seen a tower clock. Ashok had just to look out to see the time. The typical four-storeyed

European town spread out before him. There were a couple of spires and the church bells chimed every hour. Below on each floor were two workers' families. A wooden platform lay between the room and the staircase leading out past the flats.

Ashok was pleased to have at least a bathroom to himself. He had to exit his room and enter it from the platform. He had to walk between some houses to reach the bus stop, but it wasn't far. The factory was a few stops away, and the town centre next to the lake was at the end of the line A5.

Ashok began to get his bearings. The workers and their families kept to themselves. There was a silence in the house. Over the weekends, he did not see a soul as he moved up and down the stairs. Once on a Sunday evening, he knocked on the ground floor flat. He thought he would save himself the phone money. He asked if he could make a phone call. The worker himself opened the door. He was OK with Ashok making the call but wanted the money afterwards. Things were different here, every place was not India. Things that he took for granted could not be so taken here.

Ashok was terrified about one day getting bad news about his father. It wasn't just that he was getting on. There was the guilt associated with his having stayed away so long, leaving his father alone to handle things. The business was complex and could certainly do with more than one entrepreneurial hand. He was getting very useful training but wasn't he required more at home?

A few days later there was a knock on the door. It was 5 a.m. It was gray and foggy outside. There was a telegram from India.

Ashok felt dread and a chill in his heart. Something had happened. He made his way between the buildings and crossed the street to a payphone. Buses were already plying in the streets. The cryptic information given said to call a local number to get the message. He got through. It was from Brij and Radhika asking how he was and when he thought he might be able to come home.

Bergensmeiriet was as large as Valio. Some of the equipment for transferring milk here too was bought from Koltek Oy in Finland. The factory was large and airy, with huge windows at the top to make it bright. The staff dining room was on the ground floor. Ashok was to have his breakfast, lunch and dinner here. The latter was at 5 p.m. and usually consisted of some meat and cabbage. It was the worst meal of the lot and most of the staff preferred going home, but Ashok was not about to spend valuable hard currency on filling himself. He felt an angst about conserving capital that went beyond his desire to save and finance himself during the non-scholarship period.

The red Norwegian flag with the black cross was everywhere. The town of Bergen went up on all sides of the mountains surrounding the picturesque lake. The lake was a clear deep blue. There were white gulls, playing their music. There was a funicular going up to the top on the other side of the lake. The two or three storied houses with their sloping roofs, coloured red or green or a darker shade of the same colour as the rest of the house, went up the green mountain sides, all around the lake. They were of all the colours of the rainbow, in various light shades and hues, to guard the psyche against the gray light and the dark days. The houses were similar and had a harmony of design. They were pretty. This must be the only place in the world like this. How come it wasn't better known? Even Oslo wasn't like this. Probably no other city in Norway was.

They were surreal. Neat little pastel coloured fairy tale houses. Others a brighter and stronger red, green deep blue. Startling. Strong. At each long end of the lake were the two poshest hotels in town. The Hotel Norge had a discotheque, a hair dressing salon, an ice cream and coffee bar which could be entered from the outside and which also sold delicious French fries for 1 kroner.

Around the middle portion of the oval-shaped lake, Ashok found some benches where he sat and looked out at the multi-coloured houses on the far side of the lake.

The bus into town which said Centrum in the manner of all European towns had disgorged them not far from here. Ashok had walked across some grass, past what looked like a clubhouse but which turned out to be a pleasant Café, to get there.

A handsome young man with a round face and pleasant demeanour approached him. He smiled at him and said in English "Are you from Italy?" There was also another question in this - "What's a stranger like you doing here?"

Ashok went and sat with him in the Café and had a sustaining coffee and hot dog. His name was Oliver. Probably the English equivalent, Ashok thought. A group of friends joined them. They seemed to be sophisticated enough and interested in Ashok. He was pleased at the attention. He was used to it at College parties in Delhi because he had acquired a certain reputation but this was a new stage.

There was to be a Duke Ellington concert that evening at a stadium. Performers came where the affluence was. Would he join them at 8 that evening?

The stadium was packed to capacity, it was a sea of blonde hair. This was Norway after all. He filed in with Oliver and the bunch. They were not near the stage but could witness well enough what was going on. The Duke along with several Jazz musicians stepped into the spotlight, kissed the girls who came to welcome him, to squeals of surprise from the crowd. Then the well-known numbers started and Ashok forgot where he was. He was back to his growing up years.

Ashok started hanging out at the café. The curiosity in him over, he didn't immediately acquire any fresh friends. He went with Oliver and his friends to the discotheque.

The lead singer was English - a pleasant young man with dark hair in dark blue - almost black attire. Ashok started chatting to him and sat down at the base of the platform to continue the conversation. The dance floor started filling up with some people drifting in, in groups or starting off as couples. Next to the wall at the far end of the room from the entrance sat a number of pretty young blondes, taking up two tables. Ashok gauged that they didn't know each other but there was a certain social safety in numbers. They talked to each other and laughed, taking in the scene with their peripheral vision.

Ashok walked over to one of them at random and asked one of them to dance. Till he reached the table he didn't even know who he was going to ask. To his surprise and dismay she hesitated and then shook her head. As he was leaving he saw her mates making as if to ask her *pourquoi* casually. Did she know the answer herself? Rejection was a part of these things, not to be taken personally. But it was hard not to do so. He didn't feel like asking someone else on the re-bound. What would be her reaction? He went back to his position on the platform.

He looked at the girls on the two tables. Some of them were so pretty. The small dance floor in front of the band filled up. There was an intimate feel about it. Some of the girls were being held tight, now. One girl was being kissed in a way that made Ashok feel that he wanted to kiss her like that, too. Another attractive and somewhat voluptuous girl was getting into a kiss that seemed full of promise. Maybe he had inadvertently become the equivalent of a wall-flower by sitting on the platform too long. Had he by now been typed. Was he bound to get a 'no' now. There were still many girls next to those tables. They were laughing and chatting animatedly to each other. There was only one way to find out. The band paused every now and then. The lead singer chatted pleasantly to him. He had no inkling of Ashok's dilemma. Ashok put in some requests. He was buying time.

Courage is a matter of an instant, not so much of character. Ashok made to get up two or three times. His courage failed him. More of the pretty girls were on the floor, many were being kissed. It was infectious, sensuous. Ashok thought of how it was to kiss Lauren. Was he just aching for human contact. The music was exquisite.

He walked out into the fresh, cold, seaside air, out of the smoke, sweat, perfume-filled joint. The stars were bright, far. The vast ground next to the lake at the other side of which lay the other fancy hotel, was covered with snow already. It was early.

The next day he took the funicular cable car to the top of the mountain, on the far side of the lake. The brightly coloured city lay below him in various multi-coloured shades with sloping roofs. A pastry town, full of mostly light hued slices of cake, next to a blue Chinese enamel plate. He lingered savouring his cup of coffee, like it was an open air Starbucks. The bright evening lights flickered on in the town. A canopy of stars lay below him, next to him the majestic mountains, thickly wooded.

There was a flute concert later on in the week. It was at an auditorium on top of a hill. There were pleasant cottage-like houses all the way up to it. Thanks to the Beatles and the flower children, Indian Classical Music had become well known in even the smaller European towns. He hadn't heard of the performer but the music transported him far away, back to the vast moonlit plains of India. It was evocative.

Krishna, the softly flowing Yamuna and the leafy trees under which He stood and played His Magic Flute. The breeze was fragrant and made the leaves of the *peepal* tree rustle. The enchantment spread far beyond where the *gopis* did their *Ras Leela*. It reached whatever the soft moonlight and the raat-ki-raani touched.

Did this mean that he missed home or just that one could re-connect with home in an instant, so in-grained in each cell was the connection?

Back stage there was pot. Those were the days, as the song said, which all in them thought would never end. They would change the world and the change would not be reversible. Ashok was familiar with this scene. He might well have been at a party in Delhi University. There was a heady sensation of the familiar with the novel.

The next night in his attic, Ashok felt restless. He put on his beige corduroy trousers and a thick jacket and went down the stairs. He walked into one of the residential streets some distance from there. It was a cold, black night. The lights were on in the houses. There was no one on the streets but him. It was only 8 p.m. but it seemed very late. The next day was a working day. Ashok was carrying the guitar that Oliver had lent him. He strummed it and sang 'Norwegian Wood'. Did the song have anything at all to do with Norway? Oliver had thought not. Maybe it just sounded good. The street went on towards the dark mountains looming on the horizon. Surely, there would be another soul about like him. Was 'Norwegian Wood' appropriate for this setting? He strummed and sang more softly. It seemed more appropriate. There were no night bird sounds - this was not Delhi. He didn't feel lonely - but was aware of his aloneness. He walked back singing.

Hedda Gabler was on in Bergen. He had read that and *A Doll's House* and other Ibsen plays not so long ago in College.

It would be something to see it here. It would be in Norwegian but he would feel the atmosphere, see the costumes and sets, remember the plot, watch it unfold. He wasn't disappointed. It was memorable. He didn't understand a word but he understood the sense.

29

The four weeks in Norway came to an end - it was time to
make the spectacular journey back over the fjords and into
Sweden - where a fair young maiden, as the poem said would
bring him cakes and coffee on cold December morns.

His parents intervened. From the vantage point of the
protected environment of Delhi where even to go to Khan
Market his parents wanted him to take someone along just a
few years ago, this whole journey seemed like an extraordinary
exercise in endurance - deck class on the ship, long hours on
the train at night in a seat, no food.

He got a call from KLM in Oslo. KLM, because he had
liked them so much and his original air-ticket from India to
Europe and back, had been on KLM. His parents had managed
to send a plane ticket for him to fly back from Bergen to
Helsinki, instead of taking the train and the ferry again. How
had they managed to send it? It must have been exceedingly
difficult. Nothing was allowed.

Ashok didn't want his parents to spend more than a
minimum on him. He told the surprised airline to return the
Bergen-Oslo-Stockholm portion. He would fly from

Stockholm to Helsinki. The magnificent fjords would not be missed!

The return journey too started at night but the fjords and the high mountain passes came soon after the departure from Bergen. It was pitch black outside. It must be overcast. Ashok fell into an exhausted sleep dreaming of spectacular fjords below very high escarpments, full of fast flowing bubbling white water, frothing near the rocks. He woke up and looked outside. This was what he had made this journey for.

It matched what he had imagined Scandinavia to be. They swept across the width of Norway in the night, traversed the high mountains again and it was Oslo in the morning.

There would be just enough time to see an Edvard Munch exhibition. The museum would just have opened. What better place to see a son of the city than over here? Ashok was tired from the journey. He felt unshaven and bedraggled. Should he even try. It would be cutting it fine.

He dragged his heavy luggage to the left luggage and got directions to the museum. From the bus the city itself felt like a museum. There were sculptures and statues everywhere set in green parks, on top of buildings and next to descending steps. The capital of Norway felt like a modern city, steeped in history and without the overcrowding. At least he would have an impression of it.

At the museum, Ashok felt devoid of energy. He had to have some food and drink. There must be a museum café - these were generally inexpensive and had food that was reasonably good. Time or no time, he went in there. It had an immediate calming effect on him. The aroma and flavour of the coffee, the rest of the smorgasbord revived him. He would still have time to see 'The Scream'. The paintings absorbed him and transported him to the world of Munch and his mind. But he couldn't take too much of it at a go. The interval turned out to be perfect. And he might have felt depressed waiting drearily at the station.

He managed to jump into his train, with hardly any time to spare. It must have been a superfast train for within a few hours it was Stockholm, with a golden Northern sun glistening on the golden city steeples and domes. It was evening already and the plane was leaving at 5 p.m. The city was bathed in that light. Ashok checked in at the city terminal. This was the good thing about European airports. He had an hour to wander around the centre.

KLM had given him a typical sky-blue air bag, very light, pleasing. Maybe the SAS bag would be very nice too. He went back in. A very pretty girl attended to him. Her tone was provocative, personal - at the same time patronizing. What was this? Was she attracted to him? There was such little time. Ashok wanted to wander around the city. Walk as far as the port. He didn't get drawn into anything.

It would be late by the time he got into Helsinki. What would he do? Where would he stay? Valio were not looking after him now. What were his plans after Helsinki? His main India-Europe-India ticket recommenced from Helsinki.

He had to build savings in foreign exchange for a life in the West, if he ever decided to live here. Or even to have dollars to get a Polish visa again or to make them stretch for an extended stay in Poland. Maybe he would see Lauren again, their parting notwithstanding. He had left Wroclaw after about a year but it felt strangely inconclusive, like unfinished business.

There was no place in the Helsinki Youth Hostel. In youth hostels in Europe he would have as much as he could for breakfast which was included and try to make it last for the whole day - at any rate for lunch. During his training, his staying allowance in places where the Company could not provide accommodation was much more generous than the cost of a bed in a youth hostel dorm. But he would stay there in order to save the difference.

Everything else was more expensive. He started wandering around the city. He passed one moonlit monument after another. They were resplendent. There was not a soul around. The nights were getting cold now. He rang up the Police. Somebody had mentioned this as a solution ages back when yarns were being spun amongst international students. Maybe it had been just a thought in someone's mind but Ashok was going to try it.

No coin was required for calling the Police. It was an emergency number.

"I am an international student from India. I have no place to sleep this night. Please come and take me to prison. I am directly opposite such and such monument. I can see it as I speak", Ashok said in English.

A guttural voice answered, "OK, we kham, we kham."

"I am cold here in the phone booth. How long will you take?"

"10 minutes."

An eternity passed, his legs were beginning to freeze. He couldn't just stay here.

He walked a bit in the moonlight, looking all around him for a Police car. There wasn't a soul in sight. He hadn't walked far. A superb white monument reflected the moon and there was a courtyard in front of it.

He called again. It was a different voice, he explained the situation again.

"We can't do that. You have committed no crime."

He walked some more and tried again.

This voice too told him "We come, we come."

"How long will you be?"

"What?"

"How much time will you take to come for me?"

"We come right now."

He told them where he was. Again he waited. Again no one came. He couldn't bear to stay endlessly in one place.

How pretty the city was. It showed him one white monument after another reflecting the moonlight.

He remembered the Elvis song "...tired and hungry and cold and wet..." - well he wasn't wet yet.

He came across a bus stop. There was activity here. It was very early morning. These buses were going straight to the airport. He felt the warmth as the bus door opened to let someone inside. He had the money for the fare in his pocket. He was aware of a sudden urge to get on the bus and to catch a flight home. Where did that come from? He was in the West having a ball! That was what happened when people went to Europe! No, no he didn't think like that.

The next day, he got reservation in a youth hostel 30 km outside Helsinki with a number of international students in it. On an impulse Ashok decided to go there. Or was it inertia? A bus took him to a thickly wooded green area with poplars on the roadside. It was of a pleasant wood-panelled design that was evocative of a sauna. He would have to catch a bus to the air-terminal at 4 in the morning.

Ashok remembered catching a bus one weekend early morning from a similar bus stop around the end of his training. That had been the start of summer. The sun was already bright, though there wasn't a soul around. There was a feeling of freshness and brightness, of the day just starting. There was a gust of wind, with some summer leaves in it. The bus had come late but it hadn't mattered.

The youth hostel was brightly lit and the lounge was full of young people, mostly Americans and British, all there for the same reason. Ashok found it easy to talk to them and settled down comfortably, as if he'd been there for a while. The lot he started talking to were idealistic and wanted to do what they could to change the way many things were. The lounge felt cosy, as if there was a fire crackling in the fireplace.

He took down some addresses, gave his cards. Who knows where life would take him and where he might call up someone he'd met. He didn't know then that it rarely happens and people can't be collected. Even things collected don't last.

The next morning was cold and very dark. It was hard to believe that it wasn't the dead of night. Ashok stood alone at the bus stop. Nobody else was catching a flight that day. He dozed off during the hour long journey and before he knew it, it had deposited him near the terminal. He opened his things on the city pavement, already busy and re-arranged his things. The airlines could be very fussy about weight including that of hand baggage. He took out 10 Finnish Marks for the fare to the airport and carefully kept it aside.

The airport bus rolled off smoothly and noiselessly. A dark blue uniformed person, himself looking like a dashing pilot, came around to collect the fares. Thank goodness, he'd kept it aside in time and it wasn't deep inside the suitcase with the rest of his money. He rummaged around in his briefcase - papers, correspondence inviting him to various countries, travel documents - but the 10 mark note safely kept away was nowhere to be found. He looked in some of the travel documents stuffed in his overcoat pocket - health certificate, airticket, boarding pass etc. There were many passengers to be covered. This was just the front of the bus. The man waited patiently. Ashok started going through everything again. He had especially taken out 10 marks for this. A middle-aged lady who seemed old to Ashok, sitting next to him, looked on with a sympathetic expression, as Ashok's second round began. She said in English that he was having trouble finding it and she would pay. He didn't think this was OK. What had happened to the 10 marks? She did and he continued to look. Mannerheimintie, the exquisite architecture of the Finnish capital, the tall trees sped past. When they reached the airport, he asked for her address, so he could pay her back. She said it was OK, it was only a small amount. He really wanted to repay this stranger. He asked again for her address but she smiled and didn't give it.

30

"When will we get our Ashok back?" asked Brij one morning. He had gone for a walk to Lodhi Gardens with his wife. Radhika sighed. She too missed him a lot and knew how hard Brij was working and how much of a help Ashok would be.

Brij was very outgoing. He would talk to many strangers in the park and as they started going more regularly people would recognise them and greet them with a namaste. Radhika would watch in amusement as his motley circle grew.

Brij had always been a very early riser. The sacred *bramha muhurta* when all was quiet, peaceful and the sun was rising to share its cosmic energy was a time of puja, of reciting Vedic mantras and divine *shlokas*. 5 a.m. at the latest he would be up and about, followed by a bath and of late they had started this Lodhi Garden thing. Earlier they didn't even have time for that.

Then the day long battle with numbers, figures, reports, telephone calls, meetings would begin. Ideas would be implemented, schemes thought of, initiatives taken.

3 1

Out of the blue Lauren remembered one of the magical times she and Ashok had made love. She missed him a lot, she had apprehended she would, but that it would be this difficult...

Her music absorbed her but it could not take the place of a lover and a lover could not be found out of necessity. You loved whom you loved.

She tracked his movements sometimes even though she knew there was no point. She would have to fall back on her inner resources. She had been part of the choice, now she would have to face the consequences. She would pursue other things that interested her, that she had been tempted to explore but never had the time for, even though these days she didn't feel enthusiastic about much. Friends had often talked about the exhilaration one felt while skiing. She needed something physical. Come the season, she would definitely try that, especially weekends.

She was fun loving, exuberant, out-going - she would find all that in herself once again.

32

Helsinki also being in the east the ticket had been routed through Warsaw. It was too much trouble to re-route it at this stage. He would just pass through it. He was aware of an intensity with no name within him. It couldn't be about Lauren. That was a decision *déjà pris*. A big wrench already faced.

He landed in Warsaw. He phoned Barbara but she had gone to Torun for a few days. "*Szkoda*", he said. He should have written to her. All dressed up and nowhere to go! What should he do next? His flight was early next morning. The youth hostel was not far from Marszalkowska. It was in one of the row houses, set in from the main street. Next to it was a huge glass-domed eating joint called Gastronomia. It resembled an inverted fish-bowl. On the other side of the road was a main PKO, another round, glass building, part of such bureaucratic banking as was permissible in the Communist world.

As he was entering the building, a couple of attractive girls were exiting at the same time. They seemed different. The biggest wonder of all - they spoke in English. They were friendly, were from New Zealand and the conversation that started was interesting. New Zealanders often feel they are at one end of the world - so they feel compelled to travel all over, even behind the Iron Curtain - to feel that the rest of it is there.

He hesitated, he felt an impulse to chuck everything and go wandering around with the them. They seemed very nice, but he had just met them. He thought the girls would always be there. Perhaps that itself had been a metaphor, he thought later. That is how you think when your whole life stretches ahead of you. He didn't come across them again. Life is full of roads not taken.

There was still a bed available in the dorm. There were two rows of beds, filled with young boys from the countryside visiting Warsaw. They were all around 12. It seemed like a school visit. He was the only foreigner. "Cuba" they said looking at him. Everybody relates to what they know. One boy started chucking *dropsy* at them, aiming accurately for each bed. "Czesek" they all shouted not wanting to be left out. Two youths entered and chorused "Czesek" just in time, as the shower of sweets was coming to an end. They belonged to the two beds that were taken but whose occupants had gone to reconnoitre. They were from Yverdon in Suisse. He wasn't the only *zagraniczne*. They obviously didn't feel they had to know these boys. They participated in the fun. Ashok didn't think it was appropriate to ask them, nor did he particularly want a sweet. But they were not going to leave him out. One landed on him.

The Swiss youths looked at him. They seemed friendly.

He wanted to ask them something else but what came out was "*De quelle couleur...?*"

The taller one said with a straight face, "I speak English, you speak French."

Ashok had just come. He didn't have to take decisions at

once. They stepped out into the town. He let himself drift with them. They hopped on to trams. They seemed to know where they were going, though they had just arrived in the city. More importantly, they seemed to thoroughly enjoy whatever was happening, even it an ordinary tram ride to nowhere. "I am ze King," periodically shouted one of them. Their high spirits were infectious.

It seemed more comfortable to go off with the Swiss. He followed their lead and wandered around with them. It was a carefree time and he saw Warsaw through different eyes.

A G.I. with a Sundance moustache positioned in Germany joined them from the second night. He was from Pasadena. He was travelling before he went back. Poland was just next door but he had ventured behind the Iron Curtain. It was another world but quite different from what he expected to find, as is almost inevitably the way with these things. He was good company. All of them exchanged addresses at Ashok's initiative - Yverdon, Pasadena, Delhi. His meanderings would take him to these places one day.

Ashok felt a sudden pang within. He was only 21. He smiled and flirted with women, he wasn't ready to settle down but Lauren was Lauren and he couldn't get her out of his head. But he couldn't just go back there casually - it had been too deep for that.

They were walking past the Warszawa Gdansk railway station. He checked about the next train to Wroclaw. It was leaving shortly. On an impulse he decided to catch it and told the Swiss youths he would see them later. He stood outside the cream-coloured building with its slanting red roof and typical old Polish architecture. He would surprise her. He rang the bell to her floor. There was no answer. He rang it again. He was aware of an unexpected anxiety. He would try again later, phone from a booth.

Not knowing what to do, he went to the town centre. There were a number of brightly lit restaurants, full of cheerful young people. Maybe she was in one of them. This was a Saturday night. He didn't see her. He walked inside, pressed his nose to the windows of a number of restaurants. He was absorbed in what he was doing so he was un-self conscious. Which one was she in? Would she see him? He tried looking at the sea of faces but they became a blur. He entered the restaurant in the middle. The tables were packed. He inched his way between them. There were three girls on a table for four. He asked if he could join them. "*Prosze*" they said. He felt like a *pierogi* or a *nalesniki* but settled on some borscht followed by a *sznycel*. He ordered some Hungarian wine. It was the best in the Eastern bloc. He sipped his wine silently for a while. The girls chatted animatedly amongst themselves. Some of it was obviously gossip and therefore so absorbing. He felt a little more at ease. Like this he would never find her.

His thoughts went back to Lauren. He should have dessert and coffee in one of the other restaurants in the centre. She could easily be in one of them.

Was he chasing a will o' the wisp? Should he just stay in the safety of this agreeable group?

In a restaurant two doors away he had his *torty* and coffee. This too was brightly lit and full of people talking animatedly. Where was she?

Her house was not far. Should he walk past it again? "On the street where you live," I'll be singing next, he thought wryly outside her house. He stood there uncertainly. It felt strange, unreal. He felt an emptiness come over him. Wasn't it about the pointlessness of things? He just wanted to go home.

There was a 10 p.m. train. He would just be in time for it.

One of the Swiss youths was shaking him. "Wake up, you were crying. What is the matter? Must have had a bad dream."

Ashok mumbled and looked at his watch. It was almost time for his alarm.

He would finish his Training at Express Dairy and go back to hearth and home. It would take a few months. Why had he really come for this technical training? He was the entrepreneur - he could hire the best technical knowledge; did he have to know it all himself? Of course it was always useful - part of entrepreneurship came from leadership in innovation and ideas.

33

Neeru stayed away exactly one night. That night there was a party that she had long been looking forward to. She went there, the party lasted all night with delightful music flowing and the sweet smell of marijuana interspersed with earnest talk about topics that occupied the mindspace of the thinking young. Neeru danced most of the night.

The Parents had been making desperate enquiries and eventually tracked her down to this friend's party. In the early morning the Parents' blue Ambassador turned up with the driver and silently took her home.

34

Ashok's Dairy Technology and Management training lasted four months. It was Swinging London. The Co. unions had opposed any kind of stipend. They were fiercely protective but he stayed with a friend and after a couple of weeks, maybe because they saw him around, one of their leaders relented. He had enough saved from Scandinavia and these were the unions of the late 60's the precursors to the coal miners' and other strikes. So this was no mean achievement.

The first assignments took him deep into the suburbs. He caught the Tube from his friend's flat at Ovington Sq. in Knightsbridge to almost the end of the line. The journey took him about an hour each way. If he was even a minute or two late, there was disapproval. He had half an hour appointments with different department and branch managers starting from 8 a.m.

It was such a relief to be conversing in English and to be able to read the papers and understand everything. Ashok noticed their foibles, their characteristics as only an outsider can at the beginning. They really minded their own business.

He slowly started making the most of the cultural life of London. He hung out at the Young Vic and the South Bank. He saw plays of different genres in the West End whenever he could get tickets at a reasonable price. Many of the musicals were famous, he couldn't believe he was witnessing them. '*The Age of Aquarius*' re-enforced his feeling of being special. He was born in early February. He witnessed a free Rolling Stones concert in Hyde Park. He kept walking till he was really close to the stage. Mick Jagger gyrated his lean body in a really sexy way as he sang. He went to a Joan Baez concert in North London. He browsed in book shops, had his pocket picked in Foyle's. He enjoyed the clearly articulated type of English accent.

The Express Dairy training was confined to London. Most of the time he went to the headquarters. He read voraciously. The long rides were particularly good for that. It was so easy to get English books. The public libraries were well stocked too. He read *Naked came I* on the tube, a thick dark blue book about Rodin. They stirred his imagination 'and kept his mind from wandering.' Like in the Beatles song.

The vast College and party network in Delhi had given him names of people who were already abroad to get into the social scene. One of them was Neena Advani. She ran a fancy boutique near Hyde Park and their family also gave well known scholarships to Indian students going abroad. He rang her up and she invited him to a party in her sprawling house near Hampstead Heath.

"How does it feel to be one of the Beautiful People." They were spread out all over the place and the sweet smell of marijuana was perceptible in certain rooms. Gossamer nights.

He wandered over to a dissolute looking group of people. One of them turned out to be the host - the main singer in a very well known group. For all his fame he conveyed ordinariness in the most positive sense. Ashok found it easy to talk to him. He was funny and unpredictable. Ashok soon found himself in splits. He hadn't laughed like this in a while.

Somebody jumped into the pool with her clothes on. At least she had taken off her shoes. She came up looking desirable with the clothes clinging to her.

He became a personal friend of the group. This was as good as it had been in College in Delhi. He was evolving again and things were happening. The soirees were star-lit and each day was special. Time flew again, in the same manner that it had in those days. Mind and body operated as one, like when he would hit perfect shots in tennis - smooth as butter - they would come off the middle of his racquet and whip across the court, effortlessly.

But a primal instinct continued to nag at his innards. All this was all very well, but his father was getting older and he badly needed him. What was he doing here, he thought. Duty called and he should be at his side. What about his own growth, his life. His warm, loving father came to mind and he felt like Atlas, the weight of the world on his shoulders.

Neeru continued to see Vikram and though Brij and Radhika no longer tried to stop her, this added to their worries. This uneasy truce could not be long lived.

The aroma, the feel of the late 60's was still in the air. Timothy Leary, Allen Ginsberg, Herbert Marcuse and his One Dimensional Man, Berkeley, student revolutions worldwide, Japan, France, Tariq Ali and British students - so much had been happening.

Ashok threw himself into London life with the same inexhaustible energy that he had in College.

There was a demonstration in London with banners like 'Black and White, Unite and Fight'. These were issues that mattered. This was a caring, loving world - that thought about things. The young girls in mini-skirts filled up his senses. The bell bottoms, the colour, the exploration, the vibrancy of the times made it seem like this time around the world would really change, that idealism was worth it, that there was love and people were Beautiful. "All you need is Love". The three eventful years in St. Stephens and Delhi University had given him enormous self confidence, augmented his suaveness. Add to that the self confidence of youth, a person who had developed faith in himself, who had not yet suffered life's major blows.

His genuine interest in people, his sophistication and warmth opened many doors for him and he found himself meeting people in London society, he had not dreamt of meeting.

He got invited to parties in celebrity homes, not far from London. There was a large swimming pool in one such, the weather was warm, the water was blue-green, inviting. There was pot once again - he thought of it as *charas*, there was lovely music, there was moonlight mixed with the smell of a possible, sudden English summer shower. Their bell bottoms, the Indian designs on silk, the long flowing kurtas and dresses that some adorned, the colours, patterns, psychedelic designs made one want to be with the guests. But above all the people were interesting as people - their thought lines, their behaviour, the things they thought and said..., Ashok felt very happy. This was it, this was the height of it, he had made it.

He got an insight into the creative process - how songs and music emerged from the heads and hearts of artists. It was fascinating, totally non-linear. Not like the Factory management he imbibed in the day.

This was the height of the 60's before it changed. At that time it felt like it would go on forever. London tried to catch up with San Francisco. He could hardly believe it. He was part of Love-ins and wild far out parties. He remembered shouting orgy in Stephania and feeling very dissolute. But now he was part of it. How did it feel for it to be actually happening. At one party he remembered being in a room where he was part of four couples. Uninhibited by each other's presence, two of them made out on the two beds and the other two on the thick carpet by the foot. Was this an orgy? A version of?

He lay on benches with birds as their tongues darted in and out with his. The summer wind rustled the leaves in the bushes and trees overhead.

Many of the girls he met he felt he could fall for. The Beatles sang - 'Would you believe in a Love at first sight? I'm certain that it happens all the time'.

He would come across some of them a number of times and it would feel like falling in love. But he was young, was he ready for commitment? If so, why not Lauren or one of the others in France, Finland and Poland that had tugged at his heart strings.

The Stones sang 'It's so hard just to have one girl When there's a million in the World.'

There was a Summer Ball one evening. The hostess was Gillian; she had studied at St. Hugh's, Oxford. She wanted to replicate the atmosphere of Summer Balls held in various colleges around June 23rd, the end of Trinity Term. And there could be no more spectacular a setting than one of the country estates in the Cotswolds. There were dinner jackets and ladies' gowns.

The hostess decided that it was better to warm everybody up for the dancing by starting off with slow stately waltzes. They would also be more skilful at it whilst they were still sober. Ashok loved to waltz. He held himself ramrod straight like an Army Officer as one of his girl friends in India would say or like a Surd as his Golf coach would say. It was impossible to dance with everyone, (which used to be one of the objectives at the college parties), but the girls he danced with felt secure in his arms and let themselves go. They leaned back creating a tension which held them together as a couple each time, as they whirled around.

The atmosphere grew less formal as the evening progressed. Somebody sang 'Everybody must get stoned.'

Ashok felt more and more at home in London. "It takes a while," he thought, "but then you make good friends."

Brij wrote Ashok a long letter. His letters were always full of news, descriptive, moving and in very good Hindi. Letters from a father to a son. Ashok felt blessed to have such a father. He wanted to preserve them. Mr Gupta, his father's secretary, was told to keep carbon copies from the typewriter. When Ashok asked Mr Gupta much later for them, he looked totally blank.

35

Should he settle down here Ashok wondered. He had grown up reading and knowing about British and American cultures, wholly immersed in them in innumerable ways, enjoying their movies, loving their music, identifying with the free spirited, avant-garde ethos they conveyed. There had been the strong Hindu spiritual side to his upbringing at home from infancy, but the American side had got added not substituted. He loved the clearly enunciated English accent (though some of the other English ones which he heard all too often, were not pleasing at all.) English had become like his mother tongue from early school days. He could buy an endless supply of interesting books with lovely bright covers, go to the theatre and revel in the wit and repartee, there were more and more international restaurants and the Indian food could be excellent. The tandoori chicken, the chicken tikka masala were the best he had tasted anywhere. Some of the people he came across were caricatures of P G Wodehouse characters. He was charmed and disbelieving. Maybe he hadn't lived in England long enough to mind its weather, the greyness and the constant pitter-patter. He liked the evergreen grass - it was there even in winter. After months and months of extreme cold, acres and acres of leafless trees in vast snow covered landscapes, this provided welcome relief. And England gave him a sense of déjà vu, as if he had been there before. But when? In some earlier life?

Everything was so expensive. The Pound was the equivalent of so much in other currencies - Dollar, Rupee, European currencies - yet it was spent like a quid. But if he earned here things would be easier.

He had gone to the Home Office a number of times and extended his stay. The last letter from a packaging machine manufacturer who was hoping to sell his father's company a machine stated that he was required to stay in the UK till the following December. It was only July now. The young girl at the window he went to seemed not only reasonable and pleasant but above all was not suspicious, which would have put Ashok's back up.

"So it'll take you till February," she said by way of confirmation, after reading the letter.

"Yes February."

He stood waiting at the window while she digested this.

It was a tall order in those days when permission to enter was for days. This was till next February. He would be 22.

There was no governmental reason to leave now. The more uncertain he felt, the more his external circumstances configured towards his staying on.

If he met a girl and fell in love, that would really anchor him. There were so many really nice girls - it wouldn't be difficult.

Over eight months passed in that fashion. Ashok's technical knowledge grew. But then something deeper than culture began to gnaw at his sense of well being. Were these existential doubts, metaphysical angst about the meaning of life, he thought to himself. Or deep desire for another human being which touches upon and mirrors the essential oneness of all and is thence so satisfying.

He loved being in the West in the late 60's and all that it implied - the change, the freedom, the counter culture that would even after its absorption, later have a profound and lasting impact.

The extraordinary and unique creativity that was pouring out at the time in folk and pop music, in plays, cinema, books, art, philosophy, values, a way of life. In his personal life it implied unimaginable freedom - the kind he needed back in Delhi. He enjoyed the classical music performances, the chance to visit the Opera or a ballet. The picturesque countryside, pastoral, set with tall trees on the avenues leading into the countryside. The girls didn't have hang-ups or airs. It was easier to '*lagao* scope' with them.

But he missed the special way Indian girls flirted, were mischievous, the way they readily understood certain references, contexts. There was no one like them - such delicate features, such thought lines, sophisticated, graceful, gentle, sensitive, sensuous lovers - their elegance, their saris and how they looked in them.

They sat around in circles, smoking pot, saying things, sometimes witty and clever, sometimes personal and provocative, always charming - their expressions, body language, the exposed line of stomach under the sari, the dance he did with one of them moving in a circle and bending up and down with Red Indian hoops. She had even found a feather from somewhere and stuck it in her hair.

Delhi had 14 discos at the time, it had his memories and the associations that go with certain sights, sounds, smells, at the monuments you could reach out and touch the atmosphere - the strong feeling of being in another Time and Place. The moonlit nights, the bright sunshine, the colourfulness, the deep, inherent spirituality that he always felt. His work was there. He couldn't abandon it. He was producing something. He was adding to the national product. There was much scope for creativity. His father had built it with tremendous imagination and financial genius. He badly needed help. He had been a caring and accepting father, the vast cultural hiatus notwithstanding. He couldn't let him down, be so irresponsible.

36

He had to go to a new place. He had to make a clean break of it. He wasn't ready to return home and yet felt uncomfortable about that. He now felt restless in England. He had been getting training in Britain but wasn't looking after the Dairy for which he was getting training.

Brij and Radhika phoned him. In London at least they could get through to him. Radhika chatted about the rest of the family, the religious festivals that had passed, the fasts she had kept.

His old class teacher had come over, along with his Advanced Maths teacher - both Irish priests who went for evening walks from the school and had come over like they used to when Ashok was around. Ashok had been fond of them and had even discussed his girl friend problems with his class teacher.

Soon after he got an aerogramme from his class teacher. He wrote that his mother hadn't been to Ashok's room even once since he had left.

Brij briefed him on the happenings in the factory. The problems that had come up, the opportunities that presented themselves. Ashok was transported back to the shop floor. He had the energy and the risk appetite of the young. He knew what to do to be of help to Brij.

Brij told him also of the political developments and changes in India in the meantime, always a factor in India integral to business, more so than elsewhere, given the level of interference, control, mistrust the government had of productive forces (an attitude shared by politicians and bureaucrats who otherwise looked upon their political masters with contempt). The State as external environment to business was huge.

But Ashok had his own life to live, his own dreams, his own heart to follow.

Poland was Lauren. There was no one like her. He had met no one who created the same feelings within him, gave rise to the same indefinable emotions. That's why he had stuck around so long in Poland without any other purpose. But their situation was impossible. Where was the solution there?

He had to do something new and different. He wasn't old enough to stop studying. He remembered a friend and classmate from St Stephens, Raj who had gone to Paris immediately after college. Through the Stephanian network he managed to find where he was staying. It was a student hostel. He sent him a telegram there. Raj replied warmly. There was a French Language and Civilisation course at the Sorbonne. Most universities only had courses beginning in October but the Sorbonne had a term starting in February as well for which he could get enrolled. There were some telegrams back and forth. Raj would help him get admission. There was no time to lose. This was a fresh beginning. Ashok packed bag and baggage and traversed the huge cultural difference between the UK and France. Term was starting February 17th. He would have to deal with practical aspects like accommodation after reaching. It would be nice to be a student in a classroom at a university again. Start over again.

To his pleasure, he found he had a gift for languages. The large Hindi alphabet and pronunciation made it easy for him to pronounce the softer sounds that Anglo-Americans often found so difficult. The method was intensive audio-visual with a certain number of hours in the Lab as well. The cultural activity was the most fun. There were optional weekend excursions to Versailles, Fontainebleau, the Loire Valley, wineyards, etc., and during the week visits to café theatres, cultural spectacles, museums. One of the teachers was also a painter. She invited them to her atelier near Denfert-Rochereau.

Finding a place to live was much more difficult. The student accommodation had all been taken from October. *Tant pis* for those who came in February. He couldn't afford anything else.

The Cite Universitaire in the 14th *arondissement* was the best bet. Each country or most had student houses there with the cost of construction having been shared by the host country and the country whose student house it was. Only 50 per cent of the students were from that country - the rest were international and French. There were even *Maisons* of countries that did not really exist at the time like *Maison d'Armenie*, no doubt funded by the local Armenian community.

He went from *Maison* to *Maison* - same story everywhere - it was the middle of the year, everything was taken. People applied a year in advance. Most rooms were individual. Somehow he managed to find a place in a shared room in the Maison du Viet Nam at the far end of the *Cite*. Maybe someone had unexpectedly left. His roommate was a shortish, bearded English chap, who soon told him as they lay chatting in the night that his father had told him to leave when he was 19 and he had never looked back, nor had any contact with them. He was 26 now. Ashok's English accent was perfect, he said, except that sometimes the 'v' was not frenetic enough and got mixed up with the 'w'. He told some of his friends that came to go out with him that Ashok was an Indian. He too seemed to find Ashok quite fair.

37

Paris and Parisian life grew on him again. It was an incredibly delightful city wherever one looked, wherever one walked - in the daytime with the monuments, buildings, sparkling in the sun, at night the streets lit up with warm bright lights. The Metro stops became familiar - Maison Blanche, Sebastopol, Denfert Rochereau. He had to walk through the Luxembourg Gardens to get to the Sorbonne from the *Cite*. He loved that morning walk when he was hurrying to be in time for class. He readily understood Maurice Chevalier singing 'I love Paris in the springtime, ...I love Paris in the Summer, When it sizzles, ...Every season of the year....'

Half the thing that mattered in French was how one spoke it. The audio-visual lab at the Sorbonne imparted a perfect accent. From being a hesitant visitor himself, he gradually grew confident enough to start helping out visiting Japanese and Americans in shops, public places. The French girls were not only feminine and *jolie* but also *coquette, charmante*. The realm of possibilities was endless. His true love could be among the many faces milling around the junction of the *5eme* and the *6eme*, at the meeting points of Saint Michel and Saint

Germain. The potential was most definitely there. He just had to look out of the window.

He sent a postcard to Martine at her parents. She wrote back after some time. She had moved to Amiens. She had a German boyfriend now who looked like Trotsky. She gave her new phone number. She was friendly but distant when he called her. She was very busy and did not know when she could come down to Paris but she would meet him for a cafe when she did. There had been a moment but the bird had flown.

He phoned Nicole at her parents. She had got a job in a new dairy being set up in a *Departement Outre-Mer*, in Guyane, at two and half times the salary. She had just moved. South America was so far. There was a time for everything. Nothing stayed the same. He got a very warm reply. She would be there for at least some years. He must keep in touch.

His visa was about to expire. He went for renewal to the Police Prefecture. He hoped they would not say something in French that he could not understand. But the Police asked him no questions. They gave him a *Carte de Sejour*. He was a Resident now. He could go on getting extensions when the time came. He could settle down here. This was the first place where inertia would make it possible, unless he did something to alter the course of things. This was getting very close to his settling down in Europe.

He made a friend in one of the many Cafes and student eating places in the *Cite*. He went to the *Maison des Arts et Metiers* across the bridge for a croissant and a coffee *petit dejeuner*. He was an electrical engineering student. They got to chatting. Ashok found the Sciences very interesting still, though he had been clear about his decision after school to leave Science and to go to Arts. But staying up late at night in the Engineering Lab was one thing and talking about it, reading up on it, was another. *Arts et Metiers* seemed like an afterthought. The bridge was across a very noisy highway, just next to but still in a sense outside the main *Cite* campus. When crossing the bridge one morning back to the *Cite* he found himself thinking of Lauren more than usual. Why did he think about her, miss her so much still? 'The very thought of you.' What was it about her? Bright, beautiful, charming, vivacious Lauren... impulsive, quick to see the funny side of things, always ready to dance. 'I cant stop loving you though I made up my mind.'

His stream of consciousness took him to a love scene, intimate and pleasing, from a few days ago in the Maison du Vietnam. There was nothing unique about it in a way. Yet there must have been something which made him think of it suddenly. There had been an endearing quality. Something memorable. It was already night. The stars were out. Must have been 8 p.m.

They were silhouetted against the window opposite in an adjoining maison across a pathway. He was undressing her. They were very close to each other. His movements were tender, gentle. Their contact was slow, sensuous. He touched her lovingly, caressed her. They kissed. The visuals of their loving floated across the pathway. Imagination and lived moments did the rest. Unmistakable, infectious. Ashok was the guy in the window and the girl was the one he was in love with - whoever that was now.

What was it about that love scene? It reminded Ashok a lot of his own love-making with Lauren. There was something very familiar about it.

The memory was very fresh. He could feel her presence and the way they had made love. The way they had become one. The way they had wanted to become one, the unbearable feeling of love, expressing itself in joining together. The way she moved her back and arched it, the quicker to come into contact with his gliding hands, the feel of her inner thighs against his ecstatic palms....

The term ended at the Sorbonne. He got himself admitted for the next term starting October. There was time in between to go home to Delhi. It had been a long time since he had seen his parents. He missed them. It would be nice to see them. The old anxiety and worry about them surfaced. He felt guilty too. What was he doing here?

He stayed another month. Did an intensive summer course. It had a different flavour. It wasn't half as good. Classes too were not held at the main Sorbonne but at one of the *Lycees* closed down for the summer. The teacher behaved like a school Ma'am.

Then it turned August. Paris was unrecognisable. It was quite hot. The streets were deserted. A paper flew across the street. All the Parisians had left for the vacations. Only the tourists were there.

He walked down along the green slopes inside the campus and amongst the thick clusters of trees planted closely together. It is futile to try and collect things, tangible or otherwise. This is not an easy realisation. You can't hold on to people or places. He thought deeply about it. He tried to weigh the pros and cons. But rational analysis doesn't suffice beyond a point. The vast unconscious gets tapped into, instinct, gut feel play a part. Its Logic plus. You want to stay where listening to the harp is more accessible, where you can drop in at the Louvre with straw coloured blondes or the Jeu de Paume whenever you want, walk around the boutiques of the Palais Royale on an impulse.

But also its emotion. It's what your instinct is telling you. Forget calculated choices. There are also the sights and sounds of home, the straws and leaves in the wind of where you grew up.

And there were the things he found odd. Attitudes were less tolerant of children in these countries - one hardly saw them at restaurants or elsewhere. Children were supposed to keep quiet, be out of sight.

In general everything was more formal, less relaxed, more on display - the automatic smile, pleasant but often insincere. Individualism was much touted and true in terms of every man for himself but also highly conformist culturally - there could be no individualism there. There was a certain standardisation of culture, a coming off a conveyor belt. The cultural boundaries were invisible but defined and one did not step out of line. In some ways they were so tight and so repressive that it could easily lead to more outlandish crazy behaviour or symptoms of mental illness in reaction and protest.

Vignettes of home came to him - its sights, sounds, smells, its myths, its magic, its colour, the sound of the young flute player far away in the moonlit field, beyond the eucalyptus tree, evocative of infinity.

The fragrant breeze filled evening and ideal day temperature of late February spring, the unbelievable light blue of the sky, the trees silhouetted against it, the sweet smell of grass, the strong winds in the day with leaves floating everywhere, the multi coloured flowers, a hundred different shades of orange, red, crimson, pink, yellow, violet, mauve, purple matching the shades of the sky at sunset.

He loved the intensity of the summer in Delhi, with its appealing, fragrant, moonlit nights and fresh dawns, the dramatically changing colours of the monsoon sky, the play of light and imagery, stories from Puranas in enchanted forests and the torrential cascades of rain. Summer in the mountains was a high point with the hills and valleys bewitching at night, bathed in moonlight, the bushes blue-green in the light, trees swaying in the breeze, the rustle of the wind in the leaves. In

Nainital, there were the handsome smart young men laughing and talking ready to sail their sailboats, the Boat House club with its pretty, sophisticated girls, live band and dances on the wooden floor and night life in all these hill stations till late, late into the night. At 1 a.m. people would still be out in the streets of Mussoorie, outside the skating rink, in the bazaars and the eating joints.

The monsoon in the mountains had to be seen to be believed. Rainbows after sudden torrential showers which drenched everything, the extraordinary play of light and shadow, with different kaleidoscopes on different rich green hillsides;

'Kahin dhoop kahin chhaya
Yahi hai bhagwan ki maya'.

There are shadows at some places in the mountains and sunshine at others, this is all part of God's Maya - God's play.

Very dark clouds purple, almost black, depending on the position of the sun, covering the sky, enveloped the mountain towns.

Winter in the mountains was cold, clear sparklingly beautiful. Sunny days, snow covered hillsides and tall trees rising from way below or towering way above, fleecy white clouds floating on a sky of unbelievably pale blue.

Sharad was just *Sharad*, not really autumn in terms of leaves falling and preparing everyone for a long snowy winter. This was Paradise descended on earth for a short while. The fragrant flowers, the brightly lit trees specked with gold, the dew drops late into the morning, the soft, gentle breeze caressing your hair and cheeks.

Where we choose to spend our precious time makes a major difference to the way we are, he remembered saying to Lauren.

38

Neeru's boyfriend Vikram got a temporary job as part of
the public face of Lufthansa in their Janpath office. He was
smooth, polished, charming and gave confidence to anyone
who encountered him. His English was very good and he
quickly picked up the ins and outs of the ticketing business.
His white shirt augmented his Kashmiri complexion. His tie
was held in place by an elegant tie pin.

Neeru eloped. She could not wait any longer. A
Kashmiri pandit performed their marriage ceremony at the
Shankaracharya temple on top of the mountain in Srinagar.
Vikram had managed to get a week off.

Ashok decided to return to India. It had been a defining
moment on that slope. And Neeru had run away.

The flights to Delhi were full up. Never mind, he would take
the one to Bombay. He landed very early morning on the 14th
of August. The crowds waving flags and full of nationalistic
fervour walked all along Marine Drive. It was infectious.
Ashok stood at the window and watched.

Ashok thought often about it, but didn't regret his decision
to return to Delhi in the final analysis. He had been born

here and had grown up here. He was a Delhi*walla.* Some of the things that he had increasingly disliked came up again. But earlier in his idealism it had made him want to flee - to the Other place. But now he had seen there was no perfect place. There were other problems elsewhere and plenty of them. Better to enjoy the good things. There and here. No point grumbling about Delhi's chaotic traffic, road rage and rude, pushy people. It just bred dissatisfaction. Take action to contribute to starting change where you can or where you care enough and accept the rest.

39

Lauren did manage to partly fill the void through skiing. She found herself getting into it more and more. She felt the snow flakes on her face. There was very good Skiing in Poland and she felt the elation of mind, body, spirit becoming one as she became more and more skilled and sped downwards, akin to the effortless performance one can experience in Sport, being in the zone. The only other place she had felt this, besides when entwined with Ashok, was in her music. She was at the height of her youth, the trajectory of her career was upwards. Life had to be lived, her days not lost in pining for something beautiful from the past.

When she was ready for it, she would need another relationship.

40

In the dense jungles where Gita's group was operating, there was a change of administration at the local police level and the new arrivals had a much more expensive life style with a corresponding need for money. They started sniffing around. One of them, an enterprising fellow in his own way, found out that Gita who was part of the gang had a family in Delhi which owned a Dairy factory. He reported this to the local Station House Officer.

A couple of days later an emissary turned up at the shifting and supposedly secret camp with a note that the SHO would like to see Gita along with the triumvirate that ran the camp.

The SHO came straight down to business. Pay up a certain amount in cash within 10 days or they would all be in jail for interrogation.

Gita discussed the situation back in the camp. She decided to appeal to the Administration at the District level. The leaders were against this - it would bring them more into the limelight. She went quietly the next evening. The local magistrate was an IAS officer not much older than her. He turned out to be the older brother of one of the girls who had been at College with her. She was hopeful. Here was someone educated, reasonable. There was no evidence against her.

"Let me dispose of these files, Gita", he said "and come home for a drink. We'll see what we can do." It was the classic district government office complete with neon lights. The insect sounds outside the window were already getting louder. Gita watched as he went through them rapidly, chucking on the floor each file he had written something on.

"What will you have? Gin and tonic to keep away the mosquitoes. Good invention of the British."

The liveried bearer brought everything neatly on a tray and Arvind poured the drink skilfully on to the sparkling ice.

The conversation went from topic to topic but Arvind did not seem interested in her situation. He waved it aside with a "don't worry", every time she tried to bring it up, without specifying how he would help.

"You can't leave this evening Gita - where will you stay? Shall I tell them at the Circuit House?"

She saw that he had power. If he told the SHO to back off, he would.

Would he be helpful? He was from the same background.

Arvind showed off his all round knowledge. He expressed his contempt for the crude politicians, under whom they all worked.

But they had their ways and means to cleverly thwart these guys and let things come to naught.

"One of my hobbies is Photography. I have just got this new Minolta SRT 101. I almost bought an Asahi Pentax - very good, but finally chose this."

"Here let me show you some of the ones I took recently."

Arvind put on an LP titled Easy Listening.

"Relax Gita."

Gita smiled politely.

He complimented her on how she had blossomed.

He went to a shelf and came back with some shiny black albums.

He sat down next to her and began giving the background as she turned the pages

"This was when we had gone on a climb to Annapurna. The College Soc in Kirori Mal had organised it. "

41

From the early 70's India moved steadfastly towards State capitalism. Private enterprise particularly in Delhi was snuffed out. Businesses that did well were not those that were the most efficiently managed but those that managed and manipulated the external environment well. They contributed generously to the Ruling Elite and in turn enjoyed monopolies, special privileges created for them, that made it easy for them to rake in many multiples of what they had contributed even with rank bad management. Part of the mantra was to keep out foreigners. Given the history of the East India Company and how they came in as traders to the Rich East of Shakespeare, that wasn't difficult.

No new dairies were given licences. Only the government was allowed to run a factory, which it did with poor quality and hygiene, overstaffing and losses. Ashok's father's factory was slowly strangled. It was the first dairy factory set up in New Delhi, in the early 1920s and had been recognised for its pioneering role by the Indian Dairy Research Institute in Karnal. The Lt Governor of Delhi had declared it a public utility undertaking before the shift. Arbitrary and impossible restrictions were put on non-government dairies in the organised sector. The unorganised sector got by on different rules and economics. Citing a shortage of cream in the summer months, cream separation was banned for all but the government dairy. Cream separation is at the heart of dairy products production.

During the months of May, June, July, and August, every year the government started imposing the dreaded ban with a specific exemption for the government dairy. Ashok's father sought to challenge this in Court but the government was succeeding in its attempt to have a 'judiciary made to measure' in the words of eminent Jurist N A Palkhivala. At least Ashok was by his side, Brij heaved a sigh of relief.

"Brij, thank Goodness our Ashok is back. Neither of us could say how long he would stay away and who he would get involved with."

"Or what he might get up to. It seemed indefinite at one point of time, Radhika."

"It could have been. I doubt if he knew himself."

As economies of scale continued to increase, M/s Maclean's Ltd., named after the Scot who first started the dairy, were not given licences to increase production capacity. Attempts at demonstrating with facts and figures, sound logic, the justification for allowing an increase were irrelevant, as the bureaucracy did not go into the merit. Even the much lower price that would result for the customer became a non sequitur. Maclean's fell below the break even point in condensed milk being supplied to the armed forces in Assam, as in the production of spray-dried milk powder and several other products like Industrial Casein.

The Land and Development Office who were nominally the Lessors of the land given on a lease in perpetuity, started objecting even to buildings that had long been there and housed some of the major plants as "unauthorized".

Ashok's multi-coloured visions about research and development in micro-bacteriology, the techni-colours of the frontiers of science began to evaporate, like those of an eminent academic or doctor who upon becoming head finds that most of his time is taken up in administrative problem solving, instead of utilizing his knowledge. And here the problems were overwhelming. What was required was the craft of wheeling and dealing, dealing with the avarice, blatant misuse of power, a lack of concern for principles, of three disparate and culturally distinct elements of the government - the politicians, the bureaucrats and the babus - the clerks. No management principles, no dairy technology equipped anyone for handling such things, leave alone the young and idealistic Ashok.

Ashok was in a meeting with a very red-complexioned, big, square faced Mr Ashok Chatterjee, the Plant Engineer who must have been in his forties but seemed old to Ashok. A lanky milk-deliveryman burst into the room and interrupted the meeting with a couple of unreasonable demands and insisted on immediate gratification. Whatever logical answer occurred to Ashok, was stonewalled. Being difficult seemed to be the delivery man's only objective. Mr Chatterjee witnessed his young boss being cornered. Suddenly, he turned around towards the deliveryman standing behind him and told him that this was enough, he should go, Mr Chatterjee had to have his 'khana-wana'. Ashok left the room and in the verandah of the white colonial building felt his face crumpling into tears as he tried to say something again to the deliveryman, still standing outside and looking at him with a mocking smile.

On the broad roads of New Delhi he felt some sense of power returning as he sped down the wide, empty street.

Brij had faced many such situations - had had to face off with whole unions which had been aggressive and not in a mood to reason. He talked to his son at length about handling such situations. Brij had a large heart and tremendous empathy for the workers. But even he had found some situations intractable and the attitude of the leaders just plain obstructionist. He gave Ashok invaluable real life training about how to create a win-win in the end.

He also put things in perspective.

These workers were not poor. Though barely literate they had become middle class, through repeated minimum wage regulations bought in by the government for the Industry, irrespective of considerations of long term viability and competitiveness, it was something easy to do to garner votes. It didn't come out of their own pockets. One of the perils of democracy, thought Ashok.

There were people far poorer - the real poor, the actual lower class below middle class but for them the government would have to pay out of their own pocket and then how would they spend it on themselves.

42

A few days later he was in the steel vaulted butter cold storage, beyond the shining Silkeborg butter churners. From time immemorial when slender women in graceful saris pulled handis from both sides in turn and thereby churned butter, the process was the same. One was hand crafted, the other industrial. Either way the end result was delicious. He picked it up directly from the churn and let it melt in his mouth. Well meaning relatives told him how thin he was. This was one way of *banaoing sehat* – becoming healthy, which equalled being well fed in the eyes of many Indians. It was divine. Ashok stopped to put another scoop in his mouth and then another. Butter had to be stored at 4°C, not a decimal higher. The vault door was shut firmly before the cold air escaped. Ashok thought of the micro-bacteriological processes going on inside the butter, visible in the bright colours in the test tubes in the Lab.

The Plant Chief Chemist Mr Choudhury, and his deputy Mr Banerjee, mentioned the latest findings reported in a dairy scientific journal. Silkeborg in Denmark were trying to incorporate small changes in engineering design, which would enable these discoveries to be utilised. It was exciting. Mr Banerjee shivered. They had been in there 15 minutes and were not dressed for it. They decided to move to the Engineer's cabin. The handle of the vault door turned fruitlessly. The door had jammed or been locked.

No one could hear them outside. It was a solid thick steel door. The noise of the machinery made it virtually sound proof. There was an inter-com outside but none had been considered necessary inside the freezing storage. No one stayed there long enough.

It had never jammed before. Someone must have locked it. But who?

Union trouble? The butter section workers were not trouble makers. It couldn't be the deliverymen? It was so far from their beat. There was muffled shouting at the other end. The *goonda* hooligan element among the deliverymen had created trouble before. They were the most troublesome lot as it is, in the whole company. They were part of the union but had nothing to do with manufacture.

Intimidation rather than negotiation under duress seemed to be the intention. Without channels of communication there couldn't be any. Ashok was aware that in all the factories where he had got training, highly organized though the Unions were, such a thing could have been open to criminal action. Theoretically that was the case in Delhi also but it didn't work like that.

Delhi being a Union Territory had even less powers than a State in India. Even between the States and the Centre the balance of power is strongly tilted towards the Centre. The Constitution makers wanted to preempt fissiparous tendencies. The elected Delhi Assembly could not deal with real issues, specialized in dealing with non-issues. Members of the legislative assembly - MLAs often saw their election as a means of earning a livelihood, instead of representing the people and dealing with issues of concern to them. When they thought about the people it was in the context of doing things that earned them popularity. Their areas were small and their vision less than local.

The trade union of the factory, which was elected from amongst the workers, had only been interested in the workers' interests and up till now been independent, not affiliated with any political party.

Thus far the supervisors too had done a fairly good job of being intermediaries, effective channels of communication between the Management, the objectives of the factory and the workers. The workers were motivated and had graduated into the lower middle class by virtue of their skills rather than their education.

There was now however disguised unemployment amongst the deliverymen. They had become too many for the capacity, but they could not be relieved.

Arjan Singh, a car mechanic and a local tough character who specialized in extortion, was closely linked to a powerful politician on the national scene. He used every trick of the trade to get elected to the Delhi assembly.

Political parties had started aligning all unions to themselves, thus serving the vested interests of the parties, rather than those of the workers they claimed to represent. One of his sidekicks brought to Arjan's attention that the Dairy fell within his constituency and its Union was aligned with the other Party. That was an intolerable state of affairs.

He ran into a few of the most pernicious deliverymen, made friends with them and started taking more and more interest in the affairs of the factory.

Another thirty minutes passed. Ashok and the technologists were no longer near the door. Suddenly, it was opened and they staggered out ashen faced. For torture or threat to be most effective, the torturer has to talk to the tortured.

In the outside room there was a gang of mocking deliverymen. They were surrounded. It was clear there were to be negotiations and negotiations now. Somebody suggested that Arjan Singh should be called. The MLA turned up, eager to be insulting, flaunt his new found power. He had nothing to lose. He didn't work at the factory. He could not be fired. The more offensive he was, the more he demonstrated how unafraid he was.

The factory workers were side-lined and no help would be available from the Police. They dare not oppose him.

Arjan, unlike his namesake in the Gita, always went for the jugular. A rough gravelly voice spoke to Ashok. It could have been out of a Harold Robbins novel. No point bothering with the General Manger. Arjan told the young and still inexperienced Ashok that if he wanted things to continue to run smoothly, he should ask the elected union representatives to align themselves to the ruling party. Ashok said it was up to them surely. Arjan looked at him as a hired killer in a Bar in the Wild West would look at a greenhorn from the East who had just walked in and asked for a glass of lemonade.

Arjan didn't mince words. "Either you do it or we will." They stared at each other, "Or we will set up new leaders."

"But these are elected. And the next election isn't due until next year."

"Those will be too. And they'll be far more difficult to handle." Arjan didn't bother to reply about the timing of the election of union office bearers.

Ashok knew the sort - they just said 'no' to everything and bulldozed or misled the workers. There could not be any peace or smooth working, until they got what they wanted.

Ashok still had his youth and idealism. Our workers are not

like that, he thought. They are good chaps. He got up to leave. He could be blunt too. "No."

Arjan looked at him with contempt.

"Oh and one more thing, the deliverymen are really overworked. Things can't carry on like this. Their strength needs to be increased by 10. I already have trained people, you don't need to advertise."

The very next day there was a strike. Those who tried to enter were manhandled. The elected union leaders were nowhere to be seen. Some outsiders said they were the President, the Secretary and the Vice President. There was a red flag outside the main gate.

There was a time limit for the orders, especially the bulk order of condensed milk for the Army in Assam. Food in process would certainly get spoilt.

The Labour Department of the Delhi Administration too stepped in. He was served with several notices to appear before them at the Secretariat in Old Delhi.

He went to meetings in dingy detestable offices where he had to wait around for hours and then the summoning officer would have to go away in his white Ambassador - a symbol of power - for a meeting, asking him to come another day.

When he did get a hearing, Ashok who was convinced of his reason and logic found that no one was interested in listening. He started sending his lawyers who being more jaded were more phlegmatic about it all, except in their invoices.

Gita made it back to the Camp the next evening. She walked despondently towards the tent of one of the leaders. Arvind's attempt at seduction the previous evening had not succeeded. Gita had tried her best to handle it as nicely as possible without hurting his ego. Men and their fragile egos, she thought to herself. But Arvind was clearly upset. She could expect no help from him.

The leaders would also disapprove. She had not taken their clearance. Any such move was a security risk for all of them.

They were talking in low voices. She stopped.

"We need bread, man and how", said the one code named M. No one knew her real name.

"So what are we going to do about it?" said PQ.

"We've thought of everything but the need is desperate. We need immediate cash for everything - from food supplies to ammunition", said R.

"Gita has to get us money from her father's factory. We have respected her dedication and that she has gone against her family for the cause but though we have held off even thinking of tapping this source, the time has come now. "

"But how?"

"Gita will have to cooperate. She will have to demand substantial money from her father."

"But they will refuse, they are estranged."

"She will have to demand her share."

"She is not entitled to anything. It's all created by her father. She can't demand anything as a right."

"And it'll be highly embarrassing for her - it'll be a come down after she went off high-mindedly in pursuit of her own convictions."

"That's all very well but I can't think of anything else for immediate requirements."

"I don't see her cooperating in this and she has been one of our best workers. Loyal, hardworking. We might lose her."

"It might be better to kidnap her and send a ransom note. Then she is not compromised personally and we don't need her cooperation."

"We will still need her cooperation. Or were you thinking of an actual kidnapping?"

Gita waited to hear no more. She quietly went to her tent and slipped away early morning, back to Delhi.

44

It took six months for Ashok and Brij to sort out the aftermath of the strike engineered by the deliverymen in which the manufacturing workers and others found themselves unwitting participants by virtue of being part of the new Union. The Company lost some of its regular market and some of its money got stuck with distributors. It could not honour some of its supply contracts to the Army nor pay some of its creditors. Some of the best staff reluctantly found other jobs as they had to keep their households running. Ashok was left disillusioned.

At the emotional level too, things were not the same. Delhi was his city. Where he had grown up. It was easy to meet new women, every day, when he was in College. Calling them 'Women' had made them feel sophisticated and grown up. But now that he was working in his own company, social life was no longer automatic. Could not be taken for granted. Maybe if he had been working in a big foreign company where there would be others like him, colleagues. The people he knew in College, he did not see as often. It was hard to keep track of many of them. Many had left for foreign shores, lands far and wide. There was hardly anyone here, except those still in

College. He was way above them, College had been a place very conscious of seniority. Had everybody left?

He thought of the Simon and Garfunkel song, or had it been the Lovin' Spoonful - 'I'm 22 now but won't be for long.... A quarter of my life is almost past, I think I've come to see myself at last'. He knew he still wanted to go out every evening. He was not ready yet to give up that life. Was it adolescent? He didn't think it was confined to that. He wanted the thrill of meeting someone interesting. Someone new and yet not really different or distinct from us, in our inter-connected universe where we are part of the one. It had been like that in the Delhi University parties. There were new faces and the excitement of meeting that. There was a certain comfort about them. And yet many of these evenings were enchanted. Every evening held that possibility of meeting someone enthralling.

But he was no longer in College. And the parties were not so frequent anymore. Or if they were he didn't know about them. And they would be full of "kids" anyway. People who had looked up to him. He couldn't just hob-nob with them, chat with them as equals, betray an interest in them.

Evening came. The air was fresh. The evening had a deep blue to it. The blue of shadows and depth. All dressed up and nowhere to go. A whole bunch of friends had not automatically turned up for tennis and table tennis. No after sports showering with the Stones asking 'Have you seen your mother, baby, Standing in the shadows' or 'Hey Mister Tambourine Man' playing loudly.

No shaving for the party and looking at himself in the bathroom mirror under the bright lights and secretly smiling at and feeling happy about the image that looked back at him. He, Ashok Solanki had been sought after. How come no one even knew he was back?

Should he just enjoy the ever darkening evening, put on some music that he loved, float with it heavenwards? Read a book, get absorbed in it? It was no longer afternoon - otherwise he could sit in the car parked near the portico, be transported to far away situations, with the golden winter sunshine cocooning him in the car seat with its smell of fresh leather. But he felt restless. There would be plenty of time to read in his life. Shouldn't he be doing something more active, adventurous, exciting, maybe new, he wondered. He was just in his 20s. Could he just spend an evening like that curled up on a couch?

He flipped through the phone directory. Maybe the names of some old friends would pop up. Whatever happened to that very fair guy who lived near Defence Colony, who used to give lots of parties? What was his name? Tahiliani? Deepak Aga? He tried a couple of numbers. They would be in his father's name.

This wasn't it.

45

Ashok felt the urge to talk to Lauren again coming up. He suppressed it. Then one day a Chopin nocturne and the bitter sweet association it evoked had him pick up the phone and place a trunk call to Poland. But it was not like calling from Finland. A heavily Punjabi accented female voice answered the trunk booking number. He booked a call for Poland. What would he say? After three minutes the operator would interrupt the conversation to announce that his three minutes were up and disconnect the call unless she was asked to "continue". Would he even be connected? The government operators were accountable to no one. They would call back Ashok's number whenever to try the call. If he wasn't there, they would enter their attempt in the log book. After that they felt absolved of all responsibility to try it again. If asked for an indication of when they would attempt to put the call through, they would say 1 or 2 hours. But they could call, any time, in fact.

The calls to other European countries were an extraordinary example of neo-colonialism. The Punjabi operator would punctuate her conversation with the English operator with many "dear"s, in an unconscious imitation of plebeianism. The

English operator would then dial the Polish number and when she got the called person, whom only she could hear, she would ask Ashok to speak up, to literally build the conversation. In these trying circumstances, with two operators helpfully listening in, at will, what would he shout and say to Lauren, if he did ever manage to talk to her.

A letter would be much easier or a telegram. Perhaps a reply paid one. But he had this urge to talk to her. He did not try more than a couple of times. It was too frustrating.

Ashok was extremely individualistic. 'Go where you wanna go, Do what you wanna do....' as in the Mamas and Papas song. He had to live his life but not let them down. He had been showered with love. How could he think of deserting his ancestral home. He had been born in this house, had grown up in it, with its myriad memories. Its long dark corridors and high ceilings, its pillared verandas, and large drawing and dining rooms. He had grown up hearing about the family business. Its problems, its achievements. It had always been there. He started attending all meetings with Brij, both in the factory and to do with the outside world. Ashok couldn't help noticing that his father was getting older. Brij started leaving more and more to him.

He would wait for Ashok to come up with the best solution when a problem was discussed in a shop floor or Marketing meeting. It was part of his training. Some meetings on important issues he just wouldn't show up. Everyone else was there. Ashok would have to handle it and handle it well.

He was finally rid of guilt. He couldn't leave them again.

Moreover, he loved manufacture, loved working in factories round the clock - where 3 o'clock in the morning would not be too late. Loved adding to production and the excitement of the whirr and buzz of machinery in operation, with each worker doing his thing.

Marketing, strategizing, advertising, retailing, merchandising, packaging, best protection, best appearance, cost effective, selecting new distributors, going to new towns, locating old ones; Engineering, Preventive maintenance, Quality control, the lab, research, development of new products; Inventory Control, Materials Management, (FIFO-first in first out, LIFO-last in first out, JIT-just in time inventory, Re-order level, Economic order Quantity), each aspect, each facet of Business.

He could manufacture in Europe but that would still not solve his family situation, though it would give him money, if he ran it properly. Lauren had said she would help him with it, especially in dealing with recalcitrant, difficult European labour. Italians, he thought and shuddered. He and Lauren had explored the possibility when they were trying to find ways and means to stay together in Western Europe.

What would the selection of advertising agents be like in Europe? He had found the process interesting in Delhi. ASP, Hindustan Thompson, MCM, Interads, Ad Infinitum. They put forward interesting ideas, came up with creative suggestions, played around with words, both English and Hindi, proposed Mediums (at a time of Marshall McLuhan's The Medium is the Massage), showed short films which stimulated his own imagination. Would he be able to make the best use of relevant Technology? The Point of Purchase (POP) materials would be different. The outlets themselves were changing in Europe. The smaller stores were giving way. He would have faith in his ability to adapt and handle it but would he find it as enjoyable.

Smoke rising from chimneys, a cock crowing in the grey early morning - hill towns in Himachal and UP! Their products were extremely popular in the hills. These were places that worshipped *Shakti*, the Feminine Energy, were neither

Shaivites nor Vaishnavites. Their packets would have a small seal of Amba at the end. They added it to the back flaps of envelopes in correspondence. The hill folk loved it. He would meet the distributors of the Competition, meet his own, match their performance, potential. He loved the feel of a new town - retailing in it, finding out the opportunities, the threats to sales, the problems that arose vis a vis quality, shelf life. Many places they had no representation. New people would have to be found. Traders that were financially sound, understood modern marketing, at least sales. At other places it turned out to be a tiny corner store, more of a name than a presence. A replacement would have to be found. And the evenings with the smell of birch, beech, *deodar* and *cheel*, the bazaars with the sound of temple bells and the Sun setting in a myriad shades of auburn behind the hills. What would this process be like in Europe?

To have dreams and not have them destroyed.

46

Ashok had loved London the continual pitter-patter, so different from the monsoons, notwithstanding. Afternoon teas in London with a charming lady playing the Harp in the Tea Lounge. He had chosen to live in Delhi. He could still visit those places. It wasn't just a dream.

And always the unexpected, like standing at a bus stop in Warsaw on a very cold and windy night and suddenly there would be an extremely pretty girl, smiling brightly from a departing bus window. There was nothing he could do about it but the smile would remain with him.

The Romance of Europe. Erich Maria Remarque's *A Night in Lisbon* and *Heaven has no Favourites* and the impressions, images that were created. Would he too meet someone like that - be standing on a Quai or a Pont in the fog and she would be drifting past, ephemeral, waif-like? He would reach out and stop her, ask her where she was going. She would allow herself to be taken charge of by him. Would not protest.

There were times in Amsterdam when such a thing could have taken place. Girls in The Netherlands were often superb looking. He was lucky his first impressions were those of Amsterdam.

And he had taken a train and visited a friend in Bologna one December. There was a very thick fog. But there were many people about. Students mostly, as this was an ancient university town. He walked from his friend's house between six storied houses in narrow lanes and emerged onto much broader central streets and avenues past some impressive looking monuments, which suddenly appeared in the fog. There seemed to be more girls than boys, many of them rather attractive, with distinctive, typically Italian noses, noticed Ashok. In the fog, they appeared without warning and walked past him, almost touching him.

Then there was Milan and the Duomo. Ashok stayed just next to it and was amazed at the gallerias, full of life and upstairs restaurants and coffee houses up marble staircases, with tables full and a vast theatre of people talking animatedly. The tinkling laughter of a girl would punctuate this sound of people talking. But it was 1 a.m., 2 a.m., in the morning.

And more than places wasn't it Lauren he missed? Her presence, her sense of humour, her contagious laugh, her eyes, her *joie de vivre*.

An attractive girl like Lauren must have a boyfriend by now or must be going out with different boys. He had been gone a long time and there had been no commitment, no promise. He couldn't expect otherwise.

As if someone somewhere had read his thoughts, he got a letter from Zbiegniew. Ashok had introduced him to Lauren.

He had met Zbiegniew Korulski one cold and snowy December night in Wroclaw train station, as he emerged from the platform exit after a brief visit to Warsaw, in connection with registration formalities that foreigners had to do. A tall young man with a University student's peaked cap and a student's scarf looked at him. "Where are you from?", he asked in Polish. This directness didn't surprise Ashok at all, in Poland. The first month he had been there no one had looked at him and he had felt at home and unselfconscious. Then he began noticing people staring at him in restaurants, theatres but most of all in the trams and buses. The vacant stare would continue even after he looked back at them. He didn't feel inclined to get into staring matches with so many strangers. But it made him feel uncomfortable.

Even Nationalism could be narrow, if it took away individuality. Not wanting to identify with anything narrow and true to his *"Vasudhaiv Kutumbakam"* upbringing - Sanskrit for the World is your Family - he answered laconically in Polish *"Swieczie"* - belonging to the World. He thought that would be the end of that but the student had become fascinated with him and a friendship had developed.

Lauren had not gone out with anyone for a long time after Ashok left, had now become a popular and sought after girl amongst the University students and arty arty circles, was Zbiegniew's news.

Ashok had not been a good correspondent, but even the occasional letters and postcards may not have reached Lauren.

Ashok was aware of a lack, of something missing, deep inside. The life he might have had in Europe? For life passing him by? But if he had been on the other side, he might have felt the same. Or died of guilt. And there was the need for an all consuming relationship. Wouldn't it be found in time or were these feelings part of the human condition. Irrespective of the loved one.

Was this feeling a general one? Or was it for someone specific, for Lauren? The others had affected him too. That's why there had been relationships with them. He wasn't ready to settle down. And yet he thought of some of these girls he had had relationships with during his training in Europe with a twinge. Should he go back to them after some time? Explore the possibility of a long term relationship. Was he ready for that? And until then?

47

Months flew by. Lauren thought of phoning Ashok, their lives had been so intertwined, but it was very difficult to get through. She would have to hang around the phone the whole day with the probability of talking to him uncertain. Also it was 164 zlotys a minute and she could hardly afford to spend money like that.

It was compulsory for everyone up to a certain age in the University and the Arts to do a four-week stint at a factory, on the processing line. Had there been many collective farms, like in neighbouring Soviet Union, working as a peasant might have been necessary too. Lauren's turn came. She was called up to work at a fruit processing factory down south. They made squashes, jams, compote. She came across some of her old classmates. But no one had time for anybody else, other than to know that they too were there.

In the beginning she was very quality conscious. She wouldn't do anything which compromised the least bit on hygiene. Then exhaustion took over. She had to work really fast on the production line, otherwise there would be a pile-up. She was no longer in a position to care about anything.

She also saw what the others did. By the end Lauren was squeezing the fruit into jam, whatever its state and throwing it into the jar. She just wanted to be finished - the shift, the day, the yelling and meanness of some of the supervisors, the attempts to belittle in front of others.

Lauren began to feel incompetent, insignificant. A letter from Ashok came just then, redirected automatically to the factory by the post office during this period of training. She felt really grateful. It was only her. Yet he had written to her.

The weeks seemed interminable but finally the factory detail ended. She came back a different person. Ashok had always said that coming to India would change her forever. If just this had changed her perspective so much, what would that be like?

48

"*Czteri mieszance leczi*", his Polish landlady had assured him, in a context once of waiting for four months. They will fly. The days now just flew by as days have a way of doing. His work, the fine inter-woven mesh of managing and running a factory, the decisions that had to be analysed and taken, made sure of that. The things that were so important to him, that loomed so large in his life, there seemed to be no time for. The late 60's and the years that succeeded - the richness of the fabric - were an integral part of him. Those had been his formative years, in College, in Delhi University. He would go to the toilet to pee at night and a scene from Milos Forman or Ivan Passer would go through his head. He would go for a business meeting and his head would be full of Jean Anouilh or Ionescco. "Six characters in search of an author" he said under his breath. "Huh?" said the Senior Executive from a large company, trying to sell him the latest range of aluminium foil packaging. This was what he had to deal with and he found he was good at it. But the real world was where he thought about Pirandello or Camus.

This world he felt was not central to his life, to the core of who he was and it was therefore bestowed with a strange sense of unreality. 'Would you believe in a Love at first sight,

Yes, I'm certain that it happens all the time...'

There was a new system of Series amplifier and speakers, newly developed by some ex-IIT boys which was reputed to be very good, available in the Green Park market. Taking an hour off one afternoon from his Delhi office he roared off on New Delhi's wide and empty avenues, in a small Fiat 1100 which had a marvellous pick up and sounded and drove like a Grand Prix car. The sun was mellow and golden as it streamed in through the windscreen. Ashok had with him three other advisers, knowledgeable in such matters. On the side of the road walking against the direction of the car Ashok suddenly and unexpectedly espied an extremely pretty foreign girl. He was always prepared to find someone remarkable at parties or cultural events. He had just extracted himself from a discussion about Cost Accounting involving a new weight in a product. Now he was thinking about sound systems. The sight of her took his breath away. It's not just the beauty of certain people. Or their attractiveness, charm - which in any case takes a little longer to find out about. There was a great softness to her face. Her expression made him want to know her. It was indefinable. She saw him looking at her. It took just a few seconds to cross her. Their eyes met. She smiled as if in part recognition, understanding of the effect she had just had on him. The registration of whatever was happening, preceded by a certain puzzlement traversed her face in quick succession.

There were monuments littered, strewn all over the Hauz Khas, Mehrauli areas, waiting to be discovered, many of them neglected, not enumerated or protected by any government agency. The visitor had only to go a few hundred yards to stumble upon something. They immediately evoked memories of long ago, of times gone by, a different era, a different age.

Their unkemptness, their survival at random, their organic inter-relationship gave them a Jhabvalian effect, an unparalleled romance.

The chatter of his three unmindful companions continued in the car, of woofers and tweeters, watts and things that suddenly seemed far away, if not irrelevant. Carole King continued to sing 'Gotta get thru, Gotta get thru another day....' The moment had passed. He hadn't stopped the car.

The momentum of the journey propelled it. He was too busy right now anyway. He would come back and make enquiries. She must be living in the locality. Must have taken a house here.

What had that girl made him feel? A sense of something essential missing? He had to find out about her. But he also had this sense of eternity stretching before him. He was in his early 20s. He would get to know her. Her parents must be posted here. Diplomats or working for an international agency. They would be here for three years. Something to look forward to.

A month had flown by. A marketing outlet of his technical friends was in the area. They asked other merchants in the local market. No one came up with anything significant. It couldn't be. Perhaps she had just been a tourist visiting for a few days. For the day. She had seemed so at home. Poised. Settled.

He thought of her, her look, her expression. He had no clue as to where she had come from, he didn't know her name. Ashok tried again. Asked whoever he knew with links to that area of Delhi. He could not find her again.

He should not lose touch with others who had touched his life. It was the most precious thing - human relationships - self evident yet so little pursued. One reason we needed others, he pondered, was that we were all manifestations of the same

Universal Consciousness, inter-connected, different facets of the same thing. It wasn't necessary to know this. Just to give due importance to the desire for various forms of human contact, that is so strong, reaching its zenith with being madly in love where one loses all track of Time and its dimensions of *le Passe* and *l'Avenir*.

External circumstances may overwhelm all this. That remains an integral part of the equation.

Ashok could manage more and more aspects at work skilfully and creatively. His father could at long last not feel so alone. His father had been exhorting him from the days he had been lost as a teenager in College, in Vivaldi and Verdi, in Thomas Mann and Herman Hesse, to jump into battle like *Abhimanyu*, in aid of Arjun in the Mahabharat.

Surely, he could settle down to life and work, find his true love here, to meet him at 5 a.m. in Humayun's Tomb with its arches and monuments to the side of the main one, with its atmosphere - unmistakable, unique, its quads and geometry, and its romance, on a summer morning, to watch the leaves drift down in March - the season that was *patjhar*, to walk through the Delhi fog in December-January at 3 a.m. in Nizamuddin, after cold coffee in the 24 hour coffee shop at Oberoi.

The 24 hour coffee shop has to be a particular Indian innovation, mused Ashok. Where else in the world can you get things to eat and drink at 3 a.m.? A wide variety of things, tasty, freshly prepared - a chilled gazpacho, a piping hot Chicken a la Kiev. Oberoi must have been the first five star hotel in Delhi to think of this. Young ones started turning up there after parties late at night or early towards the morning. Airlines landed at Delhi at the weirdest hours of the night. It was a haven for airline crews and pilots. The foreigners living in Delhi loved it. It had charm, it had atmosphere.

Other hotels in Delhi followed suit. Delhi acquired many 24 hour coffee shops. It started becoming the norm all over the country.

So who did he feel this way about? Was it someone he had met or was it someone he was yet to meet? Would one of the girls there had been something with in Europe, be prepared to live in India? They would love it he was sure, if they visited it but would they be willing to spend their lives here? And if not could he desert his parents? Start life afresh in the West?

The economies of scale in the Dairy Industry were rapidly moving northwards. The technology in all products was becoming more efficient at much higher volumes, the machines were getting bigger and larger sales had to be generated to break-even. But there was no space in the existing buildings to expand operations. Ashok tried to get plans sanctioned for increasing the built up space in the factory but for reasons Ashok could not fathom, this permission seemed stuck. There was enough land in the premises for this to be feasible. An Industrial License from the Industry Ministry permitting a larger capacity would have to be obtained. This seemed perverse to Ashok. Surely the country badly needed more Industry, more Dairy Production. There was no need to make it so difficult. Was not the economies of scale argument clinching, why was everything licensed, what logic was there in that. Ashok felt a rage rising up.

The company would have to hone its consumer marketing skills to successfully sell much larger volumes. Extra funds for marketing outlays would be needed. Ashok tried to tie up with the machinery suppliers from Europe for payment in instalments. They were keen to sell their equipment and eager to accommodate but they wanted more down payment than the internal financial reserves of the company would allow.

The banks were no longer commercial. They had all been nationalised and had become totally risk averse.

Entrepreneurship meant managing very difficult challenges. Ashok was confident he would find a way out for the company. His father had managed far more difficult circumstances, had created factories out of nothing. Now he was getting older, in need of a lieutenant.

He was conscious of an air of unreality. This wasn't his true self. This wasn't Ashok Solanki. Or was he gradually himself changing in response to his responsibilities.

49

There was another missive from Zbiegniew, who again hinted at dark things afoot. No one could be more loyal than Zbiegniew. The sub-text was clear, either do something about it now or be content with a Lauren with whom there had been lovely days. Long distance romantic possibilities even if they involved longing that wouldn't go away, couldn't be sustained indefinitely.

How did Ashok feel about "losing" her? What was he to do? He had already been away so long. Would she come to India for the sake of his family responsibility or would she expect him to give up everything and start a new life in Europe, under any circumstances.

He was used to working hard but in the charming, hazy blue evenings of Delhi, where had all the Beautiful people of the 60's gone? 'Gone away to far off lands'. But he couldn't just turn up in America or Britain and hope to continue where he had left off in College.

Then what to do about this sense of something missing. Maybe it was an existential problem. Maybe it was a universal human problem. Maybe creativity would help. But he was being creative in his father's factory. He was adding to production, to the GNP. He was finding creative solutions to difficult problems.

Tetra Pak of Sweden was coming out with innovative new packaging that was light for easy transportation, easy to handle, visually appealing and gave long life protection. Alfa Laval of Sweden was going to introduce it in their Indian subsidiary Vulcan Laval. It would be well worth it but he would have to convince the Indian government to give them an Import Licence, so that scarce foreign exchange could be spent.

The rate of growth of the economy was slowing down still further, to almost stagnation. The ills of the economy were being addressed neither by fiscal nor monetary measures. The bureaucracy and the government tightened their stranglehold on the moribund financial system. Taxation was hiked up to absurd levels, eventually reaching a meaningless 97.7 per cent.

To mislead the masses the highest levels of the Polity came out with an opiate more catchy than intolerant religion or regionalism. "*Garibi hatao*" - banish Poverty they harangued over the pulpit. Most laudable in itself. The masses got hope, were misled. Nothing tangible was done to improve their lot. But they didn't know this when casting their votes. There was a focused effort instead to "*Amiri hatao*" - remove whatever affluence there was. Every law, every Act that was introduced one by one throughout the first half of the decade was done in the name of the poor. The right to property was taken away as a fundamental right from the Constitution. The ruling party had acquired such an overwhelming majority in Parliament, that there was no check on demagoguery. Anything would be passed. Parliament extended its own life to six years - one and a half times the term of the American legislature.

Ashok found himself working the whole day, often till 1.30 in the night. No evening survived. Only when he'd be driving home in the gorgeous, moonlit city from some recently retired bureaucrat's house in Vasant Vihar, to whom no one in the government listened any longer, would he be aware of how far he had come, in just a few years. He was still very young but he was no longer Ashok Solanki, listening to Dylan or Baez or being lost in wonderment at the creativity of Sergeant Pepper's, with a group of beautiful people at a party, sometimes sitting in a circle and smoking Pot with headbands in their hair. Or going thereafter with some of them for an early morning ice-cream at India Gate.

50

Shivratri came. He remembered his childhood. He liked Shiva the most out of the Trinity, though like his father his *isht devi* - the principal Deity through whom he focussed was Amba, also known as Jagdamba, Durga, or Shakti. He wasn't up to tricks or unfair play like Vishnu in his various avatars. He didn't want to be disloyal to Vishnu, so whenever he thought of him, he used the *Bhakti Marg*, devotion rather than *Gyan*, deep philosophical knowledge. He tried to dream about him, love him, as Ram or Krishna.

But Shiva lived on the tops of the magical, mystical, ethereal, snow bound Himalayas. He let the Ganga down from Akash through the long plaits of his Yogi hair. As was fitting, the Puja took place throughout the night. Three-leafed *bilvapatras*, from the *Bilva* tree were placed facing upwards on the Shiva *Linga* to chants of "*Om Namah Shivaye*". If one found a four-leafed one, one was really lucky. Berries and bhang - a liquid made from the marijuana plant, were offered to Shiv Ji. He would stay up most of the night along with his parents, or he would get up and go to sleep again, throughout the night. Later on his parents took to sleeping in the *Puja* (prayer) room, behind a screen, whilst the Pandits chanted. It would be February or March, so they still needed quilts at night. Ashok would get under his quilt with a sense of adventure. Shiva had such strange companions. Anything could happen.

Ashok came straight from the factory to the Puja. These days there was no time to breathe, leave alone to wonder about who he really was and what he wanted to be, whilst in this world. He had managed to get better and better quality unprocessed milk by offering higher than proportionate values to the small farmers, often owning one or two cows, who supplied their surpluses at the collection centres.

The collection centres were spread all over the hinterland of Delhi, in the states of Haryana and UP. A vast amount of milk had to be collected to meet even the existing requirements of the factory. They were essentially testing centres where each farmer was paid according to the quality of milk, especially the all important SNF (Solids Non-Fat-essentially Protein) and fat percentages. If water was mixed with milk, as per old Indian traditions, it just reduced the percentages.

They were then transported to a few designated chilling centres, where they were chilled to 4°C and quickly shipped in chill tankers which were made of aluminium and the size and shape of petroleum tankers, to the factory for processing. These tankers were well insulated and rapidly traversed large distances, very early in the morning, to be in Delhi in time for the morning shift.

He re-designed the existing internal layout of the plant in synergy with a creative young architect, who managed to re-lay the machinery so as to make much more capacity possible within the same covered area. If the government was going to be obstructive about adding buildings on his own land, he would do it in the existing space. This avoided huge building expenditure. Some office space had to be cannibalised but that only made the office operation more efficient. Some new machinery had to be added to bring about a spurt in productivity but that too added to quality and innovation. The cost of this was much lower than the civil cost would have been. Soon, the company became known for its state of the art systems and products.

As its reputation grew, its sales increased and the suppliers in Europe became more comfortable with the financing of their machinery. The references from the commercial wings of their embassies in Delhi were excellent.

A factory's problems are never over and if they are over at a point of time, it doesn't mean that things will stay that way. Nevertheless, as Ashok began to get on top of immediate problems, he again felt the void in his personal life.

Three years passed thus in work. He reached the magic figure of 25 when according to the *Yajur* Veda a man was fully a man - in his prime. He had made a lot of headway. The results were self evident but a part of him as he knew himself was missing.

51

Lauren really missed Ashok after he upped and left. Everything would remind her. It began to gnaw at her. It became difficult to remain in the city. Was she talented enough to break into Warsaw. Networks enabling entry were needed. Talent wasn't enough. Accommodation was next to impossible.

She pulled herself together.

What was this? She had met a stranger, a foreigner by chance and now he had gone back.

She concentrated her energies on shifting to Warsaw. Her break would come soon.

She devoted herself to her music and lost herself in her harp. It assuaged her soul. Her creativity flourished. She started going for performances all over Poland and began to get renown in her own right. She was invited to fraternal Socialist countries and went with a group of Polish musicians to the superb cities of Buda and Pest and to charming Prague, still full of character and creativity. And Hradny castle still felt like Hradny castle and Wenceslaus square was still vibrant and majestic.

She met interesting people and got absorbed in their

stories, sometimes their lives. She laughed, she smiled, she flirted. Spanish and Italian musicians were taken by her North European blondness and kept trying to make conquests. Some wanted to help her escape 'the Iron Curtain', to the West and *La Dolce Vita*. Once at a disco called Hybridy on Nowy Swiat in Warsaw she saw someone dancing, tall and Italian looking, some couples away and she had glimpses of Ashok from his mannerism and the way he was dancing.

She was invited to play in Lazienkowski Park, under the charcoal grey sculptured statue, next to the elegant, ornate summer palace which looked like a pavilion next to the lake. There were chairs and benches arranged in an amphitheatre format around the evocative statue. Every Sunday there was a piano concert - nearly always Chopin - the sound of which wafted all over the leafy lanes of the park. It was a big park, well designed and laid out, with benches hidden from view, strategically placed next to bushes. The lanes were walkways leading to one another. They had tall hedges on either side. There were clusters of trees. The concert was open to all and people sat on benches all over the park, as the soft sound floated around them. The sound of the nocturnes or etudes could be heard faintly in the air on every park bench next to or behind a bush. Either it had been designed like that or it was the magic of the music and the way it floated through the natural medium of foliage, bushes and trees. Only acclaimed and internationally recognised pianists were given the honour to perform there.

It sent one into reveries. It transported one to a different world. It was unprecedented that a gentle harp was asked to perform there. It was only a piano that had ever been played there. How would the much softer sounds carry all over the park? It was a singular recognition. Lauren was making it on her own.

Soon after that the Conservatoire in Warsaw accepted her pending application and gave her an assured position and Lauren made the very significant and decisive move from the city where she had grown up to the capital of Poland. Only she was to know and perhaps not even she that the reason was not only musical progress though there was clearly that, but to get away from Ashok and memories of her time in Wroclaw with him. Funny how the human mind works, Ashok would have said.

What was this bitter sweet pain she felt inside herself. Was she still pining for Ashok?

Lauren's brother too had kept up the pressure (whenever he visited home or wrote letters from Lodz) as had her parents. Wlodek's pressure was powerful peer pressure. He was just old enough to lord it over her and to have her hold him in awe. He was tall and good looking, had a way with girls. How long was she going to pine for that guy, who was from a different background and who had left and promised nothing? She was young, she was attractive, in demand. She couldn't keep her heart closed.

She had to get away from her family. She couldn't bear to hear them go on and on any longer. This had a dual effect. Pressure on the one hand to forget Ashok partly translated in this case as getting away from her family, which also meant getting away from Wroclaw. Warsaw was a fresh start. She would not have to hear her mother's relentless mean and unjustified remarks. They would ring in her ears even after her mother had gone. Whatever positive thoughts her mother might have had in the beginning, her position was clear now. Her mother was not taking any chances. She felt that implicit in her daughter's parting ways with Ashok, whether it was acknowledged or not was that they would both see how they managed without each other.

52

The politico-economic condition in Poland remained static, notwithstanding the monopoly of the party on political and economic power on the one hand or the relative freedom of many of the arts especially compared to what was possible in neighbouring Soviet Union, on the other. The accent remained on heavy industry - on capital goods (the Socialist paradigm closely followed by Nehru in India's first two five year plans). Agriculture on the other hand remained predominantly private and in small holdings. It still accounted for a very large portion of GDP. Young Poles continued to be very happy in the lively streets of Warsaw at night - laughing and getting on or off trams and buses, walking hand in hand in the intense cold, very pretty young girls punctuating the night air with their infectious laughter.

The Polish night meal *kolacja* was early. It was a cold meal, a light one. Some cottage cheese and bread, some *smaczna szynka* - cold, tasty ham slices of different types, sometimes some cold borscht-red beetroot soup, with a piece or two of red radish. The lunch was always hot, meat and potatoes being a must. The most commonly eaten meat was some form of pig meat and Polish sausages, were a match for the more famous German ones. This would be preceded by a *zupa pomidorowa* - a delicious red tomato soup full of flavour or a *zupa ogorkowa* - an equally tasty cucumber soup. Breakfast was usually a large hot mug of tea, sips from which were slurped in between bites from the large and tasty ham sandwich. What Ashok did not enjoy were the cold meat products surrounded by a large amount of jelly.

Wine was rare-the drink of choice was Vodka which was excellent and putatively the healthiest among hard liquors and of course the ubiquitous *Piwo* which too was of good quality.

The sexual revolution had come early to Poland. The 60's provided just the right context. The Roman Catholic church had lost its hold to the sexual freedom Communism had brought. Wlodek would often get dropped off at night and walk down some tree lined lane next to blocks of apartments all lit up for the night, with the rectangular green in the middle full of snow, shining in the moonlight, on the way home, to go and visit a girl friend, not always the one he most often went out with. Abortion was free, easy and legal. There was no stigma attached to it. They did not necessarily belong to the Communist Party. Lauren's father told Ashok with derision in his voice and some contempt in his eyes, that for him there was no *oborze*, no Gad (God).

This is where they are so wrong, Ashok always thought to himself. In this they are really wrong. They might be more developed, better off, compared to India which was Third World. They were in-between, the Second World by implication. But about this aspect, they couldn't be more wrong. In matters spiritual, he was really lucky to have been born in India and in his family. He felt an infinite space between him and the surrounding shores of Polska. But Lauren was different. She was so open to things.

It took Lauren time to settle down in Warsaw, to get to know the city and its ways, to meet people, to know where to go. Her music network helped as did that of her family. The Conservatoire helped with lodgings. They had a list of people. She took a room with an old lady who needed the money. An independent apartment was well nigh impossible. She would have to wait a long time. This would suffice for the time being. She had to share the bathroom but she was used to that. She was glad that it hadn't turned out to be more difficult. It wasn't far from Lazienkowski park, the location was good.

She attended some English Literature classes in the university in her free time. They had a good library which provided a useful alternative and the university overall had a different atmosphere from the Conservatoire. She gradually made some friends in the university, outside the world of music and family. In addition, Wlodek had several classmates who had gone to university in Warsaw. She also went out dancing with some of Wlodek's friends. One of them Czesek adored her - had a crush on her since childhood, and had moved to Warsaw shortly after Wlodek had left Wroclaw, in pursuit of his film career. He was short, looked a lot like Steve McQueen and liked to have a smoke in his hand. Lauren had thought him childish, though he was four years older than her, but in Warsaw, he suddenly began to grow up and change

Ashok was Ashok though. She remembered his dreamy smile, his beautiful brown eyes, his gentleness, his thoughtfulness, his olive chest.

Then there was Ryszard, a fellow musician, a pianist, a dreamer, totally lost in his own world, the world of Classical music. He had heard The Beatles' 'Abbey Road' the other day for the first time. It had blown his mind. He had to get hold of it. It was as difficult to get as a red can of Coca-Cola. Someone abroad would have to send it to him.

Then Marek came into her life. Marek had majored in Philosophy in the University of Warsaw. After his Magister which took five years, he was now a PhD student. He was tall, intelligent and had straw blond hair. He fell for Lauren from the moment he met her at a party at a Sports Bar. Lauren enjoyed his sense of humour but she was used to Ashok's and Marek's was not so infectious.

Back in Warsaw, Ashok seemed far away. Ryszard was waiting for her at the station but it was Marek who little by little came more and more into her life. Marek liked philosophers of the French Left a lot. He read out bits to her. They went out to the Opera together and to Symphony Concerts, Choirs and Quintets.

Then one day he kissed her goodnight. He lightly brushed her lips. She hesitated, uncertain, but by then it was over.

Marek was liked by his guide Prof Kowalski, a handsome young looking 54 with chiselled features and deep blue eyes. He spurred him on to good progress. Marek's self assurance grew as did his sex appeal. He became better at flirting and witty he always was. Some of the girls in the department became quite interested in him.

Marek was restrained and Lauren's attraction increased. She had him over for a meal. Her brother approved of him and her parents liked him.

"I am licking these problems," thought Ashok and slowly, very slowly, through a mixture of determination, resourcefulness, creativity and hard work things started going the other way and he found himself not just absorbed in but enjoying his work. There was no time to think of the old Ashok and his passion.

He hired more people, delegated more and more to managers, managing more and more by exception. He wanted to make himself redundant, he told them, especially from day to day management, so he could focus on the really big issues and longer term thinking. And create much more free time for himself. This was ridiculous.

Nevertheless, his interest in business grew as did his monthly profits. His business sense already acute, got sharpened like a chiselled pencil point.

He focused on cost cutting wherever possible. Every spare part had a life. No point in trying to use it beyond that, even if it looked ok. Preventive maintenance was done every Sunday. Whatever needed replacement was replaced. Ruthlessly. Machine parts were well lubricated. Precise logs of when what was serviced and when it was due next were meticulously kept and followed. The machines began to hum like the engines of a well serviced car. Engineering costs went up initially but breakdowns continued to come down. The Capital/Output ratio went up.

In finance, the company leveraged wherever Ashok reckoned that it would be advantageous - wherever the gains were higher than the rate at which they borrowed, thus minimizing their own capital requirement and making much larger outlays feasible. He dug out the soft lending arms of State financial units and worked out how his company could be eligible for those loans. Working capital requirements were minimised, the company's Current Ratio, Quick Ratio and most other Ratios which were part of the Tools of Ratio Analysis were closely monitored and the Management Information Systems made appropriate. Relevant and to the point for each level.

For these and other changes to be effected, everyone had to become highly motivated and feel part of the team. Ashok found that he was good at Human Relations and that his experience in Europe of being desperately poor at times, helped.

Brij was a constant source of guidance. He had the answers to conundrums. The objective was to solve problems at any cost - no matter what the difficulty. One had to be ingenious, resourceful, find a solution, improvise, innovate.

The biggest achievements came in the field of marketing and sales, which Ashok soon realised were at the heart of every consumer product industry. He played around with the media-mix and got help from some of the most creative minds in the advertising industry. He found some of his old St Stephen's colleagues from English Honours in a new firm and decided to risk it with them. His enthusiasm was infectious and spread to the ad agents. They came up with slogans which caught the imagination and mood of the times.

But beyond all these things was a certain indefinable sense, which cannot be taught perhaps but is developed.

55

The thought that Ashok was there in her life had made her get up in the morning and hug herself with pleasure. The thought of the blue hued evenings to come and the music in her head, not just in her instrument, filled many days with excitement, even after they had been together for a while. Sometimes, when they would make love in the afternoon, she would find herself saying '*bas, bas*' (the only hindi she had picked up from him besides *achcha*) to Ashok and a warm glow would steal over them. At the same time there would be a heightened awareness of everything outside the window - the summer smells, sights, sounds, the air stirring the leaves, the distant sound of a child coming home from school, someone playing the piano somewhere, the sounds of it wafting out through the open windows.

Sometimes, she remembered his whole back would be covered with sweat, even his chest at times. Beads of perspiration would form on his forehead and upper lip. At such times she felt she knew in her heart, she could marry this man, whatever be the difficulties.

Lauren tried to forget Ashok. They had split up. Consciously.

Now she had to carve out a life for herself in Warsaw - her new home - the unsightly, destroyed capital city of the country, built from the rubbles of Nazi destruction, without resources, without hope, in a desperate hurry. And the Soviet Union pitched in to help its newly attached satellites.

But she had her music, which filled her to the extent anything non-human can. There was plenty of talent around. Some were very talented. The Poles were a musical people. It was not just the land of Chopin and Penderecki. Lauren got plenty of stimulation, accompaniment, company, ideas, cross fertilization. She enjoyed playing with them and listening to them.

The Poles were also a lively, fun-loving lot. Their trials and tribulations, the vicissitudes of their turbulent history, where they kept getting wiped off the map had not dampened their spirit or their enjoyment of vodka.

The Communist regime had its advantages. Warsaw was totally safe at night, especially for women. A young girl could safely take a night bus at 3 a.m. Their frequency was reduced, compared to the day, but otherwise they were just as efficient and cheap. A billet, good for a bus or a tram cost 1 zloty. The odd unpleasant drunk seen in the daytime had collapsed in a heap, somewhere or the other. A nutritious bottle of Kefir - the peculiarly East European version of yoghurt could be obtained at any of the kiosks - Ruchs dotting the city, on the coldest day. Ashok remembered having it one bitterly cold January morning when it was -21°C. Varieties of hot, filling Polish sausages were easily available. There was no Coke but a bottle of Piwo was easily obtained for 2-3 zlotys. The Milk Bars were open from early morning serving *Sniadania* - the Polish breakfast to dinner time and they cost next to nothing. There was a good variety of *ser*-cheese to be eaten with ham and bread at night.

Warsaw like Cracow and other cities had a number of theatres and some of the theatre was quite clever. It had to be to convey several levels of meaning. There were a number of excellent concerts - quintets, quartets, various ensembles of chamber music. The famous film school at Lodz produced many well known directors and there were enough interesting films to be seen in the many *kino* halls. Many of them like the salon at Palac Nauki I Kultury - the very ugly layered cake like building dominating the Central Warsaw skyline generously donated by the Soviets to their comrades - had intelligent discussions before and after each film, which was treated like a piece of art. Selected Western movies were allowed in and dubbed into Polish. No one spoke anything else, except the Russian learned in schools and the German spoken by some war-oppressed old timers. One would have Richard Burton shouting in Polish. When Ashok had been there he had told Lauren, all he could hear was the 'sh' sound, of which there was such a lot in the language.

The relationship with Marek progressed and developed. He had a lot going for him. Lauren understood that a relationship with him would be steady. The romance was not lacking. Her heart even skipped a beat, sometimes when he smiled at her.

They spent a lot of time together, did many things together. He came and sat at her recitals and performances. Sometimes he brought his own work along. Her family, especially her mother and brother, encouraged the relationship. It would also shake the dust of that pesky and inappropriate Ashok off her feet.

Marek's parents liked Lauren but felt their approval or otherwise had less to do with it than was the case with Lauren. His mother, though she had never been to the West, was part of the old Polish Westernised, sophisticated, intellectual elite.

His father too came from a similar background. It would be nice if their daughter-in-law liked them and they got along, but they did not equate Marek's happiness with their approval vis a vis who might be appropriate. They were urbane, gregarious, enjoyed music and as they got to know her better liked her more and more.

But living together was not easy in Communist Poland. Not for religious or moral reasons but the practical ones of lack of accommodation even for young married couples, leave alone unmarried ones living together. The erstwhile influential Roman Catholic church had lost much of its say. The State could hardly allow a manipulative competitor like that and it was a major enemy of the Party's polemicists. Abortion was freely and easily available and there was no stigma attached to it. The State encouraged it. Like perhaps in other very cold countries, young men and women easily sought the warmth of each other's bodies. On top of that the culture and times were of the late 60's. That zeitgeist was sweeping the whole world - from Tokyo, Berkeley and Paris to Warsaw and Delhi.

Grown up children had to stay with their parents. A brother and sister would have to share a bedroom. The parents would make the larger drawing cum dining room, into their bedroom at night. This would also be where the family watched TV and the son stored his music on spools of tapes.

It wasn't easy to find fresh accommodation. "You have to make such a paper", "go to that bureau", but before that "you need such a card" which was impossible to get. This was the story with nearly everything but especially with extremely scarce items like housing. Party membership, an important job, contacts - all helped. But as a student in the university, doing a higher degree - it was out of the question, even if one was married and had children. If one was from out of town, there were Dom Studentskis. If one went out of town, like to the Film School or the Language School in Lodz, one stayed in the Student Hostel there.

They could not live together but their relationship became steady and long term. There was solidity in it. Lauren was fun loving and Marek enjoyed life too. And if not to the same extent, he tried his best to get into the spirit, to match her. She missed Ashok's spontaneity or the way he matched her fun loving spirit and acts - table dance per table dance, kiss for kiss. Marek did not have that dash. There was not the same excitement about him, or was she just looking for the same type of thing? What was her true self? She had to be true to herself but comparisons were pointless.

She thought of how it was to fall in love, to have been in Love and smiled to herself. She thought of the days to come, of her music, of her life. And Marek was there - solid. But sometimes at these moments, Ashok entered the picture. From where in the depths of her heart she did not know.

She would be fine with Marek. There was a lot to be said for it. But somehow it didn't seem enough. Was that what partnership was? An ideal bourgeois existence. Or since this was a Communist country and that word was laden, a typical, normal, middle class existence.

There was the now and then letter from Ashok. Some of his words would remind her of his dreamy eyes with that far away look. Others of his smile, with his upper lip narrowing into a thin, confident line and the corners of his mouth turning up but not enough to create an Elvis or Bobby Darin like semi sneer. And the occasional phone call. The line would be bad and it would be difficult to talk of ordinary day to day things. She did not have enough money to call him and how could it be justified. They were friends but had split up. And it was even more difficult to call *zagraniczne* from Poland. It was viewed with suspicion and the operators handling the process even more indifferent than the ones in Delhi.

56

Oscar got a much awaited promotion and moved to Warsaw. The work was better, the pay and perks were much better, he bought a Honda from a diplomat. Diplomats were allowed to bring home their foreign embassy cars. Embassies had to keep up image and appearances. It had not been used much and was in good condition. More importantly, a flat came with the job. Magda was happy, she had more time to day dream and listen to records playing romantic old time Hollywood film music and songs from the 50's and early 60's. And it was easy for Wlodek to keep coming down from Lodz. Life started converging towards Warsaw. Lauren gave up her room with the old lady and moved in with her parents. She saved on expenses even if it meant she was a little less independent. The drawing room was large enough that Oscar and Magda could sleep there, on the convertible sofa, so Lauren could sleep in the smaller bedroom meant for them.

After Ashok had upped and left, Lauren had tried not to be *en deuil* and immersed herself in her beloved music and sometime after that, somewhat fortuitously to settling down in her new domicile Warsaw. She missed Wroclaw but there was her professional career to think of. She would be more exposed in Warsaw. There was no dearth of nice young men and for a while she went out with them. But after you've been around you find yourself settling down more and more and she did, with Marek. He was sweet and she felt comfortable with him. His moodiness was still there but it wasn't oppressive. Maybe if she spent more time with him it would become a problem but when would she have that much free time?

57

He thought of Lauren, she came in his dreams.

Everything was very vivid still but they had taken a decision and there it was. He would shoulder his responsibilities to family and business. She had certain ideals about the quality of life and would not, could not compromise.

The time lengthened since he had parted from Lauren, imperceptibly and little by little. The needs of work were elastic and ate into much of his time. Seasons passed, began to stretch into years.

Then it happened. "Some enchanted evening, when you see a stranger across a crowded room...." She was a very fair Indian, tall, slim. He saw her. She was talking to another much shorter girl. It created an unbearable pain in his heart. He couldn't let her go out of his life. Who was she? He almost hadn't come that evening. Chance plays such an important part in everything. Much more than we care to acknowledge.

He felt no hesitation. The girls played so hard to get. You had to work hard. You had to be fast off the track -someone else would start. That would make a hard task even more difficult. Shyness, timidity were luxuries long discarded.

He weaved his way to the other end of the room and went and joined them, sipping his drink. The shorter girl said something to the other one. There was a slight pause. He had something to say on that. He jumped in. Naturally. The conversation proceeded. It was as if he had been standing there all along.

Her name was Aparna. He found himself talking more and more to her. He looked around to give a decent share of his eyes to the other girl but she had drifted off. She lived on the West Coast, in California, in the Bay Area. She was on a six month visit to see if she could live in India. She had very attractive greenish grey eyes, a lovely smile, long hair. She had delicate *churis* on her wrists that brought out their attractive shade. The pain in his heart seemed ever so slightly assuaged. He was there. He was talking to her.

Her parents were Sindhis. Indians left without a Province, the whole of it having been allotted by Radcliffe on his short and only visit to India to the new Muslim Country to be made. She had gone to Delhi University's prestigious LSR College. Whilst her dreams were still being formed, her father worried about settling her had put in an ad in a national newspaper. She didn't even know about it, until she was told that a young man and his family were coming to meet them all the way from America. She didn't take it seriously. She was just required to be present when they came for tea at 4 the next evening. She put in a mild protest at this frivolous exercise but then decided what the heck she would have tea. There would be home made *samosas* and that would be fun.

The young man fell for her and wanted to meet her again. After a couple of meetings they were allowed to go out on their own. It was pleasant enough and she thought why not - it's a lark. They stayed for three weeks. He, Ravi loved poetry, was even trying to write some. He wanted to marry her. Her parents found him suitable. Asked her to consider it. He was six years older. That gave him a certain dash for a girl fresh out of College. He seemed caring, thoughtful.

Boys her own age she met seemed frivolous. He wrote and phoned her. He came on a secret courtship mission. This time no one but the two of them knew. She didn't want any pressure.

They got married that winter in a grand Indian wedding spread over several functions and she moved to her new life in America.

She took to it at once and was soon driving around at great speed on the freeways, following all the complicate signage on the roads, filling up on gas herself. Life seemed idyllic. She created an adorable house full of Indian carpets rich with colours and design and delicate miniature paintings. The drawing room had a French window which looked out on the green backyard full of flowers and fruits. In the distance could be seen the brown mountains near San Jose. Music - the strains of 'Stand By Me' - filled the drawing room as the sun came streaming in from the window. They both loved music. She enjoyed being a housewife and making their hearth and home, warm, cosy, continually better.

Then one evening two years later he didn't come home. He was always so particular. He would always phone her when he got held up at work. Mostly he didn't. His priorities lay with wife and home. The young woman fretted and got increasingly anxious. And then the dreaded phone call from the hospital. He had had an accident. He was dead when he reached the hospital. The police visited shortly afterwards. He had been hit by an out-of-control van. It hadn't been his fault at all. He had always been such a good and careful driver.

Ashok stood there reeling. He hadn't expected such a tale. He didn't know what to say. Didn't want to say anything that might sound trivial. Wasn't sure that he could ask for her number - had just met her. The next day he asked his hostess but she said she didn't know her well. Their friends Rajiv and Sanjana had asked if they could bring a friend who was visiting and she had said of course. But she would make enquiries and see what she could do.

58

She got her number from Rajiv three days later and Ashok called her up. She remembered him and the conversation flowed easily. When he put the phone down they had been talking for an hour. He waited a day and then called her up again. The talk turned to love and romance. How it was between boys and girls, in so many different ways. The complex signals, the non verbal communication, Desmond Morris and *The Naked Ape*. She was liberal and he found her in agreement on many of his thoughts on these subjects. He asked if he could visit her and she invited him for tea a couple of days later. He waited impatiently.

It was a typical Delhi September late afternoon. He could already smell the promise of winter in the air. He always thought of it as *Come September*. The Alstonia Scholaris was already beginning to hint at its magic. The sun had a mellowness to it, the breeze a gentleness and the shadows were longer. An old family retainer turned up to whom she spoke affectionately and indulgently. "Dhani Ram Ji, *do cup chai ley aayenge? Saath mein kuch khane ko*", asking for tea and snacks. "Thank you Dhani Ram Ji, *Bahut badiya chai banayee*", complimenting him on the steaming amber liquid ensconced in a fine English china cup. Ashok didn't want to go but didn't want to overstay. The conversation again flowed very easily. There was an undercurrent of flirtation between them. She smiled often. It made him dizzy. He floated.

He started visiting her as often as he dared. He kissed her on both cheeks *a la francaise*. Once he lingered on her throat. They talked of exporting traditional Indian items, crafts, things precious in more than one meaning.

Sensing an opportunity he said "Let's talk about this seriously. Let's go to the rooftop restaurant in the Taj and pursue the creative ideas that come up." She hesitated and then agreed. They decided to go three nights later. He couldn't lose too much time. She was only on a visit. She might decide to up and go.

India had immense potential. The variety, the richness of products was far more than was explained by the volume of exports. Even taking into account the trade barriers, restrictions and duties put up by the West. It wasn't marketed properly. Countries like Thailand sold such a lot. Their political proximity must help. And Child Labour Evangelism wasn't misused against them in a sweeping fashion said Ashok. They identified a few items to start off with and talked about their sourcing from rural areas as he sipped his wine and she her lime juice at the start of their dinner. She was a teetotaller and a vegetarian. Ashok was serious about the agenda of the meeting but he was so charmed by her. Indian women could be gorgeous in saris and she was like an *apsara*. The orchestra started playing; they must have considered it late enough to start and the dance floor was inviting. Her sari would sweep the floor like a gown. He asked her to dance and they left the table. Her hands were so soft in his and he felt her other arm gently resting on his back. When it started resting for support on his arm he didn't know.

59

One deep blue evening he found himself automatically driving towards her house. Once he reached what then? It was already around 9 p.m. She might be having dinner with her parents. He hadn't asked if he could come. He hadn't fixed up anything. Should he just drive back. He did one two cha cha cha with the horn a couple of times. She came out laughing, in a bit. "What are you doing here, pray?" but the tone was only partly reproving. He couldn't pretend this was about exports. She slipped into the front seat beside him and they drove off, past Nizamuddin and Humayun's Tomb, onto Lodhi Road, traversed its full length and then turned back and went past Golf Links. He put on Dvorak's New World Symphony softly on the cassette player. Where were they going? He stopped the car. There was Lodhi Gardens softly lit with lamps juxtaposed between bushes and other lights tastefully lighting up facades of the ancient monument. The pedestrian gate was still open. There were a few people still going in and out. They slipped inside. There was a gentle breeze rustling the leaves. It reminded him of 'Blow Up'.

She was a *Manglik*, the Pandit Ji who had made her *Kundali* had told her and her parents. They had been worried. Whoever she paired with, unless he was a Mangalik too, had a similarly powerful constellation of stars, misfortune would fall upon him. The *nakshatra mandal* had been such at the time of her birth. She did not believe in these things, nor had her husband. Ashok knew enough about his horoscope, made at birth by a famous astrologer, the first person to have done a Doctorate from Delhi University on the subject, to know that he wasn't born under such a planetary constellation.

Something was happening between them. But he had to take it very slow. He saw her 2-3 times a week but wanted to remain careful about not imposing. She had lots of friends in Delhi, some very attractive looking women with smart young men in tow. His time in Stephania had inculcated values which included not wasting time on frivolities like gossiping or playing cards - might as well read Osborne or Giradoux in that time or listen to Chaurasia on his divine flute. He had just finished reading *Six Characters in search of an Author* and really liked it. But when she played cards in the afternoon it involved a lot of laughter and he did find himself relaxed. He had to unbend a little, not be such a stuffed shirt. He relented and joined in. It gave him her company. She loved shopping. So he endured it, even if it was in the middle of the afternoon. Fortunately his working hours were flexible. It was the output that mattered.

She was such a good dancer. She moved effortlessly to the music. And the moves expressed just what should have been expressed. He loved that. He was happy in her company, though he secretly worried that she found him too serious which could slip into boring. She liked him but sometimes in the afternoon was she yawning excessively? Didn't it also show how comfortable she was in his company, he told himself.

They both liked elegant clothes, enjoyed travelling, music.

They had had stimulating discussions on spiritual topics. She listened with interest when Ashok told her about what Voltaire, Shaw and Schlegel had to say about Indian spiritual texts with the discovery by European intellectuals of Sanskrit classics. Schopenhauer's comments she knew about. She liked the idea of being versed and immersed in ancient Indian civilisation. Her knowledge was not as deep as Ashok's, who had been tutored in it from an early age by his parents but unlike most Indians of her generation and class, who just liked the idea of it because they were Indian, she had studied Vedanta and the Upanishads on her own (*swadhyaya*). No one else in her immediate family had been like that. She knew about *turiya awastha* - that state of being and understood. *Tat twam asi*. You are that. She had read a lot out of the 18 Puranas and had enjoyed the tales within tales in the Mahabharat or the differences between the Valmiki Ramayan and the Ramcharitmanas, the much later Tulsidas Ramayan.

Impulsively, one day, he went to Mehrasons in South Extension and bought a necklace with small bright diamonds. A necklace that would adorn Aparna's slender neck beautifully. Aparna was so soft. He asked her to close her eyes, put it in her lap, in her drawing room and knelt on the carpet in front of her chair. She exclaimed and hesitated at the possible implication. She asked him to put it around her neck and as he tied the clasp at the back of her neck, his hand touched the back of her neck and they kissed. It was ecstasy. He couldn't believe it was happening. He had longed for this to be possible. Dreamt about this. Aparna had been so inaccessible in so many ways - as only girls from home can be. It was heaven - broken only when her older sister walked into the room and they instantly disengaged. Aparna told him later that she didn't accept presents like that but would keep this one.

They went dancing many evenings, to different restaurants, to the discos surviving from the many that had cropped up in the late 60's. in the heyday of the hippies and flower power and their massive inflow into India - they had to make that pilgrimage. Sensations was one of them, with its large wooden dance floor, psychedelic lights and "music that made you want to dance, that got your legs swinging and bodies swaying", said Ashok. The Cellar in Connaught Place, next to Regal Cinema and Gaylords restaurant had been the pioneer. It still had the best atmosphere, music - often live and it managed to get clientele which somehow automatically vibed with each other.

Some of the long endless afternoons, he couldn't keep his mind on work. He would leave office and take her out for a cold coffee to La Boheme or Laguna. That it was a particularly Indian concoction he was now aware. You couldn't get cold coffee like that anywhere else. Why that should be so, he couldn't understand but it could be sipped for a long time, interspersed with conversation that ricocheted from one interesting topic to another. Was it her presence that made it so interesting - probably, Ashok thought. So much the better.

The one two cha cha cha outside her window at night became a pleasurable signature tune and the relationship began to get intense. The going out with other people declined and then stopped. He didn't think he was possessive, he was a torch bearer of an emancipated, liberal movement. But sometimes when they drifted apart at parties and he saw her talking the way she talked to him to someone else, he felt an inexplicable pain in his heart and he soon went to her side. He just wanted to be with her, he told himself. Enough talking to other people. He didn't get to see enough of her, anyway.

She had a very pleasant temperament, was extremely attractive but would she be a kindred spirit?

Her interest in politics, in issues of the day, her general knowledge were not like his. Did she share his love of creative cinema, of books? Ashok remembered an animated discussion on the *Tin Drum* with Lauren. Aparna hadn't read Goethe leave alone Gunter Grass. If he made an allusion to Faust she wouldn't know. Time was to be spent in enrichment, in worthwhile pursuits. This included entertainment, like a game of chess or table tennis or laughter and talk but not about others.

How much did these things matter over the long run. Differences could get accentuated or cease to matter as people evolved and changed in different ways. Was there such a thing as a perfect fit, he wondered. Didn't relationships involve compromises.

The long annual stay of the family came to an end. At her request the family's visit was extended by another couple of months. They too flew by. That this was not a casual fling, they both knew. But what now?

61

Aparna's father worked in the Railways and thus supported his small family of a pretty Sindhi wife who loved cooking and produced delicious vegetarian food with infinite variations to please the differing palates of husband and two lively daughters. They moved around as he got transferred in different postings but he tried to minimise it to give stability to his family. As he attained seniority and acquired specialised expertise and a network it was easier to do.

In Ambala, a mid-size town with a cantonment, the last town in Haryana before Punjab started. Aparna went to the local Convent - the Convent of Jesus and Mary - an English medium school, where Reading and Writing were separate subjects, carrying 100% marks. Writing was made perfect with Vere Foster's writing books and the Reading ensured a perfect English enunciation, quite similar to the accents at English Public Schools except that some consonants like P were not aspirated and some children put more stress on D and T so that it was closer to the Hindi 'da' and 'ta'. The older daughter went to Punjab University in Chandigarh some 25 miles away. The sisters were very close to each other. There were four years between them. They sounded the same on the phone. The playful Aparna soon became a young lady, with well proportioned features, a smooth, very light golden olive complexion and expressive eyes.

Ashok later told her that he had often passed that town on his marketing trips in North India, wanting to get out of it as soon as his work was over and evening started falling, little realising that a town like that had somebody like her.

Aparna told Ashok about her sister's marriage earlier. Their parents wanting their daughters secure and settled started looking at Ads for eligible young men for Asha the older one. They also inserted an Ad themselves and put the word out in the Sindhi community spread far and wide - in Bombay, London, New York, California. They got many responses but repeated the Ads wanting the best.

A friend of their parents knew of an eligible young man, who was working as an Engineer with a High-Tech firm in the Bay Area having done Electrical Engineering from the Madras IIT. He would be visiting India for two weeks and a meeting could be arranged. That's all the time they got off in America, unlike Europe or India.

The meeting took place over Tea with fine China kept for occasions like these and hot *pakoras* and *samosas* were produced with green and red chutneys. The young man Shyam turned out to be a most presentable young man. The parents liked each other and Shyam and Asha sat next to each other and conversed about what they liked.

He was 4 years older than her, lean and tall. He had a Butch Cassidy kind of moustache which suited him. They went out on "dates" to get to know each other better. The family knew a high ranking army officer so he invited them to the officers club in the cantonment where they could sit and chat. There was a dance on that evening and Shyam proved to be an excellent waltzer, holding himself erect as he twirled her around on the dance floor, to the pleasure of the Services Officers who prided themselves on their ability to dance well, especially to waltz gracefully and expertly.

They hit it off and saw a lot of each other over the next two weeks. Had there been any doubt in either mind, perhaps a family visit to America might have been arranged later on in the year and the family would have stayed with the ubiquitous Sindhi relative in the area. They were officially engaged before he left in a simple but elegant ceremony where all family members that could attend were present.

Shyam would fly down for the wedding date which was set a few months later. So Asha got married and moved to the Bay Area. She adjusted to life in America fast and quickly learned to handle things independently and competently.

Soon Aparna's father retired and had to give up his Government flat. The family decided to move to America to be near their daughter but they couldn't get themselves to cut off completely and immediately. They had enough saved not to buy a house but to take on annual lease the ground floor of a pleasant house in Gulmohar Park facing one of the parks there. This would ease the transition and keep one foot here in case America didn't work out for them. The journalist friend lived upstairs and gave them a good rate. That way they could stay as long as they liked. They would visit once a year for several months to meet various relatives and close friends and to put the soil of Bharat Mata and thus too the lost soil of Sindh on their foreheads. It was in one of these that young Aparna's path crossed that of Ashok and things happened.

Eventually they might give this up too as they settled down more in America and intercontinental travel became more difficult with age. Grandchildren would be born and would grow up there.

62

Over time, the family felt more rooted and developed links in America. They were thankful for the plentiful sun. Indians take bright days for granted in their home land and the absence of it hits them hard. Aparna was very happy zipping around on America's freeways and felt totally at home. Her confident manner, her easy ways with people, her ability to adapt, her natural liking for America all stood her in good stead. Her delicate features got her many second glances, she was often thought to be French. She took training in Graphic Design, enjoyed it and proved to be creative. She got a job with a well known firm. She was even offered a position at the Getty Museum in Los Angeles with all its resources and prestige but she preferred to stay with her close knit family in Northern California.

Their father took Adult Education classes and pursued many of his interests. In America he actually started feeling younger, whereas in India he had started thinking of himself as a stooped old man at 58, ready to enter the *vanaprastha* ashram preparatory to *sanyas*. He finally had the leisure to do many things that he had always wanted to do. But the best thing was that he had more time with the family. In Shyam he found a supportive son-in-law, as good as a son.

Their mother who always enjoyed cooking further expanded her horizons. There were many more gadgets, things could be done a lot faster with a lot less effort. There were all sorts of spices, other ingredients that were not commonly used in India. Things could be bought at various stages of preparation. She was a gourmet cook who came into her element.

The word spread in the Bay Area. On both sides of the Bay, not just Oakland, San Francisco and Berkeley but Fremont, San Jose, Walnut Creek - first their friends, the Sindhi community, the larger Indian community, the Americans who had come to know and like Indian food, home cooking on top of that. Many in the flower power generation were returning home after pilgrimages to India and this being California there were quite a few of them.

She did it for fun and wouldn't charge her friends but soon people wanted to order this on a regular basis. She started sending out packed food. There were continual comings and goings from their household.

63

Aparna was wary. She didn't give her heart easily though if and when she finally did, it would be unreservedly, totally. Was he the right one for her?

Something could go wrong again. Bad partner karma. Despite herself she thought maybe the manglik effect might take place qua Ashok also. Maybe she would be bad for him. She didn't want to harm him. She was modern. This was ridiculous. She didn't think like that.

She had also seen friction developing in many marriages - somehow the expectations changed after people stopped being girl friend and boy friend out on dates - even of some of her friends. She wasn't going to let that happen in her life, if she could help it.

And guys could be such turncoats. Couples-sweethearts from an early age and seemingly so much in love and then there would be a shocking revelation of unfaithfulness.

But Ashok gradually helped overcome that wariness as she felt more and more comfortable. By the time of their first kiss, she felt the stirring of her heart and as time passed and the kissing became deeper and longer, she felt her heart move in ways she didn't think were possible.

She had grown up in India but things were different then. Some of them were towns not cities, the cars were less, the pollution, noise, chaos was less. There were fewer people. One could still go for a walk and see the Eucalyptus trees along the highway passing the town and elsewhere. It was a gentler life. Delhi later on was a different kettle of fish. Especially after the orderliness of her existence in California.

64

Back in America after the first encounter with Ashok, she wondered about Delhi and India. If things were to go further between the two of them, would she return to India? She loved California. She had taken to it at once and the relaxed post flower children way of life. Would she be able to adjust again? There were so many things wrong with her country of origin, so many things so hard to take. But wasn't she Indian? So many things that foreigners would find strange, she wouldn't even notice. And she had been happy in India right up to the time they had left.

She was very close to her family. She would miss them. And Asha had a son and a daughter. She played with them every morning and evening. She felt like eating them up.

Ashok had too much at stake in his family business, his father's factory, their well located family house with a lovely garden and lots of space. She couldn't see him leaving it. She would be the one who would have to adjust. Ashok even if he left everything would have to start from scratch in America. Who would look after the carefully nurtured factory.

He was very attractive, charming but was he really her

type? These things waned. Fit for a lifetime partnership? Was there enough in common? He seemed very driven. Always wanting to do something he considered worthwhile. Watching Bollywood - he considered a *perte de temps*. But she enjoyed watching these ridiculous and therefore funny movies over an endlessly stretching weekend afternoon. He was too much of a sophisticate. Would she sacrifice her real self at the altar of haute civilisation. When outside his world of management (which she understood and liked), he would think and talk about Schumann or Mozart or Haydn. In theory she liked western classical music but she didn't really enjoy it, except the most obvious pieces. His interest in folk, pop and rock music she shared though he was into it much more than her. But was he in the long run too cerebral, too much into the Arts to hold her interest? At social dos when he talked in a group about certain current Fiction or plays she couldn't participate. He read non-fiction too, avidly, books on politics and western philosophy, AJ Ayer and Gilbert Ryan, which she found deadly dull.

She enjoyed sitting with a bunch of girls and sometimes they would get convulsed with laughter about inane things. What was wrong with talking about what was happening in the lives of others? As long as it was not malicious.

She was very happy in his company and he seemed content, satisfied just to be with her. She could see that she so charmed him that he seemed to be in a daze at times. Once when they were still at the kiss on the cheek stage, he had lingered longer than could be explained. The signals that give people away - sometimes they are not even aware of them.

He had made her head swim the last time they had kissed or when she had let herself go and relaxed completely in his arms as he swung her round and round in the waltz. When she thought of him, she felt a smile coming on. And that's what mattered.

Air travel still took ages. No matter how comfortable they tried to make it and with all the advancement and spectacular progress in most areas of technology, air travel speed was stuck at the speed of the 747. It was half way around the world. If she dug a hole she would come up against Ashok at the other end! The time difference in winter was 13 ½ hours. So accessibility would always be a problem.

Ashok was in touch constantly. His letters were brief but newsy. His phone calls limited by the crackle and the time limits of international trunk calls were romantic and full of charm *malgre* all that. Sometimes the operators who were not expected to eavesdrop would openly giggle and reveal their presence. So much for human nature thought Aparna.

65

One day Ashok got a call from Neeru. She had become persona non grata in the parental home. Ashok knew that the parents thought of her and missed her a lot. Neeru must miss the family too. Even the prodigal Gita had come home and was actively looking to work as a journalist in one of the better newspapers/magazines. With her inside knowledge and contacts this was the ideal job for her. In the meantime she had already started freelancing.

They fixed up to meet for cold coffee in Connaught Place.

"Ashok, Gita and I didn't give you the support you needed when you wanted to go to Europe for training. But I saw later that parents aren't always right."

"That's alright, Neeru", he said kissing his sister's cheek. "No hard feelings. You did what you thought was right at the time."

"You must have expected support at the time - we were the same generation. We went to parties together. We did so many things together."

"Never mind Neeru. Tell me about yourself."

"I am fine, Ashok. I have to economise quite a lot but I manage.

I was also thinking of having a baby but Vikram doesn't want the responsibility as yet - ever the carefree youth.

So now I'm trying to help people with gardens and develop a landscape practice. People don't know me but I do love it and I think I'll be good at it."

"But don't you need a qualification Neeru?"

"Only to get accepted but once my work gets known, it won't matter."

"And this being the service industry not much capital will be required," said Ashok, thinking aloud.

"And life with Vikram?"

"Its fine, Ashok," and then after a slight hesitation "He is very handsome and he knows it. He is a bit of a flirt."

"Have you told him?"

"I have tried. But not a word of this to the parents."

"Come over soon and meet them. I am sure it'll be alright. How about day after - it's a Saturday? Come over at tea time. A rapprochement is just waiting to happen. And there'll be one more person besides me (and Gita of late), once again to give them support in all sorts of ways."

Ashok was already very involved with managing the factory. More and more appreciative of the interlinkage of different managerial and business functions and how they made a fine interwoven mesh.

He enjoyed most of his work. It was exciting, creative. He spent long hours at it. He liked the problem solving, the dealing with the outside world, the real world. Common sense went a long way as did a step by step, logical approach. He was good at not jumping from point to point, item to item. When other issues would come up, stories within stories, he would still put them aside, make a note to deal with them and carry on to finish the main point till it reached a workable solution.

What he didn't enjoy was most of the interface with the

government. In India it was axiomatic that it was highly intrusive, to the point of crippling action. Supplies of items were controlled, rationed, put in quotas; getting coal was a big deal. It had to be indented in the state capital, closely followed up with the Railways and the wagons chased up in Calcutta. Distribution was controlled, prices were set artificially high or low, to get economies of scale which were everchanging, new capacity could not be installed. Licences and permissions were required. This is perverse in a country like ours which badly needs to increase production. The nationalised banks were loath to give loans for capital projects or even for working capital limits. Bureaucrats never kept appointments. When they met you, it was doing you a favour.

India works at night, began to realise Ashok in dismay, when the government sleeps. The factory would be buzzing with activity in the night shift, dough being mixed in the wafer unit, cut into thin sheets, fed into the oven, packets perfectly packed coming out of the packing machines. He would visit at 3 a.m., 4 a.m., tireless like Professor Higgins. India worked despite the government not because of it. There was individual excellence, collective failure. Indians excelled in the States and in the comity of nations where was India, in particular compared to its potential? China worked in the day because the Government whatever its other faults was committed to a rise in China's economic might.

The other thing he didn't enjoy was dealing with labour (with union leaders, who were often professional union types, who did that for a living and were mostly from outside the factory) especially when it was unreasonable, which it often was. These union leaders were often not motivated by genuine interest of labour and they disrupted things particularly when things were going smoothly and the factory was flourishing. Backed by political bosses seeking cheap publicity and a quick rise to power and notoriety, they used this as a short cut. They put forward demands that at the collective level were exorbitant and untenable and therefore doomed to failure. Ashok went out of the way to share the fruits of increased productivity and performance with the workforce, whom he liked, found sincere and hardworking. Many of them were refugees from West Punjab. But at times a minority would capture power and be intransigent about unrealistic demands such that there was no solution.

Researching, testing and creating new products was a lot of fun. An idea for a new product would germinate, be tested in the Lab and on the pilot plant. Different formulae would be experimented with, while the costing was getting done. If it seemed feasible, the production team would be involved so that at least one shift could be run out of about 80 in a month. Simultaneously the packaging would have to be got ready for it, which was both attractive as well as protective of the shelf life of the product. Packaging materials would have to be carefully selected for technical properties, cost effectiveness, availability and a host of other factors. Designs would have to be simultaneously approved for the outer cover. They had to be eye catching, appealing, convey a sense of the product. The publicity campaign would have to be fine tuned - mass media was getting more and more expensive, yet essential. The media mix would have to be judiciously decided for maximum efficacy, some outlay kept aside for point of purchase. This never interested publicity agents as they never made a commission on it, but was essential. The distribution had to be well oiled and its depth and extent improved. For a consumer product, the heart of the challenge lay in its marketing, which required a high level of creativity.

Such challenges kept Ashok busy so that by the time evening came, Aparna, Europe, his life there, Lauren, seemed like distant dreams. A work out, some sports would be great. Or some dancing to shake off the hyper activity of the brain - a discotheque would be just right. The nearest large city to the wafer unit was Chandigarh. It would take at least 45 minutes each way. Would there be girls he could just ask to dance there like at a College party or would he have to create a network there, he asked. Where did he have the time for that. He could just go the Chandigarh Club - membership was difficult and as at any noted club in India involved waiting. But his membership in Delhi would get him reciprocal rights of usage. Club life mostly involved sitting around tables in the green lawn and eating and drinking. Pleasant enough after a hard day's work but it felt vacuous after a while. Sometimes he went to the movies. The Hindi movies had him in splits, he couldn't take them seriously; they were caricatures of themselves, but dissatisfying in the end. A treasure in the book shops he discovered was Russian Classics in English, excellent paper - sometimes glossy, superb printing, historical photographs of the author or his painting and his times at dirt cheap prices. He bought up the whole collection and read them voraciously. But it wasn't enough. And the journey each way was tiring and time consuming. His work life was full and challenging but sometimes in the dark watches of the night he was aware that he missed Europe and the India that was Stephania.

66

Standing before Sovereign Dairies at the corner of Khan Market and eating ham slices or drinking milk out of a bottle - looking at the very pretty girls that passed by, smiling and chattering. Or looking at the fabulous pictures in Life magazine with one of those girls sitting close to him. When Return to Peyton Place was still considered scandalous. The Hollywood movie magazines available at the corner were full of beautiful people kissing, when kissing was still something you gave your all to, because that's as far as you went. It excited him.

But you can't go back in time he knew and should be grateful for the experience, the memory. And he had taken a decision on the gently rolling slopes at the Cite Universitaire in Paris, a well thought out one, to return to India. Then why this renewed struggle, he puzzled. Was it because he was only working and in his free time he felt culturally adrift.

Or was he really a "Nowhere Man". Many things cultural that he encountered from childhood still gave him pleasure - *rasa* - roughly translatable as on going sensuous pleasure but more than that - a genuine revelling in the thing itself.

There were so many unique things about India and his

childhood and growing up. There were those illustrated picture books, published by Gita Press, Gorakhpur - somewhat like comics but with the classical text of the epics, simply and clearly explained, on smooth paper that slipped and felt good under your fingers and well drawn pictorial sketches with some text below them on the other side. He still felt a thrill the moment he saw their covers.

The association extended to many other things. There were a series of folk tales from different regions of India - folk tales from Bundelkhand, from Garhwal, from Kutch, from Saurashtra, regions which were part of large provinces but had their composite sub-culture. There were other books which he remembered being read to when he would be convalescing from fever, whilst eating *daliya* - delicious, light watery porridge, with some vegetable soup. There would be walks through forests and jungles in those stories, where one would encounter ghosts and phantoms, stories with talismans and genies, or ironical tales. There was one where two friends were walking through the countryside and one of them found two *chanas* and shared it with the other one. Thereafter every time the other one did not do what the first one wanted, he would say "*la mera chane ka dana*" - give me my chick-pea back. There were different versions of the Ramayana and the Mahabharata - studded with lovely paintings and illustrations from time to time - with descriptions that transported you to another world and which created different dimensions of Time and sometimes Space. There would be *shlokas* and *chhandas* in the Sanskrit version, stylised poetry with very strict rules. When his teacher sang them, the melody was sublime and transcendental. Then there would be *chaupais* in the Hindi version and transcendental songs, the tunes of which he would never forget. The ending of each line of a *chaupai* was drawn out to a high and then slowly brought down, accentuating the vowel each time. The effect was unique.

Then there were all the Kalidas plays in eloquent Sanskrit with beautiful Hindi translations that gave exercise to his imagination and made him reach places he had never been, at least not in this life. He read them voraciously curled up in some cosy spot in one of the many rooms in the house. No one bothered him, no one looked for him there for hours. There would only be the golden afternoon sunlight streaming in from the window to keep him company. "Here comes the Sun", though the Beatles hadn't sung it yet. His pockets would be full of English toffees, delicious, as only English toffees can be. He would keep popping them in his mouth, as he felt various parts of his anatomy grow to extraordinary sizes. They were romantic, sensuous, bare shoulders touched briefly by accident in a chariot, dupatta slipping and revealing a rounded white shoulder. The romance, the angst of parting transported him as did the descriptions of nature, of melting snows and rivulets, of the changing seasons, of *Hemant* – when the snow ended in the Himalayas, of *Shishir* – so named because the cold wind made you shiver, of the snow capped peaks where Shiva resided, where the ravishing divine *apsaras* danced and *gandharvs* and *kinnars* – the celestial singers, sang there divine songs, of the flora and fauna, the rhododendrons and violet coloured butterflies, of oak, chestnut, beech and pine, of bluebirds with red beaks and morning songs.

The shrill, sharp, metallic sound of Western flutes especially when not part of a Symphony Orchestra contrasted in his sensibility with the wooden flute player at night, playing evocative melodies near the Horizon, somewhere beyond the tall Eucalyptus trees at night, through which the Moon peeped and the sky looked silver, and behind which the flute player played. The fragrance of *madhu malti* drifted in from the Window.

Lauren would love it, he was sure. But she wouldn't live here. If home it was he wanted, he would have to be bereft of it. But isn't home where the heart is. Her exceedingly good looks flashed, her dazzling smile, with two perfectly pointed teeth at the corners, amongst fields and fields of snow - everything covered with snow, as far as the eye could see, it had made her complexion sparkle, she had looked so pure.

But he had left all that behind. He had his social contracts. His obligations as an Indian family man, with the weight of the world on his shoulders. He had come home to do right and to be good. And now he had met Aparna and that had changed everything.

Work, management, factories was not what he was all about. At least not all of him. Or at least not only. He enjoyed it though it was very time consuming.

The India of Stephania seemed to recede, become more and more elusive, as time passed.

Was he still evolving, developing to his full potential, he ruminated. He was Ashok, quite a guy about town. Was he still being true to that? And now Aparna had gone, he thought. When would she return? Would she return? Should he go to the States to continue the courtship, or was he just chasing mirages - *mrig-trishna*? Did they have a future? They had been happy together here. And when he was with her the pain of not being with her, of missing out got taken care of. He was lucky that she had responded.

The proximity of girls had given him a high in High School. Add to that fantasy, imagination and many things had led to pleasure. Girls from a neighbouring school would come not only for Socials - even strict Convent education had such institutions but their Physics Lab was not as well equipped.

Sometimes they would be paired in Practicals with Ashok and other boys. In one such experiment air had to be sucked through rubber tubes in turn, immersed in a flask of water. His partner was a divine creature with a high skirt. They did it in turns. He noticed the mouth of the tube still wet after her turn was over.

College too had been get-togethers everyday. Sometimes there would be a couple on an evening and driving around was still pleasant. And he always went in with the attitude that he would meet a fascinating stranger. There were many girls waiting to be asked to dance and sometimes he would cut in. It was easy to meet new people and go out with them. Even the guys didn't talk about work but the latest Bob Dylan or Joan Baez song and its lyrics and the latest edition of Encounter or a critique of Colin Wilson's Outsider. Everybody knew Camus'.

What was happening now to the ease with which one met people of one's ilk? Where were those intriguing creatures that he would come across at parties? It had been automatic - taken for granted by him. One met people not just in class or in the corridors of College, in the College Café, in the University Coffee House just a little way down the gate of the College behind the hostels, in the Shakespeare Society auditions, Dramatic Society readings in College, there were various other active societies in College ranging from cinema, photography and debating to hiking and mountain climbing. Then there were university level Societies like Celluloid - screening films from France like Pierrot le Fou, A Bout de Souffle, Un feu Follet, Un Homme et Une Femme and then Czechoslovakia like Closely Watched Trains, Shop on Main Street, Taking Off from Directors like Milos Forman, Jiri Menzel and a host of other brilliant and creative ones. There were readings and auditions for plays at Miranda House, Yatrik, Little Theatre Group, Youth of India. One met people after meeting whom one couldn't sleep at night, full of ideas and idealism - effortlessly, automatically. This led to invitations to more parties and Sunday morning Jam sessions where one met more people.

This world of Camus and Sartre, of Existentialism and wonderment where incredible music came out everyday, which blew your mind, (with or without a joint), was the real world. How could there be so much creativity, so many sweet melodies, such lyrics from so many different groups pouring out over a relatively short and intense time span? Mireille Methieu, Francoise Hardy, Cliff Richards and the Shadows, Herman's Hermits, Pink Floyd, The Small Faces, Elton John, Buddy Holly, The Rascals, The Loving Spoonful, Joan Baez, Dylan, The Mamas and the Papas, Carole King, Carly Simon - it was a continuum.

If he stayed he would die of lack of fulfilment, if he went away, he would die of guilt. He loved Europe but he loved India too. He missed Lauren but thought Indian girls the most beautiful. They were celebrated for their beauty.

If he fell in love, nothing else would matter. But the party scene had changed, or he was out of it. Somehow, every evening out, every party wasn't an energy field of unlimited potential. Had it been limited to that all too brief period in College? Was it because he had gone away and lost touch or was it because everyone had moved away, in pursuit of their development, their evolution? That was ridiculous. Déjà vu is also a state of mind.

Only a few years had passed. It was no longer automatic. Was it that the Times they were a Changin' yet again? He no longer came across the same sort of people effortlessly. The invitations to parties got fewer and fewer. Everybody but everybody it seemed was going for further studies, to the UK or North America or Western Europe. It was time to be out and to be doing bigger and better things in the journey that still stretched ahead. In professional life, in government offices, in the day to day world of business, he didn't come across people that he could relate to culturally. This included women. Where had everybody gone?

Into this world whence came Aparna, it was a breath of fresh air and a reminder of things lost. He phoned her and wrote to her. Her plans were uncertain. She had her creative work with a group of top notch designers, with whom it had been possible thus far to come to India for a long visit every year. The family had managed to buy their own home, with a comfortable mortgage stretching out over 30 years. She wasn't sure she wanted to re-settle in India. Her immediate family was all in America now. There were day to day hassles in India and the daily petty corruption, which was hard to accept. Buying a place to live, was getting to be unbelievably expensive. Prices matched those of New York and Paris. There was the charm of India, its uniqueness, how at home she felt here. But a house to settle down in was a factor that could not be overlooked. She could not afford to buy one at the prices ruling now.

And who would she come back for? There were her childhood memories. This was where she had grown up. But that wasn't enough. There was no one specific to return for. (There is me thought Ashok. But he would have to be clear that he was ready to make a commitment.)

Did this involve another trip? This one was Indian at least. That in itself was a miracle. And greater acceptance from his parents, though she wasn't from his state or class.

The old restlessness again began its osmotic process. Was it that he missed Europe and all that it had to offer on its smorgasbord, culturally? As if to compound his doubts, about his sense of who he was and what he wanted from life on the one hand and what his parents expected of him on the other hand, he got a letter unexpectedly from Barbara, in Polish he could understand. He remembered her dark hair, her sensuality, the promise contained in their kiss when it had happened.

There had been strong attraction between them. The sensuous tango between them had accelerated into something highly erotic. That is why their kissing had been so full of promise. That is why they hadn't been able to disengage. Maybe it had just needed more of a chance, to develop, to grow. What constituted the romance between two people could not be dissected into logical components or analysed.

Someone to live for, to care passionately and intensely about was the touchstone of his existence. And he needed to keep meeting people, interaction with whom would stimulate him, give him different ways of looking at the world, whose wit and humour he could enjoy. There were other things that were very important, living a life replete with dancing and music, cinema and theatre, literature and ideas, things that had filled his life and that gave him a sense of reality, to the extent that anyone can have that.

Not that these things had vanished from Delhi but the people to enjoy them with, the ones he knew, seemed to have all gone to points West. And though he had enjoyed these things in Delhi, the variety, the choices seemed more in the large cities of the West. Other people of his ilk must be around in the city, but it was hard to meet them. Should he again follow his heart and follow Aparna to the Bay Area and see where it took them? Live life once again in the 'real' world, like he had in St Stephen's. He couldn't go back in time and the three years in college had passed criminally fast. Before he knew it, it was over. He was on a high and suddenly everything had scattered in the four winds.

But before he could make plans for the Bay Area, she came

back to the Mughal city of Delhi. It was a short visit this time of about a month, she said.

She was devastatingly attractive. He felt the familiar twinge. What was he thinking about. He should settle down with this girl. Thank goodness, he was self-employed he mused and had been working so hard. It made his work times flexible. He couldn't concentrate anyway. It would have to do without him. That's the whole idea of a well oiled machine. It can function without him. Management systems are in place. He started spending all his time with her and life became a grand sweet song. One month stretched to two and then to three. But no more extensions she said smiling one day. She could not stay here endlessly.

Could his and Aparna's feelings, passion for each other, be ignited, catch fire, as much as it had between him and Lauren. One could be very attracted to diverse shades and hues of personae. That was part of the richness and complexity of human interaction. It could not even be measured in happiness.

If there was any city he could live in, in India, it was Delhi - the city of his birth, the city of his childhood memories, the city that he loved *malgre tout*. And out of all the metros, the mountains were the most accessible from Delhi. He adored the mysticism of the Himalayas, their untamed unkempt nature, their vastness but he couldn't live there full time. He would miss meeting people and the cultural events that was possible only in urban life. He loved Bombay too, but found its temperatures more or less the same throughout the year. He did see *Bombaywallahs* with shawls end December and that amazed him. He liked Delhi's changing seasons.

Doubts came up about India. There were so many things he wished for it. His expectations were high, he loved his country and wanted it to be perfect. He was bothered by the crudeness of many people, a large section of society in Delhi, the way they talked, the rough language they used, the way they behaved, the generally lewd attitude, the constant and open scratching of their testicles (which invariably seemed more prickly in their case) the intolerance towards something that was considered normal in most of the rest of the world, the attitude towards boy and girl closeness in public. And worse, the manner in which these objections were expressed. Particularly when he'd be dating a foreign girl. A waiter at the Delhi Gymkhana Club kept staring at them each time and when Ashok finally accosted him, he said he had almost succeeded in catching him "red handed"! Cops considered it immoral to be seen walking in the company of a girl in the moonlight, on the lawns of India Gate and would want bribes not to harass them.

In crowded areas like the shops in Connaught Place, he would have to be extra careful. There would be the sleazy types trying to touch girls improperly. Why were so many people in his country sexually frustrated? What kind of hypocrisy was this? Wanting unbelievable moral standards, which were impractical and not even desirable, being impossibly preachy which led to this kind of debasement.

But the plusses far outweighed the minuses and most of the time he didn't think he had taken the wrong decision, no matter how much he enjoyed and loved Europe.

Aparna like Lauren was an excellent dancer. All 3 of them had this in common, though Aparna wouldn't dance on tabletops like Lauren had in Poland. Ashok took her dancing to the French restaurant on top of the Taj and she just glided over the floor and her movements in the fast dances made Ashok want to do the same. With her too he felt he could have danced all night.

Aparna and Ashok began to hold hands in movies and half the time he found himself looking at her and her long slender swan like neck and lovely complexion, her captivating eyes. Once he turned sideways, they were seated in the left section of the India International Centre auditorium and they kissed in the dark. There did not seem to be anyone behind them or next to them though the central section was full. Most of the movie they kissed though they could hear and feel the movie going on. When they went out to eat and the meals took long, their silences were comfortable. She was a vegetarian despite living in California and he enjoyed Tandoori dishes, Kashmiri food, European food, most of which was non-vegetarian. But in her presence he didn't feel the need for meat. India was the best place for it. There was immense variety in vegetarian food and in food from different states. It boggled the minds of foreigners who were unexposed to vegetarian food and thought of it as boiled vegetables on the side, which had to be eaten as a balance to the meat.

It was very pleasant being with her and time just flew. They laughed a lot. Her college contemporaries from the time she had been in LSR often came over. There was a constant trickle in and out. They were all extremely pretty, but how could so many be so good looking? They smiled, they teased in that inimitable manner, most of them had their boyfriends, but it was a pleasure just to be with them and look at them.

He even found himself watching Hindi movies with them - cosily at their homes on video or on the large screen and laughing uproariously at their unbelievable silliness, which was almost a caricature. What was happening to him? The Shastras always said that one is affected by the company one keeps and extolled the virtues of *satsang* - good company that led to lofty thoughts.

There may not be a large enough common denominator with Aparna vis a vis the same intellectual and cultural pursuits but would he be happier with someone having much greater affinity - a sexy specs-wearing silk stocking? It worked differently somehow. Attraction was a very complex thing and who could attempt to understand it, leave alone dissect or analyse it.

Attraction didn't always last but who knew the quadratic equation for long term happiness.

There was no doubt about the strong pull he felt towards Aparna. When he was with her, or when he was away from her. He recalled vividly the inexplicable sharp pain and longing that he had experienced when he had just seen her for the first time at that party. He couldn't let this girl out of his life. Now was the time to take the plunge. There were no guarantees, no insurances about commitment. Matters of the heart were just that - matters of the heart. But assurance of any sort was never what he had looked for. Better to have loved and lost, than not to have loved at all.

Was this it? Did one ever really know? Sometimes one did.

The month of May had the beauty of intense heat. Hard to convey to someone who hadn't experienced it. It wasn't just the early mornings with their summer freshness and the fragrance of freshly awake flowers, or the cool evenings with the lengthening shadows and a myriad sounds and smells. The long days, dark and cool inside the high ceilinged shaded inner rooms. Lights would have to be put on when it was so bright outside. The verandahs would be covered with *chiks* - thin bamboo stick curtains covered with dark blue cloth to keep out the heat and the white light. Days which stretched out ahead and where as children they had invented stories and enacted plays - of kings and queens and gods and demons, which slowly evolved into more erotic thoughts as adolescence came and interests became more teenager-ish. The *Gulmohars*, the *Amaltas* were ablaze in the city. There were fluffs of cotton from the Silk Cotton, scattered on the grass. It reminded him of the Stones - 'Dandelion, I tell no lies, Dandelion, you make me wise...' It was a riot of amazing colours, the city was as intensely pretty as it was hot. And the nights were cool with moonlight and *raat ki rani*. The fragrance of night jasmine and other summer flowers was everywhere. But he had always liked this extreme summer - from his Tom Brown school days, with their loads of homework, caning and tough guys. It always had the connotation of long summer holidays stretching endlessly ahead, of swimming and Alphonso mangoes, followed by other delicious varieties, of lychees, plums, cherries - fruits in the summer from the hills, of parties and dances and summer romances, of movies in cool airconditioned halls in the middle of a blazing afternoon. He remembered the comics of childhood - Bonanza, Davy Crockett, Roy Rogers, Kansas Kid, Wagon Train, Maverick, Gene Autry, Buffalo Bill, Beetle Bailey, Beep Beep the Road Runner, Unca Scrooge, Thirteen Going on Eighteen, Superman - read late on the 'Sail Along the Silvery Moon' summer nights and sleeping under the stars in the garden or terrace, inside cosy mosquito nets.

The symphony built up to a crescendo of feeling. It was the first time that anything remotely like this was happening during the three factory years in India *sans* Lauren, when most of the time all he did was work

Some early May nights it could actually be cool. He remembered a Delhi girl he used to go out with a lot earlier. She would actually feel cold when walking with him on the cool green dew laden grass.

The India gate lawns were like a College fete - ice cream vendors, balloon guys, a bright moon lighting up the trees and the walks below them, the air filled with fragrant flower necklaces on sale to be tied onto the girl's hair or to be put next to her pillow or in front of the air-conditioner. As he drove off with Aparna there was a smiling girl being bought ice cream by her beau. The image stuck in his head.

It was building up to full moon. These summer nights could be so bright - an owl could spot a mouse running across the lawn. Ashok and Aparna risked Delhi's bad characters and found themselves walking in Lodhi Gardens at night around the sleeping white ducks in the pond and the monuments of long ago transporting them unmistakably to another time with its echoes and shadows.

What was it about these monuments that transported one to another time as if in a Time machine, with the romance intact, he mused.

In the days that followed their kisses grew very deep. Very intense. He tasted her throat. Their mouths got clamped together in wide circles. He loved kissing. There was no greater intimacy. It was so personal. They kissed in different ways, in an infinite variety of sucking, blowing, pushes and pulls. He gently caressed her upper lip, the corners of her mouth with his. They kissed close lipped. The kisses grew passionate, of changing intensity and face positions. They kissed gently for half an hour. Time lost its dimension. Their identities seemed to merge. In *Tantra*, they say, through union with another human being one becomes aware of one's inseparability with the rest of the world as C S Lewis experienced on his balcony. Joseph Campbell talked about this being one with the rest of the world as did the Transcendentalists of New England like Emerson. Thoreau wrote poems and prose on this next to Walden Pond.

Aparna was playful. She was like that spontaneously. Sometimes with some people it touched flirtatiousness. Ashok felt terribly attracted to this trait in her, even when he was just the observer.

Unlike Lauren she would settle down here in India but was

she *the* one for him? Would she agree to be his partner? No one kisses like that unless they are ready to give themselves. But these maddening creatures are so complex, he said aloud. You can't really tell how another person is thinking, *surtout* a girl.

His hand slid behind the garment on her back a loose fitting blue *salwar* which suited her well. Often she wore saris but she looked even younger in a *salwar kameez*. His hand felt the smoothness of her skin as it moved around her back. He felt the electricity. She felt the shocks too, he could see. He closed his eyes. He daringly undid the clasp of her bra. He wanted unfettered movement along her back - the slip and slide. His hand didn't move towards the front. He didn't want to go too far. He didn't need to go anywhere. Just sliding along her back - he could do all afternoon.

The month passed like whirlwind. He went to office but he felt in a daze. 'Dizzy, my head is turnin'… I'm so dizzy" came over the radio. He acted on important things but his mind was always with Aparna. She extended her stay by another 15 days.

He told his parents that he might get affianced to this girl. They were relieved that she was Indian, at least. They had seen her around. She was very pretty. Her complexion was smooth, very light, golden. But was she religious enough, traditional enough? They ignored the culture of their son and wanted someone like themselves. And what about the class difference? She was middle class, not from an Industrial family.

Her extended time was up and she was leaving the next day. They were lost in their feelings.

67

Neeru had started coming in and out of the parental home regularly, thanks to Ashok's initiative. When Brij and Radhika worried about the business or the family, Neeru was back as a support. She felt much better not being estranged from them. But Ashok sensed over time a heaviness coming over her.

"What is it?" he asked one day.

"Vikram's roving eye has increased with the passage of time.

He still seems attracted to me but now I wonder if I am enough. He might be starting an affair and then what will I do?" she whispered

"Maybe I should have gone by the judgement of our parents after all."

"There is nothing to say that this would not happen with a boy carefully selected by them, Neeru. There are no guarantees whether it's a love marriage or an arranged one."

"They would choose to the best of their ability. Someone appealing, suitable..."

"But how relationships work out over the long run, who can say, Neeru?"

"At least I would not have had to make so many adjustments in my life style. I don't say this to anyone else, Ashok. And certainly not to the parents. I try not to even think it."

68

Lauren had already been gaining recognition as an accomplished Harp player. And she felt comfortable enough to be inventive in her interpretations. Lauren continued to really miss Ashok, despite herself. This longing got sublimated into further creativity. She found herself writing music. In her Studio, it just happened. More tentatively at first and then as she liked it and it sounded good, she tested it on her colleagues. She began to try her hand at that whenever the inspiration struck her. A visiting Mexican painter at the very centrally located Club of Three Continents loved it. Here was praise from an artiste belonging to a different genre. Janek, the organiser of the Club, asked her to test her nascent oeuvre here every now and then.

And then the unexpected happened. Destiny or fortune took a hand. Relations between India and the Socialist countries had always been close. A group from Warsaw was going on a tour of India and Japan. She was asked to join the group. In Poland you did not pass up chances like that. It would be good for her career, for her CV.

One early morning she woke up and "She's leaving Home"

of the Beatles went through her head. She loved that whole album so much. Her line was classical music, but it was impossible not to love this Music and be moved by it. She had heard it on the radio. She would acquire some of these albums on her trip. She would save it out of her daily Dollar allowance, if required. Have a glass of cold milk, instead of dinner, some days.

Everyone was very excited, full of anticipation. Foreign travel was very difficult. Only a few lucky ones got the chance. That too outside the Socialist bloc. Japan was a developed country, the First World. This was the Second World. It would be so interesting, so different, unique. There were restaurants, they had heard, which only played particular composers. The Japanese were so good at Western music. There were restaurants each with its own atmosphere - which played only Chopin, only Bach, only Mozart, only Handel.

The restaurant would have a special shape, be brightly lit like a Japanese Lantern, with golden light coming from it. The large windows, variants of bay windows, would resemble stained glass from a church. The food inside would be Japanese, aesthetically and colourfully set in tiny plates, cups, in trays, she imagined. But the music would be so good and of that particular Composer only. His repertoire would be enough to give the variety. She had come across so many very good Japanese musicians playing. They had their traditional finesse, technical competence combined with such feeling for the music. How come they were so far away, had such a unique culture and were so good at it.

These images would stick in her head, even if the reality turned out different, as it often does.

They were to play in Tokyo, Kyoto and Nara, the tourist and cultural centres. Originally, Osaka too had been included but the tour was getting too ambitious and there were obligations at home.

In India it was to be in Bombay and Delhi and on demand from fraternal socialist states in India in Calcutta and Trivandrum. Agartala was considered too remote to be practical. Calcutta had slowly been losing its cultural prominence of the early 60's to Bombay and to Delhi, a decade later. But in the end, Bombay had been dropped and three cities retained in each country.

Japan blew her mind and that of the whole Polish group. It was green and pretty, temperate like Europe. It was highly developed and technologically advanced, more than anything she had come across or imagined. Yet it was picturesque in a way that was unique. This was clearly the East, distinctly Asia. The people seemed to belong to another planet. She didn't think they were this polite in the rest of the East. Even in trains, in each compartment before exiting, the lady checking the tickets would turn around and bow, whether anyone was looking or not.

The business suit felt like a uniform for everyone. Dark suit, colourful matching tie in the case of men, light shirt Lauren herself knowing little of business, imagined herself going around briskly in a suit, carrying a briefcase and generally being busy and pre-occupied in that particular way. In this place she felt like getting up and working, doing Business. There were huge department stores and tall, very tall skyscrapers everywhere in the cities. It was a country doing business. No wonder it was right up there with America, in being one of the largest economies in the world. The trains were the best in the world. Even the French ones couldn't be so good.

The signs everywhere were in Japanese. It was strange not to see the Roman script she took for granted in Poland. No one spoke anything but Japanese. But that was how it was in

Poland, she realised with a start. How did foreigners manage? What foreigners? The odd third world students had to learn it in Language School in Lodz anyway. At least here people connected with looking after international visitors could speak some English, some French.

Her group went to a tea ceremony. *Herbata* in a glass was popular in Poland, an auburn coloured liquid with a tea bag, lemon and sugar. More so than in Western Europe where coffee seemed to be the norm and tea an aberration. But here it acquired another dimension. It was a spiritual, meditative experience. They went to a tea house in a Park. Through the large, open windows, everywhere they could see the green of the park. The tea house was on stilts on a lake. There were the calm ripples of the water and startlingly white ducks adding to the serenity. It was open, bright and airy. It was the House of Four Winds. Shoes had to be taken off outside. There were low tables, next to mats on the floor. A tray appeared, tastefully arranged like in a flower arrangement. This was a small island with a high population density. The emphasis was on small, like in a flower arrangement or a small but well crafted zen garden. The musicians took sips of tea and looked contemplatively outside. The ritual took an hour.

They visited another zen garden. The layout, the plants, the rocks, the use of space gave rise to different moods. It was delicate, aesthetic. She felt like sitting on a rock near a small pond with overgrown hedges and meditate. She hadn't ever been initiated into meditation. Only heard about it from Ashok and in the context of the Beatles and the Maharishi. The word zen came from Sanskrit *'dhyan'* - to meditate, she was told. The Japanese couldn't pronounce it the same way and in its passage to Japan through China, this is what it had become.

Lauren found out that there was a museum dedicated

to Subhash Chandra Bose. She decided to visit it. It was a connection with Ashok. It started on the 5th floor. Strange how many things in Japan, started on upper floors, even lobbies of certain hotels.

One night for the foreign guests was planned in a *Ryokan*, a traditional Japanese Inn. It overlooked a scenic golf course, with particularly shaped trees, standing by themselves, windswept, like characters out of a Noh play. The entire side of the room facing it was a window framing it. There was a sliding partition cordoning off the sleeping area of the large room.

There were comfortable looking mattresses on the wooden floor, which was a few steps above the other section of the room. Lauren felt like snuggling into them right away. A portion of it had to be unzipped. Technology was never far away in even the most traditional aspects of Japanese life. When she finally did get into her bed and went "aah, nice to be in my bed" she witnessed a night blue sky outside with the stars sparkling over the typically Japanese trees, standing like sentinels, over the vast green course. Lauren was charmed by Japan, by the gentleness, softness of its people. How polite they were to each other and to everyone. What an introduction to the East.

There was an outdoor natural hot water spring in the spa. The water was full of minerals. There were steps leading down to it. The musicians went just before dinner. It was quite cold outside and they shivered on the way to it but the water was pleasantly warm. There were separate sections for men and women. Bathing was nude. A low wall in the water divided the sections. The men could hear the women laughing and shrieking on the other side of the wall.

Marek's letters came regularly poste-restante. They gave her news of Poland, of their friends, of the latest happenings on the cultural and social scene. He shared his thoughts, his emotions. She always found them interesting.

When she was in the *Ryokan*, he proposed to her, in a letter. He followed it up with a telegram. She could hear her family's voices. What was holding her back, she was comfortable with him. Was she not ready for marriage, was it her age?

At some places in the spring, the water felt quite hot. She felt it against her naked breasts, as if someone was caressing them. An unknown lover - a handsome stranger. Her back slumped. One day she would be back with the right guy. Was Marek he? Ashok had charm, a something very special. Or was she imagining it? Romanticizing? Projecting? Anyway that had finished. And Marek was there. And he wouldn't be forever. He was popular and there were those waiting in the wings.

If only her family would not put pressure, however well-intentioned. She could breathe, she could think. She could decide for herself, come face to face with her real feelings, without any need for rebellion, for holding her own.

Lauren stopped thinking. She let herself relax. Let the natural spring water, soothe her, nourish her, every part of her body. She put her head down under it. Could she still stay under it as long as she used to? She floated on it. Looked up and saw the stars in the Japanese sky. A celestial ensemble playing a celestial symphony.

The door to the dining room slid open. There were a number of low tables set at suitable distances. Lauren sat cross-legged before the one she was ushered to. The dinner tray was a work of art. Red, green, yellow, orange, multi colours in different hues. All perfectly balanced. A visual feast. One could just sit there and look at it. There were many small dishes, with dainty, delicate sauces and accompaniments. The quantities were small, different kinds of fish and vegetables, *sushi* and *sashimi*. No wonder the Japanese were so healthy and long lived.

With a sigh of contentment she decided to read a bit in her room before retiring. There were two levels to it. The second level was slightly raised. She left the indoor soft slip-ons she had padded about in the hotel at the lower level and climbed on to the other level. There had been a large oval shaped table on the floor with a dainty small Japanese tea set with tea accompaniments to sample, earlier in the evening. She had sipped it appreciatively and felt soothed. That had now been cleared. Beyond that, cosy sleeping mattresses had been laid out on the floor. Sliding screens with delicate designs could be used to section off the sleeping area. A very large oval shaped window overlooked a vast golf course with Japanese trees bent and shaped as if in a parable. Beyond, rushed a brook, in the distance. Woe betide the golfer that landed a ball in it. The stars were still shining bright.

A super fast train, a pre-cursor to the bullet train, took them to their new destination. It was already happening. The fastest and the most advanced trains were under development here. Whilst the musicians waited for their train, another train whizzed past them at the station, like a bolt of lightning. They saw it and it was gone. They had never seen anything like it.

Kyoto was on a different scale. In Tokyo there were skyscrapers everywhere and one could not help but feel the dominance of business. That Japan was one of the largest economies in the world was self evident in Tokyo. And the culture and history of Japan more apparent, not so destroyed by the Americans in the Second World War.

Inspired, they all played really well. Became one with their music. And the audience, knowledgeable and with an ability to appreciate both virtuosity and technical correctness, responded with passion. Lauren felt acknowledged.

The smaller the place got the stronger its surviving historical and cultural identity. Nara was even more like that. Once again the inspired musicians responded in kind.

What would India be like? It also held a special connection for her. It was also Asia. It was the same continent. Buddhism and to that extent at least, the Japanese ethos had come from India.

Was she ready for the next step?

The last few days in Japan just flew by. The temples and shrines, the winding steps leading up to them, the museums, monuments, the especially designed walks and serene parks left a strong impression but also merged into one another and became a blur.

Lauren with her thoughts flew into the clouds and looked down at the milky white ocean below, with a clearly delineated deep blue sky above. Was the sky always above everything on Earth?

69

The order of Japan gave way to the chaos of India. Lauren, like many an intrepid visitor before her, was overwhelmed at first. Was this where so many things had come from? This anarchy which seemed to function. She landed in Calcutta, the land of Tagore, Ravi Shankar and Satyajit Ray, fine music, literature, the arts. There were many skyscrapers, which surprised her. She hadn't expected that. The city had a very strong character, which she very soon liked.

An interaction had been organised for the musicians to meet some of the people connected with the Arts in the city. Lauren thought she got glimpses of Ashok as she talked to some. She would see him soon enough now. Their contact had become more and more infrequent, even more so of late. What would it be like? She had written to him that she was coming. She still had his visiting card. She hoped the phone number was still valid. Otherwise there was bound to be a Directory enquiry.

She was taken in something called Indian Airlines to Kerala. She was charmed by the air-hostesses in their saris. So gracious, the saris so colourful, with intricate designs. Everybody was so gentle. This was the East. And the women were so delicate, refined.

The venue in Kerala had been shifted to Fort Cochin - the gateway to the extraordinary and unique Backwaters of Kerala, as well as the hills of Munnar. Cosmopolitan. Lauren sensed the difference in latitude, as she landed. It was more tropical. There were swaying trees, coconut, cashew plantations, the sun was brighter. Yet there was a gentleness to it. It was different from Calcutta, yet there was a commonality, an Indianness to it.

She wandered the streets of Cochin, the Jewish quarter, the Synagogue, the one and a half streets of antique shops. Fort Cochin had a relaxed, tranquil feel to it. She sipped tea in one of the wide verandahed gleaming white stucco hotels there. The musicians were taken on a short tour of the backwaters for half a day the next morning, an introduction. She would come back one day on her own, when she would earn enough recognition and money as a musician.

Lauren and her thoughts entered a Houseboat - a rice boat which had been converted into visitor accommodation, with a shaded front deck portion. This had lounging chairs with side tables up front and a small dining table and chairs at the back. Behind this was a bedroom with a large bed and cabin views on to the water. One could sit on the front deck and look out onto the river stretching till the horizon, part of an inter-connected network of waterways, with green paddy fields on either side always visible, except when the boat was on Wayanad lake or one of the smaller lakes. Some of the waterways were quite narrow, with small, neat, interesting looking houses right next to them. Some of them were huts which looked clean and ecologically sound. Built for the environment. People spent a night or two or sometimes more on these boats depending on how much they went into the interior and how fancy the boat was. She had seen pictures of the houseboats in Kashmir but these seemed quite different.

The other musicians in the entourage had no special connection with India. They would play, perform, sight-see, shop for textiles, handicrafts, antiques - depending on their budgets and go back with vivid memories of their trip to India. But she - what of her. There was no future with Ashok. He had left. But she couldn't get him out of her system. And maybe there was a reluctance to let go of an unexpectedly pleasant past. He had a *je ne sais quoi*.

Was she projecting, romanticising, she wondered. Imbuing him with qualities he did not necessarily have. This quest for perfection we seek, especially in a loved one. This idealisation. Why was Marek not enough for her?

The Communism in Bengal and Kerala felt different from that of Poland. She did not sense the same areas of circumscription - the State would leave you uninterfered with, if you did not enter the political domain, in terms of dissent, criticism or competition in any form to the ruling party. But here she did not sense that. Why was that? Was it that it was democratically elected? Was it that it was within the larger framework of a federal state, which was not Communist? It was incredibly difficult to travel outside Poland. This may have been one of the reasons, the Party created so many demands to be fulfilled. Exposure led to education of a certain sort.

A letter arrived from Marek, breaking into her reverie. It had large, colourful, well chosen stamps from the shores of Polska. She loved it still. She had grown up there. It was in her very being. She had a lively group of friends interested in the arts who had that ability to laugh at themselves. She was comfortable with Marek. She was happy with her music and her career was progressing.

She saw so many groups of Americans and Europeans. These

ones were not comfortable stepping outside their comfort zone, even to travel alone, in a different culture. And those travelling alone would be quick to strike up conversations with others looking like them.

70

Serendipity had her sitting next to a classical musician on the 2½ hour flight to Delhi. He was a Veena player, the instrument of Saraswati, the goddess of learning. She had seen a superb painting of her in a temple. She was sitting on a swan, in a tranquil, blissfully serene lake, with a slanting Veena and her fingers on the strings. Would even Man Sarovar, that Ashok had told her about - the abode of celestial swans, lotuses and Shiva, next to Mount Kailash - now in Tibet, be as serene as this? There were Lotuses next to her. She was wearing a delicate, pure white sari, she had refined features and a pink complexion. She had bowed her head and felt at peace in front of it.

She had seen another beautiful painting, evocative of Nal-Damayanti in Calcutta. An unbelievably graceful looking Damayanti, with delicate features, dressed in an ephemeral white sari was talking to the swan, the harbinger of tidings of her beloved. The Veena player narrated the story. She wished she could re-unite them, as he narrated the saga.

When he learnt that she too was a musician, he explained to her some of the theory and practice of Indian Classical music.

How mathematical, intricate and complex the music was with its ¼ notes and ½ notes and a completely different logic from that of Western Classical. It opened up a new way of thinking. She was fascinated. Would she have time to learn it? It took years and years of practice - 8 hours a day, to reach any level. Idle thoughts.

She was put up in India International Centre, next to Lodhi Gardens. She was to perform at their auditorium. She woke up very early next morning. Decided to go for a walk in the Gardens. There were just some hues of red and orange visible in the sky. The sun was not yet over the horizon. Even the early morning walkers had not yet come.

She felt the freshness of the air, the fragrance of the night flowers was still there. She took off her slip-ons. She touched the dew on the grass, felt it under the soles of her feet. She walked on the cool moist grass. Barefoot in the Park. She had an impulse to run on it. She did. If she could have taken off her clothes she would have. She didn't feel safe enough to follow that impulse.

She reached the ancient pre-Mughal Lodhi monuments, silhouetted against the ever lightening sky. The atmosphere of long ago was palpable. One could reach out and touch it. The perception of it was so different. A different time, a different Continent. She felt like reading the history of pre-Mughal Muslim India. The invading Turks, Persians and Central Asians in pursuit of the fabulous riches and treasures of India. She thought she heard the faint sound of long ago voices, of stories being told, of *Talismans* and gorgeous women. A gust of fresh air came through one of the arches. Dawn had truly come. She was in one of the smaller monuments.

She had been reading Ruth Prawer Jhabvala's stories. They were apt. She could see where the atmosphere and the characters came from. She had felt drawn to Ashok. He would be like one of the charming, olive-complexioned young men in the stories. She imagined him appearing out of one of the monuments just then.

Her thoughts darted to Marek. He would have loved it here too. Maybe they would come here together one day. No longer the impoverished artistes, no longer as young.

And then she thought she saw Ashok, or somebody who had a profile just like his entering a monument across the field. Was her imagination playing tricks? She ran to it. She saw a pleasant looking old gentleman just outside, with a walking stick. Had he seen a young man just entering the relict? He seemed charmed by her accent in English and the freshness of her manner. He smiled and shook his head but assured her that he would keep a lookout for him.

Could she imagine living in India? She loved it. But what would it be like living long term? The people were so friendly, gentle. The culture seemed very rich. Ancient it clearly was. She had not even touched the tip of its famed spirituality. She could have fun too. There were 14 discotheques in Delhi. She loved dancing. That was something she had in common with Ashok. Marek too enjoyed it but he wouldn't get into it, the way Ashok would lose himself. Dance like no one is watching. Or everyone is. And the textiles, the silks and cottons, the Cashmere and Pashmina shawls, the richness and variety of colours, texture, fabrics. She hadn't even had time or opportunity to go deeper into these. She and Ashok both loved clothes. She could conceive visiting for a long time, even 3-4 months.

She had gone to Cottage Industries, looked at some of the pretty things, many of them she could not afford. It was a pleasure to feel the silks and the pashmina. She bought a silk scarf of a delicate violet hue. On the way back on Curzon

Road, approaching India Gate, a young man sitting at the back of a scooter turned around to look at her as it sped off in the opposite direction. This time she was sure it was Ashok. It was his profile. She wasn't seeing ghosts.

71

So she was in Delhi, this was it. After a moment's uncertainty she phoned him. A silence despite himself and then the young man quickly recovered his composure. "Good afternoon", said a familiar civilised welcoming voice, in an accent very close to English. She felt her heart warming to it and she gave a little laugh of recognition and pleasure. No, he hadn't been the young man on the scooter. The young man had even turned around, thought Lauren, but no it hadn't been him.

She ditched the official dinner. Ashok picked her up and literally whisked her off to Café Chinois, the rooftop restaurant on top of the Oberoi.

The dance floor was inviting, the music was so good that it made both of them want to drop everything and start dancing at once, where they were. When the music turned slower Ashok did not support her arm on his shoulder. He sometimes did this. It really caught the eye. It did not reduce the intimacy. But added a panache. It looked very sophisticated. As if they had always been doing this.

The band took a break. They stepped on to the terrace

stretching out on three sides of the restaurant. There was no one there. There were stars everywhere in the sky. In the distance the lights of Rajdoot Hotel, Jangpura and Bhogal glowed. They went to the edge of the terrace and looked into the distance - Sunder Nagar, Delhi Public School to one side, Humayun's Tomb in the middle, Nizamuddin after that. He looked at her and smiled. She smiled back. They kissed. It was Magic. There were no explanations. There were stars over her head. She felt like she was going to faint.

They stepped back inside. Ashok told her in India he wouldn't eat beef. It didn't feel ok. He would do it in Europe. She upbraided him in a proprietorial manner. We had decided about these things, she said conclusively, sort of also saying 'Don't be silly'. It had nothing to do with religion he felt, and the slight hesitation he felt in India had been summarily dismissed.

The band caught their mood. All the world loves a lover. The music was superb. Melodies faded into one another. 'I could have danced all night', she knew how Audrey Hepburn felt in *My Fair Lady*, a few years ago. When they went out into the terrace again, she sensed that Ashok felt on top of the world. They talked in an easy manner.

But she still felt dizzy from the kiss. She wanted them to kiss again. 'Please Don't Sleep in the Subway', 'Downtown', 'Now I've got Love going for me',..... Songs of their time together came through her head and she kissed him. This time they could not stop as their kiss grew bigger. They stood on the rooftop glued together, motionless, like statues. Time stood still. The only motion was that of the car lights below and the stars above. Neither of them knew how long they stayed there but when they came back to their corner table, the band was still playing and the restaurant was still open. She still felt dizzy and could sense that he did too. The future did not matter. She felt happy in the moment, like the *rishis* of India. Swami Ram of the Himalayas!

Ashok was very passionate. He needed someone equally passionate. Lauren was that. They both knew it. Lauren had noticed that kissing was a very big deal for Indians. The excitement it produces for them. In Bombay movies it was a big no-no. It was a cultural thing, this allowing oneself to feel and express wild passion, even when the context was of being very much in love. But it hadn't been like that in the days of the *Kama Sutra*.

They were passing the Golf Course on the Golf Links road. The wire fence was broken at one point near the bend. Ashok stopped the car and they slipped into the course. There was a thicket of shrubs, bushes and trees. Ahead lay the course around the 10th hole. They were overcome with passion. Everything happened in silence and while they were standing. She leaned against a tree trunk. There was sweat on her back and his forehead and upper lip. It was very intense. Not a word was exchanged. The only sounds were the involuntary ones of their love-making.

On the way home, they chatted about the books they were reading. She had just finished reading *The Art of Loving* by Erich Fromm. She had found it very good. He had the book, had loved it. There was the sweet smell of the night flowers of Delhi, on the now deserted streets, as they drove back. He didn't take her to the IIC straight away. They went on the charming, winding road between Golf Links and the Golf Club and then on Embassy row - Shanti Path. He drove into one of the inner lanes through the canopied road between two embassies. It was starting to rain. They went past the Embassy of Sweden, with the large blue and yellow striped flag, fluttering in the rain, in the foreground. The blue is for the sea she said, the yellow for blonde hair he added.

The next afternoon the sun shone golden. A friend of Ashok's in Kaka Nagar had on spools of black tapes of Grundig of excellent continuous analog music, quality songs from the early 60's and late 50's - "The breeze from the bayou keeps murmuring low... Tammy, Oh Tammy', 'A Summer Place', 'Everybody's somebody's fool'. They sat and listened. His friend took out some sweet smelling marijuana. "Somebody spoke and they went into a dream," he said quoting the Beatles song.

Everything seemed to be changing. They lay on some of the embroidered cushions in Ashok's room and listened to Hari Prasad Chaurasia whose flute was evocative of the vast dew laden plains with deer grazing on river banks and Mango trees with their wide canopies creating silhouettes in the night. Or Ravi Shankar with his sitar and its complicated Mathematics and improvisations producing sublime melodious serene music. The only thing missing was an innocent joint to transport them into transcendence. Something they could lie back on the cushions with and go up with the smoke. A movie called *Bobby* about young, innocent love had come out in Bollywood. Somebody had managed to get a Super 8 mm copy of it. One day they managed to catch on short wave the New Peking Orchestra. It really broke them up. 'No salt on her tail', 'Mr Tambourine Man', 'Blowin' in the Wind', 'Gotta get through another day', 'You're so vain', 'A Day in the Life', 'Sometimes you Win Sometimes You Lose', 'There's a Place', all came tumbling in, in no particular order...what was happening?

Lauren's emotional life had come full circle. Where was she to go from here? Maybe someone else had come into Ashok's life. Things could hardly remain at this point.

There was no time to talk. Just to be with each other.

72

The next day Ashok had one of the family drivers, a young lean faced driver from Uttar Pradesh. Lauren sat close to Ashok in the back of the old light blue Morris. The car was small and efficient. It wasn't intended to be a well maintained antique but was approaching that status. It was a stick shift which felt unusual at the time because most cars on the roads of Delhi had gears on the left side of the steering wheel and attached to it.

She wore a bright patterned dress which came high above her knees and provided an attractive contrast to her thighs held tightly together.

They drove out on Ring Road in the direction of the Yamuna bridge on one side and the University campus on the other. The Red fort appeared on the left. In Mughal times not so long ago the Yamuna touched its ramparts, thought Ashok wonderingly. And now it had wandered so many miles away. The sky had been rumbling for some time now. It grew very dark and then let loose.

The rain came down hard now. *Musaladhar varsha*, wrote the Puranas, the Mahabharata, referring to such sheets of rain.

The small car was getting drenched. The wipers could not keep up. It was pouring buckets. The car was being buffeted like a small boat out at sea.

The rain came down in torrents. The sky was darkness at noon. Ashok remembered being driven in the rain. The wipers worked furiously but were inadequate. They could not wipe the buckets pouring down from the heavens.

The sides and the back of the car were just sheets of water. It got extremely dark. The driver could just see ahead - barely. The driver was from a different culture. But he was discrete. Or maybe he really did not know what was going on. No interfering or uncomfortable vibrations emanated from him. The smell of the rain reminded Ashok of 'Listen to the Rhythm of the falling Rain' by the Cascades with its chiming beginning.

Ashok and Lauren kissed. It wasn't clear who had kissed whom. If it was Ashok, Lauren responded eagerly.

Leonard Cohen's 'the shoreline and the sea'. They seemed to be going to the ends of the earth. They sat close together in the centre of the seat, in the back of the small car. They kissed silently and melted into one. The car drove on and on, and the kiss went on and on. Ashok wished the moment would never end. The car seemed stuck in Time and Motion or on a steady roll. It was the same thing. It drove on Ring Road. It went on and on, in the rain, which was all enveloping. It drove into the horizon. The drive seemed unending. It went on and on, as they kissed. Time lost its dimension. They kissed as if they would die doing it and die without.

The kiss became deeper. Their mouths and cheeks merged. They could not stop. Their bodies remained jammed together

The rain was so strong around the small slate blue Morris car. It enveloped and enclosed it, shielding and protecting them from the outside world and any disturbance. It had a surreal quality to it. As if the car was going somewhere beyond the horizon and was standing still. This was it. There was nothing more he wanted. He would always remember this day, this moment. The future lay endless and full of promise. Nothing else mattered. 'Catch your dreams before they slip away' - hadn't one of his favourite people the Rolling Stones sung that?

The next afternoon they went to a couple of jewellery shops in Connaught Place and then in Tribhovandas Bhimji Zaveri on Janpath Ashok felt choked. He found something he liked. He slipped it on her finger. She really liked it. He wanted to give her something precious. It symbolised the preciousness of what they had shared.

Lauren too felt the same intensity. Could there really - in her heart of hearts, be anyone else for her either? She would have to work out her life as a Harp player, as a musician, her dreams of an idyllic life in Europe that only the very young can have, Marek and their expectations of each other... but could she really live without this guy? Life didn't mean anything without him.

Everything felt surreal. She had to return to Warsaw, sort out her Life. She was contract bound to return after the tour with the rest. Her Passport was also only for the duration of the visit.

She could not just stay back. She had come for a few days. Her visa was short term. She checked out of the IIC. She and Ashok followed the tour bus to the airport.

So whither from here? The old logjam remained. Ashok said he would come to Poland as soon as he could manage. Foreign travel and extracting himself from his work for any substantial length of time meant it couldn't be before a few months. They would take it from there. Neither of them knew more than that.

They looked at each other. There was no public display of affection on the tarmac. The days of fanatical security had not yet come. It was going to rain any moment. He looked so smart in his long raincoat, the belt wrapped around his slim body. She climbed on to the stairway and turned back just as she entered the plane to wave at him. The plane droned off into the horizon, as he stood there, with the moisture laden wind blowing his hair, a small forlorn figure, coming to terms with what had just happened. The plane sounded like a low last key of the piano struck and left to resonate. The final sound in the last track of Sergeant Pepper's! A fermata.

73

Ashok had to get things running on an even keel, so smoothly in fact that he could have a planned get away for some months. He needed at least that much time to sort out his love life. He had to work even harder than usual. Forget all else till then. Sort things out in his head and heart. Come to some sort of resolution on the practical issues for once and for all. The practical issues were not insurmountable in Aparna's case but matters of the heart were much more than that.

There were so many strands to running a manufacturing operation and marketing its products. It was a fine interwoven mesh. The work never stopped. There were always ends to be tied up, costs to be cut; too much inventory for example meant a higher than necessary inventory carrying cost, too little meant that the production process could get held up, which if anything was even more expensive. It was a 24 hour operation, 7 days a week, except for a maintenance shift on Sundays. He tried to implement the Japanese concept of JIT (Just In Time Inventory) but it was too fine tuned for Indian conditions. There were too many glitches. Standard Materials Management would have to do - EOQ (Economic Order

Quantity), Re-Order Level, etc. In maintenance, spare parts would have to be changed and noted in the register after their life as finalised by the Engineers was over, even if they seemed ok. Greasing, cleaning, turning, tuning would have to be done after the requisite number of hours, no matter what.

The unreliability of the infrastructure in India often let them down despite the best laid plans. No matter how they tried, power cuts were unpredictable and the quality losses, wastage with the unplanned stoppages severe. The capital costs of the required generator capacity was huge and would have to be capital budgeted. The present operating surpluses did not allow for it.

Ashok held engineering meetings at 11 p.m. in the plant. He went to bed exhausted. In the morning he planned for one event he could look forward to that day, a movie, an outing with a friend and often the thought was enough to satisfy him. He didn't actually do it when evening rolled around but kept working. But such self trickery doesn't work in the long run. It would have been better to keep a balance and actually allowed some relaxation into the day. He must learn not to rush, wherever he was at that point of time, to take life slower, to enjoy it more like that. The anti-thesis of multi-tasking. That too had its uses but one couldn't do that all the time.

Then suddenly a sight, a sound, a smell would remind him of Lauren. Her vivaciousness, her incomparable smile, her dreamy eyes. It had been tempestuous, intense. He yearned for her. He couldn't live without her. With her there was a sense of completeness. When she had visited India recently, unexpectedly, he had felt it in his heart of hearts. He knew as only a lover can that she felt the same way, if anything, it was even stronger. Then she had gone back and once again they were parted with their problems unresolved and without any long term solution.

74

How could Lauren ever make it to Western Europe? Maybe if she and Ashok worked on it together. But Ashok was in India, working hard on his father's business. Marek was in the same situation as her. It was even difficult to get a Polish passport, leave alone to find hard currency enough to manage outside. Zlotys were worthless. The passport was also issued for a specific and limited duration - 4 weeks for example, if the authorities were satisfied that that was the duration of the trip, after which it would have to be surrendered. Visas would have to be obtained.

Her mind was in a whirl with all that had happened again between Ashok and her. She had loved India. It had blown her mind. And she would have to return to it again. But living there permanently was still a difficult thought - she was European at heart.

She had pointed out little things to Ashok. How men still kissed women's hands, how they took off their gloves when shaking hands, how they said *dziekuje* when eating at the same table as others even if they were strangers, how they never put their elbows on the table whilst eating. How people were addressed in the third person as *Pan* and *Pani*, (roughly Monsieur et Madame) until the other person got to know them better. How they would take time to progress from the polite form of address to the more familiar. How even many ordinary housewives listened to and appreciated Opera some afternoons, how in the evening Schumann or Schubert would be playing when the teenagers came home from University, how European filmmakers like Luis Bunuel were widely known and Cinema critically analysed. How only they knew how to play Chopin. Once as part of a cultural exchange an American orchestra had played Chopin. How her mother had said it was good but still lacked the genuineness, that authentic touch and feeling in certain notes.

She and Ashok had looked indulgently upon India's "foibles" - men holding hands out of friendship and camaraderie, had related to the sensuousness of eating rice with one's fingers, loved the drama of the monsoons and the post rain clarity of the sunshine falling upon a myriad hues of green...but to give up Europe, with all that it meant, with its cultural possibilities, its opera and symphony, the post opera souper, the snowfall everywhere, the intense crisp cold of -5° or -10° with clear blue skies and sunshine. At other times, the winds of Europe and the romance of its spring. Or in some of the majestic woods with the tall trees and no one around, where it created the impulse to run naked through the woods as the heavens played Bach in the background.

They had this in common.

Marek sensed that she was far away at times and found it difficult to get back to the earlier level of their relationship. But he hadn't met anyone like her and it became clearer to him that he did love her and would have to court her if he was to get her back. The most difficult was when she seemed lost somewhere else.

Lauren was aware of Marek's feelings as well as the impasse of her relationship with Ashok. They had come full circle to the same point first in Polska and now in India. Ashok wrote to her and occasionally phoned her despite the difficulties.

Both Lauren and Ashok hadn't lost their youthful idealism. Did one ever come across a true love again?

Maybe they could live some months here and some months there. But common sense told them that they would need enormous resources for that. Quite apart from emotional resources. And vocations that allowed such flexibility. Pragmatism would take over. And her career as a Western Classical musician playing a relatively uncommon instrument, how could that progress on a daily basis in India. She knew too that Ashok couldn't lift his factory and transport it to Europe, even if he were to abandon his family.

Could he as a foreigner in Europe create even half way the same conditions, the same standard of living in Europe.

He too wanted to live in Europe especially when he was disillusioned with India, when his idealism would not allow him to compromise or accept. He came from an Industrialist background, he could not imagine doing anything else. He liked Manufacture. Maybe he would have to settle for a job. But he would have to be very well qualified for that. Build up his Curriculum Vitae. Could they only live for each other? Would that survive in the long run? Deep within herself had she felt like that with Ashok especially this time on his territory - she wasn't sure. Hadn't she felt like that, that starlit night at the Oberoi or in the car kissing in the torrential afternoon rain when there were not buckets but sheets of water on the window pane and the little Morris car they were in seemed like a little boat bobbing out at sea. Had he felt like that too?

Marek was a sweet enough boy and she could see that he cared for her. He was good-looking, dependable, solid, though life with him too, even if she contemplated it, seemed unreal at this stage. And it would mean living in Poland most probably. Was Poland preferable to India? For her career it was. But it wasn't Western Europe, which for her was the ideal. Too many things wrong with Poland. And her heart? She had been spending a lot of time with Marek, going everywhere with him during the long hiatus vis a vis Ashok. It wasn't as exciting with him as it had been with Ashok but was that her more than him?

She and Anna, a close friend from school days sat in a *Kawiarnia* near the *Stare Miasto*. They ordered *torty*, small cakes and *Herbata*. She talked about the possibility of living her life in Poland, with or without Marek or someone else. The only way she could live in the West was if she got a position with a Western orchestra or she got some other chance to develop her musical career in the West. But there was so much competition and how and why would she get selected. And even if she did, how would she get permission to leave the country. The obstacles were both ways and almost impossible to transcend without some chance event or some extraordinary luck. *Pravda* she said to Anna, who nodded. Janek from Anna's college passed by. What are you two doing, he said in a slightly amused tone, seeing them deep in conversation. Helping Socialism reach Communism?

The lure of the West was immense for Poles. It was entry into another world. A forbidden world of modernity, advancement, abundance of in vogue branded goods. And it was next to impossible. Ashok had told her once how he had once tried to change some thousand zlotys in West Germany at an airport bank. They had been highly amused at this sodden looking currency of their neighbour's and shown it to each other before offering Ashok a few Marks for it, nowhere near the official exchange rate.

So what now - would she fall in love with a West European who made her heart stir more than Ashok or Marek did? And she would not like to rely on her prospective beau for her career which she would have to start from scratch in the West. Focus on her music, which she loved, appreciate the many good qualities of her native land, forget about her childish fantasies of sensuous Italy or elegant France and settle down with Marek? And how would she run into this potential beau in Poland. Only a few people from Western Europe came. And of course individuals were different but the *Niemiecki* were *straszne* - terrible and she would make a harsh face just like her family would thinking of the unspeakable cruelty of the Germans as experienced and witnessed by the Poles.

Take things one day at a time, said Anna, articulating their common thought. Who had the answer to these things?

The *Kawiarnia* was pleasant. It had alcoves, chandeliers and very warm and pleasant lighting in the large hall like room. She and Anna chatted on as only friends can and even permitted themselves some gossip, to spice up the tea. There were so many people asking each other *wiesz* - saying you know and seeking validation of their opinion of some aspect of human behaviour.

After Lauren returned from India, Marek sensed the difference. He knew something had happened. He was patient. Sensitive. Lauren appreciated that. She needed to be left alone. She liked him. He was really nice but she had Ashok in her heart.

Her career progressed. Her dedication was immense and she loved her music. She knew how fortunate she was that she enjoyed with a passion what she did for a living. It was the best way to work and to live. How many others knowing full well the value of Time, the shortness of Life and how imperative it was to enjoy what one spent so many hours every day doing, managed to do that for a living! But she had also had the courage to take the risk and make this her vocation when no one knew her and she was uncertain of the outcome, as to how good she would be, whether she would have to do something else to earn a living, relegating this to something to be done whenever she had the time. She could spend hours practising it, playing it for the sheer pleasure of it seven days a week. She loved listening to it as well and far from being snobbish about the Popular and Folk music at the time, liked to listen to whatever she could get her hands on or hear on the Radio, of the fabulous creative music coming out in the 60's and the early 70's. It wasn't available for sale commercially but friends with connections to the West kept bringing in albums, even those who managed to travel to India or Japan or Lebanon for whatever reason. She would even in lighter moments play some of the Beatles on her instrument as best as was possible and sometimes a number of them would get together and jam. It was full of laughter and without any pressure to be correct. There was musical licence, sometimes with uproarious results as they were all talented.

Lauren was an extremely attractive girl and she knew it. Her thought lines added to her attractiveness. She had that air of sophistication combined with vivaciousness and she was unpredictable. She could dance on a table top if she felt like it. The serenity that she radiated partly through her music made her compelling.

Plus the word had gotten around amongst Warsaw's hep crowd that she was no longer going steady with Marek, albeit still friends with him. Her disinterest in a specific relationship at the moment only added to her unattainability. Rumour had it that there was some *Hinduski* chap in *Indii*. But all that seemed so far away and vague that it wasn't much discussed or thought about.

Much of her time was spent on music, hearing it when not playing it. It was time well spent. Plus she enjoyed the company of friends and the intellectual and social stimulation that it provided. She went to parties and was often the belle of the ball! She found time for reading, theatre and cinema. Her life was full. She missed the romance of the special relationship with Ashok but there it was.

If and when she was ready someone else would come along. Ashok came a lot into her thoughts and dreams but she accepted that as a witness. Or tried to. She had been there before.

She hadn't lost faith in the institution of marriage as per the zeitgeist of the times but she didn't think of it as important in itself. To be in love was all important. The rest didn't matter. And there were times in every life when one wasn't in that status. She would want children one day but only as products of love, with someone she really loved and who really loved her. Until then it could keep. And if it didn't happen again, well *tant pis*! as Ashok would say. She had had what she had had and nothing could take that away.

75

From October the Opera, Ballet and Symphony season had started in full swing. Lauren was even busier than usual. Her heart still managed to intrude when she would suddenly be presented with an Ashok flashback. The pining for him was unmistakable but she was a working woman. Her music was her self expression, her life. Even if she was to compromise about settling down in Europe, what could she do about her work? Why couldn't she have been born with an interest in Indian classical music? Impossible in a second level Polish city? More so at the time? She'd only come to know about it relatively recently.

She didn't feel angry with Ashok. There had been no commitment between them. A lot had happened during her visit to India. Her heart had done several somersaults in the air after taking off from the diving board. There had been unspeakably beautiful and intense moments. She knew Ashok had felt the same. 'We both could have died then and there' as Joan Baez sang. But they had made no plans to not part or even to be committed to each other in terms of not seeing other people. They didn't know how to create a long term. At most, there could be visits to each other's countries but that couldn't be very often or for great stretches of time. It was still extremely difficult from both their countries. Apart from the impracticality it was hardly a satisfactory solution. It seemed like all or nothing. Would that not create resentment even if one of them was to try it? It wouldn't be sustainable in the long run.

She was in her early 20s and in the prime of her life. She had blossomed into someone breathtakingly, stunningly beautiful. She came on the cover of a magazine *Moda*. Another magazine put her on their cover. If she'd been in America she could have modelled for *Life* perhaps or even *Seventeen*. But this was all incidental. She smiled and allowed herself some flirting at times. Just to keep her hand in? Or was it automatic? But what she really cared about was her music (and Ashok? A voice came from within, not acknowledged even to herself).

There were people who could find completion in their work alone. She knew herself. She did want somebody to love. Not necessarily immediately. She may not even be open enough. So would there be such a beau, such a Prince Charming who would help find fulfilment in life, brief as it was. Or could it only be Ashok (as irreconcilable as he was with her music)? That was absurd. But when was love based on logic. The workings of the heart were workings of the heart.

Could she play Music solo in India - she even thought once during a deep kiss with Ashok when her heart had gone zum-m-m. But she needed stimulation, the interaction of others, the beauty and marvel of playing in an ensemble with others, in a Quartet, Quintet, Chamber Orchestra if not a Symphony orchestra. She needed guidance, a suitable environment, the proximity of the Conservatoire.

Sooner or later someone else would come into in Ashok's life. What else could be expected? Would he want her always? There were times when she felt like giving up everything and running into Ashok's arms. Nothing else mattered. The rest would work itself out somehow.

76

Aparna was secure in herself, poised and elegant. She was good at her work and very good with people. Her people dealing was so good that she could easily have contemplated a career in Public Relations. But that didn't interest her enough.

She was fun-loving and extroverted. Ashok liked socialising too and her life with him would not be stifling at all. There would be lots of interaction with interesting multi-dimensional people, perhaps more than in the West where people she would mix with tended to be more specialised in their interests.

She valued the total freedom she enjoyed in California and whereas it would be no less in Ashok's circles, she would be interacting with many types in India. Over-all she would not feel as free. Constables still tried to extort bribes from couples at historical monuments in total contradistinction to the palpable romantic atmosphere there. In crowded places attempts could be made to touch her inappropriately. It had happened to her even on her last visit, she had bent down to look at some magazines outside a book shop in Queensway now called Jan Path and a sleazy character had touched her bum. She had run after him and hit him with her handbag, he had pretended to look innocent. She had felt disgusted and defiled.

And then there was that significant strata of narrow minded orthodox Indian society that had such a weird attitude to contact, friendship and relationship between men and women, to the most natural thing in the World. She would be dealing with them every day.

The perils and joys of living in India apart, Aparna was shocked and upset by the relationships of some close friends beginning to fall apart. They seemed so happy, so suited to each other - how was this happening? Americans tend to divorce, separate more than others, seemed to be the universal thought of non-Americans. But this seemed to be happening to both her American and Indian friends. And all too often though things seemed happy the guy just seemed to wantonly stray - "Lipstick on your collar" and "smoochin' my best friend" all over again. Or some variant of that. Were chaps just unreliable? Had to sow their wild oats? Did they realise they were risking perfectly good things?

'If I give my heart to you, Do you promise to be true...', it really was like the Beatles song. Slow to respond at first she really was falling for Ashok. He wouldn't let her down, would he? He wasn't like some of the others. He seemed so sincere. Not like the proverbial Italian Romeos always trying insincerely to prove themselves, singing "Sincero"!

Her friends' partners had seemed sincere too. She wouldn't have judged them otherwise either. So should she hold back? But she couldn't live life like that. Anyway her feelings were taking her beyond herself.

Aparna had seen her father struggle to support his family in Jamshedpur and other small towns. He took pride in his work and strove to make a lasting difference, so the system worked better for all the people. In trying to think of and implement improved ways of doing things, he got in the way of others who had different agendas. If he had done nothing, played safe and marked files up and down perennially for decision making until everyone forgot what the subject was all about, he would have got excellent Annual Confidential Reports from his seniors and his promotion would have been assured based on his seniority. His peers progressed much faster. It left Aparna with a sense of the unfairness of things, which got deeply ingrained.

She adored children but didn't want them for a while yet. She wanted her freedom plus she enjoyed going out and working. But she knew herself, she was very loving, conscientious - she wouldn't want them neglected in any sense, once they came on the scene, least of all by her or in terms of her not being at home, at least until the youngest was 6. Children should get their mother's full attention and care or not be brought into this world. Ashok too felt like that she knew.

At times Ashok was over intellectual, almost showing off. Anybody mentioned a book, he was bound to have read it. She wanted a simpler unpretentious fun loving guy who wasn't snobbish about ordinary things. She wanted company and laughter and fun, not somebody who was viewing himself to see if the activity fitted his self image. And yet in the final analysis how much did these things mean.

She missed Ashok, longed for him to hold her, for them to kiss. She couldn't pretend that her former state of equilibrium in California had not been altered. Who was she fooling? Ashok had entered the picture and there was the romance and drama of monsoon clouds on the landscape.

77

There were leaves in the breeze. Ashok read John Osborne and Arnold Wesker as he drove down the wide boulevards and avenues of Lutyen's Delhi, the Shadows played 'the Breeze and I' and 'Ole! I am a Bandit, A Bandit of Brazil...', Nat King Cole sang "the Autumn leaves, Drift by my window... The Autumn leaves of red and gold..." When it rained, he would go for a swim in the pouring rain, loving the drama and momentousness of it with the Cascades matching the thunder of Indra outside "Listen to the rhythm of the falling rain, Telling me what a fool I've been"

It was early September and the days were ambrosial. There were strong winds and purple skies with dark rain filled clouds. The Monsoons would soon come to an end at least if the seasonal pattern in North India was followed and give way to *Sharad Ritu*, appealing in a different way with cool fragrant moonlit nights and on certain days the hint of Winter. But for the moment they showed no signs of their impending abatement.

Perhaps he could spend a couple of months of the year travelling and the rest in Delhi but he would have to reach that stage in work - that level of management that he succeeded in making himself superfluous to that extent. Systems would have to be perfected such that they took care of things. Great delegation to different levels of management who took initiative and responsibility. His Motivational management would have to be excellent. He was managing people. He would have to be a psychologist par excellence. An excellent Management Information System coupled with Management by Objectives as well as Management by exception would have to be put in place. He hadn't reached there as yet. And the parameters of an on-going SWOT (Strengths, Weaknesses, Opportunities, Threats) analysis kept changing. The external environment was very important in India, where Government gave itself such a large role and had a larger impact on costs especially of Inputs and Labour - possibly much more important than in developed countries where a certain environment could be assumed as given. This kept changing the game and entrepreneurial talents would have to be employed. So his presence, for him to be proactive continually, was essential.

The stand, the view point of Ashok's parents had become more uncompromising on this issue. She was not from his Caste, his state, she wasn't even Indian. And then from a Communist country! Who had heard of Poland? She wasn't even English or French or German or American. What would life be like for Ashok. She was meat eating. Killing animals - just to eat them. Barbaric. What would happen to the carefully nurtured *sanskars* of Ashok and the grandchildren to come? They would follow their mother's culture and beliefs. She would be selfish, she wouldn't look after them in their old age. She wouldn't be respectful of the ways of the house, of tradition and ritual handed down over centuries. What did these foreigners understand of these things?

Unbeknownst to Ashok his parents wrote a long letter to

Lauren's parents. They were *Suryavanshi* directly descended from an ancient line they started. Much of the letter was Greek and Latin to Lauren's parents but they got the import. This was more grist for their mill.

Neither Ashok nor Lauren were dependent on their parents. Ashok had carved out his own niche in the business with a sufficient amount of equity in his own name and an indispensable role in the management of things. But both Ashok and Lauren loved their parents deeply and didn't want to hurt or upset them. It was their life but the emotional trauma and guilt would be too much. What they would gain in terms of their own happiness, would be greatly affected by the hurt of their parents. It might have helped if they could have thought like many Westerners in this respect. This was their happiness, their future, their decision and that was that.

Several times both thought of saying a plague on every obstacle, to blazes with everything else and just running to each other's arms. Nothing else mattered. The ache was so much, the yearning for the other was such. One had to get one's priorities right. The thought would generate such a sense of attainment.

But something in the way things occur randomly had happened just then. And as with Chance sometimes, the implications had been anything but. There were straws in the wind, from a wind blowing from beyond the Himalayas, from North west of them, which became part of a gale. Into his busy post-Aparna life had come a voice from the not so distant past. Lauren had landed in India.

78

As things moved fast with Lauren within the space of a few days it had felt like an eternity had been covered. A tempestuous relationship was rekindled and caught fire and soon went out of control. Maybe at some unconscious level they both knew that there wasn't much time and they had to move fast.

Should he let go and cast logic to the winds and let like in Zen whatever happens happen? He felt stoned. Like the Stones he felt like saying "I'm so stoned". He was high on the *charas* of what was happening with Lauren.

The time with Aparna had been intense but now all he could think about Constantly was Lauren. "All day I'm walking in a dream, I think about her Constantly, Like an everflowing stream..." a la Cliff Richards. So where was he to go from here? Follow his heart and get into the uncertainty of Lauren again. Hadn't he left that when he had finally left Poland after many months, eons ago? But now it was like Magic. Loving Spoonful and "Do you believe in Magic?"

Now Lauren had come like a Tempest, like a Midsummer Night's Dream. It was even more than it had been. If they were madly, crazily in love - nothing else mattered - they had to be together. They would find solutions ensemble.

With everything unresolved and their minds in a whirl, Lauren went back to the shores of Polska and the music of the Conservatoire. But they had experienced rapture.

79

Even the immortal music of Chopin and the timeless music of Bach seemed evanescent. Lauren couldn't get as immersed in her music as she did before her trip to India. There was only one way; she had to help Ashok settle in Western Europe. She had to be with him. She had to marry him. She couldn't live without him. But in the short term if sacrifices were involved for this long term goal of happiness, she would do it. She wouldn't be impatient or myopic. She would give herself even more to her music, so that transition to and acceptance in the even more competitive West would become a reality. He could make visits to India. She would go with him. He didn't need to be present all the time. Ashok's father's belief, which Ashok had imbibed was that control was through figures, through numbers and then asking the right questions, taking the right decisions, coming up with the right answers. Far-flung factories could be controlled and managed like that. Vast business empires could be managed, handled thus. It was neither necessary nor desirable to be physically present all the time.

When she described India to friends, her impressions of it,

the warmth and gentleness of the people, showed them her photos - a few of them asked the unthinkable, why could she not live there? But her face would take on the rigid, set look of all three of her family members combined. No, she could only live in, would have to live in Europe.

"*Dla czego nie?*" said Anna in the *Kawiarnia* after Lauren shared with her friend an inkling of the feelings involved and of how she had enjoyed India - in fact had loved it and been struck by it.

"It's one thing to visit, Anna, another to live in a place. If I could visit, even for a long time and if we could live in Europe I would do that. And this wasn't even a long visit. But I think I would be happy visiting as many months as I could take off, for the sake of love. Even that would affect my career but it's a trade off I would make."

"But Anna, to settle down? No, we would have to live in Europe. I could never live elsewhere. Call elsewhere home."

Anna continued reasoning in vain with her friend. She knew what a romantic Lauren was. This was something beyond her career. Given such a choice between the love of her life and her career, Love would have, should have won. She could still go on playing and practising the Harp in India. Ashok was well off enough that she didn't have to work for a living. She could just do it for pleasure, for self expression. She could practice and play for many hours. She could still visit Europe for performances, stints of some months at a time especially if Ashok did better in his work with her around the rest of the time.

Lauren didn't agree. She would miss the interaction and stimulus of fellow musicians and that was very important.

"Even self expression needs an audience, Anna."

She would miss the structure of the Conservatoire and

playing for a symphony orchestra. But it was more than that. She would miss Europe. This was her identity. It was very deep. She couldn't live anywhere else.

This was something obstinate, rigid in her friend. Anna couldn't understand it. But Lauren seemed so set. Anna sighed as some other friends of Lauren had done.

But not all her friends were of this view. Many fell in the other camp. They understood and agreed with Anna. There were too many things involved.

Ashok had Dairy Technology training qualifications from Finland, France and Norway. These certificates could help him be a consultant to various companies. Ashok's charm and easy manner would help. But he still had to be a citizen of a Western European country. Marrying her would not help in that regard. She herself would have a problem both with getting a Polish passport to exit and with getting a Western visa.

80

Ashok would have to bring something to the table. But machinery, technology and know-how export was allowed. It would bring precious foreign exchange to the country and would enable him to have a base abroad.

Spray dried milk powder was made in tall cone shaped cylinders with an atomiser at the top. The process was the same for both whole cream or skimmed milk powder. The atomiser used a centrifugal method to disperse at great speed into tiny atomised particles which then fell down as powder to the bottom of the long cylinder which rose to the top of the building. This atomiser was the heart of the matter. When there had been a very large order from the Army in Assam and there was no way their existing powder plant could meet the demand, Messrs Tulpulle a very fair Maharashtrian - a *Chitpavan Bramhin,* who had trained in Denmark as well and Bannerjee and Chatterjee two clever Dairy engineers put their heads together and managed to come up with an atomiser that was not bad. The rest was putting enough aluminium and steel together at the right temperatures. Maybe he could make it at lower cost. There was scope here, if he did it without making his machine suppliers feel threatened.

This process would take some time. Meantime she would have to stay put as would he to work on their respective agendas. If she wanted a life with him now, she would have to give up all her dreams and move to India. She couldn't wait but it would destroy her longer term happiness. She would have to be matured and wise. She would miss him, she would long for him, these were the best years of her life but they had their whole life ahead of them. Impatience wouldn't do. Some things are worth waiting for. She would write, talk on the phone, be in touch, maybe even try to visit a couple of times, or he could come over. But they would remain focussed on their goal and work single-mindedly towards it. Besides it wouldn't take that long. Ashok would work intensively at it. And she also needed time to make adjustments to prepare for a new life elsewhere.

At some subconscious level both Ashok and Lauren knew that this time together they had those days in Delhi was pure magic. But they wanted something perfect - wherein they would still have each other, still be young - but wouldn't have to live in India or Poland, which were both not ok. So many things were wrong with them. Nobody knows better how to live in the present than Youth but Youth also has a different perspective of time. And youth also has ambition. Ambitions which makes it stretch, strive to do impossible things. And the difficult thing of compromise, of settling for imperfection, which comes with a loss of idealism had not yet had opportunity. Thus they did not pursue the bliss they had experienced and the beauty of their timeless floating together, so that they could work hard, as young people should, towards their goal. That things might change or they might change were not things they factored in or even thought conceivable.

What Lauren did do was strive to make international connections. It was very difficult in Poland, except to a limited extent with East Germany, Czechoslovakia, Romania and others in the Eastern bloc. But if anybody could strive to have them and cultivate them, it was the artistes, the musicians. By its very nature, it was difficult to confine such people within national or political boundaries. And art flourished through interaction and cross fertilisation with others. What danger was there if music performers performed elsewhere or those from elsewhere gave concerts here? Besides, most classical music composers were from countries now falling in Western Europe. Opera with the exception of a few from Russia even more so. Segregation wasn't realistic. An Austrian Quartet performing Mozart, the most polemical ideologue could not take objection to that. And there was the propaganda value of clearly demonstrating to the West that culture was thriving under *Socializmu*.

Lauren was very talented. That combined with determination and hard work saw her getting many invitations and her getting more and more recognition in Europe. Part of her payment was in hard currency and though that was precious to the authorities and carefully monitored, she managed to squirrel away some portion of it for their future together.

If she continued to excel, she might even be able to get a permanent position in a Western country. It was very competitive and there were many good local musicians, yet she still might manage. It may not be enough to support both of them and the lifestyle they could have enjoyed in India but it would be her contribution.

Sometimes in her dreams she just gave up and was re-united with Ashok and living in India and kissing Ashok deliriously under the archway of one of the smaller monuments scattered around Nizamuddin East.

81

Machines to make *ghee* unheard of in the West could be exported. The West was already showing an awareness of Ayurveda and the benefits of certain food. Clarified butter from pure cow milk could be popularised as beneficial to health, including in terms of reducing LDL the bad cholestrol. The other idea was micro-bacteriology in the context of the semi tropical conditions existing in Delhi. He had seen in his training in the West, how much emphasis there was on micro-bacteriology as a tool of excellence in quality. It wasn't just the machines, the process, the training of the workers, the strict quality control and standardisation of the ingredients. The microbiological lab was an independent and important department, with white robed specialists and their tools for peering into and experimenting with the microcosm. The funds and the importance allocated to this Quality Control Research and Development (QCRD) department kept increasing. Ashok had been wonderstruck at the hues no less vivid than in an underwater scuba diving exploration and uniquely different. The count was always in millions. But the focus was always on conditions prevailing in temperate conditions - in France and the Netherlands, in Scandinavia and Switzerland.

Ashok made contact with some of the technocrats at the Indian Dairy Research Institute in Karnal a 2½ hour drive from Delhi as well as the Indian Agricultural Research Institute at Pusa Road in Delhi itself. The men of Science were glad to help. One of them at Karnal even happened to be Polish. *Quelle coincidence,* thought Ashok.

The temperature settings, the parameters, the range were much wider in such climates. The big companies of the temperate dairy producing countries were keen to expand their footprints, both by way of collaborations and joint ventures as well as by way of export of equipment and products. But the equipment was neither calibrated for the range that was needed under these conditions nor were the products suited to last.

Ideas flashed in his head about the wafer division of their dairy also, set in the wheat belt of India, in the Punjab. He had been working hard there as well, setting up systems and had acquired an inside knowledge of the products and their technology. Here too there was scope. The imported laminators were outdated and not efficient enough. There was a mismatch in the sheeting of the raw material mix. Better laminators could be manufactured much cheaper in India and with a better capital/output ratio. In his own workshop, when one of them had broken down and there had been the possibility of considerable down time, the resourceful fitters and engineers had come up with something which albeit make shift and crude had done yeoman duty in the interim. They could collaborate with engineering plants which had come up in Hyderabad to make laminators.

The main wafer ovens or *Waffelmaschinen* as they called them, were manufactured by Franz Haas in Vienna. There was a great demand for cream wafer biscuits and his was the only company that manufactured them in India. It was one of their USP - Unique Selling Propositions. Children loved it and they made it in different flavours - strawberry, banana, pineapple and coloured it pink, yellow, lemon green etc. It was packed in attractive foil packing red, blue, dark green. They exported them all over the world.

Ashok had seen how resourceful Indian engineers were. They had to make do. They had to manage. It was easier to do so when parts and components were readily available, off the shelf of suppliers. In India there had to be improvisation. They became experts at 'making do'. Import licences were very difficult to get from the government, even for parts. Foreign exchange was in tremendous shortage. The foreign supplier needed a Letter of Credit, which had to be followed up with a bank. The supplier had a lead time when and if the order was confirmed. There was the shipping time. Engineers learned to fabricate, to substitute, the job had to be done, there could not be a breakdown. Production could not be held up.

The demands of his work grew more and more. He enjoyed it and he could see the fruits of his labour, his ideas, initiatives and the risks he took. It also gave him no time for reflection.

Lauren's visit had been too brief and too much had happened too fast for Ashok to say anything to her about Aparna. Nor had he asked Lauren about her relationships. He could hardly assume that a girl as attractive as her had not received a lot of attention, some of it interesting. Whatever their ongoing feelings for each other that survived the parting, they had not parted with any understanding. During her whirlwind visit his world had turned topsy turvy. He was in a perpetual daze and would go to bed as if in a dream.

And what should he tell Aparna; that the thought of her still brought a smile to his lips, he still felt the enchantment, but this person from his days in Europe had suddenly reappeared and things had happened? And now it was over with her?

Was it?

'To thine own self be true'. What did his heart truly want? He did know that the last thing he wanted was to hurt anyone. But invariably one might.

It would be so much easier with Aparna. The imperative for finding ways and means abroad would fall by the wayside in one fell swoop. The cultural adjustment would be easier with his parents, with his larger family, maybe even for him, in ways yet unknown to him. He was very westernised but who knew about all the little things that constituted day to day comfort with each other? Hadn't he lived with Lauren for months? But that had been in Poland. India brought out different reactions. And didn't the older and wiser say it was different after marriage. For one thing the expectations of and from each other changed and that could lead to huge gaps with reality. Earlier the expectations were much lower and it mattered less somehow. The whole marriage thing was a thing of expectations. With Aparna there would be more of an automatic cultural comfort. Certain responses, certain ways of doing things or saying thank you through a look, a gesture, above all, certain inflections of tone, he knew would be understood.

His intentions might give him integrity and a clear conscience (if indeed something as straightforward as conscience could be brought in as a parameter in these things) but would they understand that, he said aloud. Be able to understand that. Give him the benefit of doubt.

But this was not about ease. This was about his heart which reigned in a different realm. Though even that was giving him a confused ambivalent message. During those tumultuous days with Lauren, that dizzy reunion, she had occupied his entire attention. She still did to quite an extent but as he had time to breathe, Aparna came back into his consciousness.

Nor could he hide in his frenetic schedule, his round the clock work, his success at what he was doing, forever.

8 2

Aparna continued her idyllic life in the Bay Area. She missed Ashok but was happy with her mom's fabulous home cooking, the leaves drifting past her window, the deer she would see certain mornings just outside her suburban bedroom window as she woke up. It was 'California Dreaming'.

She thought of Ashok's earlier letters, full of news and his sharp observations on the state of many things. Nobody would elect him and he would never withstand the hurly burly of politics, besides it was very dirty in India - maybe everywhere, in different ways but he felt he would do a better job than many leaders. He was good at analysing, going to the heart of the matter and finding the best possible solutions. And he wouldn't worry about popularity or being re-elected. He would make maximum possible progress especially on poverty, infrastructure—connect the rivers in a national water grid for instance, so that the absurdity of drought in one part and floods in another part of the country could gradually be overcome, etc. Delusions of grandeur? Neither of them thought so. Just an ardent desire to lift his country and help it realise its potential.

She knew he was working extremely hard and was proud

of him and his ability to focus. She knew of many of their contemporaries who though now out of College were still partying as hard - several days of the week. They worked but balanced it with pleasure, some more evenly than others. But the pot smoking, free thinking, psychedelic back drops and love-ins of the 60's continued into the early 70's for them. No foregoing the discos and the dancing come the twilight after work and a game of Tennis or a swim, the evening would still be young. 'Baby you're a rich man...'

He told her that he didn't bother to shave on certain days and though he was no longer an adolescent, pimples had appeared on his chin perhaps because of the work-only life that he was leading. Thank goodness picture phones were still a thing of the future. He didn't feel his presentable charming self.

Lots of things with Ashok had happened on impulse. Just like their first kiss. They hadn't set a time frame for anything. Neither of them was in a hurry. But as time flew by Aparna wondered why they didn't talk about it. Also she didn't like the parting for so long. She was very sensitive, intuitive. Was Ashok different now? Had there been a change in Ashok? Was there someone else? But Ashok was working so hard. Where would be the time? But that's what he said. Maybe he wasn't actually only working. He wasn't like that. He wouldn't lie. Let somebody else down.

Nevertheless, she felt uneasy. Was there an almost imperceptible change in his tone? She was conscious of impatience with herself. She was an enlightened, independent liberal woman. Why did she fall prey to these unworthy if occasional doubts? She wasn't the insecure type. He had been far keener in the early days and had pursued her single-mindedly. She had just let things happen. She hadn't even cared that much then. But he had kissed his way into her heart with his intensity, passion and charm. Their kisses had become so intimate. Had unified them, far more than any love making could.

In days of Skype she could have read his facial expressions, his body language but with 10,000 miles between them and no non verbal communication to go on, there were only the inflections of voice, the nuances of tone and possibly subtle changes in the content also.

Next time she asked him. She was American in many senses, she could be an ingénue. Wasn't naïveté a defining characteristic? That was part of her charm.

"We haven't met for so long. And we haven't made any plans."

"Why don't you come over? It's much easier for you. I'll take some time off. I've been totally immersed in work. Have not had time to think about anything else."

Leave her work, her comfortable day to day life, her family that she was so close to - to again go for some time and come back. Above all she missed Ashok. She missed him a lot. She had given her heart, somewhat reluctantly at first - Ashok had had to work hard, but given it she had. And now she felt in limbo. Emotionally. Marriage per se wasn't important to her, at least until they decided to have children. But being together was. Sure she loved India, enjoyed being there, she had grown up there, but now she had nowhere to stay. Many of her friends had scattered or had their own family lives. They were not free like before. He couldn't be with her all the time. What would she do hanging around the rest of the time sans family, sans a base, She would feel like such a *vela* when Ashok wasn't there. She couldn't stay with him yet. His family wouldn't accept that and it was a joint family house. It would be very pleasant with him but again she would spend some months and come back. That pattern had been fine till now but could not be re-enacted endlessly.

In Punjab, the General Manager of the Wafer Plant received a call from the Chief Minister's secretary. The Chief Minister desired to see Ashok 'tomorrow evening in Chandigarh at his office'.

The Chief Minister was warm and effusive. "Your father and I are good friends. The party is holding their annual session this time in our state. It is up to us to put up a good show. Last time in Patna it was extremely well organised. This time we have to do better than that. The best annual conference ever. We look to old and trusted friends like yourself to rally around. We know we can count on you."

The Chief Minister expected at least Rs 2 *Lakhs* as soon as possible. Ashok asked for some time. The working capital was tight and it would have to be taken out of operating money received from the latest sales. Since it would be unaccounted for money, some credible bills would have to be fabricated. That would take some time. The Chief Minister looked disbelieving. These businessmen always talked like this. Ashok should know better - be more sensible. The Chief Minister could help in so many ways - the indenting of coal wagons from Bihar for instance. Ashok would not just recoup his money but make many multiples of it.

Ashok was uncomfortable on several accounts - fudging bills, giving productive money for such unnecessary purposes, that too to a political party which seemed to be making a mess of the state and the country and thereby bolstering it, hurting the carefully planned smooth running of the operations.

Ashok did not call the Chief Minister back. Is this what he had learnt in management training in Norway, Finland and at home? An unrecognisable voice within him said 'This is not how Business is done in India. You have to be practical. You have to see your own good'. But he had not learnt the ways of doing business in India. Not using Harvard Business School methods but getting special privileges, preferably monopolistic from the government.

Some of his school friends in St Columbas attracted by the glamour of a convent education had come from Rajinder Nagar, Pusa Road and Karol Bagh. Their parents were refugees. They were ambitious, hard working and as aggressive in business as they had been in the professions they left behind. They came with nothing but their wits and they had to succeed anyhow.

They gave him examples of how privileges had to be bought in India. A small time dealer in an item used in many industries managed to create a monopoly through the government. The Licence Permit Quota Raj was tailor made for it. And he hoarded that item, used monopoly pricing and sold them at fancy prices to corporations operating in India. Due to his nexus with politicians no one could do anything about it. His business model of contacts, favours to the powers that be, artificial shortages and scarcity, very high profit margins, he extended to more and more specialised items. It was win-win for both him and the politicians, his business empire grew.

These school classmates weren't advocating following the

same model but this was a golden opportunity. It was all about profit, baby! They had already grown up. He still had good laughs with them, shared schoolboy jokes with them but had drifted away culturally and evolved into a different creature - his thoughts were still around theatre, music, literature and Cahiers du Cinema. He had learned to hold his own in the boisterous atmosphere of the school but the latter had suited his sensitive nature much more.

Ashok avoided the Chief Minister and focussed on the day to day problems of the factory, which were many. But they were to do with the actual nuts and bolts of factory management, difficult at times, but enjoyable and with a potential for creative solutions. This was the real stuff. The political part of Political Economy was uncalled for.

Not far from his factory he learnt of subsidised land, soft loans from the State Financial Corporation and the State Industrial Development Corporation, plus a Letter of Credit for Import from a nationalised bank for a new Wafer factory coming up. It was being set up by a small time local mafia whose real vocation no one knew but who had made enough profits to buy some small town movie halls in Punjab. Movie halls running the latest Bollywood hits in those pre video, DVD days were still money spinners - places where the family went for an evening or Sunday afternoon out. The local sugar supplier also took a minority stake in the new business. He had supplied sugar to Ashok also and knew how his pricing affected profitability since he was a major supplier in the area and sugar an important ingredient. He was in the habit of turning up frequently unannounced in his unstarched kurta pyjama the only garment that could fit around his enormous form.

The new factory bought exactly the same equipment as the existing one and copied the brands of wafers being made to a T.

There was no attempt at innovation or value addition. What was good enough for the first factory was good enough for the second, never mind its proximity and the size of the total market. The herd mentality was evident everywhere. If this was a successful way of doing business, then it must be used to make money. Shoe shops came up next to shoe shops and antique shops next to existing antique ones, until the whole street got filled with the same kind of shops. But in the case of shops there was still some kind of logic, some benefit from the whole area specialising, despite the obvious disadvantages. Factories just competed for the same resources whereas some distance away from each other they might have added value, generated more employment, created a multiplier effect.

As a first step towards good neighbourly relations they stole the closely guarded recipes, including the one for strawberry wafers the Company's most popular item, a creation the company had justifiably been very proud of. They were kept in a small safe in the company's Lab in the QCRD. A copy of the key had been made and the safe was found open after one night shift. Had this been the electronic age it would have been much more difficult to hack into. It could have been stored on a hard disk with a password.

Brij had sponsored training in England of their Production Manager with a well known English Biscuit company whose many products included wafers. The unscrupulous neighbours doubled his salary and he quietly disappeared one day.

The no.2 in the marketing management line up, who had been encouraged by Ashok and had been very close to him, was also bought at double the salary and started spreading the most vicious rumours in the marketplace about his erstwhile company and its products. He had been so devoted to this brand.

It is common knowledge that a lot of adulteration takes place in foodstuffs in India, particularly in the unorganised sector. Some of the substances used are poisonous and toxic, some are not but are still ersatz. The only reason they are used in either case is because they closely resemble the original product, are much cheaper and in abundant supply. The tasty Rasmalai soaked in milk and embellished with nuts and saffron is adulterated with cardboard. *Dals* are adulterated with a whole array of substances as are *atta* and maida. Sugar is often adulterated to unbelievable extents requiring guilt ridden middle classes to surreptitiously add more spoons of sugar to sweeten their cup of tea. Even Scotch is not spared. Indians are the last Englishmen on earth, said a friend of Ashok at the Delhi Gymkhana Club. The quantities of Scotch consumed certainly seemed to support that. Ingenious methods were developed to dilute Scotch with Indian whiskey, some of it pretty good in itself. The bottle looked like the real McCoy, the sealing was perfect. The connoisseurs could tell but didn't want to upset their hosts who were not complicit and some of the heavy drinking farm party crowd even appreciated it.

To control this there were numerous pieces of legislation. Certain foods had an Agmark of quality. The ISI mark confirming that the product conformed to the Indian Standards Institution benchmarks was an assurance of quality. There was the Weights and Measures Act, and above all the Prevention of Food Adulteration Act. But they all in their implementation managed to hit the organised sector more and not to tackle the malaise at its source. The poorly paid and semi-literate babus who were PFA inspectors were only interested in bribes and blackmail. They targeted the factories and larger companies, where they could make some money. In their testing they would find real or imagined differences, often minute ones with Standards and would call that adulteration. No harmful substance would be involved, nor any substitution by a cheaper product. If they took a sample to their Lab, chances were that they would find something. The onus was always on the producer to prove otherwise. It reminded Ashok of giving notice under the Indian Income tax law. If the Income tax officer took it up for scrutiny, it was almost axiomatic that he would find 'something' and make an addition to the returned Income, no matter how sincerely and diligently depicted. The hapless assessee would have no choice but to enter into time consuming and frustrating litigation with the Income Tax Department. Either the PFA Inspector or his boss were paid something or they would have an Adulteration case against the company the penalty for which was not just financial but prison. And prison, a criminal record for not the Quality Control Incharge, not the Production Manager but for the Managing Director. Well intended but totally misdirected and misused, rued Ashok.

Wide publicity was also given to this and the news media picked it up with relish, carrying at least a small item in their City pages, stating how such and such company or brand had been found guilty of adulteration, with no further explanation. Even if many months later the company won on merit, this was not carried by the paper. The damage would be done.

Within the next few months, a spate of such inspections and cases took place in Ashok's factory. It wasn't chance at work, it was malevolent forces at work, spending small amounts of money for disproportionate returns. The Inspector and or his boss would get paid to do it and in this case the higher bidder - the Raider or the Defendant - would determine the outcome.

One of the national newspapers in its city page said Adulteration found in Wafers, conjuring stereotypes of *halwais* looking evil and mixing things - not even remotely connected to a vanilla allegedly being 5.064 instead of 5.065. The damage was incalculable.

Perversely for a country seeking to modernise Industrial production could only take place after a licence was obtained. That was difficult enough. The Government in its dystopic socialist wisdom suddenly decided to reserve such food industries for the small scale sector, the capacity being limited to something very small. Fresh licensing and investment was banned. Bureaucrats had to come up with something with their time, the margin notes and the piles of files. A Devil's workshop. The Licence Raj was at its height.

As Brij and Ashok's wafer unit did well because of consistent quality and taste and demand far outstripped supply they found themselves hamstrung in being able to expand and get further economies of scale. Very rapidly bad quality ovens put together by local fabricators whose sole objective was to make something as cheap as possible to fit within the limits set by bureaucrats, flooded the market and a number of units mushroomed selling wafer biscuits at half the price.

The multinationals in the food sector already in the country saw an opportunity and against their previously sanctioned industrial capacity imported fancy wafer ovens. The wafer unit found itself squeezed from both sides in an uncomfortable pincer position.

Brij heaved a sigh of relief as the figures reflected a healthy black in the monthly profit and loss, despite all these difficulties. It was the result of sustained good management from preventive maintenance to Industrial Engineering. They could think of implementing many improvements which had been pending for want of funds.

The labour most of them refugees from West Punjab were excellent - hardworking, very loyal and creative about little things which added up. Relations with the union were of mutual understanding. Their bonus was linked to performance and kept increasing. The annual increments were 10%. But the neighbouring mafia had just started playing its dirty games. A lot of money was poured into this. It was worth it. A letter in Gurmukhi and Urdu started circulating setting up a rival union. Broad allegations were levelled at the management and the existing union. Some workers in the despatch and packing sections were handpicked to spearhead trouble. They had nightly rendezvous at the friendly neighbour's premises. They looked for little things to start a fire. The carefully built up harmonious atmosphere started getting disturbed.

The rival union suddenly struck. They said that leaked confidential figures said that the profits were sky high and were not being shared with the workers in the form of higher bonuses which they deserved. It was due to their hard work that this had happened. They picketed the factory and resorted to violence when loyal workers tried to work. The small town local police had been paid off and said they could not interfere in matters of industrial dispute. The sclerotic industrial disputes machinery in far off Chandigarh would take a lot of time to move and would play it safe and preach about the welfare of the workers without going into genuine depth.

The monthly profit and loss plunged into red greater than the previous month's healthy black.

The ISI type infiltration from the neighbour was handled with great ingenuity and what seemed like a large war chest though there was no naive America pouring in billions in this case.

Ian Fleming was right thought Ashok drily, the first time it's coincidence, the second time it's happenstance, the third time it's enemy action. He couldn't pretend it didn't affect them. He couldn't ignore it, much as this was not what he would like to think about. This was the dirty side of Business. He couldn't just be reactive. The best form of defence was offence. But he hated it so.

You are not fit for this world, Aparna had said.

Running Factories was multi-functional, a fine interwoven mesh of many different functions which affected each other. Ashok found himself if not quite *deborde*, occupied several hours beyond full time with the two factories in two different states.

Responsibilities had come crashing down on him. The more he took over, the more he handled with efficiency and competence, the more the burden that fell on him, the more the vistas and opportunities that opened up. Initiatives were there for the taking, they were exciting but implementation involved a lot of work, some of it dull.

His father had given him the lesson of quick decision making in business affairs. Analyse, weigh all factors - then take the plunge, no vacillation but quick, timely action. Things changed after some time anyway.

He had to move forward in his personal life as well.

Like this he was hurting himself.

He tried to phone Lauren again *Gita Govinda* in hand. It was so beautifully written, the love poems in it. He wanted to read out lines from it. He waited next to the phone, remaining on hand, so that the Indian operator would find him when she decided to try and did get through. It would be easier once he was in Europe. Even from Western Europe, Communist Europe was easier to get through to. From India every place was difficult, except perhaps England.

He remembered reading out from *Gitanjali* to her, with the smell of the rain outside and the green bushes outside the window swaying in the breeze, when she had been in India and they had lain in each other's arms exhausted, spent, complete.

But who would handle all this, there was no one really. And he owed it to his father. He could try and bring it to a point. But how long would that take, no one could say. Just a point of equilibrium where he could leave it for a little while. He had his personal life, his emotional life. What was all this about anyway, he thought. What was he toiling for. Those were his dreams but they would not remain that for ever. He had to find time. He would have to leave hearth and hame and go once again. He had to choose also. And if it was Lauren where would they live. Could he live with the guilt, if he lived in Europe?

When he was with Lauren the rest of the world didn't exist. When she kissed him, the world enveloped him, cocooned him. Nothing existed outside. But his responsibilities in the two factories, his extremely loving parents, he couldn't be oblivious at all times. He heard certain music and was reminded of Lauren. 'The very thought of you....' She came into his dreams. The fragrances of the night in Delhi, the moon hanging low between the tall trees late at night.... He longed for her beautiful thin arms, glistening in the moonlight, wrapped around his shoulder.

He had to follow his heart but there was his conscience and his sense of 'should'.

One thing was clear, he had to go, as soon as possible. It was life and death. He threw himself even more into his work. He targeted four weeks. Even that seemed interminable. But he couldn't just abandon things mid-point, half done. It took him four months. Late at night when he could he would write to Lauren. Sometimes he tried to phone Lauren with all the frustrations that entailed. Aparna was well nigh impossible, telephone connections to America were even more difficult, compounded by the 13½ hour time difference with the West Coast. He sent telegrams. Telexes came later.

He started making points for follow up - a summary of what had to be done, what the stages and options were, who had to do it in the management team and by when. It was a pre-cursor to Management by Objectives with its Key Result Areas, job and target descriptions and a PERT–CPM approach, so that bottlenecks could be avoided and things could be kept moving simultaneously. It was hard to apply it to non-scientific or non-quantifiable areas which involved Government functioning and Government interface in every sphere of Indian business life was huge, nevertheless, that approach had to be followed. The Tax part should have been quantifiable but given the approach to levy every conceivable addition to returned income, on the presumption that the assessee was a criminal, it was very difficult.

He worked flat out. His life was at stake, he felt. He had been ignoring a vital part of himself. He had been doing his duty (his *dipti* as his Nepali servant who had spent so much time with him, would call duty), but at the cost of what mattered to him most. He felt torn - in a great rush. Somehow he had to do what he had to do and be gone. He should have been there yesterday. He felt like crying in desperation. But at least Lauren was there at the end of it all. Everything would be worth it, when he had her in his arms again. They had tried giving up each other when he had left Wroclaw. It had been so painful. And then unexpectedly she had come back into his life. It had been so stormy. At least she would love him just as much. It was a matter of time. They just had to stick it out.

So finally was this where it was headed after all? Or had he just put Aparna out of his head during Lauren's visit and the mad days that followed, because there had been no space in his head or heart. Lauren and Ashok had existed those last few charmed days as if there was nothing else in their world. They were totally consumed, wholly enveloped by it.

Ashok was taking too long. Lauren remembered the love and tenderness she had experienced. Lauren knew he felt very intense. She too was like that. But her larger family, colleagues, many of her friends started putting pressure. *Kochana,* how long will you wait for this distant ethereal *zagraniczne czlowiek* who is from even beyond the large world of Europe? Is he even real? A dream? Something you've projected. You are so talented, vivacious, beautiful - inside and outside. There would be a queue of Polish men, if you were available. Is it really over with Marek? Or were you just dazzled by your encounters with Ashok.

You were naive and romantic. You are just wasting your precious life, pining away for him - the best part of your life. It's not even practical. Where will you live? What will you do? He is not even a musician.

Poland though politically not liberal was by the late 60's, early 70's a relatively free place in many respects compared to many other East European nations. There was no Classical music that was considered "unsocialist" except perhaps Wagner and artistic freedom particularly in Cinema was remarkable, partly because of the quality of film makers Poland had already produced.

"This is all American propaganda", Lauren's mother would say. "We are happy. Very happy. Polish people really know how to live." The 1968 student revolutions in Warsaw had quickly been handled. But attitudes towards sex were extremely permissive and amongst University students and age groups *voisinale* there was free sex, not just in the *Dom studencki* but even in the brightly lit small flats of Warsaw's colonies, in the lanes amongst the tall trees, the late evening visits of regular boyfriends were ok.

Polish life had its advantages. Consumer goods were not so scarce as in many other Communist nations. One could have a tasty nutritious really cheap meal at a *Bar Mleczny*. The staple *szynka* was *smaczna* and inexpensive as was milk. Even restaurants did not cost much, nor did cinema. Transport was good and there was no crime to speak of, other than the uncouth, drunk middle aged Polish men. Life was totally safe, even late at night, for girls.

Despite all this, the West held its glamour for all this side of the Iron curtain, irrespective of individual differences between countries of the Warsaw Pact because of culture and history. The standard of living was much higher in the West. This could truly be called the Second World. It aspired to a First world way of life. The grass was much greener on the other side. There were the fancy products of the West, its fashion, dazzling lifestyle, movies, hard currency which could buy anything, be taken anywhere, unlike the unattractive rumpled up notes of the Polish zloty, with pictures of workers, which was no good outside Poland, not even in other East European countries and often not even in Poland, where certain goods - like the best lead crystal - and services could only be bought in Orbis shops with impossible to get hard currency - it was the better Other.

Poles had survived so many annexations and being wiped off the map or reduced in size by large powerful neighbours Russia, Germany and even the Austro-Hungarian empire, the Turks from the Ottoman empire. They were very nationalistic, they had had to be. They were Slav but they had their own identity, they were not part of mother Russia, the mindset was different, the script was not Cyrillic but Roman, the religion was Catholic not Orthodox, December 25th was the important date, not January 6th. The erstwhile nobility, the aristocracy, the cultivated, the artistes, the litterateurs, the musicians spoke French. It was part of their refinement. They were European Slavs, not Russian Slavs.

Lauren had really blossomed. Her brother took her to a party one evening and there was Carlo. "Where have you been hiding all my life?" he said as he zeroed in on her. He was a good dancer and swept her off her feet. He spun her around faster and faster in the *Valses* till she was dizzy. In the Jive he twirled her around with one arm and then locked her in front of him with the other. He was Mediterranean short - about her height, good looking, had sharp features, honey coloured eyes and olive complexioned, a shade lighter than Ashok. Flirting came naturally to him and he could be very charming when he wanted. He had fallen for Lauren and she was flattered and despite herself was charmed. She had never met anyone like him. He lived in that most picturesque of cities, Florence and was a painter. He had come under an exchange programme to Warsaw for three months. An exhibition of some of his paintings and water colours was on at the *Palac Nauki I Kultury*. It had large salons. The vernissage was the next day and he invited her.

His paintings were winsome. They were sensuous. Some of the nudes were evocative, the expressions on their faces conveying so many things. The semi clad women were erotic. The groups of people in verdant Tuscany, Umbria landscapes and hills and vales were delicate, refined, picnicking or chatting in animated groups. His pencil sketches were a different genre but he wasn't exhibiting them this time.

It became obvious to Lauren that Carlo had already made a name for himself in Italy, *malgre* his youth. Most of Warsaw society was there. Some had even come from the far more pleasing and well preserved Cracow. Carlo only had eyes for her.

85

Carlo could be very charming and he made a fine art of it. There were a number of blonde and enticing Polish girls around Carlo. Marek's mother had described with some amusement how when they were passing through Italy and Greece, southern European men had followed them and given them a lot of attention. As northerners they had been considered something special there but here it was Carlo that was special.

He saw Lauren enter the salon from the corner of his eyes and beckoned her to join him.

"I want to take you to Italy and show you some of my sketches," he said softly. "I want you to tell me what you think of them. They are not one of my main lines but I enjoy dabbling in them. Am I just being a dilettante or do I have potential in that genre as well?"

"I thought the line was etchings," she laughed, remembering the lines of some of the English books she had read. "Goodness, he is a fast mover, isn't it a bit early for that?" she thought.

"I am no expert. I would just see them as a viewer."

"It is that I look for. I would value it."

"Italy is a bit far. Don't you have something here?" she smiled.

"I haven't brought any here. I've just started. This is an official expo."

He asked her to an official function that evening.

There were a lot of party officials drinking too much. This was not her idea of a soiree and she slipped out quietly.

Carlo didn't have her phone number and perhaps it was just as well. What would Ashok think of all this? He didn't have any claims on her though. Their situation was as usual unclear.

It was not so easy to lose Carlo. The hip, sophisticated lot in Warsaw were not yet that big. Everybody didn't know everyone but it was close to that. A few days later, he saw her at a music recital. "Where did you run away the other day?"

Would she meet him for a glass of wine at Fukier's, the famous wine cellar in *stare miasto* tomorrow before lunch? She was tempted.

The atmosphere was typical of the place, dark in a cool way when the continental East European sun was blazing outside, much hotter than the milder parts of Western Europe. It was cosy and the chatter was a comfortable hum without being noisy. The wine came out of carefully stored barrels in Fukier's cellar but it was the atmosphere and reputation that were on sale.

They went down the stairs leading to the wine cellar. It was crowded and smoky but full of atmosphere. They managed to find a table in the gallery corner. There were a number of barrels of house wine. The caskets looked old and dark.

He followed that up with lunch at Hotel Europejski and then at Hotel Bristol across the street. Both these hotel lunches were well known and had delicious soups and main meat dishes with tasty vegetables at the side, besides the chopped purple cabbage in vinegar and the standard mashed potato to go with the meat. There were pickled cucumber like gherkins, fresh red radishes, tomatoes and other Polish agricultural produce. The food was tasty, hot and not expensive given that these were two of the best hotels in town. They would usually be pretty full and one would stand and wait not far from the restaurant reception in the bright sunny room laden with white table cloths for someone to get up and there to be place.

Lunch at Zlota Rybka with its own atmosphere and specialisation in fish, in Nowy Swiat, not far from Copernicus' statue followed after a morning talk given by him at the Philosophy department nearby. Emboldened he invited her in turns to two restaurants at diagonally opposite corners of the square in *stare miasto* for dinner. They were both famous for their meat which came accompanied by sweet and sour cabbage and a host of other vegetables, presented like colours in an artiste's palette.

What am I doing, why am I letting him take me out so often, thought Lauren. Ashok came to mind but what was their future, when would he come. Irrespective of these practical aspects, the thought of him made her long for him but then again Carlo would sweep her up in a whirl of activity, much like he had swept her off her feet on the dance floor. How long would she, could she pine for him? He might never be able to come, to re-unite with her.

Dr. Zhivago flashed in her head - where he and Lara are in the same city - he sees Lara, he tries to reach her but dies before she can see him and she walks on.

He might still turn up unexpectedly, the knight in shining armour, just in time, here in Warsaw, here in Poland and rescue her. Bah! Romantic piffle!

86

Marek still thought the world of Lauren but had begun to accept that wherever he might have reached with her at one point of time in winning her affections, he seemed to be slipping out of the picture. He watched with amazement this upstart move at lightning speed. He felt jealous but there seemed to be little he could do about it. He would visit her and they would be interrupted by a phone call from Carlo. Some of the parties they were both invited to, Carlo would somehow show up he would tag and steal many a dance with her and compete for her attention during conversations. Carlo progressed from lunches to dinners, from afternoon to evening. Another day they went to a long hall which was a well known and very comfortable coffee place where ordinary people met and chatted about this and that. She came readily enough but seemed far away after a while. Eva, another friend of Lauren and Ashok, who had held her silence till now sent an epistle to Ashok. There are things happening here, she wrote, that I cannot understand. Ashok got it but did not read between the lines.

Marek did not want to give up and tried not to show

desperation. He tried to reason with Lauren about the danger of these fickle, treacherous and insincere Italian lovers. How risky, different and short lived her life and career in Italy would be. How she would be gambling her established place in the Polish musical world for an uphill struggle with much more competition in a new and unknown place. She listened thoughtfully and was touched by Marek's sincerity. But the next day Carlo would come and sweep her off her feet with some impossibly glamorous proposal or just pure unpredictability mixed with charm. To openly fight with Carlo would make him appear childish. That wasn't the way to win battles for hearts. And luck, chance, circumstance had a lot to do with it.

He felt certain that there would be a host of girls Carlo would be two timing back home in Italy - in Florence, in Rome which he would be visiting surely. But how was he to find out? He lacked the resources, the access. It would be blatant enough. If Lauren could only know.

Facebook, Google - even just the Internet would certainly have helped but even much lesser things like phone calls or permission to visit the West presented insurmountable obstacles.

Where had this creep turned up from? He would eventually make his poor unsuspecting young and gullible Lauren unhappy but how to save her? In observing Carlo manoeuvre, he was also disturbed by feeling that Carlo could be crude at another level. But Lauren wouldn't believe him. Would question his motives.

Marek felt desperate. He should forget her now. There were many very attractive girls from the University days - some no less than Lauren. There was still a lot of interest in him. He could be happy, perhaps happier. He had met Elzbieta. She was glamorous. She had modelled, was not yet attached, clever, adjusting. She would be more tolerant of his moods perhaps. There had been rumours that he may no longer be with Lauren. They had many common friends.

Necessity led him to atypical acts. The heart does not always listen to reason. He found himself in Palac Mostowski, the Police headquarters. There was a woman he knew slightly older than himself. Lauren should not be given a passport at any cost. She may not come back. Her intention would not just be to visit, no matter what she claimed. Once out she could follow other options. The State had spent valuable resources in training her, on her upkeep. She was a talented Pole. The State and the Party could ill afford to lose such people to the West. Moreover someone else equally talented would have been deprived of a career, a place, a chance to excel and make the name of Polska shine.

The official looked grim - made a noting in the file. Marek left feeling unreal. Had he just done this?

The intense Warsaw cold turned into Spring, romance was in the air and made everyone smile at young lovers. It was palpable, tangible. Carlo knew what he wanted and focussed with single minded determination.

On Mayday he knocked at Lauren's door, interrupted her practice and said "Come on, I want to watch the May Day Parade". It's all Party propaganda she said, had seen it before and had too much work to catch up with, thanks to the time she was spending with someone. But he insisted. "It's the only chance I'll get and these pictures are so well known in the West. All the Communist Party bosses standing in a row according to their ranking in the Politburo, on a podium next to the main street, wearing those hats which have become identified in the West with precisely this."

"Fine, you go but why do I need to be there?"

"You have seen it but have you ever marched in it? Come on...."

The procession was weaving its way through the principal streets, Krakowskie Przedmieście past King Sygmund's column where Carlo held Lauren's hand and joined in. In front of him was a Turkish looking fellow with a startling black beard and an Oriental looking turban on his head. "Must be a student", whispered Lauren, "a Sikh from India". Carlo didn't quite know what that was but whatever, he shrugged to himself. But whether it was the exotic sight of the Sikh as a symbol of friendly fraternal relations with fellow Socialist country India or there was something glamorous in Carlo and Lauren as a couple, the assembled big-wigs on the podium smiled and waved energetically in their direction.

How could the noon sun be so strong, it was only May and it had been so cold not so long ago. Carlo and the Sikh were perspiring. Vendors went around shouting '*lody, lody, lody*' and selling thin vanilla bars for next to nothing.

"Please come with me to Florence, Lauren. You will love it - it's dazzling and sensuous and you will still be in Europe, not so far away from home. It's a citadel of art and culture and for music and opera what could be better than Italy. It's the centre of the world for that. And there is no lovelier city in Italy than Florence and no prettier province than Tuscany."

She had been seeing a lot of him but had things moved so far emotionally? "Is this a proposal?" she asked taken aback.

He was nice, attentive, handsome in a typically Italian way, demonstrative, at times exaggerated, slight swagger.

He went down on one knee, in the middle of the marchers. They swept past them. "Will you marry me, Lauren?" his Italian accent coming out in the English.

Was this serious? He seemed to be. Was he just flirting with her?

"I am touched and honoured Carlo but I haven't known you that long. I don't know Italy at all. I don't know if I want to live there. I don't speak the language. It is Europe but I don't know if I truly want to leave my native Poland, with all its obvious shortcomings. I am well settled and happy in my profession here. The music world there is already flooded. There is so much talent. I don't know if I could make a place for myself there. And without my music, I am not me. Let me think about it. Let's talk about it. Now please get up. This is too much drama in public."

"But you yourself told me that your ultimate aim was to settle down in Western Europe."

"Dreams are one thing, reality is not so straightforward."

Thoughts of Ashok came again. If only she could have him here with her in Poland. She closed her eyes. With him engaged in something meaningful and not worrying about his parents. Wouldn't that be paradise? She didn't even want Western Europe perhaps. That was just a childhood dream, of there being gold in those streets. But what was all that glamour worth, she said aloud. In the final analysis, didn't she just want Ashok and her music. What was her future with Ashok? Or was love beyond future or was it the only *vrai* future.

"I am Italian, Latin. Women are my speciality" Carlo said aloud to himself. He pursued his objective with single minded determination but managed to do so without coming on too strong.

It helped Carlo's courtship that he became talked about by some attractive women in Warsaw. He was well regarded by the city's social elite. His eligible bachelorhood became an established fact.

With Lauren he was persistent but stopped short of being intrusive. And sometimes when she turned down his invitation, he somehow made her feel that she was the one missing out on some event that would have been memorable. "The tricks that people play", thought the down to earth Eva, but she was not in it.

Magda and Wlodek were bowled over by him. This would be her passport to the West and a new life, where she could realise her potential and reach greater heights in her profession. And he was from the Continent, with all its connotations of European civilisation.

Her father was more level headed. Just wanted his daughter's happiness. What about that nice steady boy Marek who had been hanging around for so long. And deep within himself, unacknowledged perhaps, he had noticed the sparkle, the glint in her eyes that the very thought of Ashok brought on. He had his doubts about these Southern Romeos. Once he had got what he wanted, once he had satisfied his passion, revelled in and savoured his conquest and they had settled down to domesticity, when he had finally won her heart, would he remain true? Or would his eyes wander? Italian girls could be very pretty and more likely to be what his Mama wanted. And perhaps even more to the point, more like his Mama. He didn't look the type to break his Mama's heart - his Mama who would be everything to him. And during subtle questioning, this had been confirmed.

Lauren's *Nani* - Magda's mother - her *Babcia* also expressed similar doubts. She really liked Ashok. But they didn't pay much attention to her views about such things.

She used to sleep on a bed in their tiny kitchen. She was from the Polish city of Lvov, now in the Ukraine. (Almost one third of Germany in the East was given to Poland and almost one third of Poland in the East was given to the Soviet Union, in one of those high handed acts of post War redrawing of maps. As a result totally Polish cities became Ukrainian overnight. Germany till the 1990's could not accept the Oder Neisse Line and the Soviet Union would not have bothered if they had *prevu* that Ukraine would not be part of them.)

Carlo turned on the charm during the courtship that followed. He displayed his macho side, when he thought it might impress - in showing he was in command in outside situations. And when Lauren danced on the table, her possessing beauty caught everyone's eye as did her spontaneous dance movements. Carlo and her brother stood up and clapped. People smiled at her.

She made a desperate phone call to Ashok but could not connect. Why was she doing this? Big steps in Life are decided by such little things. But there was such a thing about Ashok. He had been so self assured in those days. He would make it in time. He would sweep her off her feet - more than Carlo could ever have done and rescue her from this situation she was fast sinking in. The Universe would take a hand and help its truest lovers, the way it always did. It would unleash imperceptible, invisible forces the way it does when things are in alignment. The race against Time, if that is what it was, would be won as Time itself being a part of the Universe would start working in sync with it.

One day Carlo came all excited. He had been hard at work on the professional music front back home in Italy. He had activated his considerable social network in the interlinked art and music world not just in Florence but in Milan and Rome to explore and create options for Lauren. He knew fair maiden could not be won without this aspect getting resolved.

"There is an opening for you in the Conservatoire in Florence. Your curriculum vitae is impressive and there is place for more than one of your kind. The teaching load is too much on the present incumbent and it would be a great help to her also. The funds from the Government have been found - the application has circumnavigated the bureaucracy and is likely to get through."

"Hmmm, Mr Smart is presumptuous, leaves no aspect uncovered. Does he think all Polish girls will be dazzled by the West?"

The pay was four times, the prospects of growth the whole Western world and Japan - no Iron Curtain to negotiate repeatedly. Not a big city like Rome where despite its History and Architectural beauty, people were crass and rude and rough she'd heard and taxi drivers were cheating you, even more than elsewhere.

What would happen to Ashok? Would he ever forgive her? Understand?

And Carlo, did she love him, she searched within herself. Was she being fickle, shallow. Responding too easily, too quickly. Could her affections change so fast, what did she really feel. Did she even know him well enough. Could she sense another facet, a roughness behind the arty exterior which could surface later on in life together, she pondered. Did her sixth sense warn her the same man be macho and insensitive at times. Or were these just her fears, just her being anxious.

Would he be the typical Italian lover and have Alberto Moravia afternoons, unbeknownst to herself, after the initial years of being madly in love. He was besotted - that was clear.

The whirlwind continued - he didn't give her time to think. The three months flew. Ashok remained beyond the horizon. The old problems remained. Carlo was undeniably attractive, dashing. Prince Charming.

Her colleagues in the music world who were close enough to her fell into two camps, as did her friends outside it - the incurable Romantics still wanted to flow with the heart - they thought it lay with Ashok - they had seen them together, they had seen their eyes. The intensity of what they had had, had felt would win through in the end.

The other lot - the Here and Now lot - the Real politik flagbearers, thought she was happy enough now. They had seen them laughing. The tortured on again off again relationship with Ashok had gone on long enough.

Would Ashok come in time? Was this really happening?

She started several letters to Ashok but it was too painful and she tore them up. He had been the love of her life but that must become the past. She had been to India, loved it, their encounter had been tempestuous but at the end of the day she wanted to live in Europe and he could not find a way. It remained an impasse. Intractable. Did anything matter more than Love? Not for her. Not for Ashok. So what was the solution in the final analysis? Who would be able to compromise? Even if Ashok settled for starting without capital and getting a job, it would be very difficult as a foreigner to get one. She knew this. It would have to be in an English speaking country and England already had the most restrictions on employment of South Asians. Elsewhere in Europe language would come in the way of a job, besides legal restrictions on the hiring of foreigners.

She wouldn't let those memories come.

She suppressed it but there was a desperation, an urgency inside that would not be suppressed. Telegrams were expensive especially to *zagranica* and on an artist's earnings. She composed one. "*Je t'aime de tout mon coeur.* Come now.

I need you. It's really urgent. Your little one." But unbeknownst to her Ashok having reached a similar emotional crisis point had already left for the shores of Polska. And unbeknownst to her, his efforts to make contact had not been successful. Partly he had wanted to surprise her - to turn up and surrender. His head was in a spin. Did the telegram reach and lie in Ashok's *dak* awaiting his return, with no one especially telling him? Or got lost, carelessly waylaid in a drawer in the last stages of its trajectory in a dusty Indian post office?

She found herself responding more and more to Carlo's overtures. She had come into his life and he wasn't letting her go. Would she love him back as much as she had loved Ashok? Love was a complex web of emotions and it was different between different people. It was neither desirable nor possible to compare. She just had to be sure that it was enough.

She could always come back to hearth and home. Some risks had to be taken in Life. And what was the risk anyway? An attractive guy who doted on her, a beautiful city with many more possibilities for music. Name, fame, job satisfaction - realising her potential. Who wouldn't want to do that?

The Party and therefore the State had tried to suppress religion but because of hundreds of years of history, it lurked strongly beneath the surface, except amongst the elite - the Diplomats who had to bat for Poland, the artistes and film makers. If there was one place where it was stronger, it was Italy. It wasn't Catholic in the same way as Poland. Poland was Communist. Catholicism was part of the history, of folklore. But in Italy was there even a divorce, a second chance?

Cholera jasna! Where the hell was Ashok? What should she do? What could she do? She felt disloyal to him, but they had reached no understanding. Even during her last tempestuous encounter in India. Only passion and emotion to the deepest levels of human experience.

She put in an application for a sabbatical, as if in a dream at her Conservatoire in Warsaw. She waited. She talked to her friends at the Conservatoire. There were those who were envious or competitive. She had to be careful. The Director of the Conservatoire phoned her. She should meet him the next day prior to going into her practice. The Ministry may not give concurrence for even her one-year sabbatical. It was against the rules. If there was one thing the bureaucracy of the socialist government was, it was hide bound. Worse than most bureaucracies and as bad as the Indian bureaucracy Ashok had described. There were many talented young people waiting, wanting a place, explained the Director to soften the blow. And of course if she ever wanted to come back, her reputation would stand her in good stead and subject to there being a place she would get first preference. The Director knew of her personal predicament but purely from the point of view of her career in Warsaw, if she wanted to withdraw her sabbatical application, she could do so. Otherwise she might have to leave. Having said all this, he would try.

Carlo left no stone unturned to woo her. The Spring in Warsaw conspired with him. He hired a car and took her to the beautiful Palace outside the city, with its fabulous collections. He was entertaining, witty and made her laugh. She would be happy with him.

Carlo's Italian Mama and Papa came for a visit to Poland. His Mama was typical, plump, motherly, pampering and full of love. His Papa was amiable. She need not have fears about getting along. Anyway, they would live separately very shortly. His own flat not far from theirs and equally well located was almost ready.

They would get married in a beautiful church in Florence. It would be splendid. They would have a civil wedding in Poland, to make the entry and exit formalities between East and West easier. He would get her Italian citizenship soon. She could come and go anywhere freely. The world would be at her feet. She had a sentimental attachment to her Polish citizenship. He understood. She would always be Polish. This was just something practical, which made movement in connection with her career, infinitely easier.

He would facilitate the presence of her family, some close friends and some fellow musicians from the Conservatoire at the wedding in Italy. He had connections.

For their honeymoon he would take her to Venice.

He was taking his parents and some other visitors from Italy to Zakopane in the Carpathian mountains on the border between Poland and Czechoslovakia for a few days. He persuaded her to join the group. They stopped for a night in Sucha Beskidzka, a small town before Zakopane. There were groups of young men hanging all over town standing around doing nothing in particular. *Chlopcy*. They paid no attention to these strange looking people from Warsaw. They expected it of Varsovians. Rooms were available in a school *Dom Studencki*. The school had just closed for the summer. Dense forests, trees climbing up slopes, apple orchards, the hills behind inviting. The student house was next to a field and led up one such hill. He plucked small green apples from trees and they tasted sour and fresh. They went for a night walk into the rows of trees which got denser and denser, as they went up the slope. The densely growing trees evoked for her the power and majesty of nature. It was memorable. It doesn't take fancy places, she thought.

88

Aparna was still emotionally involved with Ashok. She had come twice to India. It was time he came for her. It was time to settle down. She had grown up in India. She would adjust to life there. There were many things about it she loved. She could always visit California every now and then. Maybe think of a way of exporting some textiles to it. She knew both places so well. She could source it well in India - ensure excellent design and quality. She understood the market in California well and could meet its demands. Anyway, career was not all there was to life. She was competent, efficient, fast and well liked in her firm. She earned well. But this was okay for the moment, at a pinch she could leave it. She was a remarkably beautiful and charming girl and even in California, already a magnet for aspiring young beauties, she turned heads. A young and already well known poet newly inducted into the teaching faculty at a prestigious University in the area, was much taken by her. There was glamour attached to his name. His work was brilliant but as a suitor...? She did not find him interesting or attractive. "No sex appeal" said her sister summing it up, "not charming, personality quite ordinary - nothing to write home about."

She was a home maker, loved children. Loved bringing them up, looking after them. Her drawing room was beautiful, cosy, comfortable, sun and music filled. She enjoyed being in the house and making it the best place to be in. A lot of time was spent there and it had an enormous bearing on the quality of peoples' lives. It was often taken for granted. It needed thoughtfulness, effort. She wanted to settle down now and enjoy that chapter of life. She had had timeless moments with Ashok. She missed him and wanted him. She wanted to lose herself in their kiss. He had to come here now and she would go back with him. This was it.

An architect friend of hers suddenly proposed one day while she was advising him on his new studio - that why not they get together. He was an old friend and she liked him a lot. But in that capacity? "Don't be crazy!", she laughed it off. "You and me?"

Another friend, a banker in the City, successful - made no attempt to hide his interest in her. He had a lot going for him, was attractive and pleasant to be with. But her heart seemed to have given itself to Ashok and would not be swayed.

A lot of time had passed. There were continuing uncertainties. But above all, she was happy with him and she could see him with her. She missed Ashok immensely and was tired of being without him. She wanted to feel his presence, to have his company. She wanted to lose herself in their kiss.

Ashok got through on the phone. He had been *deborde* with work, as she knew. Everything was on his shoulder, he was weighed down with responsibility, the call and burden of duty but was coming.

There were no direct flights to the States, he had to come

via Europe, he would follow up on his efforts there and then come.

"Where all are you going?" she asked. "All the places that I have been working on in Europe, to get a foothold."

"It's so hard to leave work and India. This time I got stuck for a long time. I've been on the verge of leaving since quite some time but it's been virtually impossible."

"If I give my heart to you,
Will you promise to be true
And help me, understand
Cos I've been in love before
And found that love was more than just holding hands", songs from her teenager days. Well, she had given her heart, for better or for worse and there it was.

89

Getting to Europe was a big deal. The dreaded P Form to leave the country even with a total foreign exchange equal to Rs. 75 was a Herculean task. It was proving to be as difficult getting to Europe, as Ashok had feared. Things had not improved over these few years. It was as difficult if not more than the previous time. And then too the last page of his passport was still stamped with the specific number of days he could be out of the country.

The Visa sections of each Embassy were suspicious and difficult. And there were so many different visas to get, each with their own idiosyncrasies. Some of them gave visas counting the number of days as if entry was being given into heaven.

Ashok's parents got a sense of things afoot and told him in no uncertain terms that he could not again abandon hearth and home and his work in which he had settled down so well and was making a real difference, as acknowledged by all. Brij had heaved a sigh of relief that his beloved son had at long last shouldered some of the burden. And now to let it adrift and to wander off again like some infatuated teenager in search of inappropriate and elusive love. Brij and Radhika loved Ashok and everything was fair in love and war. All weapons were pulled out especially the most potent one with an already guilt ridden son - that of emotional blackmail.

Sometimes he felt an immense sense of urgency and impatience while wading through the bureaucracy, while waiting for the babus to stop niggling with details. What would happen? His situation with Lauren remained intractable. But he would find a solution. All the world loves a lover. People in Europe would help them. But why this inexplicable urgency in his gut. He was sure of her love. She wouldn't ditch him. Find someone else. The commitment between them was of love, of what had happened to them, of their feelings, not of a promise articulated or of a social contract.

Was it an un-nameable yearning, he reflected. Was it reflective of a sense of urgency - that young as he was he better live life fast before it flies past.

'Young' was in any case a relative term. There had been a suitor for Lauren in Wroclaw who had been quite jealous of him. He was handsome, blond but it took a lot more than that, to win a girl's heart. He had been 24. Ashok remembered thinking how old that was.

Then Ashok got his chance and made his long awaited trip to Europe. Ashok felt more and more relaxed, felt himself de-tensing away from the *ecoeurant* Arjans of Delhi and the non business School way of doing business and the parameters for success that no business School prepared you for. The lovely part of it, the geometric rider solving, the creative aspects of better products, better distribution were the extenuations but he was glad to be away and dealing with business without those unpleasant aspects.

Ashok felt the buzz of an international flight again, from the self isolation of India. After a long time he was winging his way westwards. He couldn't believe it. How would it feel? Would he be at home again? Would he feel strange? He would be reunited with Lauren again. He would see her again. All those other things, they didn't matter, he would find a way out.

As soon as he reached Western Europe he phoned Lauren. The phone kept ringing. There was no reply. He tried the next day and the next, but he made it Person to Person (PP). If the person wasn't available he wouldn't get charged. He could ill afford it, particularly in hard currency. And he always had to go and stand at a phone booth. The Hotels put such heavy surcharges. Only multi-national company executives on expense accounts could afford to pay. Her mother wouldn't give his message anyway.

He phoned Aparna. She was on another Continent but in a way the world outside India was one - it was free.

The line from Amsterdam was clear. It was one of his favourite cities. He loved the row houses, the canals, the mist there in certain seasons, its lovely museums, the friendliness of the Dutch people. Many Dutch girls were so pretty. It was a pleasure just to look at them and to have them around. He smiled at some of them and got smiles in return. Much he said had been made of the jellied, buttered eel but that wasn't his thing. You couldn't like everything in a country. He was going to the famous Concertgebouw that evening. Alone, alas! One day he would see it with his true love. He would run out and have some sweet sherry in the break. He had had no time for such things in Delhi and now he would catch up with a vengeance.

A KLM flight, part of his round trip ticket based on Maximum Permissible Mileage between the starting and the turning point - the farthest point and thus included in the cost, bought him to Vienna. This was the beauty of Europe, everything was so near, had such richness and variation of culture but was nevertheless European.

He went and met the owners of the family business in Vienna. He was ushered into the large Old World office of the Patriarch. There were wooden cabinets behind him with objets d'art, leather bound books, period furniture. His two sons were there. Costs were rising. The mixer, the long wafer oven, other items - surely he could make something cheaper for them, that went into this machinery, to their quality standards. It would still be Franz Jens. It would still be made in Austria. It could be win-win for all of them. They looked thoughtful. They bought tickets for him to the Staatsoper. He stayed in a typical Austrian Hotel just opposite. Sachertorte, world famous, from the pastry shop owned by the Hotel, on the main street, was put on his pillow every night. The elder son would visit India after some time it was concluded at the end of his visit and they would see if they could take it further.

He let the concerts wash over him in the evenings, managed to catch some matinee performances of art movies that he may not otherwise have been able to see. He sat in the parks and enjoyed the breeze and moistness of Europe on his face. Soon it would be time to be with Lauren again. He would surprise her. He had to live his life with her. He could not live without her. He had no choice. She was the love of his life (and he knew in his heart of hearts - that he of hers) and it had been folly to try to make compromises because of all other factors valid in themselves. He had seen the same thing in her eyes in Delhi. If anything, if it was possible, he knew - the way people in a relationship do, that it was even more from her side.

He dropped picture postcards from different places in Europe - Frankfurt, Copenhagen, Cologne, Stockholm, Vienna to Lauren. She would get them faster from Europe. Know he was on the same Continent, that he would see her soon. Her mother and brother would not intercept them? Surely not. Such scary thoughts were not to be entertained.

He tried to get through on the phone to Lauren feeling strange and unreal as he did so. He did not get Lauren once. There must be a conspiracy of circumstances. Or was she deliberately avoiding him. Did not want the agony of contact with him again, with the impasse vis a vis her love of music and the importance of her career, that they could not resolve. She couldn't be that busy. He knew she spent long hours at the Conservatoire, virtually lived there, many days. That she was also running around with Carlo, he wasn't to know.

90

Lauren's passport was refused. Time was passing. Carlo got very impatient, furious. No reason was given. Meanwhile, everyday was bringing Ashok closer to her in Poland. The course of the lives of Carlo, Lauren and Ashok might take a different turn. Chance a k a the course of true love might take a hand. Carlo's own Polish visa was about to expire. He would have to shell out more Dollars per day. Besides even he could not hang around here indefinitely. There was his career and commitments back home. An important exhibition of his was coming up in Trieste.

Carlo went himself to the passport office. He had no locus standi. The Polish bureaucracy worse than even in his native Italy, would not give him the time of the day. He pulled strings. The Italian Ambassador tried. Carlo shopped around amongst his newly acquired but influential Polish high society contacts. What was needed was government or Party links, however.

In Europe, Aparna felt that Ashok sounded busy in a different way. And at least the evenings and weekends seemed to be his. Here, there was a *contrepoint* in his work - a silence which enhanced the tonality.

He had phoned her from Western Europe two or three times. They had managed to talk despite the time difference and her being on the West Coast of a different Continent. They had not talked long, these calls were expensive. Anyway, he was coming to her right after.

Then he reached Poland - why did he need so much time there? It didn't fit into this group of countries. It wasn't easy to penetrate the Socialist bureaucracy. It wasn't technologically advanced. There wasn't Capital.

Aparna felt the impatience. It was easier to wait for him to come when his arrival was vague. High time also that they ended the uncertainties in their relationship.

92

Lauren had asked for three years off at the Conservatoire. The Director had stuck his neck out and recommended one year, with a wordy justification in literary Polish. Such was the regard for her that a one year sabbatical was accepted. It was highly unusual. Her bridges would not be burnt.

The familial pressure became intense. She read E M Foster's *Howard's End* just then and saw how people arranged their own marriages. Happiness was attainable.

The job offer from Italy came in writing. It was very attractive. And it was all in hard currency. The Embassy promptly assured her of an Italian visa, by no means an automatic thing for a citizen of an Iron curtain country, in a polarised world.

No sign of Ashok. Why think about him? Pointless.

93

The clock was striking 12 when Ashok's LOT flight from Frankfurt landed in Warsaw. He had had to stay an extra day in Frankfurt. The supplier of Westphalia machines had wanted him to visit their factory the next day. The radio played Chopin at that hour everyday all over Poland, to coincide with that. He felt the familiar smell and air of the city but this time there was a momentousness to his visit. He had come to be one with Lauren again, to scoop up and carry off his fair maiden on horseback. Something he should have done ages ago. The long term would work itself out but he had to be with her at any cost. The anticipation and excitement were palpable now. Long postponed, they were allowed to come to surface. He was in the same city as her, breathing the same air, again. Never let her go - this time. He felt an indescribable intensity.

Ashok would turn up unannounced, he would sweep her off her feet. He would ring the doorbell. Armed only with flowers. She would answer. He would kiss her. Finally. Again. He couldn't wait to hold her. He gave himself up to pleasant reverie. It wouldn't be more than a few steps now.

94

At the busy crossing near Metropole Hotel Lauren bumped into Marek. She read his somewhat downcast face she felt a pang. She had always liked him and still did. Impulsively, she said lets have lunch at the nearby round dome shaped Gastronomia. Not a great place, but cheap. Metropole would have been nicer but more expensive.

In the busy packed eating place with the chatter of voices all around, they got to talking, like in the old days. She also talked heart on sleeve. Marek felt the sincerity. She still liked him. Always would. But whatever romance had been there was not there now. Could he understand that? Accept it. Forgive her, if he felt hurt. She had never deceived him.

They met three consecutive days and chatted late into the night. Warsaw was appropriately stormy - mirroring the storm within Marek. She brushed aside Carlo's objections. She didn't want to hurt Marek.

Finally he seemed to understand as much as he could and to accept. He was glad that she had spent this time with him. He had been a mainstay once, in the post Ashok days. She owed it to him.

95

Lauren's passport came through. Unexpectedly. There was no explanation. Suddenly it was sorted out. She was free to go.

Carlo lost no time, moved at lightening speed. She also got caught up in the sudden whirlwind. And before she knew it, she was ready to leave. Things happened so fast, that again she had that sense of unreality. In a daze she attended to whatever practical steps were to be taken preparatory to departure. Oscar knew his daughter was going - for better or for worse. So he took charge and supported her in all the many practical things and the running around that are an inevitable part of leaving. He knew also that she was in no emotional shape to be thinking too much of down to earth things, which are small but have to be taken care of.

Wlodek and Magda were contented that things were moving at such lightening speed. Only they knew also from his infructuous phone calls that Ashok was already in next door Germany and about to reach Poland. They even kept it from Oscar. Let her escape somehow from that boy. That he was already walking into Poland, at the very moment, even they didn't guess.

Fleeting thoughts of Marek whom she had spent so much time with, came. Other people who had been in her life from school days onwards came to mind.

Her heart ached as she left the now being renovated and modernised Okecie airport, for something lost and something gained, for her past life, for the life that might have been, for the road not taken, for something ineffable. Was it just for Poland or was it for Ashok and the life she had had with him and their love. How long could she wait for him, have waited for him? With no solution in sight. Music, her career, Europe, his family responsibility - she felt weary at the thought. Going around in circles. Love should have conquered all. Maybe it would have in the end. It had been all consuming but how long could she hang around waiting uncertainly for him. There had been no sign of him. Would he come one day and find her sudden and unexpected departure incomprehensible, inexplicable?

It was a beautiful golden day. 'Why are places so hauntingly and symbolically beautiful, just when you are leaving them? Is it to etch them in your memory?' Was there a shadow somewhere in the distance but not too far off, of Marguerite Duras' L'Amant standing next to his trademark car and uniformed chauffeur, as her ship left Port and she stood on the railing watching those who had come to bid goodbye?

Oscar and Magda felt drained after the departure of their daughter. Oscar had enough leave due to him. They needed to get away. They needed the beautiful mountains. They badly wanted a break. They would go for 10 days to Zakopane. It would be cold, it would be full of snow. It would be refreshing. It would mark the watershed. They took *Babcia* and even Wlodek managed this much time off.

Ashok held off calling the familiar number till he had settled down in the Hotel and unpacked. He knew its Polish pronunciation by heart. He had had to say it so many times - *Czterdzieści trzy*, etc. He hoped Lauren would pick up. "*Sucham*" whoever answered would say. He had always found that strange. I mean 'listening' - surely there were more refined ways of commencing a conversation.

No one answered. Strange. Was no one at home? Not even *Babcia*? He tried again after 10 minutes and then half an hour later.

He went back to the room, took off his travel clothes, got into comfortable pyjamas with a sigh and went to sleep with the sound of children playing outside in the afternoon. As he drifted off to sleep the Rolling Stones played in the background 'It is the evening of the day, I sit and watch the children play... All I hear is the sound, Of rain falling on the ground.' The Naipaul he had been reading, lay half open next to him.

He woke up, it was already evening. He called again - fully expecting to hear the loved sound finally. He asked the hotel operator to check if the number was out of order. He took a taxi and went to the address, climbed up to third floor. The door was firmly locked. He rang the bell a few times sans espoir.

He slipped a note under the door. He didn't know any of the neighbours. The whole family must have gone on vacation. They never travelled.

Ashok had called from the Hague one day. The next day he was to leave the Netherlands but one of his potential collaborators could only meet him the following day. Their headquarters were in Rotterdam. He would pick up Ashok and they would lunch in a windmill in Rotterdam. Very pleasant but it would mean the day spent in Rotterdam. The days were adding up. Deep down inside he was dimly aware of an underlying tension. When would he reach Warsaw and surprise Lauren? It was so difficult to get to Europe from India. And things were happening on the business front. These opportunities may not come again. He had to see things through, if possible. It had been so long since he had seen Lauren. He could wait another few days. No point losing patience at this stage.

Even from the Hague it had been easier to get through to America than across the Iron Curtain. He missed Lauren by a minute. She had just stepped out. Her mother picked up. He was in Europe. She would give her the message. Ashok knew she couldn't call back. Too expensive, too difficult. Wait by the phone, not knowing when the operator would try. Same story as India. The next time he got through he was glad to hear the voice of *Babcia*. At least she was *sympaticzny*. But she didn't speak a word of English and Magda took the phone away from her immediately as if anticipating a call from Ashok. "She is not here, I will tell her," she said.

Even if he found out the number of the Conservatoire, they would not disturb her sessions. Many evenings too he knew she would be performing or busy in connection with her music. He got her brother.

Ashok asked him to tell her that he had been swamped with work in India. Lauren knew that in fact. She knew how difficult it was to talk on the phone. He had been writing with his news. Her brother did not mention a thing to a soul.

Ashok had known many colleagues and friends of Lauren but most of them had been in Wroclaw not in Warsaw. Even the ones who had been here might have gotten married or otherwise moved on. He didn't know their phone numbers or addresses. Some of her girl friends whom he had really liked and who had spent a lot of time with them, he knew well by face, by first name but how to contact them now. One in particular tall, beautiful had spent three nights with them in the countryside. They were to go in a foursome but her boyfriend had ditched at the last minute. She had been very disappointed but they had decided to go ahead anyway. Lauren and Ashok had both encouraged her. It hadn't at all been a ménage a trois but in the cottage there had been two beds. Ashok and Lauren had shared one and she had the one across the window. Lauren was very careful to see that her friend didn't feel left out and she wouldn't let Ashok kiss her as long as her friend was awake. There had been undercurrents. She had liked him a lot. But he couldn't even properly remember her name now, leave alone how to find her.

They must have gone out of town - *quelle coincidence*! Never mind, they would be back soon. He would wait it out.

He went back to the hotel. At 10.30 p.m. there was still light and he heard the sounds of Friday night revelry. He slept fitfully. At 5 a.m. there was already light. He went for a walk which took him all the way to Lauren's silent flat.

It was the weekend. He couldn't get anyone in the reception or office of the Conservatoire.

Monday morning and the situation in Lauren's flat had not changed. The Director of the Conservatoire was on leave for two weeks. He was vacationing somewhere on the Baltic coast, near Gdansk. The next in command did not know him and could not reveal anything about the private lives of their musicians. However if he left a note she would pass it on.

He even tracked down number of Adam in Wroclaw. He had liked him from the start and had been instrumental in his initial contacts with Lauren. But Adam didn't know. He wished he had a friend like that in Warsaw.

Ashok hung around for 10 days. He had finished his work in Western Europe and there was little point returning there. He could not return to India - it would be very difficult and expensive to leave again. In any case, he had come for a purpose and that was entirely unfulfilled. He had no desire to go anywhere or to do anything else. All he could think of was Lauren. Everything in Warsaw reminded him of her. Where was she. What was he doing here alone, he said aloud. People would think he was crazy - hanging around Lauren's apartment.

On the 11th day, he ran into the Director's secretary, at the Conservatoire. She too had coincided her leave with her boss' and had come back to be prepared for her return. She instantly recognised Ashok and told him everything. She had not seen him for a long time. She had assumed, that things had not worked out and they had split up. She saw from the shock on Ashok's face that this was not the case. She felt bad but did not know what to say, which would not be trite.

Lauren had finally left the very morning Ashok had landed. He had not been wrong when he had thought that he was finally breathing the same air. Her flight had been around 12. They might have been at the airport at the same time. If he had spent one less day elsewhere. Ashok had missed her by a whisker. What if they had actually met at the airport? The course of their lives might have been different, or would it have been too late?

He wished he hadn't spent the extra day and night in Rotterdam or gotten stuck in Frankfurt longer than planned. Every minute is always precious but we forget that, he thought.

The secretary sighed. The affairs of men and women only they themselves understood. She like many others who had seen them around thought that they were the perfect pair and would be inseparable. If she had had any inkling of Wills made for each other contest in India, she would have entered them and thought them sure winners!

She sent for some restorative *herbata* with lemon in a glass with the tea bag dangling in it, waiting to be squeezed with a spoon and taken out.

He drank it silently. His whole world was crashing about him. Did she not know that he would be devastated, shattered. Could she really not have thought of him, Ashok puzzled. It was truly hard to believe. When had she left. *Where was she?* In his growing up years he had heard Cliff Richards 'All my love, Came to nothing at all, my love... I woke up to find, You were no longer mine' and loved the melody. Now it was happening in real life to him. Lauren had loved him so. He wasn't mistaken about that. How was this possible, what had happened to her, why didn't she tell him, talk to him. Why had this never come up in their phone calls, why had she never given any inkling in her letters. She was such a decent sort. 'Oh Darling! Please believe me, I will never do you no wrong,' - they had heard that together in a Beatles album he had bought in the West, whilst the snow fell outside their window in Warsaw, in heavy drifts. She had had tears in her eyes. They had shared the intensity and the pain and longing of love.

Had she done this to him? How could she do this to him? Incomprehensible. He couldn't believe it. He couldn't understand it. His Lauren, his little one, could never, would never do this to him. It was totally inexplicable. It wasn't like her. It was out of character. She had been so in love with him. He knew it. She showed it. He knew it deep within him. If anything, if that was possible, she had been more in love with him, than he with her. There was no mistaking it. She had been *so* in love with him. What could have happened? She would never do it to him. And would she be capable of this ultimate cruelty to herself and to him? She was so loyal, true blue. He loved her because he understood her, for her myriad qualities. This was part of it. She was the best of the best. She would *never* do it to him. He couldn't imagine her falling out of love with him. He hadn't misread her, misunderstood her. In the last few weeks they had not been able to connect. But that was only some weeks. She wasn't *like* that. He knew her. Oh Lauren, Lauren, Lauren...

97

Numbly, he walked out and fell face down on his hotel bed. He couldn't think, couldn't feel. His plans, his dreams, his whole life had collapsed. Run back to India - to hearth and home, to work and parents. He had been fulfilling his obligation. He had worked hard in the family business. He had seen what a difference it made. He could plug in back into that.

It had all been part of a plan, part of his dream. Go back alone. Empty handed as it were. What would inspire him? Nothing to live for. It was unthinkable! When the moonlight had filled his room very late on summer nights in Delhi, and had woken him up, it had had enchantment - Lauren would witness this for herself, share it, at least some of their time together. She liked visiting India. Just not living in it full time. That would be a let down from her ideal of living in Europe. The dream of a bourgeois young woman, growing up in Europe - it hadn't seemed so then. It had rubbed off on him. He was part of the quest.

What was he doing in this place? He had to get out of there.

He looked at his watch. It was 4 p.m. He told the hotel he was checking out. At the most they'll try to charge me for another half day or day. He couldn't bear to be in that hotel one second longer. But the hotel didn't fuss. He caught a taxi to the airport. He would take the next flight out of there. To wherever. Of course as an Indian, he would have to have a visa for that place. The way visa and Immigration fussed in many Western countries, you'd think they were giving you entry into God knows what, he had said once to Lauren. "Never mind", she had said. He didn't have head space for checking flights and timings. There was a flight going to Copenhagen in an hour and a half. From there he would get a connection to Frankfurt. He found himself in the transit lounge sipping coffee. It had to be paid in Western currency. 25 cents. That would be worth a lot in Poland but he had officially left Poland. He saw the haze in Warsaw as the sun sank lower and the city lay below him.

From Frankfurt he was to catch a connection to San Francisco. On an impulse he went to Rome instead, his Italian visa was still valid and turned up at the doorstep of two friends from the partying days in Delhi who were now studying architecture here. They worked very hard, from morning to night - they had undertaken some teaching assignments to partly finance their stay. It suited him. He couldn't really engage with anyone. He lay in their flat in a stupor most of the time. Wandered out sometimes - Trevi Fountain and "Three coins in the fountain"- he would have come here with Lauren, "...make it mine, make it mine". Once she had told him, "don't worry, I'll handle the labour", when he had said what if we end up running a factory in Italy but the workers there can be so difficult.

He existed like that for what seemed an indeterminate time but was in fact a month. The architects knew their old friend was going through trauma and time would numb the pain. They encouraged him to cook for them, have dinner ready by the time they came home in the evenings. The time passed in a daze. His parents, his family, no one knew where he was. Then, tired of living in limbo, he left.

98

They would soon be touching down in the Bay Area, the pilot announced. It was glorious California weather. It was 72 degrees. Another world, another life. Aparna would be there with her softness, gentleness. He had gone to an in between place. The where and how long of it had been unimportant. He had done nothing. Existed zombie like for a while. "Oh Lauren, Lauren... you've let me down so badly." He said to himself as he walked across one of the bridges in Rome. He cursed, he swore under his breath. He couldn't believe it. Recover would be the wrong word. She had coloured his world. Just reached a different point of numbness.

The Golden Gate Bridge came into view. "If you are going to San Francisco... Be sure to wear some flowers in your hair... some gentle people there... there'll be a love-in there...". He associated it with Lauren. They used to hear it in the car together. One day he would go with her there. There would be a direct flight from Delhi. The flight announcement system would be saying your flight to San Francisco. He would feel a sense of marvel, of adventure, of his whole life lying ahead of him.

He had fallen for Aparna. It was easy to see why and how. In between a tornado had happened with Lauren. It had been tempestuous, it had been real, it hadn't been ephemeral. The last time with her in Delhi had been indescribable, paradisical. Memorable, timeless. It was those moments that had made up his mind. Just.

It had been way beyond any conscious reasoning, logic, analysis - even if that had been possible in such things. There it was.

And now inexplicably it had fallen through. That had been part of the shock. But how, why, how come - the earlier questions reverberated. Hadn't she at least owed him an explanation, an understanding - to better come to terms with things. That much decency.

He had planned to come to the West Coast after Europe. To work out things with Aparna. To tell her about Lauren in India. To let her know that he had truly fallen for her Aparna and that whatever they had felt had been for real. But things happen to the heart and that has its own ineffable way of deciding.

Now where was he? Did he know? It had been so close for him between Aparna and Lauren. Yet he had chosen. And now that was gone. It was easy to love Aparna. He had never really stopped loving her. And then life had played one of its tricks and it hadn't worked out. It was a very big thing. But now what did he want? Should he still tell Aparna about Lauren? Tell her what now?

Taking it forward would be the natural and expected outcome for Aparna.

Maybe for him too. Maybe what happens, happens for the best. There was no defeat, no giving in, in this.

99

Where were the certainties in life, the guarantees? Least of all in relationships - the main man woman relationship at that. Was this a falling back because Lauren had gone or was this a natural outcome? In the final analysis did it matter? Was he happy? Was he content?

Would thoughts of Lauren still come? Pangs? Yearning even? Would he ever come across her again? How would he react? She?

Her letters, photos? Intensely bitter sweet. He wouldn't go through them, he would keep them, they were lived moments. They were part of him. He couldn't, throw them away.

"How come they named you Lauren?", he had asked her one day. "Its not a Polish name."

"Ask my parents," she had replied facetiously and then more seriously, "They were going to name me Agnieszka - almost did."

"Oh that's a beautiful name", he had said, as they sat on a bench in Lazienkowski Park "typically Polish and unusual elsewhere, with a resonance of Sanskrit. It would have become *Agni* for short."

"They chose Lauren because my father liked it enough and it was cosmopolitan - it could be French, it could be American. It sounded nice."

"It almost doesn't sound Polish."

"Doesn't it?" she had smiled engagingly and he had kissed the corner of her mouth.

100

Aparna was there at the airport. She was wearing a delicate light violet sari. She looked even thinner than before. She looked incredible. No one would have guessed that Ashok had chosen someone else. She had the love light in her eye. She was clear ever since he had succeeded in winning her heart. It had taken its time and she had been careful in protecting it and then in giving it. He would feel so good with her. Could he have forgotten?

Aparna's sharp features, her soft face, her light brown hair falling over her shoulders, her exquisite smooth light golden complexion, her expressive greenish grey eyes came into focus. Who would not fall for her?

How could he not be happy with her? Where was the doubt? Why had he gone astray - looking for something else - when he had someone like this waiting all this while?

This time he kissed Aparna, felt the sweetness of her breath and the softness, the sensuousness of her mouth. The blood went to his head and he felt like fainting, like an adolescent first kissed. His knees buckled. Did this happen to guys?

He wanted to do nothing but kiss her. They stood against

each other kissing at the airport as if they had discovered it. Insatiable. She drove him to a small boutique hotel with soothing light blue decor, not far from Telegraph Avenue in Berkeley and started helping him unpack and they fell impatiently on the bed in a tangle. They weren't aware of some of their clothes coming off though Ashok was aware of thinking how desirable she was. The golden afternoon sunshine of California came streaming in through the window, like notes of music. There was a breeze and the swaying trees outside made patterns on the wall with the leaves and the sun. Somewhere in the distance someone's radio played Simon and Garfunkel or was it just in Ashok's head?

GLOSSARY OF FOREIGN WORDS AND PHRASES

Pl. – Polish
Fr. – French
Hin. – Hindi
S. – Sanskrit

Abhimanyu – son of Arjuna and one of the heroes of the ancient Indian epic Mahabharata

Agni (S.) – fire

A la recherche du temps perdu – *In remembrance of times lost*

Approfondir (Fr.) – deepen knowledge of

Asana – (S.) yoga posture

Atta (Hin.) – flour used to make Indian breads such as chapatti, roti, naan.

Aube (Fr.) – dawn

Auberge de jeunesse (Fr.) – youth hostel

Babcia (Pl.) – granny

Bandgala (Hin.) – Indian coat closed at the neck

Banlieue (Fr.) – suburbs

Barfis (Hin.) – a sweet confectionery from India made with milk and sugar.

Bar Mleczny (Pl.) – litt. Milk bar, Polish form of cafeteria

Bas! (Hin.) – enough!

Behenji (Hin.) – (in this context) not up with latest trends

Bien-connus (Fr.) – well-known (people)

Bise (Fr.) – a kiss on the cheek

Brasserie (Fr.) – type of French restaurant with a relaxed setting, open every day of the week and serves the same menu all day.

Cadeau (Fr.) – gift, present

Carte de Séjour (Fr.) – residence permit

C'est dingue! (Fr.) – it's crazy

Charas (Hin.) - marijuana

Chhanda (S.) – Hindi and Sanskrit poetry with a particular type of metre and rules

Chłopcy (Pl.) – boys

Cholera jasna! (Pl.) – bloody hell!

Cholernie zimno (Pl.) – bloody cold

Chowkidar (Hin.) – watchman

Chaupai (Hin.) – verse of Indian poetry, especially medieval Hindi poetry, that uses a metre of four syllables.

Chukker (Hin.) – a round, « take a chukker » – go for a walk. Also chukker in Polo.

Churis (Hin.) – Indian bangles

Côté pratique (Fr.) – practical side

Coup de foudre (Fr.) – love at first sight

Croque-monsieur (Fr.) – a grilled ham and cheese sandwich served in French cafés and bars as a quick snack.

Czarnuszku (Pl.) – dark and attractive one

Czlowiek (Pl.) – man

Czterdzieści trzy = 43 in Pl.

Cztery miesiące zlecą (Pl.) – four months will pass quickly

Daj! (Pl.) give me!

Dak (Hin.) – mail, post

Dal (Hin.) – lentils

Débordé (Fr.) – very busy

Déjà pris (Fr.) – already taken

De quelle couleur? (Fr.) – what colour?

Dlaczego nie (Pl.) – why not

Dobranoc (Pl.) – good night

Dom studencki (Pl.) – student dorm

Do widzenia (Pl.) – good bye

Dropsy (Pl.) – traditional mint candies

Du bon vin (Fr.) – some good wine

Dzień dobry (Pl.) – good morning

Dziękuję (Pl.) – thank you

Écoeurant (Fr.) – horrible

En deuil (Fr.) – in mourning

En même temps (Fr.) – at the same time

Fraises (Fr.) – strawberries

Glaces (Fr.) – ice-cream

Garj, garj kshanai moorah, Madhu yavat pibamyaham (S.) – roar for a second while I drink this elixir

Gopis (S.) – Krishna's companions

Gulmohar (Hin.) – typical Indian tree known as Flame tree; In Persian "gul" means "flower", and "mohr" means "coin" or "stamp". Also "mor" means "peacock", which seems to be most close to physical appearance and beauty of this tree.

Halwais (Hin.) – the traditional sweet makers, found in India and Pakistan

Herbata (Pl.) – tea

Interdit (Fr.) – forbidden

Invalides (Fr.) – a complex of buildings in the 7th arrondissement of Paris, containing museums and monuments, all relating to the military history of France, as well as a hospital and a retirement home for war veterans, the building's original purpose.

Je ne sais quoi (Fr.) – I don't know what/with something indescribable

Je suis tombé amoureux / j'ai eu un coup de foudre / mais il y en a deux (Fr.) – I fell in love / it was love at first sight / but there are two of them

Je t'aime de tout mon cœur (Fr.) – I love you with all my heart

Jeunes femmes (Fr.) – young women

Jolie(s) (Fr.) – pretty

Kawiarnia (Pl.) – café

Khana-wana (Hin.) – food, meal

Kir-champagne – A drink made from champagne and cassis (blackcurrant liqueur) named after Félix Kir (1876–1968), mayor of Dijon in Burgundy

Kochana (Pl.) – dear

Kolacja (Pl.) – dinner

Kolezankas (Pl.) – girl friends

Kundali (Hin.) – Indian horoscope

Lakh (Hin.) – one hundred thousand

L'avenir (Fr.)- future

Le passé (Fr.) – past

Le piège (Fr.) – a trap

L'étranger (Fr.) – foreigner

Livres de poche (Fr.) – paperbacks, pocket size books

Lody (Pl.) – ice-cream

Madhu malti (Hin.) – a vine with red flower clusters and is found in Asia

Maida (Hin.) – a finely milled and refined wheat flour

Maison (Fr.) – home / house

Malgré tout (Fr.) – depite all of this, after all

Manglik (Hin.) – difficult and powerful constellation

Matinée (Fr.) – morning

Matka (Pl.) – mother

Ménage à trois (Fr.) – household of three

Mieszkania (Pl.) – flat, appartement

Miłość ale (Pl.) – love but …

Morceau (Fr.) – a piece of

Mleko (Pl.) – milk

Myna (Hin.) – medium-sized Indian bird

Naleśniki (Pl.) – polish pancakes

Nakshatra Mandal (S.) – Star Constellation

Nani (Hin.) – granny

Niemiecki (Pl.) – German people

Niveau (Fr.) – level

Nowy Świat (Pl.) – litt. New World ; here : name of a street in Warsaw

Om Namah Shivaye (S.) – Salutations for Lord Shiva

Pakoras (Hin.) – fried snack found across South Asia

Pałac Nauki i Kultury (Pl.) – The Palace of Culture and Science in Warsaw

Panchatantra – an ancient collection of allegorical animal fables

Papierosy (Pl.) – cigarettes

Pathjar (Hin.) – season when leaves fall - typically late spring in India

Peepal tree – sacred fig tree

Perte de temps (Fr.) – waste of time

Petit déjeuner (Fr.) – breakfast

Phus-Phus (Hin.) – whispered to each other

Pieniądze (Pl.) – money

Pierogi (Pl.) – dumplings

Piwo (Pl.) – beer

Pont (Fr.) – bridge

Pourquoi? (Fr.) – why

Praca magisterska (Pl.) – Thesis, dissertation

Prawda (Pl.) – truth, "…, prawda ?" – really?

Prévu (Fr.) – predicted, due, foretold

Proszę (Pl.) – please

Quartier (Fr.) – quarter, district

Quai (Fr.) – quay

Quelle coincidence! (Fr.) – what a coincidence!

Raat ki rani – (litt. Queen of the night) night-blooming jasmine

Rencontre (Fr.) – encounter

Raj Guru (Hin.) – the royal court's guru

Rishi (Hin.) – Hindu "sage" or saint

Rues (Fr.) – streets

Samosa (Hin.) – tasty Indian flour patty filled with a mixture of potatoes and peas

Sans (Fr.) – without

Sans espoir (Fr.) – hopeless

Sanyas (S.) – the life stage of the renouncer within the Hindu system of philosophy of four age-based life stages known as *ashrams*

Shakar-paras (Hin.) – a sweet Indian savoury

Shastras (S.) – Hindus sacred texts

Shivratri (S.) – special night of prayer for Lord Shiva

Shloka (S.) – verse in a particular meter

Smaczna (Pl.) – tasty

Śniadania (Pl.) – breakfasts

Souper (Fr.) – light meal served late in the night

Soir (Fr.) – evening

Stare Miasto (Pl.) – Old City

Surtout (Fr.) – above all

Sympatyczny (Pl.) – nice

Świat (Pl.) – world > "Z całego świata" – from the whole world

Sznycel (Pl.) – Schnitzel (fried veal chop)

Szynka (Pl.) – ham

Szkoda (Pl.) – pity

Tant pis! (Fr.) – too bad ! never mind !

Torty (Pl.) - pastries

Toujours (Fr.) – always, still

Très vivant (Fr.) –very lively

Très intéressant (Fr.) – very interesting

Très léger (Fr.) – very light

Turiya awastha (S.) – Pure consciousness - the fourth state of consciousness

Ulica (Pl.) – street

Une grande ville provinciale (Fr.) – big provincial town

Une semaine à l'usine (...) à la fabrique (Fr.) – one week in the factory of this (…) in the plant of that

Vanaprastha (S.) – the third stage of life in the Hindu ashram system, when a person gradually withdraws from the world - literally 'goes towards the forest'

Vela (Hin.) – someone who has nothing to do, jobless

Vive la différence (Fr.) – An expression of approval of difference

Voisinale (Fr.) - close to them/neighbourly

Vous aimez votre travail (Fr.) – Do you like your job?

Vous êtes les enfants terribles (Fr.) –«The Holy terrors » (cf. Jean Cocteau's novel)

Vrai (Fr.) – true

Zagranica (Pl.) – abroad (noun)
Zagraniczne (Pl.) – foreigner
Złota rybka (Pl.) – gold fish

ACKNOWLEDGEMENTS

Ameeta Rathore, Manju Kapur Dalmia and Ira Singh for going over the script and offering suggestions.

Anita Bali for believing in me.

My family Manju, Maya, Katyayani and Agastya for their ongoing support.

Marta Maniere for her help with the glossary.

Manish Purohit of AuthorsUpFront for his all round support and Arpita Das also of AuthorsUpFront for her faith in me.